HERO FORGED

Book One:
Ethereal Earth

by Josh Erikson

Hero Forged by Josh Erikson

Published by Josh Erikson
www.Josherikson.com

© 2018 Josh Erikson

All rights reserved. No portion of this book may be reproduced in any form without permission from the publisher, except as permitted by U.S. copyright law. For permissions contact: Josherikson@gmail.com

Paperback ISBN: 978-1718910652

This is a work of fiction. Names, characters, places, and incidents either are the products of the author's imagination or are used fictitiously. Any resemblance to actual persons, living or dead, businesses, companies, events, or locales is entirely coincidental.

For Jenny, who believed.

Author's Note

Wait! Don't skip this! I promise I'll make it super quick. And if that's not enough, I slipped a little compensation for you into the main story by way of a rather sophisticated poop joke. So hear me out.

First, I want to thank you for taking a chance on this book. Quality is tough to gauge by just a cover and a blurb, and I genuinely appreciate you giving this one a shot. I'm just a regular guy trying to make this writing thing work, so the fact that you're reading this right now is incredible to me. Also, I made you imagine poop just a second ago, and I'm thrilled that you're letting me have that kind of power. Thank you. Seriously. You are awesome.

Second, I want to tell you where I'm going with the Ethereal Earth series. When I started out, I met with an agent to tell her all about my grand plans for a big Modern/Urban Fantasy series that delved deep into difficult truths and philosophies beneath a thick sheen of smart-assery—starting out in the exotic locale of Lincoln, Nebraska. And she was thrilled! But only because she hadn't laughed so hard in a while. Yet that's what I'm doing. The second book is already written and awaiting revisions as of May 2018, and the third book will quickly follow. I might even keep going beyond ten if enough people want me to. Plus, I have some short stories planned to fall between releases. So if you get invested in this book (and I hope you do, because I've loved writing it for you) you don't have to worry that I'll leave you hanging. I'm doing this all the way, and it only gets better from here.

And finally, I have a bunch of people to thank. But those long acknowledgments at the beginning are always super boring to me. I'm in the mood for a story at this point, not to read the credits. So I've put together a little section in the back that explains who helped me drag this story into existence. If you find yourself reflecting on life at the end of this book and you want to read about some cool people who helped make it happen, it's worth a minute.

Please consider checking out www.Josherikson.com for more information about me and my upcoming releases. I have a mailing list where you'll get news, updates, and the occasional short story. And hey, if you happen to like this book, and you happen to be talking to friends, and the title *happens* to come up organically in the conversation...that would be really cool of you. Thanks again.

                    Josh Erikson

PROLOGUE

Haley wasn't sure when the night had gone off the rails, but the feel of cold ground beneath her back made her realize it must have. The sky was dark through the curtain of leaves above, and the wind cutting through the trees bit at her bare arms and face. She idly wondered when she'd lost her jacket, and the question suddenly lit a series of unfamiliar memories that unfolded in stuttering images like movie stills of a stranger's life. She watched in growing horror as she went places she'd never been and did things she'd never done—until finally stumbling out of a house to fall there to the grass. It was like a different person had been driving her body for the night. Like she'd been drugged.

A dozen questions and fears tried to roll through Haley at once, each one shouting for their own explanations or actions, but it all quickly gelled into a general panic that left her only with the single need to run. Her mind flashed ahead to envision standing, then to finding help, then to finding answers. But when she tried to sit up, something cut into her neck and yanked her painfully back down. She tried to reach up and grab it, but couldn't move her hands either—nor her feet. The cords were tight and drawn taut to the ground. Struggling did nothing but hurt.

"You shouldn't be awake yet," a man said.

Haley sucked in a terrified breath and tried to wrench her head around to find the speaker, but he saved her the effort and casually moved to where she could see. He was tall and slim with expensive-looking clothes and slate gray hair slicked back against his head. He almost looked "normal" despite the circumstances, and she enjoyed a flicker of hope that this might be some weird mistake or terrible joke she could talk her way out of. But then she noticed his bare and dirty feet, and the livid purple bruise darkening under his right eye...and that he was holding a big, shiny hammer.

The man crouched next to her and let the hammer thump to the dirt a few inches from her mouth. "That makes it harder," he said. "Though I did want a special one. The process needs a sturdy constitution, and anyone able to fight through my geas certainly must be *sturdy*." He reached up and gingerly touched his bruise, then shook his head and laughed lightly.

She remembered giving it to him. This wasn't a joke. She was in trouble. Haley could feel the scream waiting there in her chest, ready to burst out and loose some of the pressure of her panic. But it wouldn't come. The terror in her gut and the cord at her neck had already conspired to close her throat, and it took all her concentration just to keep breathing. She wouldn't get much more than that.

The man's laugh settled into a smile. "It didn't have to be this uncomfortable," he said, then gestured with the hammer back to a massive house in a clearing beyond the trees. The front door was standing open, and a little light spilled out across the threshold into the night. "I could have firmed up the geas for you and marched you back inside. Finished this on a comfy bed." He closed his eyes and took a deep breath, then sighed long and loud. "But now that we're out here, I can feel how much latent power the land has stored. Always a new surprise with magic. So I hope you don't mind if I save some work and skip straight to the main event."

Haley barely heard the words. She swallowed hard and sucked in a breath that burned all the way down, then tried to force herself to speak. She wanted to beg or cry or curse or do *anything* that might help, but all she managed was a weak sob that scarcely splashed across the man's amusement. He was going to kill her, she realized. This was what a murderer looked like. The man watched her for a moment as she struggled with herself and her bonds, studying her like a project. Then, inexplicably, he began to sing.

Haley felt tears spring from her eyes as she strained desperately against the cords, but even as the panic built, the music wormed its way in. There was no tune or words or even rhythm that she could follow, but it was loud, and it seemed to cut directly into her like nothing ever had. It sounded too rigid and layered for a human voice to produce, yet it flowed from the man like a clockwork lullaby, pulling her in and wrapping her up in its sharp edges.

And the more she listened, the more she wanted to. She knew she was still in terrible danger, but the sound seemed to wedge in the cracks of her brain and spread the solid blocks of logic wide to let new thoughts grow up like weeds. Suddenly she wanted to stop fighting and listen. She wanted to stop being so unreasonable. She wanted to obey. A warm, pleasant fog was falling over her, and she wanted to sink into it and relax. There was no trouble. Everything was fine.

Haley felt her muscles go slack as the slow drip of music spread through her. Her throat opened to let the breath come easier, and the hard ground suddenly softened like a cradle. All her thoughts drifted apart and frayed away until there was nothing for her to hold onto and she was floating free within herself. She was coming undone, she knew, but that was good. Her consciousness was dissolving, but it was *supposed* to. It was the only way to make enough room for the door that had appeared in her mind, and for the new thing trying to get through it.

When it finally came, the rupturing was barely noticeable. The music filled Haley until it burst the seams of her psyche and cracked her whole self wide like an overripe fruit. And through that wound—that door—a dark worm slithered in. It began gathering up her memories as it entered, and she felt bits of her life and knowledge vanish from her grasp as it munched merrily to her core. But she didn't care at all. The pain and fear and worry were gone, and that was a fair trade. And there was a door open now.

The new thing settled in her brain with tentacles and barbed hooks and an alien weight of intelligence, and Haley let it. She was done with her body. There was a way out through that open door, on to something vast and glorious beyond anything she'd ever dreamed. It was white and peaceful and calling to her. It was a light to go toward. So she did. Haley Schram passed from reality and into the Ether, leaving her body behind. In her place, something much larger and much older remained.

The music stopped and Gwendal took a deep breath. She struggled briefly with the sensation of flesh after so long apart from it, but that first bite of air—cold and painful and gloriously real—filled her with a pleasure unlike anything else.

"Now, succubus, we can have some fun," a man said nearby.

A binding spell brushed across her, and Gwendal looked to find its source even as she shattered it with the barest portion of her strength. The man—a sorcerer—fell back with eyes gone hard and bright before gathering himself to try again. This time Gwendal let the spell linger for a moment before shredding it, and the recoil of the snapped magic slammed into the man to throw him back with a screech of pain. She laid her paralyzing geas on him to keep him there, then pulled herself up, yanking on the ropes to easily tear the foot-long stakes from the ground. She ripped the cords from her wrists and dropped them in pieces to either side, then stepped forward to loom over her prize.

A look of utter shock bloomed on the man's face, only to be smothered by horrified realization. He was smart enough to understand that he'd drawn much deeper into the Ether than he'd intended, if not so smart as to avoid doing so. He'd wanted something minor to dominate, but had used far too much power and found her instead. No simple succubus. Not even close.

His fear was intoxicatingly thick, and she considered taking him right there to slake her new hunger. But souls were much easier to come by than sorcerers. And pitiful though his power might be, it could prove useful for what she'd come to do. She needed to stay focused on the greater goals. She couldn't let her hunger dominate as it had before. She laid her own binding spell on the man, breathing him in until he was hers.

Gwendal lifted a pale hand to her face and studied it. It was good: young, and firm, and strong. She would shape this body, of course, but that would come. The important thing was that, after hundreds of years in the quiet dark of the Ether, she finally had flesh again.

CHAPTER ONE

Gabe drained his hot chocolate and scrolled back to the top of the page. He wasn't all that proud of what he'd written so far, but he knew he didn't need to be. It just had to be compelling enough to sell. He frowned and read the intro again:

"**CONscience: A Shepherd's Guide to Sheep**

```
I'm a conman. In fact, I already have some of
your money...assuming you actually bought this
book like a sucker.

My name is Gabriel Delling, and I've been
running scams on people just like you for
fifteen years. I'm one of the best, but now I've
decided to put all that behind me and give you,
the "marks", a look behind the scenes. Some of
my life may shock you, and it should. But most
of it, I hope, will help keep you safe from
people exactly like me. I'll give you the tricks
to…"
```

His phone rang and he closed his laptop, leaving the sentence unfinished. He'd have to remember to revise "the best" to "the best in the world". He'd read somewhere that you were supposed to hook people on the first page, and the latter sounded more epic. And it wasn't like there was a con artist regulatory board to dispute the claim. "Most Profitable Fraud" was a tough category to give out trophies for. He also made a mental note to somehow work nudity and violence into the intro. He figured he might as well pull out all the stops while he was shamelessly selling out anyway.

"This is Tony. What can I do for you?" He hadn't recognized the number, so he'd defaulted to his good-guy persona. Tony was Southern, and likeable, and nice for dealing with the bill collectors that always seemed to find his number. Plus he said fun things like "reckon" and "sure's shootin". People love a good stereotype.

"Hey, it's me," the caller said.

Gabe sighed and dropped the Southern accent. "James, come on, man. Are you calling me from a burner phone? I thought we were best buddies?"

James chuckled without any humor. "You get me the money you owe and sure, we'll be chums. We'll talk about cute boys, eat raspberry sherbet, and frolic through flowers and shit. 'Till then, I use a burner to call people who make me want to check my wallet several times a day."

Gabe slid his computer into his bag. "You're hurting my feelings here, brother. I'd never stoop so low as picking pockets. I have standards."

"Don't call me brother," James said. "It sounds weird when you say it. And I didn't call to talk about our relationship. You know you're not my type. I'm giving you a chance to earn."

Gabe sat back and lowered his voice. The coffee shop was relatively empty this time of day and the music would probably cover him, but caution never hurt. "Well, that's the nicest thing you've ever said to me. How much?"

"Ah, now he's serious. About twice what you owe me. Maybe more if you're smart."

"You know I am, J. How much in numbers?"

"They're offering five, but I bet you could get seven. Minus what you owe, obviously. Plus my regular fee for delivering this to you on a silver damned platter."

"That's not bad," Gabe said, thinking it was actually great. He picked up his hot chocolate and found it empty except for some syrup on the bottom. He grimaced and glanced at the other patrons, finding only three loud teens who should probably be in school, and an older woman who had been sitting by herself for some time. "And that would make my take..." He paused. "Carry the one..."

James made a disgusted noise. "Man, I am not your accountant. You owe me two-and-a-half. I take ten percent off the top so that leaves you with just under four. That'll pay all those bills of yours for another couple months, plus get you some of that disgusting cherry shit you're eating all the time."

"Pie, J. It's called pie. And I eat it in perfectly normal, human amounts." He stopped and ran his free hand across his stubble as if deliberating. After a moment, he realized that nobody was watching the fake body language, so he dropped it with a silent curse. Sometimes it was hard to turn off.

He did need the cash, James wasn't wrong about that. His latest scam was a tell-all book about his seedy criminal past, but he was quickly learning how much legitimate effort went into writing. Every day it seemed less like a con and more like a job. He'd only managed about ten mediocre chapters so far, and even those were getting away from him. In the meantime, he needed to keep all his plates spinning.

But it never paid to seem too eager, so he injected a little skepticism and bored superiority into his voice as he responded. He was still an artist after all. "Huh. That sounds okay. But a pay rate like that for a few hours of work makes me itchy. There's a catch, right?"

James made a sound like a noncommittal shrug. "Maybe. But you know how this works: I just bring clients and vendors together. You bid out the job. If there's a trap, I'm sure a smart guy like you will be able to figure it out."

Gabe allowed himself a laugh which he hoped could be taken as either agreement or doubt. "Well if I can't, you don't get paid. And for all I know, this might be how the Lincoln Serial Killer lures his victims. How about some details before I jump face-first into this mysterious brown liquid?"

James hesitated a moment longer than Gabe was comfortable with. In that pause, the older woman rose and went toward the bathroom, leaving her food and drink behind. She also left her purse. The Midwest never failed to amaze him.

"Hey, I admit it's a weird one," James replied, "but those murders were, like, two months ago. You gotta figure that psycho moved on by now. There are only so many handsome young hunks you can kill in Lincoln, Nebraska before things get too hot. Also, you're not young or that handsome. I think you'll be fine."

"Ouch," Gabe replied. "Thirty-two is still young...relatively. And don't dodge the question."

James sighed. "Okay, it rang alarm bells for me too. You'd want to keep your eyes open. Head on a swivel."

Gabe rose and pulled out his pocket knife, palming it. "Super. You know how much I like vague warnings and opaque platitudes when my life is at stake. Let me just put these two birds back in the bush so I can light some midnight oil and stitch something in time."

"Man, if you shut up for a second I'll explain," James said. "A rich dude needs stuff stolen from a house. Basic B and E. In and out."

Gabe glanced at the baristas as James spoke, but they were both engrossed in their phones. He moved toward the condiment bar and slipped six packages of liquid creamer into his jacket pocket, then he casually grabbed a few napkins, using them to cover the knife in his hand. As he passed the glass water carafe, he rubbed the cuff of his sleeve against the condensation beaded on the outside, soaking the fabric. "I'm sorry," he said, "the number you have reached is no longer in service. Please hang up and call a petty thief. This is not a recording."

James waited an extra beat. "You are obnoxious as shit sometimes."

"I work at it," Gabe replied. He thumbed open the knife in the napkins and drifted back to his table

"Yes, your majesty," James said, "I am aware that your shit is of the finest quality and scent, but this is more than just a smash and grab. Easier, even. Apparently the guy behind the job is some rich bitch who wants to keep his wife from getting a bunch of expensive art in the divorce. It's his house. To screw over his own wife. Not how I'd do it, but then I'm not stupid enough to get married either."

As he passed the woman's table, Gabe glanced down at her unattended purse. He couldn't believe she'd left it there. Some people were almost too naïve to live. Then he lowered the blade to her cup and pierced it just along the seam before moving back to his own seat. "And a little insurance fraud as a bonus, I bet."

"I don't think so," James said, thoughtfully. "He doesn't need the money. He just wants to keep his wife from getting the art. A real bitter marriage, I guess."

Gabe grunted and sat back down. "Not a bad plan, actually. The art disappears and insurance pays out. The divorce is settled in the meantime. Our guy hires an investigator, and a year or so later the P.I. magically turns up a line on the collection—maybe from an art dealer who's happy to return the lot for a small finder's fee and the warm fuzzies of doing a good deed. The ex presumably took the settlement, so the guy gets back his unicorn watercolors. It's not entirely stupid."

"Uh huh," James said, "that sounds about right."

Gabe picked up his receipt, then started pouring the creamers into his empty cup. "You also said this job rang alarm bells."

James sighed. "Every damn job rings alarms for me. That's what I do. I don't like working for rich amateurs, is all. Something goes wrong and they hire a fancy lawyer. Let us take the fall. Fucking rich people."

"I happen to agree," Gabe said. He swirled the creamer around until it picked up the leftover syrup, then he poured it all onto his tray.

He used his pocket knife to punch a hole in the paper cup just along the seam, then he folded the blade and put it away. James was clearly waiting for more, but Gabe let him listen to dead air while he worked.

As expected, James grumbled a moment later. "Hey, you don't want it, that's fine. But you still owe me. Rich amateur this guy may be, but 'rich' is the operative word. Another easy one might not come along so quickly, so I hope you've got something else cooking."

Gabe put the cup down on the tray. He'd pushed James as far as he dared, and he wasn't likely to annoy any more details out of him. "When's the job? Can I think about it?"

James's phone beeped with an incoming call. "Nope. That's the other thing: It might be as soon as tonight. In or out, I gotta know in the next hour. I'm gonna answer this other call, and then I'm picking up a sandwich. Call me back before my post-lunch guilt sets in and the job is yours."

The line went dead and Gabe saved the number. James usually only kept a phone for a month at a time, but it would likely still be good for the day. He watched the woman come back to her table and find that her cup had leaked most of its contents. She went up to the counter and loudly complained until they gave her a free replacement drink. Gabe rose immediately after.

There was no helping it. He hadn't pulled off anything significant in months and he was running low on cash. He owed money to more people than James, and he had been hoping for some kind of hook-up to fall into his lap. The job being weird didn't make it any less worthwhile. The only other downside was that it would completely clear his debt with James, giving the man less incentive to throw him plum gigs. He'd need to find a way to accrue a little more debt to keep that relationship mutually profitable.

Gabe slammed his tray down on the counter in front of the young barista, sloshing some of the chocolate creamer in the process. He showed her his wet shirt cuff and the little slit in the side of his cup

—the one that matched the woman's. He handed over his receipt and got back a fresh hot chocolate free of charge. Four dollars and seventy-nine cents. He was a real criminal mastermind.

    He sighed and pulled out his phone as he shouldered open the door. There were quite a few benefits to his leisurely lifestyle, but one thing remained constant no matter how you lived: sometimes you just had to go to work.

TWO MONTHS AGO

Gwendal was already settling in to the human body after one night, but bits of Haley were still intertwined within the years of memories that had come with it. The actual human soul was gone of course—cast into the Ether and likely annihilated—but the shadow of it was impossible to ever fully scrub away. It was a fact of flesh that the soul left an indelible imprint. Taking on the memories of a human would always leave an Umbra's spirit altered, no matter how strong it was, but she didn't have to like it any more than she had during her previous manifestations over the centuries. Regaining her true form would help.

She sighed and glanced down at the body of the handsome young man. His blood was already congealing in a wide puddle that almost covered his dorm room floor, but the sight of it did nothing to cheer her. He should have been her first sacrifice, her first drink of power in this new form, but something had gone wrong. Instead, his life had faded away uselessly and she'd gained nothing. Her will had faltered, or she wasn't yet seated as firmly as she thought. She didn't know.

"You will complete the next ritual," she said to her pet sorcerer, "as is fitting for my servant."

The man barely grunted his reply from where he sat crouched in the corner, but Gwendal didn't bother chastising him. Her priests would have done this for her, had she any left, but they were long dead and dust. A leashed and broken sorcerer was no replacement for the truly devoted, but it was better than failing again. She was starving, and the clock was running on her mission.

"I could serve you in better ways, mistress," the sorcerer said, his voice barely above a whisper. "I could prepare my plan to—"

Gwendal forced him to silence with a thought. They'd only been bonded for a day, but already she could pull his strings like a marionette. However, she did prefer willing obedience. She had explained her plans to him once he had calmed down, and he'd been only too willing to strike a deal with her in exchange for his own petty desires. Whether he believed her story didn't seem to matter. Sorcerers were basically human and blinded by the same base lusts. He would help her perform the ritual to summon another Umbra from the Ether, and all he wanted in return was access to the carnal magics. A succubus or qarinah would do, and one would be easy enough to deliver once she had the strength.

She'd forgotten how rigid the physics of reality were, and her power was taking much more effort to manifest than it should have. She'd expected to have a group of believers ready and waiting the next time she emerged, but much had changed about the physical world since she'd last walked it. She'd been born a goddess, but felt much less now.

The sacrifices would help. If nothing else, they would feel good. A few hundred years might have dulled her power, but they had done nothing to quiet her hunger. And once she was back to her old self, she could begin in earnest. There was much to prepare if she was to serve her purpose, and she only hoped the world had enough time left to wait.

Gwendal frowned down at the body again. It was still early in the day, and if one idiot man had agreed to take her back to his room, surely another would. This flesh was quite pretty, after all, and it would only get better as her shaping took hold. Everything would get easier.

She snapped out a quick mental command and the sorcerer jumped to his feet. "Time to try again," she said. "Tell me if you spot a lonely or frightened one. They break quickest."

CHAPTER TWO

"All things considered, Lincoln, Nebraska is a fine place to live. Nice even. It doesn't have the nightlife of the larger cities, but then it doesn't have the crime either. For someone like me it's essentially a wash. Fewer opportunities but less competition. I might have chosen something a little more romantic like New York or Chicago, but it isn't my call. And while part of me hopes I won't need to make that decision anytime soon, there's always that small selfish piece that resents being tied here. But even though he wasn't anything close to the best father in the world, he stuck around for a while. Better than my mom. So I have to stick around too."

-Excerpt from Chapter One, CONscience

    Gabe stepped into the gravel lot and surveyed the weird little industrial complex. Fast Frank's Food Ferry was doing its usual brisk business in sandwiches and salads at its location of the day, and it wasn't hard to spot James on the hood of his car, eyes glued to his phone and mouth working to dismantle what looked like a reuben sandwich.

    "Gross," Gabe said as he approached. "Do you know how they make sauerkraut?"

    James barely glanced up as he swallowed. "Yep, they bury mouthy little dudes in a pit for six months, then dig up whatever's left over. Been thinking about making some homemade, actually." He took another bite and smiled around it.

    James Jackson was a handsome guy, and even the act of eating a smelly sandwich on the hood of a Lexus in a warehouse parking lot was somehow stylish when he did it. Today he was wearing a lavender button-down with the sleeves rolled up to avoid potential stains, and the color offset his dark complexion in a way that had to have been intentional. Put Gabe in that color and he'd look like a package of bread dough, but on James it was striking. The man just knew how to dress well and make it look like an accident that happened every day.

"Eh, clever-ish," Gabe said, waggling his hand from side to side. "Did you order anything for me?"

James shrugged and swallowed. "Didn't know you were coming. Also, we're not friends."

Gabe glanced over at the truck and saw that the menu for the day had some kind of German and Indian fusion theme. He waffled for a bit, but the thought of curried liverwurst made him decide to go hungry. "Still not serving hot dogs. I swear the guy's missing a golden opportunity with that name."

James snorted. "The day he takes your culinary advice is the day I stop following him around the damned city. What do you want, Gabe? You got an answer?"

Gabe moved to sit next to him on the car, but stopped at a warning look. "I wanted to talk to you first."

James took a swallow of what looked like lemonade, then wiped his mouth with the back of his hand. "Go for it."

"Okay, first, why the rush? Shouldn't there be some plan time?"

"Already done," James replied. "You're just a body on this one, not the brains—luckily for them. The dude requested six people, and the professional crew is only three-strong. They need three more and asked me to round them up. Two guys and one girl. Very specific. Besides, not everyone takes a year to come up with a viable plan, Gabey-boy. Some people have lives."

Gabe shrugged. "I'm not going to apologize for being thorough. The client specifically requested the number? And the genders?"

James nodded. "Couple of other weird requests too. But I've had weirder, and the job basically checks out."

"Huh. Who else is on the crew?" Gabe asked. "Anyone I know?"

James lowered his sandwich and gave him a reproachful look. "Does that mean you're in? Because you know we don't talk details until you're committed. And I know you wouldn't try to sneak info out of me like some kind of amateur. So that leads me to believe—" He cut off abruptly as he glanced at something over Gabe's shoulder.

Gabe took the cue and invented a conversation on the fly for the benefit of the person approaching, just in case. "...uh, probably shouldn't be green, man. I mean, I'm no urologist, but I'd have it looked at."

James turned back to him with narrowed eyes, and Gabe took the opportunity to pretend to notice the new arrival. "Hey, we're trying to have a conver..." he began, but stopped when he recognized the woman.

He only knew her by Heather. It was probably an alias, but it was one she'd used often enough for it to stick. She was roughly his age—thirty or so—and smallish without being delicate. She dressed like she had a desk job, and her dark hair was almost always back in a tight ponytail. Along with her thick-rimmed glasses and vague air of intellectual superiority, the whole thing gave her the unmistakable and obviously intentional aspect of a sexy librarian. He suspected that she was a con like him, and had to admit that the persona worked well. It was simplicity balanced against a hint of something much deeper, and though he could spot the manipulation from a mile away, it still worked.

"Am I that predictable to you damned people?" James asked as he wrapped his sandwich back into its paper.

Heather sidled up to the car and leaned against it, getting no warning look of her own. "It's the job," she said. "It makes you numb to social niceties like pretending not to notice your preference for a sexy culinary artiste named Frank. Lots of sausage on the menu today, I see."

James gave her a wry smile, and she accepted the scored point with a wink. Then she turned to meet Gabe's eyes with something that landed exactly between interest and annoyance. "Hi," she said.

Gabe wavered between several of his personae before finally settling on just being himself—or the closest approximation he could ever recall. "Hi," he replied. "Thanks for stopping by. We weren't having a private conversation or anything. I just like to stand here and watch him eat."

Heather only smirked and looked back to James. "Can we talk?"

"That depends." James said, turning to Gabe with a raised eyebrow.

It was decision time. Gabe didn't like the feel of it, but the job paid well and was about as low-risk as it ever got. Yes, the entire situation had a sticky film over it like a movie theater floor, but it came down to necessity. While he preferred to follow his gut, his wallet almost always got the final vote. And Heather possibly being involved made it twice as intriguing.

"Sure," he said. "I'm in." He'd had worse feelings about jobs and come out fine on the other side. There was no reason to think this one was any different. Also, no ominous thunderclaps followed that thought, which was nice.

Heather glanced at Gabe and seemed to size him up, then gave a small shrug. "Me too. Give me the details."

James grinned and pulled out a small notebook embossed with his initials: JJ. "Two-for-one. I feel efficient as hell today. Let's see... It's clear north of town. The meeting point is a little row of tin buildings with a welding shop and assorted other blue-collar shit." He turned his notebook to them and waited until they each nodded that they had memorized the address. "The pros are out of Omaha. They'll meet you there to go over specifics. Once I call them with your names, the job could happen any time. A guy named Paul will complete your trio of subcontractors. He's weird, but okay. Full disclosure: he used to be a dealer."

Heather groaned, and Gabe barely stopped himself from following suit. Common opinion around the criminal watercooler was that drug dealers were among the lowest in the professional food chain. The majority were unpredictable amateurs at best and violent morons at worst, and Gabe normally did everything he could to separate himself from them and the Jimenez Cartel most of them worked for. But while it certainly did nothing to ease his reservations, he knew it was already too late to back out. Nice guy that James might be, he hadn't carved out his little niche by letting people walk away with sensitive information unless they had ample incentive to keep quiet. James might let him loose for old time's sake, but his future prospects would be shot—and he'd count himself lucky that nothing else was. It took a special kind of ignorance to believe that a man who wears fancy clothes and gets regular manicures can't also be terribly dangerous.

Heather apparently didn't have the same fears. "I thought you told me that this was a professional—"

"Stop," James said, cutting her off with an upraised hand. "I told you this would be easy. I didn't say it would be a trip to candyland. Are you really backing out because of one dude?"

Heather met James's stare for a long time before clicking her tongue in annoyance and then waving the last few moments away like a swarm of gnats. "Keep going."

"Gee, thanks," James said. "As far as I know, you're leaving from there, so prepare accordingly. The meeting point is supposed to be secure, so you can use your own vehicle to get there. Questions?"

Heather shook her head and Gabe did the same.

"How about names?" James asked. "You using an alias?"

Heather shrugged, apparently unconcerned, but Gabe took longer to consider. He had a whole list of fake identities and personalities he could use, but most were tailored for specific cons. For something as ambiguous and potentially dangerous as this, his best bet was to use one that was fully fleshed out and easy to wear. "Viktor," he said.

James smirked and shook his head. He'd seen the character a few times. "Nice. I'll warn the neighborhood watch." He slid from the hood and snatched up his food. "I'll text the go-time once I have it, but they're moving fast. Could be tonight."

With that, James got in his car and pulled away, leaving Gabe and Heather standing there together in the settling dust. He searched for something clever to say, but Heather spoke before he could make a fool of himself.

"Does this seem weird to you?" she asked.

He almost made a quip about his whole life seeming weird to him, but he throttled it just in time. "Yeah," he said, then surprised himself. "Do you want to get lunch and talk about it?"

Heather looked him over and seemed to honestly consider the invitation, then she cracked a smile and slipped her professional demeanor back on. "Thank you, but no. I have some important things to do before this starts. Can't leave loose threads hanging." She dropped him a quick parting wink. "See you later, Gabe."

He shook his head as he watched her walk away. The words had been simple, but they'd still left him feeling like she had just promised something that hadn't really been there. He ratcheted up his respect for her by another notch. A man could make dangerous assumptions with just that tiny bit of inflection. Probably *expensive* assumptions. Heather was good, and he'd have to watch out for that. Interesting and beautiful though she may be, he held no illusions that her wholesome, honest facade extended any deeper than his own. She wasn't a woman to cross lightly, let alone to casually take out for lunch.

He glanced once more at the food truck menu, almost considering the bratwurst and chutney, but came to his senses and got in his car. He had important things to do too, and he was already overdue for the biggest by a few days. Putting it off anymore wouldn't make it go away. It was time to deliver groceries.

SEVEN WEEKS AGO

"Please! I swear I won't tell anyone!" the man whined as he struggled uselessly against the paralyzing geas.

In answer, Gwendal drew her index finger across his throat and let her nail bite deep enough to open the artery. She stepped back fastidiously to spare her shoes, then watched for the full minute it took for him to stop thrashing. She felt the body weaken and fade as the blood drained, then let the moment linger as she tried to find the exact instant the spirit began to slip free.

At her gesture, the sorcerer stepped forward to weave his spell song. "Taken, spilled, and gifted soul," he intoned over the body. "Worthless life made worthy. Sup of strength and make you whole. Worthless life made worthy. Be you more with pittance paid. Worthless life made worthy. May you never be unmade! Worthless life made worthy!"

The words were a translation of a translation pulled from memories a thousand years old, but with the weird musical power behind them Gwendal felt the connection actually form this time. She took up the offered spirit and breathed deeply, and was elated to feel the old familiar pulse of energy enter her like a lover. It wasn't perfect yet, but it filled the empty spaces in her, and she inhaled until she had every bit.

Then she collapsed back onto the bed to bathe in the afterglow as the power burned through her like an inferno in an abandoned mine. It cleared cobwebs from corners and shed light in the dark places, and suddenly it was so much easier to think and remember. Flashes of her true self came crawling back from where they'd been scattered through millennia of dispersion in the Ether, and she took each shard of herself up in a delicate mental grasp to piece it all back together.

Her homes came first, beginning with the last and moving back. A dark altar, soaked in terror and blood, hidden beneath a Christian church. Then a grand castle built in her honor by a beloved who promised more than he could give and had died for it. A small village in the mountains where her name was spoken with lust and reverence and pain. A cave on an island now lost beneath the waves. A mud hole in the savannah. A dark desperate place in a mother's fear. A glimmer of hatred. A whispered curse.

But her true home, the one which had never crumbled or burned, was still there in the noise of emotion that filled the city. It wasn't as thick here as it had been in less enlightened times, but what it lacked in potency it more than made up for in sheer quantity. There was more than she would have guessed possible, and it seemed now to come in many unimagined flavors. The humans, for all their new wonders, had not yet learned to conquer fear. They had only invented new ways to distract themselves from how deeply in it they were buried.

The old power sparked within her again, and her oldest names returned. Dread Wife. Night Mother. Fearling, Wail Witch, Womb Stalker. All of it was still out there, waiting for her, and she breathed the surfeit of it in as the last of the dead man's life curled lazily into her nostrils. She was still worshiped, in a way. The humans just didn't remember how to name her.

She used her new strength to part the veil between reality and the Ether for an instant, then sent a brief brush of her presence skirting past the wall of the precept bindings. The protections were weaker now that the old gods who had placed them had fled the physical realm, and that would help when the time came. But she still needed more power to pry it all open.

"I am coming," she said into the mists.

The reply came back only as an impression of his fierce hunger and vast power, but it was enough. He was ready and waiting. All she had to do was loose him, and together they could fulfill their grand purpose. Side-by-side, they could save this universe.

The clarity faded and her thoughts settled back to the plodding human pace. She had been gone from the solid world for too long, and she needed a better way to gather power. The foolish sorcerer had spent every scrap of magic within the old fairy circle at the mansion when he'd inadvertently loosed her, and even that much wouldn't have been enough for her purpose. The veil was still thinly drawn there, but she would need to bring more power to tear it and break past the precepts. Sacrifices would be needed. Enough blood to wrench forth a god.

CHAPTER THREE

"I don't steal from poor people. This isn't fake nobility for the sake of book sales, (Tell your friends!) it's just that poor people have less to take. I could clean out a poor guy and walk away with a thousand dollars and a vocal enemy, or I could get ten times that from a rich guy who'll never want anyone to know about his stupid mistake. Which do you think I prefer? Plus, which makes you angrier from the outside looking in? The inherent injustice of wealth inequality seems to cancel out the theft for people. I call it the Robin Hood effect: we don't mind seeing the rich lose something, no matter how it happens, even if the only needy person benefiting is me."

-Excerpt from Chapter One, CONscience

    Gabe stared at the building, listening to the traffic go by behind him as he worked up the courage to go inside. He'd stopped for the groceries on the way, taking more time than he probably should have, and now they sat in the back seat taunting him. This was something he didn't have a knack for, something his father ironically had never taught him how to handle, and he dreaded it every time.
    He sighed and put on his happy face before getting out of the car. The door buzzed and he pushed through, wrangling his grocery bags past the heavy steel monster as it tried to shut on him. He recognized the receptionist from the dozens of other times he'd slipped past, and he nodded to her like usual. She nodded back, but this time seemed to linger on him a moment longer. She mumbled something that Gabe didn't catch, and then he was moving past.
    "Mr. Delling?" a voice called from the back offices.
    The receptionist's mouth twisted into a frown, and she gave Gabe an apologetic look before bending to her computer as if removing herself from the line of fire. A moment later, the director of the facility, a woman named Cyndy, came around the corner. She led with a fake

smile and trailed the kind of purposeful air that usually meant trouble or money.

"Good, Mr. Delling. I've been meaning to call you," she said, her tone carefully free of any edges or burs of inflection that might cause offense. "Do you have a moment?"

Gabe hefted his bags. "Actually, I'm just dropping off today. I have a shift starting soon."

Cyndy pursed her lips. "Hmmm, well, I do need to discuss some things—"

"No problem!" Gabe interrupted, drifting down the corridor. "I'll come by in a few days and we'll have a chat. Good to see you!"

"I'm trying to save you embarrassment, Gabriel," she said, loudly enough for the whole office to hear. "It's about your payments. I have contacted you several times."

Gabe stopped and dropped his goofy kid act. "I think I'm paid in full to the end of the month."

Cyndy nodded and tapped her fingernails on the counter. "Yes, you are. But the new management company is insisting on at least three months of deposit on record at all times. It's something that's been policy for several years, but you were given some special leniency in the past. That is no longer possible."

Gabe stifled his initial anger and moved back toward the counter to where Cyndy stood. Then he took the chance to really look at her, letting his only real talent do its work. She was partially obscured by the desk as if not fully willing to commit to a confrontation but wishing that she was. Her face was carefully blank, awaiting the expected battle, but her eyes showed the glisten of fear around the edges. She didn't know him or how he was going to react, but it looked like she suspected the worst. She was ready for him to yell and rant and maybe even get physical. So he had to do the opposite.

Gabe knew the woman wouldn't respond to normal manipulation, but that didn't mean she was untouchable. One of the first lessons he'd learned was that stupid people have no idea how stupid they actually are, but that smart people tend to know their exact IQs. So while it was hard to lead a clever person by the nose, buried clues and dropped incentives could lead even a genius into conning themselves. He siphoned off the rest of his anger and sent it into the mental closet where he kept his non-productive emotions and spare personae. Then he allowed himself to deflate. He didn't have one complete personality for this, so he took pieces from several and made something on the fly. The tears came automatically.

"I don't understand, ma'am," he said, letting a hitch enter his voice as he tried to walk the narrow line between helplessness and fragile pride. "I thought I was keeping up. Three months is... That kind of money..." He trailed off by shaking his head and lifting the bags to his stomach as if searching for something to hold onto. The trick was to play out just enough net to tangle her.

The effect on Cyndy was immediate. She had girded herself for a battle, but here instead was a tragedy. The armor visibly fell away from her to be replaced with something very near sympathy, and she even took several steps toward him as the new scene came into focus. "Oh, I..." she stopped and looked around for backup that wasn't coming.

"Why don't we go to my office?" she asked, reaching for him.

He took a small step back and let his eyes widen as if he was afraid of her touch. Then he pretended to catch himself, and he gave her an apologetic look that he hoped would appear long-practiced. It was subtle. And it felt so dirty.

Cyndy's eyes narrowed, and Gabe wondered if he had overplayed it. But as she slowly lowered her hand, a new comprehension was entering her gaze. He watched as she created an entire story from the few scraps he'd given her, and he molded his expression to match. It was a mix of shame and defiance and fear, and over it all he layered the sudden desire to be absolutely anywhere else—which he didn't have to fake at all.

He moved to leave the facility, but allowed himself to be stopped when Cyndy called after him and stepped into the trap. She now looked at him with pity and understanding instead of resolve. And though it was exactly what he'd wanted, he still felt guilty beneath that caring gaze. With this kind of con, he could never help but feel he was stealing something worse than money—as if compassion was a finite resource.

"Y...Yes?" he asked, shifting his bags in real discomfort.

She moved close to him and lowered her voice for the first time. "Just stop in next week, okay? I'll see what I can do about some kind of deposit that's less than standard. Maybe half or less. If it were up to me..." She spread her hands.

Gabe let a few more tears fall as he smiled. Then, still fighting the bags, he leaned in and shocked the woman with an awkward hug. He might have imagined it, but it almost felt like she sank into it. And that, more than anything else, made him feel like a complete asshole. He made himself whisper, "Thank you" as he pulled away. No sense wasting the bait if you weren't prepared to set the hook.

She patted him on the shoulder, then slipped an envelope into one of the sacks. "This is an invoice of what they're asking for. See what you think and we'll talk. I'll buy a little more time until then. Have a good visit, Gabriel."

Gabe nodded and walked away, allowing his steps to grow more purposeful and confident as he went. He'd let her think she had just saved him. From now on he'd be her personal project, and she'd be more likely to bend the rules for him. She'd be invested and connected, and wouldn't want to see it go to waste. It was more work for him to keep up appearances, sure, but that deposit really was quite a bit of money. That, at least, he hadn't had to lie about.

Feeling like the worst kind of genius, Gabe followed the well-lit hallway to the sixth door on the right and the last place on earth he ever wanted to go.

CHAPTER FOUR

```
"My father taught me everything I know.

I've never forgiven him for that."

-Excerpt from Chapter Two, CONscience
```

    Gabe could hear the television even before he got to the door, so he knocked loudly enough to be heard over it. A moment later, a balding man in a flannel shirt and track pants peered out nervously.

    "Hey, Dad," Gabe said, holding up the sacks. "I brought supplies."

    Alexander Delling grunted in reply and shuffled back toward his worn brown chair to continue watching a game show.

    "How are you?" Gabe asked as he pushed in and searched for empty counter space. The unit was small—more like a dorm room than an apartment—but it had a kitchen and was fairly cozy.

    He cleared a spot for the bags and started stashing the canned stuff before he finally heard the grunted reply from the chair. "Are you having a bad day?" Gabe asked. There was another grunt, this one surlier, and Gabe balled up an empty sack. "Well, we got soda this time, so that should improve your mood."

    In response, his dad stood and shuffled over to take one of the orange cans from the counter. He avoided Gabe's eyes the whole way, then went right back to his chair and the acoustic guitar that always sat propped nearby. He fumbled with the can's tab a bit, as he always did, but eventually muscled it open with a crack and hiss. His hand shook as he brought it to his lips, but only a little spilled today.

    Gabe sighed and grabbed a candy bar, leaving the groceries for a moment. He could see they'd shaved his dad recently, and the scar from the accident was clearer than usual. It ran in a thick pink ridge up from his jaw to disappear into his receding hairline, marring the perfectly nondescript Delling features that had once served him so well as a conman. It wasn't the only thing that had killed that life for him, but it was the easiest symbol. And Gabe still couldn't look at it without remembering that first night at the hospital. The blood and the impossible trauma were still etched in his memory, and the story of a drunken car accident as told by a tired doctor was still as clear as if he was hearing it for the first time. The fear and the guilt came too, but he pushed it all back down where it belonged.

"Did you steal something again?" he asked. "Are you in trouble?"

Alexander shrugged and stirred uncomfortably, reaching over to the guitar to run a finger up and down the A string to elicit a low buzz.

Gabe crossed his arms and waited, but the tactic didn't work well when the other person had nowhere else to be. It was the same ritual they always went through: Gabe trying to get any words at all flowing, his dad refusing or unable to be drawn in, Gabe trying to pretend like he knew what he was doing, and his dad oblivious to most of it.

Gabe decided to shift gears. "I brought candy," he said, lifting the chocolate like a priceless jewel.

Alexander's face lit at once, and his hand moved from the guitar to snatch the snack. Their eyes met for an instant in the transfer, and Gabe thought he caught the hint of a smile. It was enough. He moved back into the kitchen to finish unpacking.

Halfway through, he found the invoice envelope and slipped it into his pocket. "Hey, I have another job coming up. It's quick, but it should cover us for another few months. Pay for this place and groceries and keep the house going. I thought you'd like to hear."

Alexander grunted past his candy, and Gabe went on. "It should be simple. Just a one-day thing." He shifted a bag of marshmallows before it fell out of the cabinet. "And there's this girl that's pretty interesting. Smart and cute—also a little scary. I know you used to say I'm not supposed to get attached to anyone, blah, blah, blah. But I'm thirty-two, dad. I should probably be thinking about this stuff. Of course, I'm fairly sure she thinks I'm a complete moron, which—" The moment the word came out of his mouth he regretted it and he held his breath. His dad didn't seem to notice any more than he did anything else, but Gabe felt ashamed anyway. He knew better.

He finished unpacking in silence, then decided he should probably atone. He could play the good son for a few minutes, and these days there was only one way to do that. He pulled a kitchen chair up next to his dad and carefully lifted the guitar from its stand. Alexander watched him warily, poised to defend the only thing he seemed to care about anymore, but all of that changed when Gabe began to tune.

The first chord was like a magic spell. He only remembered a few songs anymore and he'd never been a great player, but he knew he could stumble through the same ones over and over again and his father wouldn't care. It was the sound the man loved. The warm hum and curve of the dark wood seemed to reach places in him that words no longer could. His dad had been a decent player once upon a time, and some of Gabe's only good childhood memories were set in the dive bars they'd played between jobs. He had learned about the guitar and about life while drinking cherry cola and making friends with felons who had treated him better than his own dad had. Happy times for a ten-year-old. But Alexander's skill was yet one more casualty of the accident—along with most of his memories and the ability to take care of himself—and now the only vestige seemed to be the love of the thing.

The songs came without thought, and Gabe sang quietly with them. He could at least do that well. He played until his fingers hurt and his dad's features and posture softened. Then he brought the song to a soft close, retuned the guitar, and propped it back in its stand. Alexander's hand went right back to the neck as if longing to pull the same sounds from it, then he finally stirred and looked over to Gabe with real recognition. His eyes were wide and wet, like he'd just appeared in a strange place.

"Oh," Alexander said, his voice a mix of surprise and annoyance. "Stephanie? Where?" The words were thick and slow in his mouth as if he hadn't spoken for the whole week between visits. He looked to the door.

Gabe swallowed hard and rose. He hated this part more than anything else. "Mom's gone, dad. Long time ago."

His father looked back at him and that spark of recognition had already fled. "Oh." The animation drained from his face, and he turned back to the television."You can go."

Gabe started to scold him for being rude, but then just nodded. He rose and replaced the kitchen chair, then cleaned up the trash of the week and put away the laundry. All things considered, it had been a good visit. There hadn't been any outbursts, nothing was broken, and he hadn't had to explain his mother's utter abandonment of them for the hundredth time. Plus his dad had spoken a whole seven words. It was about as much as could be hoped for. Hearing the word "degenerative" and watching it unfold in real time were two entirely different things.

Gabe moved to leave, but then turned at the door and just watched. His father had changed nine years ago, and Gabe had been forced to change with him. Alexander Delling had once been ruthlessly clever, and had used it to ruin every life he'd ever touched. The kid he'd never wanted was no exception, and their relationship had been one of distance and disappointment on both sides. But while being wanted was a luxury Gabe knew he might never know, it was something to be needed. And day-by-day, he was trading the long-hardened hate for something he grudgingly considered better. Tarnished as it was, there was still a magic for him in the word "family". This was the bit of it he had, and he wouldn't let it go now that he'd snagged it.

His phone buzzed and kicked him from his reverie. It was a message from James. "Bye, dad," he said as he closed the door. He quietly walked out of the nursing home, keeping to himself and avoiding eye contact with the staff. His dad was safe, and life was normal for another week. He'd overcome his fear again and done his duty. Now it was time to do his job.

FOUR WEEKS AGO

"I love Detroit," Gwendal said, admiring the high vaulted ceiling of the living room. "So many beautiful old houses like this just sitting empty, waiting to be snapped up." She grasped at the air to illustrate her point, then turned back to her captive audience. "Don't you think?"

The younger man nodded vigorously, ready to agree with anything. He'd been the easiest one to get there. A bottle of vodka and a smile and he'd jumped like an eager puppy. The couple had taken more effort and money to lure.

"And so many people desperate for an opportunity," she said. "It's much better than where I came from. All I did was eat four little college boys and the whole town went crazy. I felt like some kind of criminal. Not like here at all."

The woman sobbed through her gag and the older man struggled to free himself from bonds he couldn't see. Gwendal looked again at the young man. He was dirty and smelly, but he seemed relatively strong compared to the pudgy man next to him. It certainly wasn't the cream of the human crop, but she would take what she could get for now. She'd risen higher from less. And since she'd left her pet sorcerer behind to make arrangements in Nebraska while she sought safer hunting grounds, she'd had to go entirely without help. The successful sacrifices back in Lincoln had done wonders for her strength, and now it seemed improper that a goddess should have to run down her own meals.

"Oh, you're no fun," she said to the couple. "Fine. I won't part two lovers. Women aren't usually to my taste, but I can find a use for you."

The relief on their faces was almost sickening until Gwendal stepped up to the older man and shoved her thumb nail into his throat. The blood came at once, hot and vibrant, and his soul quickly followed.

The woman next to him tried to scream through her gag, but with her body numb from the neck down, it only came out as another weak sob. Gwendal ignored it as she fed, pulling the freed energy deep into her and letting it mingle with her growing strength. She'd gotten much better at it over the last few weeks, as the old ways slowly came back to her, and she could now finish a meal long before the blood stopped flowing. His life was hers before the body slid to the floor.

Gwendal moved past the sobbing woman and blessed the younger man with a sweet, sated smile. His eyes were wide with fear, and he was pulling hard against his bonds. "Oh, don't worry, sweetheart," she said, stepping forward and running a long dark nail down his filthy cheek. "I'm keeping you. You will serve me, and help find my lover." Then she reached back without looking and punctured the woman's throat.

The energy spilled out at once, a tempting treat to gorge on, but this time Gwendal redirected it instead. She took up the raw power of the sacrifice and shaped it into a wedge to part the veil, then propelled her will back into the Ether for the first time since returning to Earth. It was barely deep enough to matter—and not anywhere near to where she longed to reach—but it was enough for today. Another step.

She seized something wild and wriggling, then turned her attention back to the young man. Her true power had yet to return, but he wasn't any kind of challenge either. He'd lost his will to addiction long ago, and it was no trouble to follow his fear and enter him without a fight. There was little else but desperate terror within, and it was only a matter of moments to scour everything clean and pitch the human soul out to leave an empty shell for her new pet. Far from perfect, perhaps, but Hounds weren't picky.

The man went limp as his spirit fled, then the Umbra Hound took over. At first it settled poorly, like a bear forced into a tuxedo. But after several minutes of jerking limbs and acclimation, the head snapped up and Gwendal saw a Hound looking out through the eyes. She'd done it. She was rather proud of herself, in fact. It had taken far more energy than she'd expected, and only confirmed how much she still needed the damned sorcerer, but she'd still succeeded. It was a good start.

"I am your master," she said to the creature as she dropped a bond on it. It struggled briefly, testing the length of its leash, then it quieted just as the woman in the chair finally finished dying. "Good," Gwendal said. "Now you need a shower."

She released her paralyzing geas, and the Hound jumped to its feet and sprinted away. It hit the front door in two long strides and burst through the wood with a great crack that sent splinters scattering across the front lawn. But Gwendal had only to tug on the bond to drop the creature to its knees. It squirmed and squealed on the floor as if it had been kicked, but it didn't try to rise again without her permission. Eventually she'd find one that was more mature and stable, but this one would work for now. It just needed training.

    She spotted a man jogging through the neighborhood, and she pursed her lips. "You are now bound to serve and protect me with your life, little one. And I will most certainly ask that of you." She watched the jogger come to the end of the block and turn down a darker road. "But first, let's grab a bite."

CHAPTER FIVE

"I rarely get involved with people. They just get in the way and bring messy complications like the kind of relationships that last longer than a weekend. To that end, I never go on a job as myself. I've built up a stable of alternate identities over the years that I call "personae", and after being worn for so long, they've basically become personalities unto themselves. I know that makes me sound like I need some psychiatric help, but it makes me damned convincing too. My character is easier to believe if it's not totally an act. It's like the difference between a prop sword and the real thing: they're both fine from a distance, but only one will stand up to close scrutiny. If my life depends on how well I pretend to be someone else, I'd rather be using the sharpest version. Even if carrying around a metaphorical sword makes me a teensy bit crazy."

-Excerpt from Chapter Three, CONscience

    Gabe pulled up to the warehouse after dark and parked away from the main road. His car pinged and popped as it cooled in the evening air, and he took a moment to prepare himself. Someday he'd finish his book, or get that big score, or take the traditional path of con artists and go to law school, but for now this was his job. It was time to shut up and do the thing.

    Given that he didn't know or trust anyone on his team, he had decided on a tough-guy persona he'd developed as a kid when he'd still thought his dad's talent was worth emulating. He'd never been the strongest or fastest, but his mouth had always been both, giving him plenty of opportunities to learn how to talk his way out of things he'd talked himself into. For everything else in those early days, he had relied on Viktor.

    The persona was all bluff of course—Gabe could fight about as well as he could crochet doilies—but the character acted just close enough to psychotic that it didn't matter. And on the playground, when most kids were willing to believe anything said loudly enough, bluff was all you needed. If he couldn't weasel out of something, Viktor came out to play. He couldn't recall why his twelve-year-old self had chosen the name, but it somehow still fit. The Russian accent had disappeared awhile back though. The 1990s had been a simpler time.

Gabe gave his steering wheel a few hard smacks to get himself into the proper alpha-male mindset, then he tried a few experimental phrases in the sanctity of his car to settle the personality into place. "You fuckin' want some? I'll fuckin' kill you! I'll dropkick your fuckin' fuck ass from a fuckin' overpass!" He pitched his voice lower and spoke like he had a marshmallow in his mouth, and the man started to take shape in his head.

The character was completely over the top, he knew, but bad situations rarely left time to communicate. If you wanted to use your only given instant to stop violence from happening to your face, it was best to make every word and cue pack the biggest punch. The keys were novelty and volume. He snarled once for good measure and smacked his chest a few times before pulling it back from crazy to merely questionable. Being given a healthy distance was one thing, but there was no sense in getting shot as soon as he walked through the door.

He pounded the steering wheel again until his palm started to hurt, then just happened to glance over to find Heather staring at him through the window. Her arms were crossed and she wore an expression that managed to perfectly bridge horrified amazement and girlish delight. He briefly considered a less embarrassing excuse to salvage the situation—like saying he'd seen a really scary spider—but eventually settled on just pretending like it hadn't happened. Best not to mess with the classics.

"What's up?" he asked, as he got out of the car.

She watched him with mock-wariness. "Too much coffee? Or did I interrupt your pre-game ritual?" Then she gave him a half-hearted muscleman pose before breaking into a laugh.

He smirked and gestured for her to go ahead on the sidewalk. "Yeah, well, we both have our methods, right? I was putting on my armor. You of all people should get that." Then, to his own horror, he found himself gesturing meaningfully to the tight shirt that hugged what was possibly an extra layer of padding in her bra. As soon as it happened, he couldn't believe he'd done it. Viktor was in his system now, and most of his normal restraint had been pushed out to make room. He managed to keep his face neutral, but inside he couldn't think of much beyond a constant refrain of "No, no, no, no, no!"

Heather though, seemed amused, and she brushed by him with a new twinkle in her eyes. Either she was so used to being objectified that she'd developed a resistance to it, or Viktor's natural jackassery genuinely worked for her on some level. Either one felt wrong to hope for, and he came out pretty bad in the equation regardless.

As they approached a set of slate gray double-doors, Gabe felt Viktor's manic energy taking over and he began rolling his shoulders and clenching his fists as if he couldn't contain it. He wished he'd thought to add a few fake tattoos for a better ex-con look, but it was a little late now. Heather turned and nodded as she noticed the change.

For her part, she pulled back her shoulders and tightened her stomach like an impossible pinup model, then she let her eyes go cold and distant—daring stares and wilting them. Gabe tried to limit his reaction to the same professional nod he'd gotten, but Heather's satisfied look told him he'd failed. So far he wasn't coming off as a very nice guy, but he reminded himself that it was for the best. Theirs wasn't an industry for polite young men, nor for women who preferred them. If he was playing a stupid jerk tonight, he needed to act like one. The "bad-boy with a heart of gold" archetype was way too cheesy to work outside of comic books and romance novels.

Then they went in. The smell of oil and metal hit him first, reminding him of a mechanic's shop, but the place appeared to be a storage facility for industrial equipment. Huge, shrink-wrapped machines lined up in rows that ran the length of the building, and at the end of the center aisle was a platform that rose above the main floor and held a single-room office, like a sentry tower over a field of battle-ready steel behemoths. Heather moved straight for the office and the silhouettes within, and Gabe followed her at a middling distance. He didn't want to give the impression that they were together, but didn't want to dispel the notion either. That kind of ambiguity could be useful when dealing with strangers. The fact that she smelled like warm strawberries and trailed it in her wake was totally coincidental.

They reached the stairs, but before they could ascend, a shorter man in fatigues noisily entered the building and finally drew the attention of the those above.

"Call out your names," a male voice said from the office.

Heather replied first and Gabe followed with "Viktor." A moment later, the short man got close enough to shout, "Paul" in a gritty baritone, and the plank door above them opened to reveal two men outlined in the entrance with a female behind them. The taller man beckoned, and they went up.

The room was barely an office. It was roughly the size of a double-wide supply closet, holding a desk, a chair, and enough pegboard on the walls to hang all the wrenches in the known universe. The rest of the space that wasn't already occupied by people was filled with cigarette smoke, and Gabe slipped in behind Heather just as they heard Paul hit the stairs below. The man who'd beckoned them was tall and had a shaved head that was clearly meant to hide his balding. He stood like the leader of the three, which probably meant that he wasn't, and he seemed awfully proud of the gun at his side. He was the muscle of the group. Maybe not the brightest, but that could be a dangerous assumption with big men.

The other man was older and shorter, but overall better-looking —though he was closer to overweight than he'd probably like to admit. He seemed like the smarter of the two, but perhaps allowed Baldy to play at leader as it suited him. This, to Gabe, was what a real professional thief looked like. The woman, on the other hand, was blonde and slim, and immediately seemed like she might be the smartest of the three. It would explain why she let the men play their little posturing game between themselves. As the brains she would be scary enough, but as a woman in the business she would also be the hardest and most dangerous. Weakness didn't last long among predators, and women had to be twice as strong. She noted his stare and winked as she took a pull on her cigarette.

"So," Gabe said as he looked away, "do we get your names or what?"

Baldy let his own gaze linger on Heather for an awkwardly long moment before turning to Gabe. "Trevor," he said. "This is Maxwell, and that's Laura."

"A pleasure," Maxwell said. He didn't exactly have a British accent, but he clearly wanted to sound refined. Like maybe he had a cravat hidden in his closet at home. "You three come highly recommended by people we trust. Are you up for this tonight?"

Gabe scoffed as Viktor. "We'd fuckin' better be. It's a little late to call a temp service."

Maxwell smirked. "Fine. Ask a stupid question, I suppose." He picked up a folder from the desk and moved to hand it to Gabe, then seemed to think better of it and gave it to Heather. Gabe didn't blame him.

Heather opened the folder to show a satellite photo of a house somewhere out in the country. It was big, but the main distinguishing characteristic was the way the wind-break trees surrounded the property almost in a perfect circle that was broken only by a long driveway. "This is the place?" she asked.

Maxwell nodded. "It should be pretty standard. I'm told you've been briefed about the odd nature of this job, so I won't go into that. The way is clear for us, and we've ensured that the house is unoccupied tonight. The goal is to be in and out in twenty minutes, which is just shy of the police response time to this place."

"So it's out there a ways," Heather said, settling in to her assumed position as leader of the three independent contractors. Paul apparently minded about as much as Gabe did.

Maxwell nodded again. "About thirty miles northwest. A third of it on gravel."

"When do we leave?" Paul asked. He had a distinct accent that Gabe couldn't quite place in so few words.

Maxwell glanced to a clock on the desk. "A little over two hours. Eleven is shift change for a few of the factories up north, so it's not unusual to see traffic moving through the area at that time. We want to be heading home when the bulk of the traffic is active. A small detail, but every little bit helps cover the trail."

"And the pay?" Gabe asked. "When does that come in?"

Maxwell glanced at Trevor, but before either of them could speak, Laura blew out a cloud of smoke and stepped in. "You'll be paid once everything is safely packed and onto the next phase. You can stick around tonight until that point, or you can wait for the check to come in the mail."

Heather was the only one who chuckled at the joke. "Fine. So what do we do until go-time? Play board games?"

Laura took another pull on her cigarette, and Maxwell stepped in smoothly. "There are a few more formalities. We need to set some ground rules and establish a security baseline."

"First," Trevor said, jumping in like this scene had been rehearsed, "I'm carrying the only cellphone and gun on this trip. If you have either or both put them on the desk right now."

Gabe and Heather both placed their phones down and then spread their hands in similar gestures that invited scrutiny. Gabe never carried a gun. He hated them as a matter of principal, but practicality had a bit to do with it too. People tended to shoot at you when you carried a gun, and bullets were notoriously difficult to talk down. Plus he was naturally a bad shot, which didn't help his disposition at all. His whole life philosophy was based on the idea that things weren't worth doing if he wasn't effortlessly good at them. It had worked so far.

Paul, on the other hand, removed three large handguns from about his person and mutely placed them on the table. Gabe wondered if the job had been pitched that much differently to the man, or if he just routinely went strapped for urban combat.

Trevor seemed to understand and gave the smaller man a brief nod of respect when the last hand-cannon came out. "Good. Thank you. Now we need to establish a security baseline."

"Which means fucking what?" Gabe asked, allowing some of Viktor's perpetual irritation to come through.

"It fucking means," Trevor said, "that we need to make sure you're not wired." He held up a wide black wand that had an LCD display on the base.

"Just a quick scan and pat-down for anything we forgot to mention to one another," Maxwell said. "It picks up RF and wireless transmissions. You'll be checking us too. We'll all trust each other better after."

Gabe suddenly remembered his little pocket knife and slowly pulled it out for inspection. "How about this?"

Trevor glanced at it, then smirked and shook his head. "That's adorable. You can keep your nail file, man." He turned his gaze back to Heather and his smile became something oilier. "So who wants the first patdown?"

For some reason Gabe was unreasonably annoyed at that. He blamed Viktor. "Me," he said, stepping forward.

The scans and mutual pat-downs went smoothly, then it was just a matter of waiting for the time to come. They were instructed to stay in the building but without access to their phones—a special kind of torture which he found he liked even less than being groped by strangers. He looked to Heather, but found her already off to one side, going through some kind of martial art forms. She seemed unreceptive to company, and he doubted his clumsy flirting would improve that. So he settled in for a boring two-hour wait and ran through contingencies with the new information he'd gained. Had he known then how the night would turn out, he might have better appreciated the calm.

TWO WEEKS AGO

Seven in one night had been too many. She realized that now. But even as Gwendal fled through the dark neighborhood, her Hound's breath coming fast and hot at her back, she couldn't deny the exhilaration at the power she'd gained. It was more like the old days when there had been proper altars and supplicants. It had felt like a real ritual again. She almost felt like a goddess.

Gwendal spared a moment to imagine what she might have done with the power had she been given time to properly consume it. The depths of the Ether might have been within her grasp with such a large sacrifice, allowing her to skip all the machinations to wrest her lover back with brute force. But then that damned soldier had burst in on her and forced her to abandon the feast. He might even have sent her screaming back to the Ether had he expected her Hound. Her servant had bought her time to flee, but she knew the pursuit wasn't far behind. She would need to find a place to hide or she'd have no choice but to stand and fight. That might go well for her, or it might not. She didn't know what was chasing her, and she couldn't afford to risk it.

She vaulted eight feet into the air, clearing the next fence and landing mid-stride into her sprint. She heard her Hound hit the ground behind her, and his breath came out in a harsh rush when he landed. He was still keeping pace with her, but she could hear him starting to struggle. Gwendal glanced back and saw that his lovely white shirt was now stained with dark blood, and that just past him, the soldier in black was coming on quickly. She turned back and weighed her options, then took firm hold of the bond and forced the Hound to stop in the middle of the yard. It was a pity to lose him, but it was his purpose. She felt his dumb affection for her through the bond even as she left him behind. Then there was a pulse of sudden fear before the soldier slammed into him and the connection snapped.

Gwendal ran. She snatched up a rusty bike and launched it behind her with blind hope, then sprinted through an overgrown garden. She jumped the next fence, and the bright streetlamps of a busy road came into view just beyond some chain-link and a weedy field. A long row of businesses lined the far side, and she followed her instincts toward the humans she knew had to be there. She had not yet sculpted her flesh into her true form, and she had glamour enough to hide herself to the casual observer. She could still pass as a human. It might work.

Suddenly a weird buzzing gunshot sounded behind her, and a jolt of sweet pain registered in her shoulder as something both magical and not. The bullet passed straight through, but the force of it still pushed her forward and off her feet into a graceless tumble. She hit the ground hard, then her power raged to life in a black web that splayed out to carry her around and back up to standing. Another shot rang out and hit the ground where she'd just been. Her choices were gone.

Gwendal threw out her hands to bend the raw power she'd gained that night, forcing it out in thick, black tendrils that snaked like rotten tree roots in search of living flesh. She hadn't wanted this, but it did feel wonderful to be harnessing such power again, and she nearly laughed as her coils dragged the soldier to a sudden stop. There was nothing so heady as utter domination. Then some kind of charm pulsed from his body, and her magic rebounded with a jolt. She stumbled back in shock as the leftover power retreated into her gut like a kicked cur, then took another step back when he brought his huge weapon up to bear. The gun glowed with a faint power of its own, and she could sense at once that she wouldn't withstand many more shots from it. The thing had been specifically designed to kill an Umbra like her, and she wasn't strong enough yet to resist. She'd run out of time.

In desperation, she threw her whole strength into a glamour greater than any she'd yet attempted in this body, making herself an object of lust and terror that an entire nation might be ready to die for. But the soldier only paused and shook his helmeted head to shrug it off. Then he said something muffled by his mask: "Target... Terminate... Catherine." He paused as if waiting for a response, then nodded and prepared to fire.

Gwendal braced herself for release back into the Ether, back into another five hundred years of the constant struggle to maintain cohesion bereft of faith or fear. She snarled her defiance and started to weave a curse from a language centuries-dead. Then the man suddenly dropped to the ground as if someone had cut his strings, and there was a dark blade protruding from the thin line where his mask met his armor.

She backed against the fence and followed the trajectory up to a black shape sauntering across the pitched roof of the house. The thing dropped from two stories up, then continued walking toward her without missing a step. It was long and lithe, at least seven feet tall, and featureless from head to foot. At first Gwendal thought it was obscured in darkness, wrapping it around itself like a cloak. But as it neared, the thing began to look like a charcoal drawing come-to-life. As if it wasn't merely veiled in shadow, but made of it. It was a construct, she realized, and practically a work of art. She found herself appreciating the incredible craftsmanship even as she gathered the power to destroy it.

But the thing stopped well short of her and raised one smear of a hand for forbearance. "I bring an invitation," it said, its voice as empty as its body. "He would like to meet you. And help, if he is able."

Gwendal tried to ask for clarification, but was cut off abruptly as the creature fixed her with its eyeless gaze and spoke a single word of power: "KNOW."

Her mind lit with a flash of pure knowledge—too much at once—and she found herself on her knees and weeping from the pain. She might be a creature of creation, but the brain she inhabited had its own limitations. Flesh had never been intended to bear the weight of what Umbras demanded, and such things were at the outer limits of what was possible. Whoever had prepared the magic was immensely powerful.

Then the pain faded, and she knew much more about the world. It was a remarkable feeling: five hundred years of progress and power struggles, dynasties and disasters, all implanted directly into her brain in an instant.

"A gift," the Shadowman said, "in good faith." Then it came apart and blew away on the next breeze, discarded like an empty wrapper. Its animating force grounded itself and dissipated into the earth, and the blade disappeared from the man that Gwendal now understood was a Knight of Solomon named Archibald Deminov. He had once been quite feared among her kind. No more.

She walked over and kicked the body out of spite, then tasted the air for any remnants of his soul. For a moment she eyed his weapon and armor, tempted with the notion of such easy power, but the idea was preposterous. There were too many limits to such charms and hexes, and they rarely existed without a price to be paid by the bearer. The devices had likely fed on the man's own life force, which would explain their strength. But trading years for power was foolish in the extreme. And she would soon surpass the need for such toys anyway.

Gwendal sent tendrils of magic into the weapon and armor plates, exploring them until she found places where they were not impervious to her strength. She probed and pried, then surged her power to shatter all of it from within. There were many more Knights like him out there, she now knew, but leaving such a message would hopefully make them think twice about coming at her again.

She turned and made for the nearby road. There was a car waiting for her there, and in it, possibilities.

CHAPTER SIX

```
"We take because we can. I wish I had a better
explanation for you, but that's it. Maybe
upbringing and genetics play their parts, but
ultimately it boils down to the fact that we're
capable and willing and most other people
aren't. You hear about crimes of passion or
opportunity, but that's not guys like me. We
know exactly what we're doing when we're doing
it, and we planned it in advance. Every choice
has a consequence, and part of my job is to
foresee each path so I can follow the one that
nets me the most of your money. Cold and
calculating. We're like Wall Street bankers,
except… No, I can't actually think of a good
difference."

-Excerpt from Chapter Two, CONscience
```

At ten o'clock, the group came back together. Heather found Gabe first and nudged him with her foot. "Time to go," she said. She held out her hand to help him stand, and Gabe tried to hide his shock when she pulled him straight to his feet.

He grimaced and shook out his hand theatrically. "Powerlifting?" he guessed. "No, it has to be daintier than that. Log tossing."

"Tai Chi."

He nodded in appreciation. "That's slow motion martial arts, right? Like underwater karate? I thought that was for old people?"

She nudged him with her elbow as they turned toward the main exit. "Yes, sort-of, and no, in that order. It's more like dancing, and it's an amazing core and leg workout. They do some watered-down stuff with older people because it's low-impact, but the real thing is hard. And I get to kick ass. Win-win."

"Well it works. Plus, you'll be able to protect us from the world's slowest ninjas."

She pursed her lips, but there was a hint of a smile there. "I don't like to waste my time. If it isn't useful, valuable, or sexy I don't bother."

Gabe opened his mouth to reply that he was at least two of those things, but suddenly realized that they were flirting. Normally he would have tried to keep it going—probably ruining it in the process—but it was a stupid thing to do given the circumstances. So instead of making the witty, insightful remarks that definitely would have come to him, he simply said, "Good policy."

Professional that she was, Heather picked up on the hint and slipped her own mask back on. He wondered if she'd been trying to butter him up or if it had been a real lapse and she actually did like him. Either way, it didn't matter now. Something for later maybe, but now it was time to work.

Trevor stood at the main doors and opened them like a bouncer when they walked up. The outside air had grown cooler as the autumn night had settled in, and an old green pickup with a topper over the bed and dark tinted windows was idling nearby. Gabe noticed right away that it was a standard cab, leaving room for only three to get cozy up front while the others would be flying cargo. But before he could point that out, Maxwell slid in behind the wheel as if it was a foregone conclusion, then Laura slipped in next to him, followed shortly by Heather. None of them had walked particularly quickly, so it was a testament to their unwavering confidence in their right to the first-class seats that neither Trevor nor Paul had made even a cursory protest. Gabe thought about whining a little, but decided to bear it in manly silence instead. It didn't seem like good company in which to argue traditional shotgun rules.

He rode for twenty minutes in silent darkness while awkwardly avoiding conversation with the two people in the merry bunch that he liked the least, until the truck finally turned and he heard the crunch of gravel beneath the tires. They were headed into the country. Roughly ten minutes later, they turned again, and the sound of the gravel changed to a softer, finer crunch. If there was such a thing as a better grade of rocks for rich people, this was the driveway. It seemed like a silly notion, but then he had once sold dog-kidnapping insurance to a rich lady in Chicago. Wealthy people buying stupid stuff had kept him fed for most of his life. Premium gravel was fairly tame compared to Platinum United Pet Protection Services.

After another minute, Gabe noticed the darkness outside wavering, indicating that they had reached the trees encircling the house. The truck slowed and veered left before finally rolling to a stop and creaking into park.

"Let's go," Trevor said. He popped the back gate open and hopped out.

Gabe followed and suppressed a groan of pain as his legs and back protested. As he stretched, he noted that the trees there had all dropped their leaves already and stood eerily bare against the moonlit sky. He knew it wasn't late enough in the season for that, but the grass too looked ridiculously dry. It was like someone had sprayed everything with herbicide, and it gave the whole place a distinct haunted-house vibe that he didn't care for. They were one black cat or slamming shutter away from being in a bad slasher movie.

Heather came around the truck, crunching through the grass to meet him. "Comfy ride?"

He considered a few different replies, then remembered that he was being Viktor and simply grunted. It should have been automatic, but it was amazing how easily she threw him off his game. This morning he would have said he never slipped out of character, but now he found himself doing it constantly. And that didn't make much sense. While the life of a con artist wasn't nearly as sexy as the movies made it seem, he'd met plenty of beautiful women who hadn't had the same effect on him. There seemed to be something about Heather that stuck in his head like a catchy tune, annoying him relentlessly until he was humming it over most of his thoughts. It was like a kind of magic, and his only consolation was that he might be doing the same to her. Maybe it meant there was something between them—or, he realized, maybe it meant she was that much better at the game.

Gabe examined himself and realized that, yes, if something went wrong he would almost certainly side with Heather. That made his feelings for her stupid and dangerous, regardless of their authenticity. And it was likely the exact reaction she was looking for. She would have an effortless ally if things went sour. Or maybe not. Maybe it was real and she thought he was an adorable rogue and wanted to kiss his face. It was impossible to know for sure with someone like her—or with someone like him, in fairness. The whole thing was exactly why people like them stayed away from one another: mutually assured distraction.

He turned his attention to the actual reason he was there. The house was a big, two-story mishmash of Colonial, Victorian, and Roman architecture, with pillars and gabled windows crammed together everywhere. It was clearly expensive, and practically a proper mansion, but it looked like it had been built by three different architects who all hated each other. He silently wished the owners of the house good luck in selling the thing off in the divorce. He doubted there would be many people interested in the Little Bathhouse on the Prairie. Trevor unloaded several canvas bags from the back, then handed them to Maxwell to distribute. Laura followed behind and gave each person a photocopied list and a small flashlight with an amber filter taped over the lens.

Gabe took his paper with a frown and inspected it. Art had never been his thing. He knew many conmen had historically been artists and vice versa, but he had neither the talent nor interest in it. Just then, however, he was wishing he'd done a little studying. Nothing on the list meant anything to him aside from the notion that most of the names looked vaguely Slavic, and he didn't think that would be terribly helpful.

"Do you know what you're looking for?" he asked Heather quietly.

She leaned over and pretended to acknowledge something he was showing her. "Of course. Don't you?"

Gabe grunted as if impressed by the collection. Then he whispered, "Not a damn clue."

She hissed softly and gave him an unreadable look, then she moved toward Laura. The two women talked for a bit and Heather pointed at Gabe, and then at Paul and Trevor in turn. Laura seemed to consider for a moment before nodding.

"Max, get us in," Laura whispered. "I think it would be best if we pair up Trevor and Paul, Heather and Gabe, and Max and me. That way we stand the best chance of finding the right items and getting them hauled out in the quickest time. Is that okay?" She asked as if she would be fine with objections, but also somehow made it clear she didn't expect any. Max gave her a questioning look, but then jogged across the lawn to a window near the entrance.

Gabe watched Heather as she returned to his side. Her face was frozen somewhere between satisfaction and annoyance, so he decided to speak first. "Thanks, but I would have figured it out."

She raised an eyebrow and blinked at him. "In the three years of Art History I took, we only talked about some of these obscure Polish artists once or twice. You were just going to figure that out? With what, magic?"

Gabe shrugged, "If Percocet Paul can sort it out I should be able to."

Heather rolled her eyes and moved to join the rest of the group near Max, who was just then shouldering the window open. "His last name is Nowak," she said, as if it should mean something to him. Then she caught his blank look. "Lord, how have you convinced so many people you're so good? Laura and I had some girl-talk on the way over. The name Nowak is like the Johnson of Poland. Paul was born there. Also, he sold weed and acid, not pills. Sorry to kill your alliteration."

Gabe tipped his head in acceptance. "Okay, fine. I guess I owe you one. You are spectacularly talented and the queen of everything."

Heather looked away but let her mouth curl into a wry smile, and Gabe turned back to watch Max haul himself into the house. The man was much nimbler than his frame suggested, and he was through the window surprisingly fast. Gabe imagined the guy moving quietly to disable the alarm system, and he wondered what Max had been earlier in life. Maybe a locksmith or an electrician. It was hard to tell with professional thieves just how they'd found their way into the business, but disappointingly, it wasn't often a penchant for striped shirts and black eye makeup.

They all waited there on the grass, listening to a night that was eerily bereft of cricket chirps or bird-song—or any noise at all beyond the wind and their own shuffling feet. But soon a full minute had passed with no signal from Maxwell, and Gabe noticed Laura showing growing signs of agitation. They were subtle cues, but his real job was noticing that subtle stuff. He nudged Heather and directed her attention to it, confident he wouldn't have to explain.

She looked for a moment, then let her mouth turn down before meeting his eyes with a hint of concern. "I thought the alarm was supposed to be a pushover?"

He nodded. "Supposedly Max has the code. Maybe he stopped for a snack."

Heather didn't respond at first, but then whispered, "Time to worry?"

Gabe shrugged. "Not quite, but eyes open."

"Always."

It wasn't until five solid minutes had passed that Trevor seemed to pick up on something amiss too. He and Laura held a whispered conference that resulted in him going in through the open window next. Barely thirty seconds later, Laura seemed to run out of patience and waved the rest of them forward before she too slipped inside. It didn't seem like part of the plan, but Paul followed right behind without question, like a puppy. It left Gabe and Heather alone outside.

"What just happened?" Gabe asked, glancing down at the item list in case he'd missed instructions.

"I don't know," she said. "Do we follow?"

He almost responded with a resounding negative, but then realized that Maxwell had the keys to the truck. He sighed. "If a neighbor called the police when we pulled in we only have about fifteen minutes now. I'm not looking forward to a hike back to town dodging every set of headlights that crests the horizon."

Heather crossed her arms. "Better than jail. We could hotwire the truck."

Gabe had considered that, but had already discarded it. Mostly because he didn't know how to do it. "What if Maxwell just twisted his ankle in there and we bolt? How would we look?"

"Like traitors," she said wearily.

"And dead meat. So that leaves us with either waiting out here like idiots, or going in there like different idiots."

She still looked doubtful, so Gabe stepped forward first and positioned himself to climb in. "It's cool if you want to stay out here. Nobody will think less of you. Taking three whole years to pass Art History class though? That's a little harder to ignore." And with that, he pulled himself up and through the window with, what he hoped, was just enough flair to look really cool while making relatively sure he wouldn't land on his face.

He heard Heather shuffle outside for a moment, but she didn't follow. He shut her out of his mind. Now that he was actually inside, things had gotten serious and his love life would have to wait. First, he pulled out the flashlight and looked to his left to examine the foyer. He assumed the alarm panel would be there, and that made it the best place to start looking for the rest of the team. That it was also the location of the fastest exit out was coincidental.

The carpet of the hall changed to expensive tile as the entryway opened up before him, and a shadowy staircase appeared to his right. To his left was the front door, dark and closed, and next to it blinked the single red LED of an armed system. There was no sign of the team.

His paranoia flared immediately to fire a series of worries through his brain. The plan had either gone terribly wrong or he was being played. Suddenly Heather's reluctance to enter the house seemed suspicious—as if she'd known something. Maybe he'd just walked into a trap. Maybe the job hadn't been about art at all, and he was about to take the fall for something larger. Anything could be happening right now, and he was the ignorant jerk standing right in the middle of it.

Gabe glanced at the door and considered running. If it was a setup, he might still have a shot to make it out. But if it wasn't, and his team was in danger... He caught himself at that thought. It wasn't *his* team, now or ever. He had no responsibility for them regardless of what might have happened in the last five minutes. This was a one-time job, and they'd screwed it up. He could safely write them off and save himself.

He moved toward the door and gripped the handle, then paused. If the rest of the team were all caught—which they almost certainly would be if he opened the door and set off the alarm—they might lead the police to him. On the other hand, if he stayed and helped and they all somehow got away, he could demand a hefty bonus. This night could save him two or three more months of work if he played it right. It was a gamble either way, but the best he could hope for by running was that he'd be free with a ruined reputation and no money. That was a bad result. If he stayed, he had a shot at playing the hero and really cashing in. And that, more than anything else, was what decided it. He could almost take the thought of being stabbed to death in a serial killer's mansion, but he hated being broke.

Gabe let go of the door handle and moved back into the foyer. He swept his flashlight around to get a better picture of the layout, and was just deciding between going up the stairs or deeper into the main floor when he heard Heather's scream.

TWO WEEKS AGO

"What a pleasure," Phillip said, taking a seat opposite her across the cheap desk.

Gwendal knew his name from the packet of knowledge she'd received, but had found to her dismay that it was all she knew about him.

"Can I get you something to eat?" he asked. Then he laughed lightly. "Or are you still full? I heard you had a big night?"

Gwendal gave him a cool smile. She knew enough about his offer to keep herself in check, but she didn't like being mocked.

"I'm just giving you a hard time," he said, jovially. He was short, but gaunt like a devoted runner, and his hair was a lank blonde that was styled to match his fashionable shirt and khakis. He also wore several pieces of gold jewelry that were just on the far side of good taste. In all, he looked like he might actually belong in the small real estate office they were in—if it weren't for the air of power about him.

"I am in your debt, Phillip," she said, inclining her head a fraction. "What do you want of me?"

He grinned, showing plenty of white teeth. "Straight to the point. Good stuff. What we want is to help you." He steepled his fingers and sat back. "My group seeks those in our population who might merit an investment of our time and resources. You seem to fit our profile nicely. How long have you been back?"

Gwendal stirred in her chair, uncertain if she should give away anything that might hand the man an advantage. "Two months," she said, her mouth betraying her. She wondered why she'd said that.

Phillip whistled. "And have you kept current, or..."

He was asking her how often she'd been able to manifest in the world over the millennia, which was tantamount to revealing her level of power and ignorance. Obviously he thought he knew something about her to gift the knowledge he had, but that didn't mean she had to confirm anything for free. She closed her mouth, then immediately opened it. "It's been almost five hundred years since my last manifestation," she said, involuntarily. She slammed her teeth together and stared hard at the man. "What is this?" she hissed.

He only smiled again. "That's a little while. You probably have all kinds of questions. The information we supplied will have filled in the worst of your blanks, but you'll need much more than that to catch up completely." He leaned forward and rested his arms on the desk. "But first, I need to know what you're after. To make sure we're going to be a good fit for each other."

She was searching for it now, and so finally felt the power flowing through the room—a thin thread of it that had silently slipped into her mind. She manged to keep her mouth shut this time, but the force of his magic battered at her will as she fought it. It was incredibly powerful, and she feared that she only resisted now because he didn't actually care that much. The man obviously already knew what he needed to, otherwise she wouldn't be here. It was nothing more than posturing, which made the effortless domination even more humbling and infuriating.

She tried to force herself to say something evasive, to redirect the magic and keep her secrets, but she quickly lost the battle. Whatever this man was, she wasn't his match. "I wish to bring my counterpart, my lover—*husband*—through from the Ether. We will reclaim what was ours and wrest humanity back to its knees where it belongs. We will harvest the power of these cattle, then pull back the veil and throw wide the gates of Earth to finally bring all of creation under our sway. Every Umbra now born or yet to be will unite beneath us, and together we will march against the Emptiness that threatens the perpetuity of this universe. We will save this plane from the Endless Dark, and all will worship and sustain us forever in flawless balance."

Phillip nodded. "Sounds about right. A little bolder than usual, and a little flowery, but that's a pretty typical outline. Though, I didn't think you dark goddesses ever had male counterparts? Doesn't it, I don't know, ruin the whole thing if you have a husband? Girl power and all that?"

Gwendal lowered her eyes to avoid letting Phillip see her fury.

"The world changes. So do we."

"And the Ether is slow and lonely," he said, nodding. "I understand. I really do." He rubbed his hands together as if preparing to make a big sale. "Well, I think we'll get along just fine. I mean, I should tell you right up front that the whole *world domination* thing isn't how it works anymore, but we'll get there. Our overall goals are similar enough. None of us here are very excited about the prospect of being rendered down to fuel the eternal engine of entropy, but I assure you there are other ways. Once upon a time it might have been nice to have a throne of skulls to sit on as you glutted on the blood of virgins, but there's only so many times you can do that before it gets old, you know? And skulls are not terribly ergonomic. The teeth are particular murder on the thighs. Besides, these humans are so much more fun to play with now. Trust me, modern society is a big upgrade once you get used to it."

The dismissive note and sliver of humor didn't escape her. "You don't believe me," she said, lifting her chin. "The threat to this universe is very real, I assure you. The Silent Maw threatens us all with not only death, but eradication. When it comes—and it *will*—the consumption will be total. Matter, energy, spirit, time: all of it gone forever. For all your power, you will be helpless. The strongest of us will fall alone. It is only if we seize control and unify that—"

"Yes," he said, cutting in, "my goodness. You are in deep, aren't you? I've heard the stories and theories, and I've seen what little proof there is. But true or false, frankly it doesn't matter either way. We'll talk about that once we've gotten to know one another better. But there are plans in place already, I assure you. Old plans. For now, let's get your fella sprung, huh? Who did you say he was?"

She stared hard back at the man, this time bending all of her strength against the compulsion. "I didn't."

Phillip smiled again, and Gwendal could see he had far too many teeth in his mouth. He'd mastered his flesh. Then he shrugged and the magic evaporated from her mind.

She tried not to sag in relief. "Why help if you do not believe?"

He looked at her like it was a foolish question. "Power, obviously. We have our own agenda, and your magic and outlook are both unique to this world. That's an advantage we'd like to add to our arsenal. We'd rather have you with us than against us. See? Just because we don't share the same endgame goals, doesn't mean we can't be partners until the last turn around the bend. We're willing to provide money, documents, political power, physical muscle—whatever you need to make it in this new world. And all we ask is that you think favorably of us at a later date. Come to help if you're called. Easy as pie. No explicit bond, just the hand of friendship."

She eyed him carefully. "And what must I pay for this *friendship*?"

He shrugged. "Now? Very little. The only issue I have is that you're a bit of a liability in this city." He laughed. "Seven men tonight? Eighteen total in the last few weeks? That's not great, even for Detroit. You're a growing girl, I get it, but the humans think there's a serial killer on the loose, and that makes life harder for our other partners. There are far more Umbras here in this age than you're used to, and most just want to carve out a little niche and get comfortable. Snag a bite here and there as their legends demand, but otherwise stay under the radar. We encourage that, but you're making it difficult by bringing in so much scrutiny. There will be a day when we need and encourage chaos, but right now the last thing we need are more Knights running around. So you need to find another home-base for a while."

"You've been following me?" she asked.

"Of course," Phillip said. "My organization keeps close tabs. You'd be surprised how easy it is to track an individual Umbra once you have the scent these days. A bit of blood or hair for the old ways, or a GPS tracker for the new. We use it all. When eighteen people are ritualistically murdered in a few weeks, it doesn't take a legion of Hunters to find the source. Let's just say you're lucky most of the Knights in America are fairly stupid." He sighed. "Do you have some place to go, maybe do your thing with a little more subtlety? The Templars, in all their bastardized manifestations, are generally only an annoyance. But they're an annoyance we do try to avoid. With the death of one of their more prominent agents, they'll get..." He waved the thought away like a bothersome insect.

"I came through in the state called Nebraska," she said, as if the idea of casual exile meant little to her. Inside she was seething at being told to do anything against her will. "A sorcerer overreached in his attempt to enslave a succubus. He is still bonded to me there."

"Nebraska," Phillip said, grimacing, "is perfect. I don't even know if there are any Knights active there outside of Omaha. You should be fine." He pushed back from the desk and rose holding out a fat envelope and a cell phone for her to take. "I look forward to working with you, Night Mother! The cash in here is to see you anonymously to your destination. The credit cards are to see you set up like a queen once there. I'll be in touch again once you've secured your boyfriend. Then we can talk about our mutually beneficial relationship. And if you need more help, call me on that phone." He spread his hands and smiled. "My friends are your friends now."

Gwendal shook her head. "I am not some petty spirit come begging for a hand to hold. I was ancient when man was yet young. Your cabal does not interest me beyond this temporary alliance, and I will ask for no further help from you or yours."

Phillip nodded his acceptance and made as if to leave. Then he stopped and raised a finger. "Please use some creativity and subtlety, if you can. Detroit is one thing, but I imagine in Nebraska it makes front-page news when a cow gets a cold. Understood? Small bites."

Gwendal watched him go, then looked down at the cellphone in her hand. Despite what she'd said, she *would* use it and anything else if it would bring her god to her. With him at her side, even Phillip would be forced to show more respect. The man was a fool. The world would end—was ending even now—and she had to stop it. For that she needed her Aka Manah.

She left the building and called her sorcerer. "Whatever this ridiculous plan of yours is, proceed. I am tired of being careful. Just make sure there is at least one healthy male body left for his vessel."

CHAPTER SEVEN

"Most of life is about embracing the choices you make and making something of them. Even your mistakes. And if you're really good, you can own your errors so thoroughly that they actually become advantages. It's another thing that separates con artists from normal people: we go all-in all the time. It doesn't matter what you're doing, act confident enough and people will believe anything. Act confident for long enough, and you might start believing it too."

-Excerpt from Chapter Four, CONscience

    Gabe's mind snapped down hard when he heard Heather's cry, and everything came into sharp focus. He killed his flashlight and held his breath as he waited for the sounds of struggle or running feet, but nothing rushed in to fill the vacuum except a terrifying silence. His better judgment shouted for him to stay there and weigh his options, but his body overruled it and moved toward the window. It was the opposite of what he should do, he knew, but he consoled his protesting common sense with the idea that he might be in for a *really* great bonus now. Saving the day had to be worth another grand at least. It was a pretty thin argument next to the more plausible suspicion that he was willingly walking into a trap, but he already felt foolish enough for being in the murder-mansion in the first place. The thought of a grateful Heather plunging into his arms for comfort was just a nice extra.

    He reached the window and poked his head outside to whisper for her, but no reply came back. She was gone. He grabbed for his phone to check the time, but cursed as he felt his empty pocket. He guessed that maybe ten or fifteen minutes had passed since they'd arrived, which gave him another ten at best until the police showed up. It wouldn't be enough to salvage the job, but it might let him figure out what the hell was going on. Five minutes. That was all he'd take. After that, he told himself, he could run away guilt-free. He pulled out his tiny pocket knife and started counting down.

Gabe followed the hall a few steps farther and found that it opened into a huge kitchen that occupied the entire east side of the lower level. Stone countertops and stainless steel appliances filled the room, but there was no sign of anyone having been through recently. No team, but no ax murderers either. And he'd chewed up nearly three minutes in the process. Investigating one more room should do it, then he could go with a relatively clear conscience. The prospect almost made him giddy, even if it meant he was facing a long walk home and leaving bodies in his wake.

He was about to turn away when he noticed a door ajar on the other side of the room. He moved carefully over to it, leading with his little blade, then peeked inside to find that it led to a set of steep spiral stairs descending into darkness. He suspected it was a wine cellar, given the size of the house, but he wasn't ready to discount a dungeon either. Rich people were weird. But then he spotted a darker patch of something partway down the stairs, and he froze. He slowly brought the dim glow of his flashlight up, and his heart almost stopped when he saw the black bag that matched the one slung over his own shoulder. The kind Trevor had handed to them all.

If Gabe was nothing else, he was pragmatic. He lived his life by a set of rules carefully crafted to result in the most amount of money in his pocket with the least amount of damage to his face. His current facsimile of heroism was an obvious exception, but near the top of his list of taboos was this exact scenario, written in bright red letters. He didn't mind occasionally pretending to be a decent guy when the situation wasn't too risky, but there was absolutely nothing to be gained by exploring a dark cellar in an abandoned country mansion at night. In the history of all the stories ever told, nothing good had come from going down the stairs.

Gabe hesitated, then closed the door. He had maybe six minutes left before he started pushing his luck, and he wasn't sure how long it would take to wipe down anywhere he might have touched inside the truck. That was his main concern now. The team meant nothing to him, and there was no reason to take any crazy risks for them. Heather might be something more, but the hard fact was that he barely knew her. Almost everything he felt was an invention of his own overactive imagination and no older than that morning. To her, he was a goofy but charming acquaintance whose temporary company was better than nothing for this one job. After tonight, they'd go back to nodding in greeting at chance encounters. They weren't in love. He owed her nothing.

He made it back to the open window in only a few seconds, then moved to pull himself through. His mind was already racing ahead: first to the truck, then the driveway, then the long walk home through the fields. But when he tried to climb out into the night, he found that he couldn't. There was nothing stopping him, but for some reason his arms couldn't quite get the leverage, and his fingers felt clumsy. He shook it off, calling it nerves, then tried again. And again he failed. He stepped back and stared at the window as if it was somehow defying him, but it was clearly no different than when he'd come in. Something else was wrong, something inside of him, and he feared he already knew what it was.

Gabe glanced down the hall to the kitchen and cursed silently. It was all too perfect: the short notice, the easy job, then everyone disappearing one-by-one. There were too many questions, and it seemed too easy for him to run away from them. It felt like the plot of a badly written book, which meant it was probably a con. Bailing on the botched job was exactly what he should do—the logical response—but if there was a bigger con here, the architects surely would have counted on that. *He* would have. He stood there motionless, trying to force any of it to make sense, but he simply didn't have enough information. He could force himself to run, sure, but then he'd be leaving behind the kind of regrets and mystery that he might not ever live down.

Or he could do the unexpected thing and dig deeper until he figured out what the hell was going on. His brain was already out there in a field a mile away, but his gut was anchoring him there in the house, telling him to keep looking. To beat the game. And he'd survived and thrived on those instincts for too long to ignore them. If he rescued Heather in the process, so be it. But he swore to himself that it wasn't altruism keeping him there. It was the need to *know,* and that, he could justify.

He hefted his flashlight and let Viktor loose. Sometimes pretending to be something was as good as actually being it, and for Gabe that was doubly true. Channeling a persona like Viktor couldn't actually make him stronger or faster, but it was a well-worn pathway in his mind that worked a kind of magic of its own—like standing behind someone bigger while you shouted insults. His personae weren't separate personalities per se, but they weren't *not* either. And he had always been able to walk that fine line along the distinction.

By the time he reached the kitchen again, he was more Viktor than Gabe and stupid-brave with it. He pocketed his little blade, then upgraded to a long chef's knife from a line of them stuck magnetically to the wall. And it was a testament to his new confidence that he scarcely considered what the hell he might do with it. Viktor's help or not, his combat skill was precisely zero. But then his hand was on the cellar door before he could think too hard, and he was suddenly moving down the stairs.

The flashlight was small, but even with the filter it was more than enough to brighten the deep dark of his descent. He stopped at the black bag, but it was just as featureless as his, and it was impossible to tell who it might have belonged to. So he kept going down, and it didn't take long for his feet to hit the stone floor.

Gabe pressed his back to an empty shelf and panned his light across the room to find a small wine cellar with a single door set in the rear wall. So far so good. There were no murderers or monsters around, which was just how he liked it. He took a quick glance back up the staircase, already lamenting the convoluted rationalizations that had led him there, but Viktor squashed the thoughts for him before they could blossom into cowardice. Then he rode the emotional momentum to carry him the last few steps to the door. It was rough and unfinished, and it was held closed with a simple latch that told him it probably hid nothing more than a storage room beyond. He'd take a look and find nothing there, then he'd run away as fast as he could to escape the much more realistic threat of the police. But when he pressed his ear against it, he knew he was wrong in so many ways. There was something inside.

He stepped back and examined both the door and his resolve. He'd come to find answers, but even Viktor's stupid confidence had its limits. He shouldn't be here. He was risking his life for the sake of curiosity, and that was worse than stupid. He was in a dark cellar staring at a closed door, holding a flashlight and a knife. The danger couldn't get any more cliché or obvious, and yet there he was.

But then...he *was* already there. He'd already gone this deep, and the door was right in front of him. No light came from around the edges of the poorly fitted wood, so he assumed it had to be dark inside. It could be nothing more than a mouse in there, and it would be easy to take a look and find out. Just a peek, and then he'd know. One tiny step more, then he could go.

He reached for the door, ready to slide it open just enough for a brief glance inside, then he froze as he heard a thump like something heavy hitting the floor. There was a grunt. Female. Then nothing.

Viktor took over. He ripped the filter from the flashlight and popped the latch on the door, bathing the room in a blast of white light as he rushed in. There was a tall man standing just inside with one arm thrown up to shield his dark-adjusted eyes, and his whole demeanor was of someone caught in the act. Gabe felt himself advance, leading with the knife. He meant to merely look menacing, to stop a violent reaction before it began so he could force some answers, but just then he spotted the bodies.

"Stop!" Gabe yelled, struggling to keep his voice from breaking as he took in all the information at once. "I'm armed!"

The five people were laid out in a neat row at the end of the room, shoulder to shoulder and feet toward the wall. One was large, several shorter, two women... And Heather's dark hair.

Then the tall man was moving, and Gabe couldn't spare any brain power for anything else. He opened his mouth to let Viktor bark a threat, but there just wasn't time. The room was too small, and the man was only steps away—his face a carnival mask of anger. There were no choices, no loopholes. Too fast. There were bodies in this room, and he was about to join them unless he fought back. Time to act. The knife or his life. Not a choice at all.

Gabe firmed his grip and planted himself just as the man barreled into him, and momentum did all the rest. The world became chaos and he could only follow along for the ride as the blade sank, and the pain came, and the breath fled, and the floor rose. Then darkness fell.

CHAPTER EIGHT

```
"You could do worse than believing in nothing.
It's not a bad philosophy to live by. Though
admittedly not great to die by."
```

-Excerpt from Chapter Four, CONscience

    Gabe smelled blood. And he was crying for some reason, which almost disturbed him more. He certainly didn't feel great—that might be part of it—but he thought he was forgetting something larger too. Something he should be worried about. Something bad.
    A heavy weight suddenly rolled off of him and he gasped in a breath he hadn't known he needed. The air filled lungs that felt long-deprived, and with it his memories came rushing back as if they'd been waiting their turn. His thoughts lined back up to remind him of where he was and what had happened, but it certainly didn't make him feel any better to know the exact consistency and depth of the shit he was in.
    He needed to get away. But when he tried moving his arm to push himself up, it only flopped limply over his chest and stayed there. He could barely even feel it. He tried his other arm and got the same result, then moved down to his legs in a growing state of disbelief. They didn't so much as twitch. He knew the commands were going through to his limbs—he could feel that—but nothing was working right. He should be sprinting up the stairs already, but he was still staring at the ceiling. His body wouldn't respond no matter what he tried. He was paralyzed.
    Gabe had panicked before, so he understood the scent of it on the wind, but he'd never felt the uncut terror of reality's official "Game Over" screen. He'd always found a cheat or workaround before anything got too serious, but this was too much. He was about to die. His mind hung there for a moment, tipping toward panic, but then Viktor yanked him back and planted him several steps from the edge, refusing to accept something as minor as reality. The breakdown still yawned out before him, ready to swallow him whole, but he wasn't falling yet. The persona then systematically squashed the fear like a

mechanic pounding out dents, and it left Gabe with enough mental room for rational thought. That was good. Logic was safe.

It was dark, but his light was still shining where it had fallen, and roughly half of the room still glowed in its stark white cone. He heard a whimper next to him and wrestled his head around to look at his attacker lying nearby. Black blood covered the floor around the man, and he had rolled onto his side to curl around the knife sticking out of his stomach. Gabe tried to recoil, forgetting that he couldn't, then settled on wrenching his face back toward the ceiling. They might be stuck there together, but he didn't have to watch the man die. That was when he heard the footfalls in the next room.

He instinctively stilled himself just as a young woman appeared in the doorway. She was well-dressed and perhaps in her twenties, and she didn't seem at all alarmed to find two men lying in blood on the floor of what might appropriately be called an abattoir. She surveyed the scene with something like disdain on her face for a moment, then she sighed and crouched down by the bleeding man.

"I told you these theatrics were stupid," she said as she inspected his wound. "We could have snatched them off the street, taken what we needed, but you had to have your layers of intrigue. Protecting the precious reputation of your flesh and of the ego you've adopted. Working within the rules of humanity as if they will mean anything for much longer. This is why your people are so few now, sorcerer. You've made everything so complicated for yourselves. You could rule the humans with just a scrap of effort, but you are all so afraid. And now you've ruined this body for nothing. Had I not stopped the human, you would be dead. Remember that."

A large part of Gabe's brain was freaking out. He wanted to scream and demand answers, but the smaller and smarter part of him in charge would allow no such thing. Demanding anything in his position was an obvious dead-end, and he knew screaming would be about as effective as peeing himself in the hope of being too moist to kill. His only real option was to bide his time and wait for the odds to improve. It was maybe the first time in his life he hoped he'd been sloppy enough to draw the police down on the job.

The woman clicked her tongue in disappointment. "You'll have to replace this one now." Then she carelessly tore the blade from the man's stomach. He groaned and writhed in agony, and she held the knife up with a look of wonder. "So fragile, this flesh. Reality can be broken so easily, yet we Umbras yearn for it above all else. Sacrifice all to save it. Why do you think that is? Because we crave the embrace of the womb from which we sprang? Or is it simply because the alternative of the Ether, safer though it may be, is just so damned dull?"

The tall man groaned again and rolled to his back, then painstakingly dragged himself to his feet. It seemed to sap him of everything he had left, and he fell back to lean against the wall as he sucked in quick, shallow breaths. Being able to stand at all should have been impossible with something like half his blood on the floor, but his expression showed no actual fear. He seemed no more concerned than if he'd pushed himself a little hard on the morning jog. "I haven't started yet," he said in a hoarse whisper, "I can take whichever body you do not need. I was always set to replace this form at the end of this escapade. Too many have seen it, and much of its native power is now spent."

The woman rose and waved him on with the bloody blade. "So be it."

"It will have to be fast," he said, closing his eyes. "Entropy wants this form. I have minutes only."

The woman let the knife clatter to the floor near Gabe's leg, then she smiled grimly. "Pick one, but be quick."

The man looked down at Gabe. "I have." Then he started humming.

Gabe felt something flicker at the edges of his mind as the weird, atonal music began. It was a sound that a voice shouldn't be able to make, and it made the danger seem suddenly so much worse. The noise felt wrong and heavy and imminent, building to something terrible that he couldn't pinpoint or understand. But whatever it was, he knew his time was running out to stop it. He focused all of his attention on his right arm—the one he'd already managed to move—and lifted it with what felt like fifty pounds of weight attached. Then he swung at the man's legs with all the strength he had.

His forearm connected feebly, then bounced off and landed heavily on the ground. By all rights it should have only annoyed the guy, but he was struggling to stand as it was, and the force buckled the knee to drop him. Gabe's heart leaped in victory as the music abruptly stopped, but then his mistake became clear as a mountain of bloody man came falling down toward him.

Then the woman was there, her hand clasping shirt fabric to hold the man suspended a foot above Gabe's face. She looked no more troubled than if she'd snagged an errant beach ball.

"What the hell?" Gabe's mouth said before his brain could stop it.

The woman lifted the tall man off of his feet and walked him several paces before leaning him against the wall. "Strong," she said, watching Gabe but still talking to the man. "Few humans can fight through my geas like that. I think you should pick one of the others."

The man groaned and pressed a hand to his wound. "He stabbed me. I want him. The honor of my order—"

The woman turned to the man and her face darkened. "Enough. I know very well about the so-called honor of your order and precisely how much it costs to buy. Or have you forgotten our own arrangement? I also know best which vessel to choose for my love, and I think he'll want this one." She gestured to Gabe. "Of course, you may challenge him for it when he arrives if you'd like to pit your feeble skills against those of a god."

The little color left in the man's face drained away, and he turned without another word to stagger deeper into the darkness of the room. The woman bent to Gabe and regarded him fully for the first time. She was pretty, and fairly normal-looking considering the circumstances, but her eyes were lit with something Gabe couldn't identify. Something old, he thought. Something painful or wrong.

She reached down and gripped his jaw tightly, then turned his head to examine it from several angles. "He will like you," she said. "Young and reasonably fit, but plenty of room for improvement. A little short perhaps, but the shaping will take care of that. Still, resilience and cleverness are worth far more. Minds like yours have so much more room to spread out in."

Any reply Gabe might have constructed to that nonsense fell to ribbons as he heard a body hitting the floor. He imagined what might be happening there in the darkness, what further horrors, then his breath caught as he saw Trevor step into the light. He'd never imagined he might be glad to see the thug, but suddenly the guy looked like a guardian angel.

"Better?" the woman asked without turning.

Trevor flexed his hands and rolled his shoulders as if just rising from a nap. "Yes," he said, staring down at himself. "I'll miss the hair, but youth is a gift of its own."

Gabe glanced between them, his heart falling and confusion settling back in.

The woman grunted. "You do not understand what power you hold in that skill, sorcerer. Such a small creature you are next to a true Umbra, yet in this you exceed even the most powerful of us. Someday you will teach me to swap flesh at-will, if it can be taught. And if not... There are other ways to gain such powers."

Trevor looked down evasively, but nodded like someone swallowing a bitter pill. "There are many limits. And an exponential price. But I will try."

Gabe glared hard at Trevor as his last bit of hope died. The bastard had been in on it the whole time. It was the only explanation. He wracked his brain to find the angle, the reason for this elaborate trap and show, but he found nothing. The location, the job, the murders—none of it made sense. Which made it even worse. With nothing to gain from this terror, it left only one possible motivation: fun.

The woman smiled and let go of Gabe's face. "We should begin. He has already waited for too long."

Trevor stepped forward quickly and loomed over the woman. "We had a deal. Mine first, then yours."

The woman's smile spread into something closer to a snarl, and she slowly lifted a single finger to Trevor's chest. A small spot of blood blossomed on his shirt where it touched. "Remember the bond and the difference in our power," she said, her voice deepening as she spoke. "You may have some secrets, but what I know that you do not could swallow you entire. You are not an Umbra—not really. You are still human at your core. That makes you weak. That makes you food."

Trevor pulled himself up as if ready to argue, but it was clear he was genuinely scared now. "You need me to split the veil," he said quickly. "And to bypass the precepts. They are there to stop creatures like you from doing exactly this. He is not meant to return, and you are not meant to reach him. Without me you would need ten times this power. More, even. If you could do it yourself, you would have already. This...this," he stammered, "this isn't like dipping into the shallows to fetch a Hound. You need my magic."

The woman seemed to grow and darken as he rambled, then suddenly she receded back and her smile became sly again. "True enough, and well bargained. Be my guest."

Trevor practically sprinted back to where he'd come from and melted into shadow. Gabe had reached the limit of his ability to push insane details down for later examination, and the pile was overflowing. So he decided to finally speak up. Words were all he had left.

"Okay, I'm lost," he said, his voice raspy but thankfully not broken with fear. "What's the endgame here?"

The woman cocked her head to the side as she regarded him. She almost looked impressed. "The best kind: Love and salvation."

"Right!" Gabe said, then coughed out something like a laugh. "You seem like a real lovable lady."

Her smile went a little odd. "You have no idea."

Gabe grinned as confidently as he could while lying broken on the ground and fighting off terror pee. "Come on. You got me. Whatever game you're running here, it's cinched. You won. Just fill me in on the details for my peace of mind. Kill me if that's the deal, just don't leave me hanging. I am literally dying to know."

The woman laughed and turned to watch Trevor drag two bodies into the center of the room. Gabe gasped as he saw Heather's still form come to rest several feet away, but then he spotted the rise and fall of her chest. She wasn't dead after all, which was interesting. It didn't make a bit of difference in the situation at large, but it was a small flicker of hope nonetheless. Maybe a bolt of lightning would strike in the cellar. Or the A-Team would show up. You never knew.

Trevor moved around Heather and tossed the tall man with the stomach wound down next to her. He was still breathing too, but looked like he wouldn't be in a few minutes. His eyes were glazed over like he'd already slipped into a coma, and the blood from the knife wound had stopped flowing.

"Make sure you aim well this time," the woman said, almost playfully.

Trevor shot her a scornful look. "I couldn't have known this land held so much latent power. I reacted..." he stopped. "It was a miscalculation of the veil's thinness here. A fairy circle of unique potency. A rare but foolish mistake." He paused for a long moment, then met the woman's eyes. "Also fortuitous of course, mistress."

The woman ran her fingers across the side of her face. "One that blighted the land here for a generation and forced us to these measures. But, yes, fortuitous." Then she gestured toward the dying man on the floor. "Make it quick or you'll lose him. Thin veil or not, you still need his energy to pierce it. It would be quite a shame to go home with no prize of your own after all this hard work."

Trevor nodded and bent to retrieve the kitchen knife from where it had fallen. Gabe tensed for an attack he could do nothing about, but then felt a sudden sickening surge of relief and horror as Trevor turned back to draw the blade across the tall man's throat.

There was very little blood, but the gurgling sound more than made up for the lack of gore. Trevor placed one hand over the new wound, and the odd humming music came back with a fresh vigor. He put his other hand on Heather's brow, then knelt there while the sound filled the room with an unsettling and alien pressure. Seconds passed, and Gabe nearly succumbed to blind panic in the midst of the confusion and terror, but then the pressure fell all at once, and Heather suddenly convulsed up.

Gabe watched in fascination as her arms flexed and released, her legs kicked, and her head lolled crazily. Trevor did something over her with his bloody hand and she gasped before going limp. There was a long pause. Then finally, as if coming up from under water, she took a *deep* breath.

Heather blinked and looked around, taking in the room with a clinical interest that showed no hint of alarm. Then she turned to Trevor to inspect him like a horse she might buy. The animation slowly seeped back into her face as she looked him over, and she grimaced as she turned to the other woman. "A sorcerer? Honestly?"

The strange woman stared back. "You are part of a bargain made by your betters. Be thankful only that you have flesh once more, and do not dwell on the why. Many would trade you for this chance, little one, unpleasant though it may be. Consider it a small price to pay."

Heather sighed and closed her eyes. Then she gracefully slid up into a kneeling bow toward Trevor. "How may I serve, master?"

CHAPTER NINE

```
"Relationships are messy. Romantic partners
always want to know private things like your job
and your interests and your real name. It
doesn't work for people like me. Instead, I
usually have flings. And by 'flings' I mean an
unsatisfying night with a woman I just met. And
by 'usually' I mean one time a few years ago.
I'm just not a good catch, and I've become okay
with that. No sense shackling anyone else to my
sinking ship. Plus I'd have to trust someone for
more than five minutes at a time, which frankly
sounds really stupid."

-Excerpt from Chapter Three, CONscience
```

Gabe wanted to let himself shut down. He was out of his league, and giving up seemed like the least painful choice now that Heather had betrayed him too. But as usual, his mouth had its own opinion. "Probably too late for me to ask you out to dinner, huh?"

She didn't react the way he expected, and only spread her hands as if she had no idea what he was talking about.

"You know all the flirting we've been doing tonight?" he ventured as he looked up at her. "I thought we might have been able to make something of it, but now I probably seem a little beneath you."

Heather studied him, then snapped her fingers. "Ah. I am sorry. It will take me time to integrate these memories. She liked you, this Heather. She wouldn't have grown attached to you, but you might have been allowed a brief physical encounter, if that is any consolation."

Gabe could only stare back in confusion.

"Enough," the other woman said. "Let's begin."

Trevor had been staring intently at Heather from the moment she'd knelt, but tore his gaze away. "Which ones?"

"Leave the Slav," the woman said, staring into the darkness like she could pierce it. "We will need at least one new Hound."

Trevor nodded, and a moment later came back dragging Maxwell and Laura by their feet. Both were still breathing, but again they were otherwise motionless. Trevor dropped Laura against Gabe's right arm, and Maxwell fell against his left. Then he produced the knife, and without any fanfare, drew it across Maxwell's throat.

"Wait!" Gabe yelled. But it was already too late. He quickly looked away and felt the panic surge back over him in an icy rush. He wanted to close his eyes, but didn't dare. He didn't want to see the knife coming for him too, but he couldn't help it. This was it. The end.

Maxwell was still dying as Trevor circled around to Laura. This time Gabe had time to steel himself for it and pour all of his focus into not hyperventilating. She was gone a moment later. Two people he'd been talking to twenty minutes ago. Two lives. Dead.

Then the humming began again. It was soft at first, like a faraway choir, and he had to strain to hear it. And desperate as he was for any kind of distraction, he listened carefully this time. It wasn't his paralyzed body, and it wasn't the corpses to either side of him, and it wasn't the prospect of violent death. So he bit down hard on the lure and let it pull him under.

There was no tune or rhythm; it was more organic than that. It sounded like a beehive in a coffee can underwater, but there was nothing random about it. It felt like there was an intense structure somewhere within, like the mathematical blueprint of a melody or the wire mesh beneath a sculpture. It was one-dimensional, but it ran deep—maybe forever—and he followed where it led. Down and down and down.

As he dropped, Gabe found that he no longer felt sick or scared. Those emotions stayed behind in the framework of sound as the rest of him ran through it like water through a sieve, draining into emptiness. Down and down, into a place of peace. For every pace he fell, he shed a little more of the worst of himself. Down and down, and growing cleaner and calmer as he went. Soon he couldn't remember why the concern had ever been there at all. Down and down. He'd been so afraid just a moment ago, but the reasons were gone. Down. In that non-place that had always been and hadn't, worries held no sway. Down.

And then he stopped. It felt like he had fallen to the end of the universe, and the concerns of the world suddenly seemed distant and ridiculous. Where he'd gone, there was only the vast quiet and the empty expanse...and a door that called to him. The music told the story of something wonderful beyond it, and all he had to do was go through willingly. It was where he belonged. He should ignore the small knot of pressure throbbing in his mind. He should ignore the pain that was building and warning of something wrong. Those worries were nothing. A past life. The door was his life now. He should go through. Now.

But that wasn't true, was it? He stopped. Just a bit of reflexive skepticism holding him back. He *should* be concerned—he almost always was. It was too easy, and easy things were never free. He wasn't thinking clearly, and he was losing track of himself. He wondered if he'd been drugged, or if he was dying and this was a coma. Then the music and the door harmonized that he should abandon those cares and enter, and the worry faded. But the knot of mental pressure had built more by then, and the background ache of it started souring the notes and clearing the fog. It felt like a massive thumb pressing into the plastic wrapper around his thoughts, and he knew suddenly it wasn't right. None of it was right, and he wanted to know what the hell was going on. The door called again, promising release.

He wanted to seek out the problem, and he also wanted to succumb and flee from it. Both thoughts warred within him, pulling him to opposite sides until the edges of his sanity were stretching and creaking beneath the force. A pressure grew at the walls of his consciousness, trying to break him. It was like something wanted him out of his own mind. Like something else wanted in.

Gabe pushed back suddenly and a spike of retaliatory heat immediately followed. It drove straight into his mind like a searing knife and tore down the remnants of that peaceful place as if it had been nothing more than window dressing. The outside pressure flooded in all around him, and his thoughts were pushed out and back toward the door until all that was left was one simple directive: *"Let go."*

Gabe flailed in his own mind, trying to find the source of the pain. *"Let go."*

He gathered himself and pushed back, only to be penned in tighter. *"Let go."*

He felt himself shrinking, becoming bits of personality and scraps of story tied to memories. He compressed into a placeholder of himself, like the personae. Like Viktor. He slowly eroded into little more than a construct, shoved into the same niche where he kept his other personalities. Then something massive surged in to fill the waiting space. It whispered, *"Let go."*

He didn't. But the new thing came anyway.

"Yesssssss," it said.

Gabe watched from his tiny corner with horrified fascination as a sea of alien thoughts and images filled the space he'd vacated. Raw information swelled up and threatened to suffocate him, like he'd been jacked directly into the internet or given a glimpse of the mind of God. He felt himself being pulled in and stretched far too thin, being absorbed into something much greater as bits of memories and knowledge were ripped from him. It was all he could do to keep himself whole beneath the onslaught.

Then it stopped. Everything went quiet all around him as if a hurricane had passed, and he was left floating in a vast expanse. He was alone except for some bits of random memories and the impression of Viktor's framework somewhere nearby. Then someone high above him spoke.

"I am returned," a man said.

The voice didn't belong to Trevor or Paul, but it was male, and it echoed in his head like his own. Because, he realized in horror, it was. He was speaking, and yet he wasn't. Then his arms were moving too, and his legs—and he was standing. Yet he was doing none of it. Something else was in control, and Gabe couldn't stop it. His body was *occupied*.

There was no other way to describe it. He was aware and thinking, able to feel and hear and sense, but he was no longer in command. It was like two distinct programs were running on the same computer, but his was far in the background and impotent. He felt the edge of panic wash over him again, but it was dull and distant like the memory of the emotion. By rights it should have been mind-numbing, ball-clenching fear, but he realized that the glands that would have fed him the fight-or-flight juice were apparently no longer affecting his thoughts.

His eyes opened without his permission and he was suddenly looking at the strange woman again. And try as he might, he couldn't look away. He felt a smile form on his lips, and a surge of revolting desire cascaded through his body so strongly that even the backstroke of it was enough to nearly knock him under. Lust and memory and relief all roiled through him, but none of it was his. He watched through his own eyes as her face drew closer, leaning in, and there was nothing he could do to stop it.

The kiss was brief but intense, and when it broke off, Gabe felt himself speaking again. "You remain first among my wives, dear Gwendal. You have fulfilled your vow, and for that you will be rewarded beyond all measure when this world again lays at my feet."

"Thank you, lord," the woman named Gwendal said with adoration in her eyes.

Gabe felt his lips part into a grin and his hand went up to stroke her face. His fingers rubbed hard, digging to the bone beneath her flesh like a sculptor molding clay, and Gwendal's eyes closed in pleasure. Then Gabe's body turned, and Trevor and Heather came into view.

"You have served well, sorcerer," Gabe heard himself say. "To circumvent the precepts is no small feat. There is power here yet from this blood. Call for me a Hound with the final flesh and bind him to my will. For this and all else I will grant you such power as you have never known. It will serve you well in our fight against the Endless Dark."

Trevor looked nervous, but bowed deeply. Then he walked back to where Paul lay motionless, and it was only then that Gabe realized he could see everything perfectly. The far end of the room was now completely clear, and he was able to watch as Trevor picked up Paul's left leg to drag him.

Gabe felt his head incline in acknowledgment. "You are weakened?"

Trevor straightened, but then sagged a little. "Yes, Great One. I did not expect to slough my previous flesh tonight. It has left me diminished."

Gabe felt himself nod again, and then something new happened within him. Until that exact moment, he might have been able to rationalize himself through this when he came out the other side. A huge dose of LSD, a big con, and a room full of crazy people—it all could have added up to account for most of what had happened. It wouldn't have been a clean theory, but it might have been enough to keep him out of the nuthouse. But when he felt the raw power surge up from within him like a tsunami cresting the horizon, all of his queued logic and careful explanations were swept away.

The feeling was beyond description. The closest comparison he could find was to drinking hot chocolate while winning the lottery during an orgasm. The power was everything he had ever been missing: every dropped opportunity, every suspected destiny, every treasure over the horizon was suddenly filling him like a breath of rocket fuel. It was pure, uncut wonder. It was magic. And it hurt like hell.

Gabe watched as the smallest portion of that roiling sea of potential separated from the whole and left his body to roll out toward Trevor. It took on a gold-red glow that rivaled the sunset, and then it sank into the other man to lend him its light. It was a gift of strength. A blessing from a god.

Trevor took a deep breath and seemed to swell with the infusion, then he bent to Paul and started to hum. This time Gabe could hear it properly, as if his ears had finally been tuned to it, and he realized that it wasn't random at all. It was dozens or hundreds of sounds all overlapping to form a latticework of power. He watched as it sank deep into Paul, first threading through him, then rising a moment later with its tip coiled twice around something spectral and dim and wriggling. It arched back like an adder, then struck at the air to slide gracefully into an invisible space there, taking the dim thing with it. When it returned, it was holding a feral glow that raced along the lattice and back to Paul. It spread and sank in gratefully—hungrily. And the man became something else.

This wasn't a con. It wasn't fake. He wasn't hallucinating. Something had taken Heather and Trevor, and something had just taken Paul, putting him on like a coat. He was possessed. In hindsight, Gabe realized he would much rather have been drugged. The realization crumbled all the solid ground around him until he felt like he was standing on an island in a void. He was in territory here that he had never planned for, and nothing in his repertoire would help. He didn't need a new accent or a fake ID; he needed a goddamned ghostbuster.

Instead, he got Viktor. Like a computer virus that refused to be deleted, Viktor reloaded in his mind and started mentally slapping him for being such a weenie. Then he took hold of all the scraps of what remained between them and thrust it all forward like a dagger into the hulking mass of alien thought that had stolen their body.

Gabe flew from the perch in his subconscious and dove directly into the massive well of power. The warm, sensual sensation filled him again, but this time he was a part of it. He could tell that it was hopelessly beyond his strength to control, but even as he fell forward, the stuff seemed to do all the work for him. It reacted to his wish to get his body back and caught him up to propel him through the layers of consciousness until he stopped just behind the writhing mass of the invader's thoughts. Then the power shrank back to its reservoir, leaving him alone to face the terrible and incomprehensible intelligence turning toward him.

"The soul was not cleansed!" Gabe heard himself scream suddenly, and then he felt the full weight of the invader's attention fall onto his own tiny spark.

The thing was enormous, and the weight of it almost overwhelmed him in the first rush. It felt like sitting at Beethoven's piano with Einstein inside the ruins of a concentration camp—impossible greatness and horror and malice, and it radiated out to buffet him like an ethereal wind. But somehow he held on.

"*Let go, human,*" the thing thought, shaking Gabe's mind like thunder. It would have shattered his eardrums had he still possessed them.

"No," Gabe replied, finding to his shock that his voice was almost as powerful.

"*You were to be cleansed,*" the thing said. And this time there was a hint of uncertainty in it.

That gave Gabe a little hope. Like maybe he held more cards than he thought. "Apparently I wasn't," he replied.

The thing seemed to swell as it inhaled more of its power. "*You must go! This space will not hold us both for long.*"

"Nope," Gabe returned. "This is my head." He hesitated before going on, but then realized how little he had left to lose. "What are you?"

The thing vibrated in what felt like amusement. "*An Umbra. Child of humanity. And greater than you can possibly imagine.*"

Then, as if the cosmic animator of this nightmare had suddenly added it to the scene, the door reappeared next to him. It was plain and white and closed, and it was by far the most real thing in his mind right then. In fact, it was far too real, and focusing his attention on it for too long made him feel lost and afraid—like standing next to it diminished him by comparison. It was like a splinter of reality had been ripped from the outside world and pulled into his imagination.

"*This leads to your new home,*" the invader said, apparently trying to approximate calm with his apocalyptic voice. "*Enter. What you find beyond will please you.*"

Gabe felt an urgent need to follow the instructions. The door was tugging at him, wanting him to be within, to finish this process and be at peace. And it didn't seem all that bad. Maybe he would be better off. It couldn't hurt to look at least.

He took a step closer, and the door flew open, revealing a blinding white expanse of formless mist. It was not the promised paradise. He reeled back, and at the same moment the invader pounced, throwing the full weight of its consciousness toward Gabe to push him in. Gabe tried to slip away, but found himself penned in between the press of power and the waiting embrace of what felt like eternal purgatory. There was nowhere to go but through.

Then Viktor appeared out of nowhere and shoved Gabe back hard, and the invader somehow hit the persona instead. Viktor shattered like cheap glass, providing no resistance to the attack, and suddenly there was nothing between the stampeding invader and the open door. A sudden wash of alien terror filled their shared mind as the massive consciousness realized what had happened, but then it slammed full-force into the portal, and the mist within hooked it like a waiting maw.

It was like a black hole capturing a sun, and the full gravity of it easily pulled the invader in. The god tried to arrest its momentum, scrambling against it with gold-red power that flashed and cracked through Gabe's mind, but none of it helped as it was all siphoned away into that waiting door. The slow pull became a stream and then a flood until the flickering energy was spiraling down into that hungry mist, and with every bit that vanished, the presence of the invader seemed to diminish. Within moments, there was nothing left of that vast power but a thin line of it that clung to the frame. He felt the invader reach out, to try to gain more purchase, to try to claw its way back into Gabe's head, but the mist pulled back almost gleefully. An instant later, the door closed with a gentle click.

Gabe's mind went silent, and he found himself left only with the echo of a final mental cry and the image of a closed door sitting placidly in the center of his every thought. Then he expanded suddenly like air filling a balloon, becoming himself again in an instant. He could see through his own eyes and was standing on his own feet. His brain felt stretched ten sizes too big, but otherwise there was no sign of the struggle he'd just gone through. The physical world casually reasserted itself, and he was back. And everyone was staring at him.

CHAPTER TEN

"There's nothing so satisfying as pulling off a good con. Being the smartest person in the room is intoxicating, and it's tough not to want that again and again. But true perfection is in conning someone so well that they never suspect you. You win by leaving them thinking *they've* won. The only shame is in never being appreciated for how good you are. My eternal curse. That being said, I will also take plain dumb luck any day of the week."

-Excerpt from Chapter Two, CONscience

    Though he felt mostly normal, Gabe remembered that the situation was still anything but. He took a quick assessment of the calm, expectant faces of strangers who had tried to kill him a moment ago, and decided that very little time must have passed. It had felt like hours in his head, but it appeared as if nothing had changed in reality. He thought about using the surprise to get the jump on Trevor, but discarded it at once. Even without the gun and substantial difference in ability, Trevor still had nearly seventy pounds on him. And that was discounting Gwendal, who he definitely shouldn't. He needed to play to his strengths.

    His thoughts were jumbled and chaotic, and he needed time to put things back into meaningful shapes, but luckily his instincts were as strong as ever. It only took him a moment to pick up the thread of where the invader had left off. "The situation is resolved," he said, doing his best to affect the odd cadence.

    Relief passed over Gwendal's face and she smiled with that alarming affection. "You feel diminished, love. Was he truly so resilient?"

    Gabe fought with several answers before replying, "Quite." There was no reason to get too fancy. He just needed to talk his way out the front door.

    Gwendal touched his face and Gabe had to use all of his remaining willpower to avoid flinching away. "You must rest," she said. "Your Hound and I will guard you as you replenish." She gestured to

Paul who was now crouching against the wall near the door. Then she looked at Trevor with a powerful hatred. "But first, this worm endangered you with his idiocy. Allow me to dispose of him."

Trevor wailed and fell to his knees, and Gabe had to hide his shock at the outburst. He barely managed to turn it into a look of disgust. "I would not have you spend even that effort," Gabe said, digging deep to play the character. "He is nothing now. Go from my sight, vermin."

Trevor fell prostrate and scrambled forward to kiss Gabe's feet, but Gwendal kicked him back. "Truly?" she asked. "To leave a soul in the flesh is incompetence! There are any number of ways you could have been damaged or banished back to the Ether! Two souls in one body, even briefly, could have left you broken. Allow me, love. I will bathe you in his blood so you may sup from his pittance of power."

Gabe waved away her protests as if they were childish ramblings. "Let him go on his way in the knowledge that his debt can never be repaid. His services may be required again soon, and I would not throw away a useful blade because it once cut me." Suddenly he got a stupid hunch, and he couldn't help but follow it. "However, she is no longer his," he said, nodding to Heather. "I will take charge of her."

Gwendal looked puzzled for a moment and turned to him with hurt in her eyes. Gabe fumbled for an explanation, but just gave her a reassuring look. "Trust me, my love" he said, forcing the words out while recalling the exact wording of the line he'd heard earlier. "You... remain first among my wives."

Gwendal's eyes widened a little, then she turned back to Trevor. "Do it," she hissed.

Trevor let out another sob, but it came out as part relief and part loss. There was no telling what that meant, but Gabe didn't have time to consider it before Trevor waved a hand toward him and a wash of something warm and clinging ran through his body. It was like walking through a hot spiderweb, and he had to fight the urge to wipe at his face. When it had settled, there was a new knot of pressure in his mind, like a string tied to his finger. It felt loose, but it gently pushed him back when he probed it.

"There," Trevor said bitterly. "I have fulfilled my every promise and have nothing left but my life. May I leave with that much intact?"

Gabe didn't deign to answer, so Gwendal hissed and flicked a hand toward the door. "I release your bond, worm. But know that I do so only as a favor for my husband. Run."

A look of pure relief flashed across Trevor's face, then he sprinted from the room. Soon the sound of his footsteps faded into the night.

Gwendal turned back to Gabe. "We should leave this place. I will take you—"

Gabe held up a hand to stop her, hoping he wasn't pushing his luck. "I will take myself. You may go prepare the way. I will find you soon and we may *begin*." He had no clue if that meant anything, but Gwendal nodded as if she understood. His luck, it seemed, wasn't quite played out after all.

"Very well," she said. "And her?"

Gabe avoided looking at Heather. He didn't dare let his thoughts about her fully surface, but he wanted to help her if he could. If she was possessed, or whatever, he didn't want to leave her to Gwendal. He knew it was probably a stupid choice, and he was suddenly glad Viktor wasn't there to call him a dumb-shit for it.

"I will allow her to accompany me while I recover," he said. "She may serve as my..." he struggled for the word and almost panicked when Heather herself jumped in to help.

"Attendant?" she supplied.

Gwendal eyed her carefully, then slid up to press herself against him. "As you wish. But see me soon. There are things I would give you now that you are flesh."

Then she grabbed him roughly by the neck and kissed him with shocking violence. Sharp nails dug into his skin and served to drive him even harder into her embrace until their teeth ground together. The pain was immediate and intense, and he tasted blood on his tongue. He forced himself to hold back a grunt of pain, afraid of breaking character or encouraging her.

When they finally parted, Gwendal held him skewered there as she tenderly licked the blood from his lips. She swallowed and then her smile curled out like smoke. "This will serve for now," she whispered. "But do not keep me waiting, my lord. There is so much more of you I would have inside of me."

Gabe allowed himself a wry smile to hide his revulsion, and then he gestured that Gwendal should take them out of the cellar. She nodded and hissed a command to Paul, who immediately shot up from his crouch and loped up the stairs like something closer to a wolf than a man. The women followed, and Gabe bent to stoically take the truck keys from Maxwell's cooling body. The horror of doing so was only outweighed by the prospect of freedom, and as soon as his finger slipped through the ring, he bolted without looking back. He could still see in the dark for some reason, but there was nothing in that room he wanted to remember.

Gwendal and Paul stopped for a brief conversation in the foyer, and then the man ran back into the house. Gabe was too relieved to care where he was going, but Gwendal watched him carefully as he trotted away. Then she led them out into the night, and he had to forcibly keep himself from gawking at the outside world as seen with his new vision. It was lit like a clear dusk, and the sudden sense of openness rekindled some of his suppressed terror. Something had changed in him, and it wasn't going away.

He wasn't sure what he had expected Gwendal to do when they got outside—maybe teleport or fly off on a broom—but he definitely hadn't considered that she might get into a small car and just drive away like a regular person. But that's exactly what happened. There wasn't even a puff of smoke. As she pulled away, she met his eyes and touched her lips in an odd gesture, and he felt something electric pass between them. It felt like a promise, and like a watchful gaze. She winked, then hit the accelerator. But even as she rounded the bend to turn out of sight onto the gravel road, Gabe had the unnerving sense that she could still see him if she wanted to.

He shook off the feeling and waited until Gwendal's car was long gone before heading to the truck. "Get in," he said to Heather, not yet dropping the act. He felt a slight tug on the knot in his mind as the command came out, and Heather nodded and promptly got in the passenger side. Another weird thing for him to examine later.

The engine started on the first try and he put it in gear, anxious to get the hell away. Now that he was almost free, the idea of police catching him at the scene of a triple murder wasn't quite as appealing. And that thought followed him as he chased the gravel road back to the highway—the motionless faces...the blood. He'd known people who'd been killed on jobs, been to their funerals and heard the stories, but he'd never actually seen it. Nothing had prepared him for what he'd endured that night, and he couldn't help but feel that everything was going to be different now. He might be physically getting away, but the rest of him might be too changed in too many ways.

The weight of all the terror and panic of the night suddenly caught up to him and hit him like a body blow. He'd slogged through the whole ordeal by pushing everything back like he always did, keeping it together by sheer will. But in the cool quiet of the country road, the dam was cracking. Real people had just been murdered. *He* had almost been. He'd stabbed a man. Something terrible and impossible had tried to take his body. It was too much.

Gabe gripped the wheel tightly as his hands started to shake. He blinked back tears. He hadn't really cared about Maxwell or Laura, but that didn't make witnessing their deaths any easier to cope with. He had been so scared. The memory of their faces felt like venom burning him from within, and he could feel their blood crawling over him where it had soaked into his clothes. The dam broke and he pulled the truck to a quick stop as they came to the edge of the highway. He threw it into park, took one shuddering breath, then began to cry.

Gabe knew it broke the character, but he couldn't help it. Even with his command of emotions, his essential humanity refused to be denied this time. It all came bursting out of him in quick succession: first for the grief and fear, then for the anger, then for the relief. The whole thing only lasted a few seconds, but when he was done, he felt as if some of the poison had been drawn from him. His thoughts came together more cleanly, and his hands stopped shaking. He wiped his eyes and took a deep breath, then risked a glance over at Heather. He didn't know what he had expected to see in her, but the puzzled, horrified expression wasn't it. She looked like her dog had just spoken a few words in Latin and she was still trying to decide which one of them was crazy.

A look of questioning defiance was all he could muster. This was her chance to come clean and give him some answers or expose him for a liar. But she didn't. She merely frowned and shook her head, then turned back to stare at the road. So he collected himself and put the truck back into gear, joining the highway and the world again.

Heather finally broke the silence when the lights of Lincoln were on the horizon. "Will you release me?" she asked.

He shrugged, suddenly very tired. "Where would you like me to drop you off?"

She took a long moment to reply. "There was a vehicle?" she asked as if she couldn't remember.

It was probably the best idea to cut her loose and let her make her own way, but he still couldn't shake the sense that she needed some kind of help. If he'd had any fight left in him, he might have tried harder. Getting her out had been his good deed. It was time to look after himself. "You want me to take you back to your car at the warehouse?"

Heather seemed to seriously consider the question. "Yes, the car. I have the memories to drive, though perhaps not with any great aplomb."

He almost asked her what the hell that meant, but he left it alone. He could feel the finer mechanisms of his mind shutting down as his brain realized that the worst of the danger was past and that the repairs could begin. He didn't dare trust himself to handle anything else with subtlety or grace for a while. Drop her off, then go home to sleep forever—that would be the best thing. Heather, or whoever she was, could take care of herself the same way he had.

Gabe pulled up to the warehouse with a sigh of relief and parked next to their cars, then began wiping down anything he had touched. He cringed at the thought of how much DNA he'd probably left back at the house, but it was a little late to burn that bridge now.

"Don't take this the wrong way," he said, not bothering to look at her as he cleaned, "but I hope we never see each other again."

"That's as easy as releasing me," she replied.

Gabe inspected his work, then waved his hand through the air. "Fine. Go home."

She sighed. "If it were that simple I would have already forced you to it. You must release me."

He dropped the last tatters of his patience. "I don't care, lady," he said as he shouldered open the door and hopped out onto the gravel. "You do whatever psycho, murder-fetish bullshit you want, just not around me, okay?" He moved toward his car. "You assholes dragged me into this, so if I ever owed you a damn thing, I certainly don't anymore. You can now go promptly to hell. Do not pass Go, do not collect two-hundred fucks, because I have zero to give. You go find your buddies and leave me alone. I'm a ghost now as far as you're concerned."

He wrenched open his car door, but then stopped just short of getting in when the sound of sirens came wailing toward them in the night. He tensed and looked up just as three firetrucks, an ambulance, and four police cars went speeding past on the highway. They were headed north, and Gabe had a strong suspicion where they were going.

"Paul," he said, numbly. Three firetrucks probably meant he didn't have to worry about any DNA evidence, but it also meant that there was no more proof of what had happened. Even if Gabe did decide to put on his upright citizen pants and report the murders, there wouldn't be anything left but ash and a story that sounded crazy even to him.

"I believe so," Heather replied, still staring after the fading emergency lights.

Gabe shook the thoughts off and pounced on the momentary distraction to slip into his car. He fired the engine and reversed out of the spot just as Heather turned toward him. She yelled for him to stop, but he slammed on the accelerator and swerved around her, kicking up rocks and leaving her standing in a cloud of dust. It felt like the first smart decision he'd made all night.

He took precautions on the way, parking in a grocery store lot for a while and spending some time exploring the far south of town. But eventually his paranoia lost out to exhaustion and he drove home. He pushed into his blessedly quiet living room and slammed the door closed, triple-checking the locks before he felt safe enough to turn his back on it. Then he got in the shower without so much as taking off his shoes. He turned the tap to hot and got in to stand beneath the water, letting the blood and memories of the night wash down the drain. He gingerly touched the split in his lip Gwendal had given him, then rubbed hard to wipe away the taste of dried blood and of her.

Time slipped away from him there in that cocoon of safety, and he only remembered how tired he was when the water finally turned cold. He quickly stripped and tossed his clothes to the back of the tub where he could dump a gallon of bleach on them later, then he scrubbed until his skin hurt and he was shivering. He barely had the presence of mind to pull on a pair of shorts before crashing onto his bed in a hard, desperate sleep.

LATER THAT NIGHT

"It is finished," Paul said, "The house was aflame as I left. No trace to track you." His voice was rough and stilted, but Hounds weren't known for their ability to communicate. The fact that he could speak at all, let alone use a cell phone, was a testament to his relative power. This one was a pack leader at least. The sorcerer had done well in his last service for her.

"Good," Gwendal said. "I am almost back to the hotel. I trust you can find your way?" The Hound grunted and hung up as she pulled into the parking garage and shut off the car. The hotel she'd chosen as a temporary base wasn't ideal from a strategic point of view, but it did put her very near the town's main university. She'd found the proximity to so much primal fear and lust impossible to resist. Later she'd have a proper temple again and could wade neck-deep in blood and offal, but for now, the ambient emotions generated by so much shattered innocence in one place would have to do.

She closed her eyes and allowed herself a moment to revel in her victory. She'd done it. Her god was free from the Ether, and they could at last pound and sharpen this world into the blade it needed to be. There was so much to prepare if they were to save this place from itself, and any small delay felt like too much time wasted. She could only console herself with the knowledge that the Endless Dark had not yet touched reality. There was still time.

She thought of her conversation with Phillip and almost laughed at his imagined reaction when he realized who his money had helped her free. By then, any measures the little man might hope to take against them would wither in the face of the sheer power they would command. Forcing his casual skepticism of her back down his throat would be a pleasure. Perhaps he and his organization had given up hope of harnessing this world to bring to bear against the Emptiness, but that was only because they weren't proper gods. They weren't like her Aka Manah. Or her.

The thought made Gwendal miss his presence already, and she was tempted to reach out to him. She could still taste his new body's blood on her lips, and it pulsed in her belly with the distant flicker of his spirit. She could use it to seek him out, the Sanguine Fetter, but she stopped herself. She remembered how she'd felt in those first few days, lost and fragmented and weak. Of course he needed time. Of course he'd taken a slave to serve him. It made perfect sense. And yet...

She reached out the barest tendril of power into the world, seeking his unmistakable presence. She couldn't trace his location precisely, but she could taste of his spirit for reassurance. Of all who walked this earth, he could take care of himself. But she couldn't help a twinge of worry. For five hundred years they had drifted in the Ether, intertwined and sharing themselves utterly until their separate desires and lusts beat together in harmony. For five hundred years they had felt the onset of the coming end of all things, and for five hundred years they had planned how to stop it. She knew him as well as she knew herself, and she couldn't shake the feeling that he had acted oddly after expelling the human soul. He had felt diminished, less fierce and less gleeful. And then, for no reason at all, he'd taken that slut with him. Yes, she had a perfectly good reason to check on him. Let him be wroth with her if he wished. It had been too long since she had been properly punished anyway.

Her power brushed across the city, fanning like a breeze to match the scent of his presence to the taste of the blood in her belly. That's all she wanted: a nibble. She would just feel him, maybe subtly remind him of what waited with her, then she'd let him be. He would come to her when he was ready.

But though she scanned wide and slow across the expanse of her range, she felt nothing of what she should. His body was out there, she could feel that moving somewhere south, but the more she tried to find his spirit, the more frustrated she became. He was too distant and too quiet. It was almost as if he was back in the Ether again, back where she couldn't quite touch him. It was like...

"No," she said, her eyes snapping wide. "No!" She slammed the car into drive.

It only took her ten minutes to get back to the warehouse, but even upon cursory inspection she could tell it was too late. She ran to the old green truck to find it abandoned and her love nowhere in sight. She wanted to believe that he'd prudently switched vehicles, fearing that the truck might have been spotted during the night, but she doubted he'd have cared. He had no need to fear the laws of man.

She closed her eyes and turned in a circle there in the lot. She reached out and searched for him again, this time throwing herself fully behind the effort, but only got back a faint echo in reply. He wasn't in the Ether either, she realized. He was trapped somewhere between and impossible to trace. Who knew what danger he might be in? The human, in the meantime, had crisscrossed all over the city in a tangled trail that she could never unravel by herself. Not quickly enough. She had been tricked.

Gwendal felt for the bond with her Hound and found that he was still miles away, likely picking his way through fields as he fled the arson. He would be hours in returning to help, and she was not built for hunting. She searched for her bond with the sorcerer, then remembered that she'd released it. She was alone again.

She screamed in rage and flipped the truck onto its side. Then she left the warehouse in a rush, wrenching her car into the street and furiously punching up the first number in her phone. It didn't even ring.

"How can I serve?" Phillip said on the other end.

Gwendal gritted her teeth, but managed to spit the words out. "It seems I will need more help after all. Now."

CHAPTER ELEVEN

"Avoiding romantic entanglements has its benefits. I get to keep all my money, for instance. And I can sleep on either side of the bed as it suits my whim. Try not to be too jealous of my sexy single life."

-Excerpt from Chapter Three, CONscience

Something moved in the dark of his subconscious. *"Where am I... Why can't... Wait, No... No... NO!"*

The nightmare broke and vanished, and it shifted immediately to a dream that was much more pleasant. A soft hand ran across his stomach to his hip where it lingered teasingly at his waistband, and fingertips brushed against his ear as they snaked back to grip his neck and pull his mouth to hers. It started slow, lips brushing once, and again, testing. But then it deepened as they found a rhythm, and soon his breath was hers and the world was spinning as her nails grazed skin to pluck at fabric and slide beneath and down...

Gabe woke with a start to find someone's hand down his pants.

It took him a moment to connect the dream to reality, but when it finally sank in, he managed to vault the bed and a pile of laundry in a single leap to hurl himself to the far side of the room. "What the hell?" he yelled. He'd been shooting for anger and was annoyed when it came out borderline plaintive. He slapped at the wall until he found the switch and flicked on the lights.

Heather sat up and stretched, letting the blanket fall away to reveal that she was topless. She practically purred as she pulled herself taut. "I'm trying to get some sleep," she said. "We had a long night."

Gabe looked away and stared firmly at a water stain on the ceiling.

"That wasn't... What are you..."

She laughed sleepily, then let her arms drop to her lap. "Close your mouth, Gabe. Unless you plan to put it to better use."

He wiped his hand roughly over his mouth to cover closing it. The alternative had been to snap it shut like a cartoon character, and he was already scraping for dignity as it was. Then he looked her right in the eyes just to prove he could. "That did *not* feel like sleep," he said, this time injecting what felt like the proper amount of anger. "What are you doing here? And how the hell did you find me?"

Heather sighed and slid out of bed to retrieve her shirt, and to Gabe's relief she was still wearing the leggings from the night before. At least things hadn't gone that far. She eyed him slyly, then reluctantly pulled the dark shirt over her head as if making a concession for him. Once covered, she bent and reached into her pile of things to withdraw a black phone—the one he had left at the warehouse.

"Fantastic," Gabe said with a sigh.

She smiled sweetly. "It was foolish of you to leave it behind for anyone to find. You cover your tracks well, but Heather knew all about finding hidden things."

Gabe tried to make sense of that, but was still too groggy to do any complex analysis. "Yeah, well, I'm not making that many great decisions lately."

She yawned and stretched again before flopping back onto the bed as if it was her own. She rolled to her stomach and lifted her feet up behind her, then propped her chin on her hands as if posing. "Though I didn't need it. I could have found you almost anywhere. Returning this device was more of a peace offering to get you to talk."

Gabe crossed his arms, refusing to be distracted. "Great, let's talk. But you need to say something that makes more sense. I asked what the hell you're doing here."

She pouted and made a hurt sound. "Awww, aren't you happy to see me anymore? Your kind are so much more honest in your dreams." Gabe ignored that nonsense too, waiting her out, and she rolled her eyes and let her hands and feet thump to the bed. "Fine," she said, her voice losing some of the artificial sweetness. "I'm here for the bond. Release me and I'll get out of your life."

He shook his head. He'd already walled up the memories from the night before, and he wasn't about to drag it all back out. Some things just couldn't be explained, and he would be alright with that. It would totally work. "Stop it. Don't even start with that horseshit. I'm not as fragile as I was last night. Here's what I know: I got conned hard and given some nasty drugs or something. Maybe the plan went wrong, or maybe that's exactly how the night was supposed to play out for some god-forsaken reason—I don't care. All that matters is that I'm out. So quit trying to play this sick game with me. Get your stuff and go, or I'll call the police right now."

Heather looked disappointed. "Oh help, Mr. Constable, a beautiful woman wants to put her hand down my pants." She scoffed. "Is that how that call goes? Grow up," Then she rolled off the bed onto her feet and pushed past Gabe to leave the bedroom.

"Hey..." Gabe said, then reluctantly followed to where she'd stopped in front of the open fridge. "You're just going to make yourself at home, then?"

Heather grunted in disgust at his food selection and nudged the door shut. "Until you release me, I have little choice."

Gabe pushed down a sudden surge of fury. "Just once, before I throw you out of my house, I'd like you to be straight with me. You owe me that much. Last night was..." He almost shuddered, but mastered it in time. "...bad. You can give me two minutes of honesty in exchange."

Heather leaned back against the fridge and crossed her arms. "That's all part of the deal, isn't it? Ask any question you'd like and I will answer truthfully." She said it as if reciting from an instruction manual.

Gabe stared at her for a few seconds, then nodded. "Good. Why are you here?"

Heather sighed and her voice went bitter. "I must be. I am bound to you. If I stray too far without your permission, I will cease. Foolish question."

Gabe decided to try a different approach. Sometimes the best way to pick apart a lie was to search for the farthest edges and find the frays. "Okay, fine. We're bound. That's... Whatever. We'll come back to that. Tell me about that Gwendal lady. Who is she?"

Heather shrugged and let her eyes drift away from him. "I'm not sure. She might be a higher demon or goddess in one of the lesser pantheons. Though, she seemed subservient to that other one, so maybe not. Perhaps an old nameless one. Who knows how many of those there are. I'd have to spend more time with her to know for sure."

Gabe veered another direction. "What did they drug me with to make me have those hallucinations? LSD?"

Heather gave him an odd look. "Oh, somebody's progressed to denial, huh? No drugs, lovely. That was a geas on your spine to paralyze you. Magic. Whatever else you think you saw, I don't know. Gwendal's work, probably. I can't do that kind of thing."

Again Gabe shifted. "Who did that house belong to?"

"I would guess the sorcerer—or, at least the body he was using first. I assume that's what he really was, anyway. He certainly wasn't an Umbra or I'd have sensed it on him. In fact, I suppose I should thank you for freeing me from a lifetime with that man. Sorcerers are notoriously poor masters. He probably wanted me for carnal or blood magic. I might have lasted a year at most. Asshole." She brightened as she said the word, as if just hearing it for the first time. "Ah, I like this one. English is crass, but it does have a great deal of color."

Gabe nodded along as if he understood every ridiculous word. "Sorcerer and sex magic. Got it. So what was the point of the whole thing? Why the big show?"

Heather shrugged. "Who knows? I came into the mess after you, right? I could ask you the same thing."

Gabe chewed his lip and looked away—then realized his cut was gone. Somehow it had healed completely overnight, and his lip was now perfectly smooth. Unfortunately, he couldn't afford the mental bandwidth to wonder how just then. He had bigger concerns staring right back at him from his kitchen. The conversation was getting him nowhere, and he had no idea what to do next. But Heather knew where he lived now, and that made her incredibly dangerous. Regardless of their true motivations, Gwendal, Paul, and Trevor were demonstrably insane. They'd killed people. And as the only loose thread in the job, there was a good chance they would want to snip him too. Heather might not have anything to do with that group, but he couldn't afford to take that risk. He'd have to somehow secure her silence long enough to work out an escape plan that allowed him to relocate with his dad. It was all he could do. The only alternative was to kill her.

He almost laughed out loud at the idea that he might be able to kill anyone. It was out of the question obviously, but recent events put it uncomfortably close to his thoughts. She might be a complete nutball, but she was also the only one of the bunch who wasn't a verifiable murderer or arsonist. The worst thing she'd done so far was try to be the world's best alarm clock. Bottom-line: he needed her on his side for now. His well-developed justification center worked overtime for a few seconds to help him deny that those leaps of reason had anything to do with her being easy on the eyes. It was about getting an informational edge, he assured himself, not getting sexy with the second-most terrifying woman he'd ever met. There was logic in there somewhere, he was sure of it.

Gabe sighed and wiped the sleep from his eyes. "Fine. Let's go get something to eat."

She actually looked surprised at that, and her demeanor softened a little. "That would be nice. Steak, maybe?" She licked her lips. "Yes. Definitely something wet and chewy."

Gabe turned back to the bedroom to find some clothes. "Whatever. I almost died last night, so I'm having bacon and pie. Where we're going they don't judge."

It turned out to be early morning when Gabe stumbled outside. And fifteen minutes and an awkward car ride later, they were seated in a booth at Barbara's Cafe. Gabe left his menu sitting on the table and played idly with his straw wrapper as he waited for Heather to decide.

"It's not life-or-death," he said, choosing to keep the conversation casual. "I thought you wanted steak?"

"Oh, I do. But that's not all. It's been two centuries since I've had a body. I intend to try one of absolutely everything while I'm here."

Gabe swallowed a snide remark. He just needed to string her along until he could pry out what he needed to know. Nice and easy. "Well, you look pretty great for two-hundred."

She looked up from her menu in confusion.

"I don't get it," he elaborated. "Explain to me how you're somehow not Heather anymore."

She placed her menu on the table. "Are you still playing with me? I honestly can't tell the difference between your cleverness and your ignorance. Do you get that reaction often?"

Gabe couldn't quite subdue the incredulity. "*Me* playing with *you*? You've done nothing but con me from the minute we met..." He stopped himself with a sigh, then placed his palms on the table to let the anger drain away into the cool surface. "No. I'm not playing with you."

She leaned forward and narrowed her eyes. "How can you not know?"

He stared straight back. "I don't know," he said. "Get it? I don't know how I don't know because I *don't freaking know*."

She searched his eyes more desperately and carefully than any cop he'd ever met, and whatever she found obviously didn't please her. She broke off and sat back with a groan. "You really don't."

He spread his hands and Heather pushed her menu to the side. A bitter little smile creased her face, and she blew a stray strand of dark hair from her cheek. "I can't believe this," she said. "I thought you were some kind of genius manipulator, and that we were..." She threw up her hands, then ran her fingers roughly through her hair. "I thought we were sparring for position. I thought you were testing me!"

Just then the waitress edged up to the table with the wary look of someone accidentally walking into a domestic dispute. "Are you folks ready?"

Gabe tried to ask for a few more minutes, but Heather smiled sweetly and patted the menu. "Absolutely! I'll have two steaks, three cinnamon rolls, two bowls of fruit, and seven sides of bacon. Oh, and a coffee."

Gabe stared at her for a moment, then gave the waitress a "What are you gonna do?" look. Suddenly he didn't feel so weird about his own order. When the waitress left, he turned back to Heather. "Are you going to start speaking in complete thoughts again, or should we wait for your buffet to arrive?"

She dropped the fake smile and shook her head in disbelief. "I'm sorry, I just... You're a regular human?" She asked as if the admission would get them both arrested.

"As opposed to what?" he whispered back. "An ocelot?"

She blew out a long breath. "This is great. I finally manifest again, and within five minutes I'm tied to the biggest moron in the room." Gabe tried to protest, but she talked right over him. "You have stumbled into something that is so much larger than you know. And it just worked! I mean, how? I thought you were... You should be dead!"

Her voice had gotten steadily louder as she went, and Gabe stared pointedly at her. She looked around, then raised her hands to placate him. "They can't hear us," she said. "My glamour hides anything that... Ugh, I'm sorry. I'll use complete thoughts." She stopped and frowned to herself. "Where do I even begin? This is so bad."

She seemed to deliberate for a bit and Gabe let her. He watched for any signs of deception, but it looked like they might be getting through the mutual acts and down to some real answers.

Then she finally nodded and leaned forward. "Right. How much do you know about the Ether and Umbras?"

He gave her a tight shrug. "Are those, like, astrology terms?"

The question seemed to hit her hard, and her gaze fell to the table. "Wow. My fucking luck." She again pronounced the curse as if trying it out for the first time.

"Oh, *your* luck?" he asked. "What about—"

Her hand flashed up to place a finger over his lips. "I know," she said. "I'm sorry." She took a breath and brought herself back into focus. "You've had a rough introduction to something that humans were never meant to see."

Her touch sent a little tingle through him, and there was at least a portion of sincerity in her eyes. She looked honestly shaken. He let his anger drain as quickly as it had come and told his common sense to just hold on for a minute while he worked things out. "Fine," he said. "I've got nowhere to be. Make me understand."

Heather opened her mouth to speak, but then turned it into a smile as the waitress dropped off her coffee. "Thank you kindly," she said. Once the waitress was out of earshot, the smile melted again. "You have a serious problem, Gabriel. And before I give you any more information, I would have a bargain from you." She took a sip and groaned in pleasure.

Gabe was torn between asking about the bargain and what kind of coffee she was used to if she thought Barbara's was worth that kind of reaction, but he ultimately decided on the life-or-death thing. "That's more like it," he said. "I know how to do bargains. What do you want?"

She took another long swallow, then put her cup down to add an obscene amount of sugar. "I've already told you. We are bound, and I want to be released. You let me go, and I will give you enough information to keep you alive for at least the next twenty-four hours."

"Let's say I believe you," he said. "Why would I let you go before I got the information? By your rules you would have no obligation to tell me the truth after that, right?"

Heather smiled as she added a seventh packet of sugar. "Not completely hopeless, then. Maybe you'll live forty-eight hours. I am obligated to honesty now, so any bargain I strike will be in the best possible faith no matter when it is executed. Is that good enough?"

Gabe tossed his mangled straw wrapper to the table. "I'm working blind here. How can I make a fair deal unless I know what I have? But you're bound to honesty, right? Let's try this: You to tell me who you are, where you're from, and the details of this supposed *bond*. Then if I feel like I understand things enough, we'll bargain. Go."

As he said the word, something electric flashed between them and he nearly jumped out of his seat. He looked to Heather to see if she'd done it somehow, but she only flinched, then grimaced in annoyance.

"I shouldn't have told you that part first," she said. "Fine. My name is Shanti—at least it was. I am from..." she stopped to consider for a moment, "outside of the material plane. A state of being without substance called the Ether. The bond we share was placed by the sorcerer, and it links us body and spirit so I may protect and serve you to my fullest ability until you release me or one of us falls. It will only strengthen with time, and I know of no way to break it short of death or your willing dismissal. For the latter, you must have knowledge of and access to magic. Which, since you're human, you can't possibly have. And I can't kill you or lead you to harm. This leaves me screwed from every conceivable direction. How was that?"

Gabe sat back while he processed, but just then the waitress arrived with their food and they spent several seconds arranging plates. When the woman was gone again, Gabe looked back up at Heather. "So you're...possessed?"

She picked up a piece of bacon and chewed slowly. "Sort of. Except the other way around. I possessed her."

"Which means you're not Heather?"

She chewed thoughtfully. "No and yes. It's difficult to explain. This is unbelievable, by the way. Bacon. Oh my."

Gabe picked up his silverware and took a large bite of cherry pie to cover his need to compile. He felt like he hadn't eaten in days, and the quick hit of sugar went straight to his head. They ate in silence for a while, and he was hungry enough that he didn't care. That he was alive to eat at all was a reason to shut up and relish the simple pleasure, and even this insanity couldn't dampen that for him. He knew it would still be waiting for him on the other side, but the quiet was nice.

Unfortunately it didn't last. Halfway through her second steak, Heather seemed to notice something in the cafe and sat up to fold her hands on the edge of the table. There was suddenly a new urgency in her that she was clearly trying to suppress, but Gabe caught the subtle lacing of fear in her expression. Something had changed.

"The bargain?" she asked, her voice just a bit too high.

Gabe took another bite and shook his head, purposely drawing it out to make her squirm. Just because she was afraid didn't necessarily mean he had to be. And it was the first time he'd had the upper hand all morning. He swallowed. "What danger am I in that I need your information? Who are these people?"

She leaned forward. "Dangerous. But they are not even your primary concern. You say Heather is possessed, yes?" She held his eyes in a way that suggested no doubt or deception. "Well, so are you."

Gabe's fork stopped halfway to his mouth and he let it hang there. "Oh yeah?"

"Yeah," she continued. "Except apparently it didn't take. Which is not something I've ever heard of. But I still sense an Umbra in you, which is why you had all of us fooled for a while last night. Whatever came through from the Ether, it's still linked to you somewhere in there. And the power of it is incredible. So that's your first problem: you've trapped a tiger in your bedroom. Second, Gwendal is dangerous in her own right. And while you might have tricked her last night, she will come looking for you. The geas she used to shut down your spine is probably the least of what she can do. She's something much older and stronger than me, which makes your situation pretty damn hopeless without my help."

Gabe finally took his bite just to prove that he wasn't scared, but it tasted like styrofoam.

The main entrance bell rang, and Heather's eyes darted over his shoulder toward the noise. She didn't appear to like whatever she saw.

"Quick," she whispered. "Your answer. My information for my freedom."

"I thought you said I needed magic, or whatever?"

"We'll figure that out," she snapped. "I just want your promise to try. Now."

But Gabe had stopped listening when the rear entrance bell rang and a man in a horrific costume entered. His mask looked like a flayed face, all muscle and sinew, and his clothes were covered in very realistic burn damage. It struck Gabe as odd. Halloween was still a few weeks away, and there weren't any conventions in town that he could recall. It was also clear that the guy was agitated about something. His eyes were roaming everywhere in the skinless sockets, and his steps were quick and short like he had somewhere to be but didn't know how to get there. He clearly wasn't at Barbara's for an egg sandwich, and there was only one reason to wear a mask like that in the middle of the morning.

"Robbery," Gabe hissed. "Stay quiet."

Heather glanced over her shoulder, then reached out to grab his hand. "No," she whispered back. "Hunters. Looking for us." She met his eyes, and her gaze was honestly terrified. "We're about to die."

CHAPTER TWELVE

"I like the police. They clean up the riffraff that are too stupid to avoid getting caught, and they create a nice sense of societal security I can exploit. Cops aren't looking for professionals like me in their day-to-day; they're after the dangerous amateurs. I can generally smile and nod as they pass. And it's definitely not because I'm innocent, but because I'm good."

-Excerpt from Chapter One, CONscience

Gabe heard the unadorned sincerity in Heather's voice, and for the first time all morning he completely believed what she said. He didn't know what a Hunter was, but their costumes certainly didn't make them look like kindergarten teachers. The one at the rear of the cafe glanced around at the two dozen diners, then started casually walking by the booths as the one at the main entrance began on the other side. They nodded politely at people as they passed, and shockingly, most smiled or waved back instead of screaming in terror. One little kid even saluted, which was weird.

"For the sake of argument, let's say I'm on board with whatever plan you have," Gabe said, sliding down a little in his seat. "What is this?"

Heather nodded, seeming to pluck the specifics of the question from his mind. "Hunters use glamours to hide in plain sight. It's a kind of magical illusion most of us have. You and I are only seeing their true forms because we're meant to, but humans see constables."

He looked back at her incredulously.

"Police officers," she said in annoyance, as if that was the weirdest part of the statement. "Focus on the moment, please. We need to get out of here."

He stared hard at one Hunter, and for a second he caught a glimpse of a uniformed officer smiling tightly at a table of older women. Then there was a haze and shimmer, and the man became terrifying again. Gabe had to look away. "Fine," he said. "That makes as much sense as anything else today. So what do we do?"

"I don't know. I'm a succubus. Heather had some surprising facility with combat that I'm still processing, but I'm not used to doing the fighting thing."

Gabe tried to suppress the urge to ask more follow-up questions on that line of nonsense, but he couldn't stop himself entirely. "A succubus. Geez, lady, this is getting thick." He took a breath to focus. "Okay, well I don't do the fighting thing either—especially not with cops. Should we play it cool or try to sneak out?"

She glanced at the Hunter on her side and shook her head. "Talking won't work. They hunt. That's it. As for running, I don't know. I've dealt with them indirectly, but never like this. They used to be enforcers for the Umbral Council, but that was two hundred years ago. There's no telling what they are now. They're older than most gods, and they exist only to fulfill their purpose. All I know is that they can kill us in about two seconds if they see us running. And that if it starts to get cold in here, we should try to run like hell anyway. There's no time for more, but I promise to tell you everything else once we're out."

Gabe growled under his breath. He didn't know what he believed anymore, but it was tough to deny the tactical merits of a good retreat. He glanced around quickly and spotted a group that might have possibilities, and it only took another moment for a plan to come together. "When you see the distraction, get up and go out the back door," he said. "Don't go to the car. Four blocks south of here there's a big mall. Meet me in the cookie shop on the lower level. I'm going to hold you to that explanation after this." Then he slipped about a hundred bucks onto the table and stood.

Barbara's Cafe occupied what had been meant as spaces for four smaller boutique shops. Over the years, as the place grew in popularity and one failed dog sweater store after another left the surrounding shops vacant, the cafe had sprawled out in a winding floor plan that any fengshui master would have hated. Consequently, the booths and tables were all crammed in wherever there had been enough space, and any dead spots had been filled with potted ferns and random room-dividers. He had often thought the place would do well to clear it all out and start over with some kind of forethought, but today the crazy setup proved to be an asset.

Gabe carefully moved across the cafe, staying nonchalant but always keeping a pillar or plant or wall between himself and the Hunters. He did up the top button on his shirt as he walked, then snatched an empty tray from a vacant table and tucked it under his arm. Then he shifted his path to *accidentally* bump into a waitress, and they shared a brief chuckle as he palmed the ticket pad he'd lifted from her apron. It would be a quick and dirty con for sure, but he only had to pass as a manager for a few seconds. He made his expression grim, then leaned over his target table as if he had something serious to say.

The trio of young guys had been talking with their heads together, but at seeing Gabe, they all leaned back with identical looks of thinly veiled fear. One was wearing a frat shirt and had a lanyard hanging out of the pocket of his patterned golf shorts. Gabe had eyed them on his way over and decided he was the most awake of the three. "Good morning," Gabe said. "I see you're still a little drunk from last night. Did you drive here?"

All three looked like they were drowning in open air for a minute, but then the de facto leader got some words out. "No, no. I... We didn't drive."

Gabe realized he was also smelling just a hint of the sharp tang of weed, and he tilted his head in mock-disappointment. "Would you gentleman be able to pass a drug test? Or breath test? Because if not, you should have stayed home with your Fruity Pebbles. Those cops are going to tag you." He nodded toward one of the Hunters. "They already know who they're looking for. They're just making you sweat."

The two guys on the other side of the table were way worse-off, and after checking out the officers headed their way, they stared back at Gabe like little kids caught standing over a fresh Kool-Aid stain. They really did see cops where he saw monsters. That implication threatened to topple his little tower of denial right there, but the existential crisis would have to wait. He could blubber about it later in the bath or something.

"So what?" the first guy asked. "You gonna narc? Because cops can't just randomly—"

Gabe held up a hand. "Shut up. You don't know what the cops can or can't do. I'm here to help you. Keep you from going to jail. How does that sound, brother?"

The guy shrugged and fiddled with his flat-brimmed hat. "Brother? More like my dad, dude. But okay, why?"

Gabe checked the Hunters again and realized that he was almost out of time. He needed to hook this fish. "No, moron. *Brother*. Sigma for life." He slapped the ticket pad against the guy's fraternity shirt and silently gave thanks for the command of Greek letters he'd taken from his otherwise ill-spent college days. To his surprise, the guy nodded, taking the dubious lifeline without a second thought. No secret handshake required.

"What do we do?" the guy asked.

Gabe glanced to the Hunters and found them both nearly to him in the center section of the cafe. How they hadn't seen him already was a mystery. "I disabled the alarm on the emergency exit. You guys slip out the back and drive away before they know you're gone."

All three exchanged glances and came to a blessedly quick consensus. "We owe you, man," the ringleader said. "We just walk out?"

Gabe stepped back and let them rise from the booth. "Just act like your normal selves. Objectify some women and make a few boner jokes on your way out. Nobody will suspect a thing's wrong. Just hurry!" Then he turned and walked purposefully toward the front of the restaurant, hoping the bait was good enough for both traps he was trying to set.

He stopped at the hostess stand by the front door and pretended to check the seating chart. The Hunters had joined up at the table he had just left, and they seemed to be lingering there as if sensing something interesting. He still couldn't believe people weren't screaming in terror at them as hideous as they were, and the idea of being caught by them made him bend lower to his fictional work. If those things were real, and they really were using some kind of magic to hide in plain sight, then it might *all* be real. It might all have *really* happened, and he wasn't sure he could handle what that meant. Suddenly this wasn't just a precautionary retreat; he badly didn't want to be there anymore.

A puzzled-looking waitress approached just as his first trap went off. "Can I help—" she began. Then the alarm sounded through the whole restaurant and every eye in the place looked to the emergency exit. The three guys stood shocked and frozen in the doorway, outlined in morning sunlight as the red light above them flashed and the klaxon blared. The Hunters sprang into motion faster than Gabe would have thought possible, and as soon as the frat guys saw them, they bolted like rabbits, letting the door slam closed. The Hunters quickly followed and the door slammed again, and Gabe used the confusion to drop his props and slip out the front door. He looked for Heather as he left, but she was already gone.

Thirty-seven minutes later, Gabe was nursing an underbaked cookie on the bottom floor of the city mall, and he was close to convincing himself to run without looking back. Then Heather finally walked in wearing a new outfit—tight jeans with black flats and a billowy, floral-print top—and she had several more bags dangling from her hands. She smiled as if this was just any other Wednesday.

"Hiya," she said, settling into the chair opposite him. "You changed your shirt."

Gabe glanced down at the blue t-shirt he'd picked up in a three-pack for six dollars, then looked pointedly at her entire morning of shopping. "So did you."

She tossed her dark hair theatrically and somehow it fell perfectly into place. "Do you like it? I have to admit to missing the formality of Victorian fashion, but there is something to be said for comfort. I was a little nervous that I didn't understand the memories correctly, but from what I've seen, most women eschew dresses for trousers now. How odd and wonderful."

Gabe pushed his cookie away. "Okay, let's go find somewhere safer to talk."

She stood and dropped the bags into his lap before he could even think to object then tapped him on the nose. "Such a gentleman."

Gabe saw an older woman smile to herself when she overheard, and realized that he'd just been effortlessly maneuvered. So he gathered the bags and rose to lead Heather from the mall to a frozen yogurt place he knew of a few blocks away. When looking for complete privacy at ten in the morning on an Autumn weekday in the Midwest, you couldn't do much better than a frozen yogurt place. Unfortunately, they didn't make it anywhere close.

They barely got out the door before Heather hissed and pulled him roughly against the wall of the car-park. "They found us already."

He followed her gaze and saw a white utility van pulling into the parking lot. He could just make out a red face behind the wheel before she was pulling him back into the mall. "So quickly?" he asked, as they started jogging up the escalator.

Heather was right at his heels. "I don't know. It's possible they're just casing the most logical spot for us to run to. But given that they've shown up at two of the places we've been, I think it's more likely that they can trace us somehow."

Gabe lowered his voice as they made it to the upper level and tried to blend in with the sparse morning crowd. "Can they do that? Maybe a GPS tracker on one of us?"

She took his arm and slowed him to a more natural pace. "They don't need technology if they can track us by scent or blood. But they shouldn't have had access to either of those. Did you leave anything behind? Any fluids?"

Gabe's tongue went to the healed spot on his lip. His thoughts raced as they moved past kiosks selling brightly colored junk, but then he realized the absurdity of the question. Had he left anything behind for magical boogeymen to sniff? It was ridiculous, wasn't it? Except he was still running away as if he believed it. It couldn't be real, but it had to be. He'd *seen* it, and he'd definitely felt it. The door flashed in his mind again, then it was gone. It was too much. He needed to decide which side of the crazy train he was going to sit on, because he was collecting way too much baggage to keep standing in the aisle.

Heather seemed to pick the fear and confusion directly from his brain. "They do have your blood, don't they?" She didn't wait for confirmation. "When she kissed you. Damn."

"Okay, how do I hide?" he asked.

"It's not like that," she said. "It's a spiritual trail, and Hunters can and will follow it anywhere. That's what they do. There's nowhere that's far enough away."

Gabe felt dizzy and sick all of a sudden. "Then what are my options?"

At first she looked like she was going to lecture him more, but then she stopped and turned to him. "Do you trust me?"

"Nope," he said.

She sighed. "For heaven's sake. What do you not understand about this bond?"

He shook his head. "*Any* of it."

"Well, let me clear up the most important bit for you," she said, pulling him back into a purposeful walk. "I have to protect you with my life. That precludes hurting you directly or intentionally leading you to harm. You're safe with me. So would you please relax?"

Gabe didn't reply until they'd made it into one of the big department stores, just out of sight of the main corridor. "Fine. What's your plan?"

Heather took his arm and led him through the store, weaving through displays of clothes and kitchenware before finding a secluded spot near a shoe display and turning to him. "I need to kiss you."

Gabe shrugged. "That's not so—"

"And take some of your soul."

"...bad," he finished, darkly. "What?"

She glanced around and moved nearer to him to speak in a whisper. "Only the smallest portion. I'll take some of yours and give you some of mine. The new spiritual profile should render your blood useless for tracking."

"My soul?"

"Yes," she said. "I swear it won't harm you. Though, you will not be unchanged. And we have to kiss for it to work. My magic is specific that way."

He stared at her. "This is the succubus thing?"

She nodded.

Gabe realized that he had come to a decision point. If he still wanted to try to justify everything away, then letting Heather kiss him wouldn't be a big deal. She was pretty, if completely insane, and millions of guys with Harley Quinn fetishes would say there were worse combinations. Plus they'd started the day with her hand down his pants, so he could really think of it as more of a lateral move. But if he *did* believe any of it even a little bit, well, then he had way bigger problems than a little soul swapping.

"Okay," he said. "Let's do your thing. I've had worse dates."

She nodded again and led him out of the store into a long, glass-covered walking bridge that crossed a road and connected the mall to the parking garage. Cars slid silently below them, but the corridor was empty. Heather grabbed a sign advertising a sale on purses as they left the store, and in one quick movement she snapped the top frame off, leaving her only with a metal pole and heavy base. She let the glass double doors close behind them, then she shoved the pole through both handles to barricade them closed.

They reached the stairwell at the end of the hall, but she grabbed his arm and stopped him there. "It won't do us any good to go on until this is done. They'll just keep chasing."

Gabe let the shopping bags fall to the ground. For some reason he felt the need to have his hands free for this—though whether it was in preparation for an embrace or a battle, he couldn't quite decide. He looked at Heather to say something along those lines, but the words fell apart in his mouth.

She had changed. It wasn't any one thing, but more a series of tiny adjustments that added up to something staggering. Her hair seemed to have thickened and taken on a darker sheen, curling over her face in soft spirals, and her skin had gone paler and her lips redder until the two contrasted like blood on snow. Her smile was shy but sly, and it was willful and tentative and real all at once in a way that should have been impossible but was there for him to see. And her eyes were...more—larger and deeper and sparkling with mischief and old knowledge as they danced over his face to read his every desire.

He couldn't believe he hadn't noticed this before. She was staggering, and the longer he looked the more he wanted to. He moved closer, wanting her, loving her, and complying without reservation to the pull of her. It was like nothing he had ever felt, and his body was happy to embrace it. He knew better, of course. Blemishes and small compromises are a part of reality, and nature has no such thing as perfection. But he didn't care. He went to her and breathed in the scent of her and was lost.

At first it was nothing more than vanilla, simple and clean. But then the memory rose and smothered him beneath its weight, and years fell away to drop him back into his first rush of real lust. She came back vivid and powerful in his mind, a girl he hadn't thought of in years, and now he could see every freckle beneath her blush. Discovering themselves together, there in that closet. A first glimpse of skin. The first tentative touches. The fumbling, the giggling, and the awe of forbidden magic. He'd never felt the same way before or since.

Then in the same breath the scent changed, becoming a sweet perfume like fruit and lilacs. And suddenly he was in his old dorm room, drowsing next to a girl and feeling his first true taste of love. And then it was strawberries, hot and ripe in the sun, and he smiled up lazily from the lap of a woman who had never loved him quite enough to stay, but had wanted to, and had tried. The taste of her kiss. The first desperate desire... Then it was soap and clean skin, wet hair on his cheek and water slick between them. Then warm chocolate drizzled down a pale stomach, candles flickering and laughter at the mess. Then a fireplace and wine and a long goodbye. Then summer heat and fresh-cut grass... Then... Then... Then...

Then he was kissing Heather hard, forgetting everything and wanting nothing more in the world. She was all of them and more, and she had never left, never changed, never hated him or pitied him or knew the lie of him. She was there, and she was his, and she pulled him in hungrily.

CHAPTER THIRTEEN

```
"Most con artists get their start by being
conned themselves. At least once. For me it was
my dad. He convinced me that running from city
to city and never having family or friends and
never knowing where your next meal would come
from was fun fun fun. He was great at it too.
Until he wasn't. For other people it's a
boyfriend, or a boss, or a buddy. You don't
usually just wake up one day and realize you
have this skill set. You have to hear the
language to understand that you can speak it.
You have to feel it to know it's there. Almost
like becoming a vampire: somebody has to bite
you first."

-Excerpt from Chapter Four, CONscience
```

    Gabe sank into the kiss. Nothing had ever felt so good, and he couldn't imagine why he had ever wanted to do anything else. The world was perfect as long as Heather was in it. She was everything he'd ever need, and all he had to do was stay right there.

    Then the pain started. It was subtle at first, growing as a soft ache in his chest, but soon it rose to fill his entire body with an unpleasant buzz of sound and heat that made the shimmer of the moment fade and tear. The illusion soured, and suddenly Gabe was fully aware of what was happening. The scents and memories fled as if they'd never been, and instead he was left with every bad breakup, every tragedy, and every insult he'd ever experienced: His father's accident, his mother's abandonment, the women he'd lost, the friends he'd left. It felt like all of his self-pity, pain, selfishness, and grief were swirling to the surface like grit stirred up from the bottom of a pool, and the idyllic swim had left him wading through his own filth.

    Then his soul ripped apart. The pain was beyond anything on the human scale, and after the first full second, Gabe's brain refused to acknowledge it. It was then that he knew for certain he was dealing with things that couldn't be rationally explained. One moment the idea of a soul was something half-believed and half-understood, and the next, he could have said exactly where it was within him. The previous night came screaming back to him in full, high-definition play-by-play, and the voice of the invader echoed in his mind, telling him that his soul was to be scoured clean. The door was still there, waiting for him. It had never left. It had all happened, and it was all real. God help him, it was real.

Gabe tried to pull away, but his body wouldn't respond. Then Heather *exhaled* into him, and a warmth spread through him, dialing down the pain until he could get his hands around it to find that he was still a whole person. There was an ache there yet, like long-past loss or regret buried beneath drink, but there was something new as well. It was jagged and alien, but it was there. And it was his now.

He studied his new spiritual center with utter amazement, but found it already fading from his awareness. He tried to hold on, but it slipped from his mental grasp and fell back into the furthest depths of his mind where even his subconscious was a distant point high overhead. Soon he only had the memory of what had happened, and through the lens of it he could suddenly see that his ideas of what constituted rational explanation were about to become greatly expanded. The world had changed beneath his feet, and he had no freaking clue what to do about it.

He was finally able to pull away, and he took a deep, cleansing breath. The entire thing had happened in a moment, but in that space he'd come to understand, deep down, that he was in a whole bunch of trouble. He looked at Heather and saw the thing inside of her for the first time. The tiny details had been there all morning, in her eyes and language and demeanor, but he had refused to really see. She wasn't human anymore.

"Oh my God," he said, falling back against the glass wall.

Heather was breathing hard and fast, like she'd just run for her life. She kept her eyes down. "It worked."

Gabe shook his head. A succubus had just entered him and performed some kind of psychic surgery on his soul. That wasn't something that happened in real life, and he certainly didn't have a scripted response anywhere in his repertoire. "What are you?" he managed to ask. "This is—"

But before he could articulate the world-altering thoughts in his head, Heather grabbed him and threw him staggering down the hallway toward the parking lot. He had a moment to look back as he regained his balance, and it was just in time to see the two Hunters burst through their makeshift barricade as if it had been made of styrofoam.

The pieces of the metal pole and broken door handles went scattering to either side as the monsters rushed into the walkway, and Heather was already racing toward them. She pivoted away from the first one with surprising grace and sent it sprawling with a well-placed push in its sternum. Then the second Hunter hit her hard at chest-level and bore her to the floor.

Gabe watched, frozen in fear as Heather struggled beneath the Hunter. She slammed her fists into its sides and legs as it crouched over her, but the creature seemed barely to notice. It raised a clawed hand to strike at her, its mouth pulled into a rictus grin and its fingers stiffened to drive into her chest. The thing had been strong enough to shatter a metal pole without stopping. It was going to kill her right there.

He had to do something. Despite everything, he didn't want Heather to die. He didn't know how he felt about her anymore, but she might have answers to the thousands of questions racing through his head. She also owed him about eighty bucks for breakfast. So he improvised. He leaped forward to the Hunter and booted it in the head, scoring a glancing blow across its jaw that scraped off a chunk of meat to splat nauseatingly against the glass. The creature fell back just enough to give Heather the leverage to throw the flayed thing back with shocking strength, and it landed on its side several feet away.

By then, the first Hunter had gotten back to its feet, and it dismissed Gabe to move to Heather as she rose. Gabe set himself in what he hoped looked like a defensive posture and tried desperately to remember the few months of judo he'd taken as a college elective. Unfortunately, nothing popped to mind as a solid defense against skinless monsters. Luckily, Heather had it covered, and she grabbed the Hunter's lapels as she came up, then twisted like a dancer and sent the thing flying into its companion back at the entrance of the hallway. The two collided in a stumbling mess, and it opened a brief window of freedom.

"Come on!" Gabe said, grabbing her arm.

She wrenched from his grip and started a careful backward retreat. "We can't outrun them. This is what they do, Gabe. They have our new scent now. I can't..." she paused as the Hunters disentangled themselves, "I can't do that soul thing again. It's a one-time deal, unless you want a really pleasant way to die. That means these two can track us and pass the information on to their friends. If we're walking out of here alive, they can't."

Gabe had so many questions, but there wasn't time. "How do we beat them?"

Heather shook her head tightly. "I've never seen one die. They're way beyond my level. Old before written history. The only reason we're not already dead is because they haven't bothered to try that hard. No Rime Blades yet."

"Not helpful in so many ways," he said.

They had almost reached the door leading into the parking lot when the Hunters got back to their feet and started pacing toward them. A sudden rush of cool wind preceded them, and Gabe saw that they both held out a hand to one side as a thick crust of something white began to form in their fists. It looked like ice, and as they came on, it was extending into a club—or a sword.

Heather groaned but stepped forward to meet them. "Run," she said.

CHAPTER FOURTEEN

```
"Few things in this world scare me anymore. When
you learn to see into people's hearts, there
aren't that many monsters left in the dark."

-Excerpt from Chapter Seven, CONscience
```

Gabe watched death stalk toward him, then looked at Heather standing between them. She had told him to run, and he wanted to, but his logic screamed that it would be futile. If he was believing what Heather said now—and there was no reason not to anymore—then running away would do no good. They would only find him later when he was all alone. He needed to stop them now.

He looked to the windows and tried to construct a scenario in which he could throw the monsters through the glass, but the variables and hurdles were too many. He considered luring them to the stairs and somehow pushing them and letting the fall kill them, but another look at their gruesome faces made him doubt the efficacy of a simple two-story tumble. He needed more. He needed a weapon or a trick or an advantage. He needed *anything.*

The world stopped.

Gabe had been tensed for battle—or more likely a wild flailing while being stabbed to death—but nothing came. Everything just paused, hanging there in space and waiting to resolve. Heather was poised low and ready for the attack, one leg behind her for balance and both hands up competently as if she had some kind of chance. And her dark hair was floating partway through a defiant toss. The two Hunters were mid-stride and mid-snarl, both holding what Gabe assumed must be their Rime Blades: gray-white swords sprouting organically from fists covered in hoarfrost. The edges of the weapons didn't gleam so much as glower, but they looked deadly sharp. And it was all just hanging there, paused.

He glanced wildly around, expecting something to break loose and set everything back into motion. But as the moment stretched longer and longer, he was eventually able to accept his place in whatever this frozen world was. Some new torture, he assumed.

"How very interesting," a voice said behind him.

Gabe turned and saw a fuzzy outline of a man coming up the stairs. He blinked rapidly and started to back away, but the figure didn't resolve no matter how hard he tried to focus on it. It was like a low resolution image taken in the dark that had suddenly come to life.

"Who are you?" Gabe asked, only barely keeping his voice from breaking.

The image came to a stop several paces away, then stretched his arms as if he'd just woken from a long nap. "Ahhhh, wonderful," he said. The voice rolled out like a wave of warm syrup. "You have no idea how long I have been waiting for you."

And then Gabe recognized the voice. The image of the man wavered for an instant and became a white door, infinitely sided and far too real and sharp from every angle. Then it snapped back to the blurred man again, the invader. And Gabe's brain threatened to break. "What..." he began, but the questions crowded in all at once so that none made it out.

The invader chuckled. "Indeed. A good question. One which I would also like answered."

The door flickered back again, and this time the entire world seemed to jitter like a bad computer game. Then everything settled back into place and the man returned as if nothing had happened. It was like none of it was real. The place, the man, the door—it was like they were all constructs of his own mind. Like his brain was laying a simpler operating system over an impossible situation to protect itself from shutting down beneath a computational problem it was outclassed by. It meant running and fighting were worthless here, and that he might not even be in charge of his own mind anymore. He supposed he could try pinching himself to wake up and get back to the business of being brutally murdered, but... Well, it couldn't hurt to have one little mental chat with a hostile extraplanar monster who wanted to banish his soul and seize his body.

"What do you want?" Gabe asked, defaulting to flippancy. "I'm busy."

"I see that!" the invader said. "Quite a situation. Hunters, I believe. Very interesting."

Gabe glanced back to make sure nobody was moving. "I guess so. If you call being stabbed to death interesting. Are you here to gloat or something? I thought you'd gone back to where you came from."

The invader's face was blurred beyond any hope of spotting facial cues, but he seemed to be staring past Gabe. "Gloat? No. I'm here to talk and make you an offer. A small thing, but rewarding for both of us, I hope. You have but to listen."

Gabe could hear the calculated pleasantness of the voice, encouraging friendliness and making rejection seem like a silly overreaction. It was like seeing an old professional in his element, except that Gabe knew the trick better than most. "Who are you?" he asked again.

The invader continued with the sugary, placating tones, but seemed irked that Gabe hadn't just crumpled. "I am old and powerful, and I am your salvation."

Gabe felt the tug of the words, trying to draw him in and smother him, but he was aware of the effect even as he felt it. The lens of Heather's gift surprised him again by letting him sense an energy edging near him: the red-gold power trying to nip at his thoughts. But it was far weaker now, and once he knew it was there, it wasn't much trouble to sidestep it.

"That's not what I asked," Gabe said. "Who *are* you?"

The invader now seemed truly annoyed. "Time unspools at a different rate here, human. What feels like minutes for you, may be years for me here. My identity spans—"

"Stop," Gabe said. The thing was deflecting and trying to gain control again, and the reaction gave Gabe enough confidence to go on the offensive. He didn't know what kind of stick he held, but he poked with it all the same. "Answer me truthfully or I'll leave. You brought me here, so that means I have something you want. Tell me who you are and we can talk. Answer with more vague bullshit and you can go back to whispering to yourself in the dark. If time passes differently in here, maybe I'll go park myself on top of a mountain for a few months and see how well you like the sound of your own voice then."

The figure of the man stilled at once. "Very well," it said. The sweet overtones disappeared, replaced with something that sounded like grudging respect. "I was ancient before gaining a name, but my first true name was Aka Manah."

Gabe felt the truth of it, and the tiny part of him that was now Heather cringed. "And why are you here..." He meant to repeat the name, but even in his own mind the words simply wouldn't form.

Aka Manah rumbled. "There is no point in denying it. I am temporarily trapped by my own design. You now play host to a power that will eventually burst you like an overripe melon. Congratulations."

The door and the world flickered again, and Gabe tried not to shudder. "That's great. Why are you here in general though? On earth? What the hell do you want?"

Aka Manah seemed to consider for a moment before replying, "No. I could answer that. And may yet if you prove worthy to know. But it is not the right question, Gabriel."

Gabe faltered at first, but then the words formed in his mouth of their own accord. "*What* are you?"

It was like hearing someone smile over the phone. Gabe couldn't see it through the blurred features, but he knew it was there: the big, toothy grin of a predator who had just gained a perch above his future lunch.

"Yes," Aka Manah said, rolling the word out like a long bolt of silk. "What am I, indeed? That is why I summoned you here."

Gabe felt the situation slipping from his grasp, but he had no idea what to do about it. "Explain," he said, simply.

"You need something, human," Aka Manah said. "Had you no need I could not have asked you here. Your desperation opened the way. Therefore we are in a perfect position to make a bargain. And what *I* am, is what *you* need."

Gabe suddenly remembered the tableau just behind him. A minute ago, he would have accepted help from pretty much any cosmic source willing to give it—he just hadn't expected to get a reply. But he also wasn't in any hurry to go back and get eviscerated. He squared his shoulders and nodded. "Fine. Make your offer."

Aka Manah almost purred with satisfaction. "Wonderful," he said, stretching the word out to lick every syllable. "I can provide what you need, provided my needs are met."

"Elaborate," Gabe said, using short statements to hide his ignorance.

"It is simple. I will grant you a measure of power to deal with this problem. In return, I gain your help in restoring my freedom. Two lives bought with one. Quite a deal."

Gabe might have been ignorant, but even to him it sounded like a trap. "You know, I'm getting this offer a lot lately. But for one dose of power that I don't know how to use, you get to try to take over my body again? What's behind door number two?"

Instead of sounding annoyed this time, Aka Manah actually seemed delighted. "Oh my, a negotiator! What luck!" The laugh that followed was part giggle and part snarl.

"Come on, man," Gabe said. "We don't have all day."

"Oh, you're wrong on that account," Aka Manah said. "In this place we could speak for an eternity before a single grain of sand dropped in the hourglass. I told you that time flows differently here. Yet you are partially correct in that we two are not in stasis. We will continue to change even as all else in the universe is still and silent, and this cannot be sustained indefinitely. The space here will not contain us both without fracturing, and then we will expire quite horrifically." He laughed again. "Or we will combine into something unspeakable and slaughter everything in sight—after a period of insanity and agony and so on, of course. I am frankly amazed it hasn't happened already."

Gabe let the following silence hang longer than he should have. "...Sure."

"And don't worry about your little demoness," Aka Manah said. "She is factored in as a courtesy to you. A bonus. Here, try this: I will grant you power and the knowledge to use it in exchange for freedom, with the caveat that your body is no longer available for occupation."

Gabe was thankful his instincts were still working. "No. You'll just take Heather. She's off limits too. And you have to guarantee my complete safety. Try again."

Aka Manah squealed with glee. "Yes!" The word was almost orgasmic, and Gabe cringed. "Very good! Try this: Power, knowledge, guarantee of ability, and certainty of safety from me and mine for both you and your friend. And I get freedom. I think you'll agree that this covers all concerns."

Gabe had to admit that it did, but something still nagged at him. "Why do you care? Why not let me die? Wouldn't that be the quickest way out for you?"

Aka Manah grew quiet, regrouping just like a conman who'd been thrown off the script by a savvy mark. "Does it matter?" he asked, finally. "Events on the human scale are but trifling flits and glimmers to a—"

"Shut up," Gabe said, recognizing the redirection again. "Why can't you let me die? You've been here since last night, right? You had all morning to talk to me about this, and you're just showing up now. Is the question too complicated for you? Or is there something you don't want me to know?"

There was another period of silence before the voice resumed in a more casual tone. "You are in danger. I need a small amount of assistance from you and offer my help in recompense."

"Not good enough," Gabe said, scenting a trail to follow now. "Try again."

Aka Manah only paused a moment this time. "I wish us to work together to find a solution that will benefit—"

"Wrong," Gabe interrupted. "You don't want to work with me any more than I want to work with you. But the roles are reversed from last night, aren't they? This time *you're* the little fish in *my* ocean."

There was a long, long pause, and then finally Aka Manah responded with deadly calm. "Would you like to make a counteroffer, smart little human?"

"I have a theory," Gabe said, ignoring the implied threat. "I think you need me way more than I need you. I think you're stuck to me like a parasite, and that if I die you die too—or at least go back to where you came from. And you don't want that, do you? Or maybe if I die you get stuck where you are forever, which might be even worse. And maybe you don't know either." He let his voice rise with his confidence. "I think we're here, talking now, because you are in just as much danger as I am. All this bargain crap is just an old pro trying to get as much as he can out of every deal, but either way, you can't afford for me to die. Maybe these Hunters are here to take me back to Gwendal. But *maybe* they're here to kill both of us. You don't know, do you?"

Aka Manah grew very still, almost seeming to freeze with the rest of the surroundings. At first, Gabe thought he had missed badly and that his argument was based on too many guesses. But then the door burst into incandescence and flew open, and the blurred man-shape was there within the vast white mist stretching into infinity behind him. Aka Manah held onto the frame by only his fingertips, and his power thrashed all around him in an effort to gain more purchase. But it was like watching someone snatch at running water. Every effort slipped through his grasp, and the tendrils of power that reached out from that white expanse to cross the threshold were pulled right back in. He would not let go, and neither would the grip of his prison.

Then the struggle peaked in a great burst of sound and heat, and with a final cry of impotent rage, the door slammed closed and silence fell again. Gabe wanted nothing more than to curl up in a corner and have a little cry at how broken and insane his world had become, but then the fuzzy shape reappeared.

"I see," Aka Manah said, as if nothing had happened. "My Gwendal chose a more appropriate vessel for me than even she knew. Shrewd and ruthless. Very well, human. Make your bargain."

Gabe found himself in a difficult spot: on one hand, he was elated that he'd somehow outmaneuvered the thing. But on the other, he had no idea what to do about it. "I have no reason to trust any deals you make," he said, taking a gamble. "So how about you prove your worth and reliability? Give me this one for free. Then, in future, we might deal in good faith."

The god remained silent for a long time, and Gabe worried that he'd overplayed it. So he tugged on the line a bit. "Or let me die and we'll see what happens to you," he said. "Your call."

A low rumble started in his mind, and Gabe was afraid the whole fire and fury thing would repeat itself. But then the sound resolved into a close approximation of a chuckle—albeit as heard through the teeth of what sounded like some kind of demon.

"Agreed," Aka Manah said finally. "But this is the only time you will get such a bargain, mortal. When next we meet, I will want something in return."

He began to fade from view, but stopped when he was scarcely a smudge in the air. "Oh, one tiny thing more. I understand your reluctance to give up your body, though I do think I would put it to better use. But I suggest you find a way to separate us before your fragile psyche fractures beneath the strain. I would say two days, perhaps three before the both of us are irretrievably insane or dead—or fused into a monster the likes of which the world has never seen. Good luck!"

Then he was gone. Gabe barely had time to register that he'd won before reality lurched back into motion and he suddenly had two Hunters bearing down on him. He sucked in a frightened breath, and the world became fire.

CHAPTER FIFTEEN

```
"In the end, the only unique talent I have is
apathy. Guilt is a powerful motivator among the
normal, which basically makes the lack a
superpower. The most dangerous people in the
world are the ones who just don't give a crap."

-Excerpt from Chapter Two, CONscience
```

"There is always a price for power," Aka Manah whispered. *"You will learn."*

He did. Aka Manah's gift hit him like a gut blow and spread until it filled him to bursting. But it was too much, and Gabe feared he would drown in it before it finished expanding.

And it was changing him. Awakening.

Liquid flame raged through his brain to scour pathways there, leaving behind in the agony the knowledge that these places were not new, but old beyond accounting. The power lit ancient memories like hieroglyphics on forgotten walls left by ancestors lost to the tumult of time, and each one came to life in quick succession to fill his mind with images too raw and alien to comprehend. Titans. Gods. A humanity that had been and could be again. Beautiful and terrible and powerful and impossible to look at or away from. Humans, but nothing like it. The beginning. They called to him.

Then the images withered and died, their ashes first dispersing then coalescing into an ugly, stunted approximation of the originals named Gabriel Delling. Him. *He* was the worse, lost, bastardized version of what they'd become. No glory, nor strength, nor power—just meat. And then the memory fractured, becoming incoherent and fading from him until he was left only with a few shards of knowledge that he clung to as the flood blew through him. The surfeit of it scoured him clean on its way out to expand into the infinite, to where it would be consumed by an endless waiting hunger that was coming for them all, and that he immediately forgot existed. He held his shards tight, aware that they were cutting him even as he did. But they were not to keep, only to use. He could hold them for that long. He knew the questions would come, agonizing and unanswerable in his forced ignorance, but even that knowledge was melting away. For now it was enough that the torrent had left in its wake the thing he needed: the temporary and impossible magic of a god.

When Gabe's sight returned, his right hand was full of light. The red-gold power surged from within him and coalesced in his palm as he stepped in front of Heather and raised his arm. At the sight, the Hunters actually tried to pull up short, but Gabe had the magic fixed in his mind by then, running on the fumes of the fleeting enlightenment, and it was far too late for them—or him—to escape. Their fates had already been sealed, and Gabe couldn't hold back if he wanted to.

The power was incredible. It filled him with a joy that nearly broke his heart and threatened to ruin him for any other earthly sensation, and at the same time, it filled his stomach with a sickly weight. He was holding pure potential. He knew he could do nearly anything with it—create or destroy in equal measure—and that capacity was instantly intoxicating. But he also knew he was playing with something far beyond his ability to control. He might be holding a fragment of a god, but he wasn't one. So he kept it simple. He allowed the power to take the shape it wanted to be anyway, then he let it loose with a cry of despair.

The blast of raw entropy hit the Hunters with a physical thump that shook the suspended walkway. Windows fractured down the length of the hall, and the metal wailed ominously as it bent to accept the force. The Hunters flew back into the glass doors, and the panes shattered with the impact. Gabe felt a massive pressure lift Heather and send her rolling back to the stairs, but he alone was left unaffected in the eye of the storm. Then he watched in horror and fascination as the Hunters' grotesque bodies degenerated under the influence of what he'd unleashed, sagging into themselves with what looked like months of decay hitting all at once. One creature tried to stand but fell to pieces with every effort, dropping fingers, then a leg, then half of its torso until it was nothing but parts. In a matter of seconds, the two bodies melted until they were moist smears defiling the floor, suddenly posing no more of a threat than that of giving some janitor a really bad day.

Gabe would have stayed there awhile longer, trying to comprehend what had just happened, but his survival instincts finally kicked in and realized for him that he should get down. It might not be the best idea to be the only person still standing in a glass hallway after what must have looked like some kind of explosion. So he dropped into a crouch and scrambled to Heather as fast as he could.

He found her gathering herself in the safety of the covered stairwell. She seemed fine, but she looked at him with an unreadable mix of emotions that he didn't have time to speculate on. "We need to get out of here," he said, moving past her to go down the stairs.

The walls there were brick, allowing him to stand and race down as fast as he could without risking a headlong fall. A moment later, he heard Heather following behind him amidst the rustle of the bags she had remembered to pick up. His original plan—before he'd cheated a god and played with the underpinnings of the universe—had been to wait on the top level of the parking lot, out of view, until the Hunters gave up and moved on. But he didn't think that was so smart anymore. There were about to be a bunch of really awkward questions from people who saw two police officers follow a young couple into the hallway, so it wouldn't be a good idea to be a young couple anywhere nearby when the officers were found to be protein pudding. They slipped out of the stairwell and into the parking garage without trouble, but before they could hide, three security guards came sprinting from one of the mall's main-floor exits.

Gabe stood and pulled Heather in tight to him as the three men approached. "What's going on?" he asked the guards, injecting as much panic and fear into his voice as possible. Unsurprisingly, he found a wealth of it there just for the asking.

The three guards glanced at them briefly, but only one peeled off while the other two carried on into the stairwell to survey the battleground. That one approached with the familiar swagger of ex-military or a moonlighting cop, and his hand rested on a can of pepper spray at his belt as if wishing for a gun. The threat of violence wasn't hidden very well, but Gabe was fresh off of liquefying two supernatural monsters. He found it a little hard to be intimidated just then.

"Are you folks hurt?" the guard asked, keeping his distance.

"Just scared shitless," Gabe said. "Are we safe here?"

The guard studied them for a moment. "Probably not. Come with me. Now, please."

The tone was clearly *ex*-something; Gabe knew the command voice anywhere. But he also knew that to follow the guard would be to step right back into the mess they'd just escaped. There could be more Hunters anywhere. Maybe. He actually had no idea since he was making this up as he went along. What he *did* know was that they only needed to get rid of this one guy and they would be home free. It had to be fast and quiet, and then they could get away.

Gabe felt an unusual anger building within him at the sight of the approaching man, and with it came a flicker of energy playing over his hands. He suddenly couldn't believe the asshole rent-a-cop would dare, *dare,* to stop them. To get in their way, to question them. Not when they were this close to being free. For someone so fragile and weak to presume to give them orders... It was unacceptable. Gabe rode the anger, and he groped for the entropy he'd wielded moments ago. It came at once to his call, and light gathered in his fingers. He idly registered that the guard didn't notice the power, and his contempt for the man grew. It must be like the Hunters' glamour, hiding the magic from those too stupid to look, he realized. Or maybe his own eyes had just been opened widely enough to see the real world now that he was something superior. He suppressed a smile. Either way, the guard wouldn't see it coming. It would be quick and easy. It felt wonderful to have the power to make his own choices.

Gabe raised his hands as if asking the guard to wait, readying the energy and focusing it down to a pinprick of destruction. But before he could loose the killing wind, he saw himself as if from a distance and realized what he was about to do. He was going to kill a man just for doing his job. He'd talked his way out of situations like this a thousand times without ever needing his power, but now apparently he just killed people. And had he just thought of it as *his* power? He'd claimed it, and the death had come running to his call like an obedient dog.

In horror, Gabe let it all drain away, dropping his hands as it went. But before the light faded, he could have sworn he heard Aka Manah whispering somewhere deep within him. He took a breath and then another, then tried experimentally to call the magic back up. To his relief, it didn't come. And the unfamiliar rage had sunk with it too. Back down past his reach. Back down to the thing inside him.

"...right now, sir!" the guard yelled.

Gabe snapped his attention back to the moment and realized that the guard had been talking for a while. Apparently the time-stopping thing didn't always work.

Heather shot him a quick glance and then stepped forward into the scene like an actress hearing her cue. "Oh, officer!" she said, stumbling toward the bigger, stronger man.

She dramatically dropped all the shopping bags as she moved, and the guard barely got out a strangled "Ma'am!" before Heather was in his arms and weeping. She cried beautifully—that Hollywood crying that left the makeup and hair intact but brought a rosy blush to pale cheeks—and Gabe himself almost wanted to ask the little lady what the problem might be. It was a master class.

Apparently the guard saw nothing cliché about it though, and he pulled Heather in like a true hero to complete the romance novel pose. He did at least have the grace to give an apologetic look, but he pointedly didn't let go either. Gabe had gathered himself by then, and was just gearing up to play a complimentary role as the annoyed/litigious boyfriend, when he saw the guard's eyes glaze over.

Heather stopped crying all at once and slipped out of the man's hold. She caught up his hands and led him like a sleepwalker to the far side of a gray minivan parked several spaces down. Gabe began to follow, but she met his gaze and shook her head. He caught the whiff of perfume and nostalgia, and the impact of it stopped him cold. Whatever was about to happen, he probably didn't want to see it.

A few tense minutes later, Gabe watched several police officers pull up and begin to fan out. He knew he should have run when he'd had the chance, while the guard had been *distracted*, but something in him no longer wanted to leave Heather behind. He was connected to her now, like it or not, and she was the only person in the world who might answer some of his questions. She was his guide in this foreign country, and you didn't leave your guide behind when you could barely speak the language.

Just as the police were spreading through the mall and cordoning off the parking lot, Heather and the guard returned—she with a satisfied little smile and spring in her step, and him with the blank look of a ventriloquist's doll. Gabe shot her a questioning glance, but she waved it away and walked to the outer edge of the police cordon as confidently as if she were the lead detective on the case. The guard followed like a puppy.

As soon as they got to the lone police car on that side of the lot, the guard came back to life and stepped forward to get the officer's attention. "Hey, Kyle," the guard said.

The officer had to look twice to recognize the man. "Jimmy? Are you undercover or something?" he asked, obviously joking.

"Moonlighting," Jimmy said. "Christmas money, you know? This is some shit, huh?"

"No kidding," Kyle said, visibly relaxing and leaning back against his car. "Not a bomb though, right?"

Jimmy the guard shook his head. "Nah. Some frickin' kids, we think. Who knows? I'm supposed to lead these people back to their vehicle. They're cleared."

Kyle the cop nodded in acceptance and waved them through. Jimmy looked to Heather, appearing for all the world as if he was just a normal guy acting out a normal conversation. "You good, ma'am? Sir? There's really no danger here anymore. Those kids'll be long gone. I can walk you the rest of the way if you want?"

"Not necessary," Heather said. "Thank you so much, officers." The wink she dropped to Jimmy was nothing short of miraculous, making a thousand promises that would never be fulfilled. Gabe even got a little hot under the collar standing outside its influence. But Jimmy the guard only smiled politely and waved them away, and he and Kyle started a separate conversation as if nothing weird had just happened.

Gabe waited until about a block past the mall before speaking. "What the hell was that?"

Heather glanced at him and seemed to take him in, studying him in a new light before responding. "I'll tell you when you're older. Shut up for now, okay? We're in big trouble and I need to think."

"But the Hunters are gone, right?" he asked, feeling like a little kid in truth given how little he suddenly knew about the world.

Heather sighed and picked up her pace. "Yes. Those are gone," she said, her voice a little hollow. "But there are more where they came from. Lots. And whoever sent them isn't gone. I'm afraid we both know who that probably is."

"Why would they want us this badly?" he asked, fearing that he already knew the answer.

Heather met his eyes, then glanced down at his hands—the hands that had just fried two monsters with something that had looked like a portable sun. A single raised eyebrow was all he needed for confirmation.

"Right," he said, picking up the pace as they walked back to his car. "I'll shut up."

ELSEWHERE

Gwendal idly inspected the little carving with her fingertips, searching out imperfections in the wood, in the dimensions, and in the care with which it had been prepared. The man was elderly, almost on his deathbed in truth, but there was no doubt that his hands had once held tremendous skill. The sculpture was nothing like the marvels she'd once had, but it would do for now. She needed real power, and that only came from worship in *any* form.

"Fine," she said, placing the carving on the desk. "Make them until you bleed."

The man's mouth worked, and he looked from side to side, as if searching for a way out. "My family," he said, his voice shaking a little. "I've been here for two days. Do they at least know I'm alright? Can I talk to—"

Gwendal slid up in front of him serpent-quick and put two long fingers over his mouth. She used her other hand to slowly wipe the tears from his eyes, then she licked them clean. She'd been waiting for hours to hear back from the Hunters, and she was getting restless. Hunters were unpredictable at their core, and though she'd ordered them to leave the human alive for fear of losing Aka Manah forever, she couldn't trust them implicitly. They weren't truly hers. She needed to distract herself.

"I thought you were ready to be devoted only to me?" she asked, dropping her voice low and giving it a razor edge. "Did you not accept my employment?"

The man tried to back away, but the Hunter standing behind him lifted a cold, ragged hand and held him in place. The man made a noise of desperate protest but quickly dropped his head. "Yes, of course," he said, "but you promised..."

He didn't elaborate. Gwendal found that men rarely did when they were attempting to collect on a promise from her. The quirk was rather convenient. "Ah, yes," she said, lifting his chin to stare into his cloudy eyes. "I believe I said that you would never need to fear for the well-being of your family again."

The man's eyes went wide, as if he only now heard the potential negative connotation in the phrasing. Gwendal smiled. "Relax. Your family will be fine. Probably. I don't actually care."

The man sagged, and the relief gave him a small measure of courage. "And my pay? I told you, my daughter-in-law needs a surgery."

Gwendal let her smile lengthen. "Who said anything about pay? I said *reward*." She grabbed his collar and pulled him into a long kiss, ripping his shirt from him as she threw him onto the nearby bed. He fought back, but his muscles had long since abandoned him to age and illness, and he was nothing to her.

When she rose several hours later, the Hunter silently handed her a bath robe. The thing had stayed there in the room as she had taken her worship, just staring numbly at the wall as if seeing nothing. She knew little about Phillip's creatures, only that they were nearly as old as she was, and that they were as powerful as they were mindless without something to chase. She'd heard of them over the years—dark riders stalking the night, wild and fierce and deadly focused—but she'd never had cause to cross paths with one until now. It wasn't a working arrangement she intended to abide for any longer than she had to.

She turned back to the man to watch him dutifully crawling from the bed, dragging his now-useless legs behind him as he made his way to the corner where he kept his knives and wood. There were much easier ways to do what she had done, but none as thorough—or fun. The process of breaking was where all the best fear was. "Are you concerned for your family now?" she asked, unable to resist the small cruelty. It had been so long since she had used one of the old rituals, and she was still flush with it.

Confusion passed over his face, then he turned to look up at her like a flower facing the sun. "You are my only family, Mistress," he said, smiling wide around the broken remains of his teeth. Then he set to work carving her image with a mindless devotion.

"I need more," she said to the figure crouched in the corner. "Bring me a strong one this time."

"And the others?" Paul asked, nodding to the bodies behind the bathroom door.

She waved her hand. "Pile them in the other rooms. Take whatever scraps you like."

Paul grunted. "There is a creature wishing an audience. A pishtaco vampire. He claims to work for a Baron of this city. Name of Jimenez."

She tapped her lip. "Send him out, but do not harm him. We don't wish to start a war, but neither do I have need of any more allies at this juncture. The old power structures will not matter for much longer."

Paul loped out to do her bidding. She breathed in the scent of the room and suppressed a shiver. It felt more like home every day, and she'd need that to grow. She had no idea how to retrieve her Aka Manah from where he'd been trapped, but when her Hunters returned with the human, she intended to be strong enough to tear his soul apart in the trying.

CHAPTER SIXTEEN

```
"It doesn't matter that I have no clue what I'm
talking about. Competence and confidence are
farther apart in spelling than they are in
perception. My mom taught me that, actually.
About my dad. It took me a lot of years to
realize that she hadn't meant it as a good
thing."

-Excerpt from Chapter Four, CONscience
```

    Gabe had considered taking Heather to the anonymous safety of the nursing home, but had thought better of it. It was the only place on earth that none of his contacts knew about, which made it an ideal bolt-hole in case of an emergency—or rather, some bigger emergency than the constant state of it he'd been in lately. Instead, he took her home.

    "What do I call you?" he asked, staring into his root beer. "Heather or Shanti or what?"

    Heather was at the stove preparing some kind of egg dish, and she glanced over her shoulder at him while she worked. "Shanti was my first name, but not my only one. I've had some for longer and I've liked some better. Heather seems most appropriate given the circumstances. And I like fresh starts. You certainly seem most comfortable with it."

    Gabe shuddered at that word. There was nothing comfortable about a succubus wearing the skin of a girl he'd been flirting with yesterday. "I guess," he said. "So she's really gone? Heather, I mean." He'd tried to make the question sound casual, but it came out with an accusatory edge.

    Heather threw a handful of chives into the pan. "I'm not sure. I don't get to know what happens to a soul once it departs. Maybe it goes to a better place. Maybe it's gone forever." She got quieter. "I don't know."

    Gabe wiped idly at the moisture beading on the side of his glass. "Huh. So she might still be in there, like I was?"

    Heather shook her head as she scraped around the edge of the pan with her spatula. "I really don't know. But I doubt it. Normally a body is vacated naturally or artificially prepared by removing the original spirit. They call it 'purification' or 'cleansing' or...other things. What you did wasn't ordinary."

"Nothing about this is ordinary," he said. "I just thought—"

"I understand," she said, cutting him off. She used the edge of the spatula and sliced two thick wedges out of the dish. "But you should know I'm just as much Heather as she ever was. Aside from the spirit itself, I have everything she had. All of her memories, experiences, and skills were here when I arrived. It's part of the deal. Like Heather and Shanti had a child who was the total of all their parts. Does that make sense?" She turned and placed a full plate in front of him.

Gabe eyed the dish dubiously. "I guess."

Heather slid onto the stool across from him. "Okay, imagine you're twenty years older and you go back in time to meet your younger self. You have more knowledge and experience now, but which is the real Gabe? You from this exact moment, or future you?"

"Both," he said, grasping her point and not liking it, "but it's not the same thing."

She shrugged and pushed her food around with her fork. "It's close. I didn't ask to take her body, Gabe. It just happened. I also didn't ask to be what I am. We all live within the constraints we're given, and I won't apologize for being here, if that's what you're after. But I won't pretend I'm the victim either. I didn't forcibly take her, but I didn't fight. If not me, another would have come."

"Okay," he said, "it's who you are. I can cope with hard justifications. But at least help me understand this stuff."

"You're right. You should know more than you do, and that's not a bad place to start." She picked up a pen and started drawing on the back of the envelope from the nursing home. First she drew a large, amorphous blob in the center and labeled it "Physical". Then she added a bunch of squiggly lines around it and in the crevices and wrote "Ether".

"See?" she said, pointing to the diagram as if it made any kind of sense. "You live here, on the physical plane. Everything you touch and experience is real and solid. It's the axle upon which reality turns. But Umbras—that's us—live in the Ether. We have no physical form or even spiritual cohesion until we're given a seed of consciousness to nucleate on, and we need humans to supply that."

Gabe had taken a bite while she'd worked and found it was surprisingly good. "So you're spirits?"

Heather took her own bite, then covered her mouth as she spoke. "Sort of. We're like blank slates. Basically pure potential. Think of Umbras as the stem cells of the universe, and we only gain cohesion and purpose when an idea gives us form. In my case, it was the superstition of Succubi. I'm more than that now, but initially I was a two-dimensional caricature. The seed. It all comes from your collective will."

Gabe ran his fork through his eggs. "Wow. And there are more of you things?"

She nodded. "Maybe infinite. I have no idea. But only a very few ever gain enough traction to matter. We're the lucky ones."

He sat back. "So what does that make humans?"

"Well, in one sense you're our gods. We couldn't manifest without your legends and myths and belief. And in another sense you're..."

"Food?" he supplied.

She shrugged and took another bite. "Some of us are more dependent on humans than others, yes, but you created us this way. We're working from the blueprints provided."

"Let me get this straight," Gabe said, dropping his fork and crossing his arms. "You're saying that there's this pool of potential out there just absorbing random thoughts and becoming them? So there could be characters out of books or movies walking around because enough people thought hard enough about them? That's ridiculous."

"Gabe, I can't answer all of your questions. I know I exist, and I know of a few others, but otherwise I'm not a scholar. I will say that belief is a powerful thing, but an Umbra requires a great deal of it to manifest. Your world seems more steeped in fiction than at any other time before, and I suspect the wealth of it may dilute modern belief too much to produce many new things. Maybe it's just the old stuff that has enough weight. Who knows? Again," she pointed to herself with her fork, "*not* a scholar."

"Great," Gabe said, standing and moving into the living room. "So what do I need to do to get this thing out of my head and go back to normal? According to him, I have maybe three days before I go crazy or die or become some kind of monster myself. That's kind of tough to run from."

Heather put her fork down and folded her hands on the counter. "I don't know."

He laughed bitterly and dropped onto the couch. "Up to me, then. Super. Maybe I'll call up Gwendal and offer her a trade. See how that works out."

Heather stood suddenly, making the stool scrape loudly on the kitchen floor. "No," she said. "That is the last thing you should do."

He kicked his feet up to the coffee table and reclined, suddenly enjoying a quick dip into defeatism. "She seems to know what she's doing, and obviously she wants this guy back. Let her have him. I have a time bomb curled up in my brain and I want it out. You said you can't help me. What else should I do?" Gabe felt a surge of reinforcing emotion come from somewhere within, and it stoked his apathy.

"Not her," Heather said, moving into the living room, "because you have no idea what any of this is about. The Umbra in you could mean to destroy the world for all you know, and then where would you be? Where would any of us be? It could be truly evil."

"*Says the succubus,*" something whispered to him.

"Says the succubus," Gabe repeated.

Heather's eyes narrowed, and she crossed her arms. "Okay, Gabriel, I get that you're upset and out of your element. But if you're going to get out of this alive, you'll have to trust somebody that knows more than you—even if she doesn't have every answer to every question that pops into your little head. That person can either be me or someone like Gwendal. Of the two of us, I'm the only one who hasn't tried to kill you. Technically, yes, I can take a human soul like plucking a grape. But *technically* you can buy a gun and shoot someone in the head. Being capable of something doesn't make you guilty of it. So pull it together."

Gabe stayed silent, and he felt the bitterness and negativity receded a little. It was a tough point to argue.

Eventually she sighed and joined him on the couch. "I'm a succubus. I need to absorb human life energy to survive. But I don't kill people. I'm not evil or good, Gabe, I'm somewhere in the vast expanse between. Just like you. And I certainly don't want to see the world destroyed." She turned and looked at him until he reluctantly met her eyes. "Do you know what I *do* want?"

He shook his head.

"Cake. And pastries. And sausages, and the sun, and cool rain, and silk, and art, and dancing, and laughing until I can't breathe, and sex until I can't think. I want all of that every day until this body dies, and that's it. I don't want to hurt anything or dominate anyone. I just want pleasure while I'm here. You tell me where the evil is in that."

He made sure she was finished before putting his feet back on the floor and sitting forward. "Got it. I'm sorry," he said, forcing the words out. "You're right that I need your help. And if what you say is true, I guess I can come to terms with..." he gestured vaguely at her, "this."

Heather seemed to lose her fire almost as quickly as it had come. "That's a good start. And so eloquently put."

He folded his hands and stared down at the floor. "Let's keep it Heather. That's easier for my brain right now."

She nodded agreement. "You don't think I'm crazy anymore?"

"I didn't say that." They lapsed into a brief silence, then Gabe threw up his hands. "So what do I do now? I can't just sit here. You saw me wipe out those Hunter things, then I almost killed that guard for no reason. I don't want this in me anymore."

"I did see," she said, "but I still don't believe it. You shouldn't have been able to do that."

"I'm thrilled to be the exception."

"Indeed," she replied. "I suppose my first suggestion would be to research your new houseguest. If he gave you his name, perhaps something will turn up."

Gabe realized that he should have thought of that and reached over to the edge of the table for his laptop. A few minutes later, they had learned everything the internet could tell them about Aka Manah. It did nothing to ease his fears.

"The Zoroastrian god of evil," he said, sitting back.

"Also lust," she added, as if that made it better.

"Definitely not great. I have the prototype for Lucifer in my head."

She shrugged. "Well, at least you didn't have to research for a month in a poorly lit library to gain this knowledge. I'll need to spend more time with this internet."

"Yeah, you'll fit right in."

She tried an encouraging smile. "It doesn't mean much. I'm bound to tell you the truth, but Aka Manah can lie all he wants. Even if he once was the original god, which I doubt, he could have changed a hundred times over the years. Maybe he's a friendlier version. Or a more modern, mellowed one. Or something else entirely. That happens all the time. Faiths and legends change, and by our very nature we change with them. I myself haven't eaten a man's heart in more than a thousand years."

Gabe glanced over at her, but couldn't quite tell if she was joking. "Sure," he said, "just a friendly god who goes around hijacking bodies and handing out the power to unmake life. Seems like a cool dude."

"Well, you certainly shouldn't trust him," she replied. "Don't make any more deals."

"It wasn't for fun," he protested.

"I know," she said. "You saved us. But regardless of what he told you, there will always be a price for his power. That's how it works."

"He did tell me that, actually," Gabe said. Then he thought back to his willingness to kill the security guard, and realized that he might still be paying that price. All it had taken was a single drink of power to push him almost completely into the well. Maybe the promised insanity was already closer than he thought. "Well, we can't just sit here waiting for me to go bananas. We have to do something, right? Find help?"

Heather ran a hand through her dark hair, and the tangles fell free like magic. "I guess we'll have to. We need someone who can give us answers, but we'll be running a huge risk in exposing ourselves. There's no telling who's working with Gwendal. Unfortunately, my knowledge of the current power structure is depressingly outdated, so we'll need to make some new contacts. That means exploring, which could be dangerous."

Gabe stood and grabbed his keys from the counter. "It's either that, or learn to live with Satan's creepy uncle trapped in my head—you know, for the rest of my whole three days of life. Between the two options, I'll take the one that will only *probably* get me killed."

Heather stood. "Good attitude. We'll start with groceries."

Gabe pulled up short at that, but Heather was already heading out.

"Just come on," she said. "Sometimes it's okay to not voice every single question. Leave a little mystery."

CHAPTER SEVENTEEN

"People will challenge your worldview every day, and normally it's up to you how or if that fits into your life. But a good con artist won't challenge you at all. He'll make you feel like a genius with secret special knowledge that nobody else has. By the end, you'll be totally sure that up has always been down and black looks remarkably like white. Reality is malleable if you know which buttons to push. Don't take your eyes off of it for too long."

-Excerpt from Chapter Five, CONscience

    Gabe stopped the car in front of the little grocery store and squinted at the sign on the door. "Eleven a.m. to four-thirty p.m. Hey, this one's open when normal people shop! Now if we can just find something other than disconcertingly large root vegetables, we'll be in business."

    "Would you relax?" Heather replied, checking her perfect hair in the visor mirror. "I told you that markets were an option, not a sure bet. It took me months to make good contacts last time I was physical, and that was two hundred years ago. You want me to find Merlin in a day?"

    Gabe grunted, and then his eyes widened. "Wait, that's not really who we're looking for, right?"

    She closed the visor and stared back at him. "It was a joke, Gabe. And a bad one, so I'm surprised you didn't recognize it. If Merlin did manifest, do you really think we'd find him in a strip mall grocery store in Nebraska?"

    "I mean..." he said, trailing off sullenly.

    The day had faded to mid-afternoon as they'd made the rounds to every small grocery store, specialty market, and out-of-the-way shop Gabe could think of, but Heather had yet to find what she was looking for. She claimed that markets used to be gathering spots for her kind, but Gabe suspected things had changed somewhere around the advent of the Pop-Tart. All things considered, he felt justified in begrudging every minute they'd wasted. If he really did only have three days left to live, they'd used up one eighteenth of it already. And he'd figured out that math by wasting another one four-hundredth of it. He needed some progress before he started tearing out his hair.

The store's glass door had a large handwritten sign forbidding pets, and he almost made a stupid joke about leaving Heather outside. Fortunately his mouth betrayed him and stayed shut as he held the door open for her. The smells of curry, cinnamon, and several kinds of incense filled his head as he followed her in, and Gabe had to blink a few times to keep his eyes from watering. They were good smells, but too many and too much. Soft sitar music played from a blue smartphone on the register counter, and next to it, her hand working to scribble notes into a ledger, was a small round woman in a bright green and black sari. She looked up and smiled as they entered, showing teeth that were very white against her dark skin.

"Hello! Can I help you?" the woman asked with a cheerful Indian accent.

Gabe smiled to greet her back, but Heather stopped him by patting his shoulder, as if sending him to scamper off to the toy aisle.

"Good day," Heather said, her voice tinged with a slight Indian accent of her own. "I was wondering if you could help me find something?"

"Certainly," the woman replied.

Heather launched into the same series of inane questions she'd been asking all day as a cover to study the shopkeepers and patrons, but Gabe could already tell that this one would be another bust. He turned to inspect a display of curried nuts on the nearest endcap.

Several minutes passed before the woman finally waggled her head from side to side at Heather's question about aurochs yogurt. "I'm afraid not," she said. "Would you like to try one of our other brands to see if they suit you? I will open one—"

"No, no," Heather said, reaching over and patting the woman's hand. "You have helped us as much as possible. Are there any other employees here, or perhaps frequent customers who might know about old things?"

The woman slipped on an amused smile as if she thought she was being toyed with. But before she could respond, the door chimed, and an overweight Caucasian man wearing a metallic blue kimono and a beaded necklace walked in humming what sounded like Battle Hymn of the Republic. It was weird enough that Gabe noted his arrival, but it wasn't until the man stopped abruptly to stare back at him with wide eyes that Gabe realized there was something wrong. The air around the man shimmered for a moment, and then the tip of a dark blue tail was poking out just past the hem of the robe. It was all Gabe could do to keep his jaw from dropping.

Fortunately Heather had the presence of mind to do more than stare. "Good afternoon, sir!" she said in a too-loud, too-polite voice. "May I have a word with you outside?"

The man in the kimono glanced at the shopkeeper as if searching for help, but though the clerk had smiled in recognition as he'd entered, she seemed happy to go back to her ledger.

"Do I know you?" the man asked, his voice soft and a little shaky.

Heather slowly closed the distance between them, almost seeming to grow taller as she went. She was somehow filling the little shop with her presence, and the lights even dimmed as she passed. Gabe couldn't be sure, but he thought he could actually feel a hint of the power she was exerting to bend reality. It was alarming.

"Just a talk," Heather was saying, her voice deep in her chest and smooth as chocolate icing. Her smile was still there, touching her lips at the corners, but it didn't look pleasant anymore. The man clearly saw it too, and he carefully placed his basket down where he was standing. He gestured for Heather to lead the way, but she stared back coolly and he deflated. Then he turned and exited the shop with her on his heels.

Gabe followed. Once outside in the sun, he could see that the outline of the man's body beneath the kimono wasn't quite right, and he found himself trying hard to look past the surface. Heather hadn't bothered explaining glamours yet, but he suspected he was seeing another one.

Their little group stopped at the far end of the strip mall, near a line of dumpsters, and for lack of knowing what else to do, Gabe stood behind Heather and tried to look scary. He wouldn't fool anyone into believing he was the muscle of this operation, but he couldn't just pull up a lawn chair and gawk either.

"Do you know what I am?" Heather asked.

The round man attempted to gather himself up for a moment, then he sagged back all at once. "More or less."

"Good," she said, taking a few steps closer to him. "Now tell me what you are."

The man's eyes darted around for an escape route. "A hobgoblin—or hob, if you like. But then you already knew that, I think." The creature then twisted his head to the side, and several things popped in his spine. When he straightened again, his neck was much longer and thinner, and his head seemed to perch atop it like a dandelion puff. "Ah, apologies. So long as we are doing this I will take advantage of your glamour's radius for a measure of comfort." He spoke quickly and mechanically with a cadence Gabe had never heard before. "What little glamour I can conjure works better if I'm the right shape to begin with, but it gives me terrible cramps. Not all of us have your effortless facility with illusion, mighty one."

Gabe felt his eyebrows go up, but he knew he should play it cool. "Your tail was showing," he said, trying to make himself sound totally comfortable about a man with a tail.

"Oh my," The hob said. "I don't make outings often, and am consequently out of practice."

Gabe tried again to pierce the glamour or illusion or whatever still surrounded the man. It was shimmering there, wanting to fray apart and dissipate, but it held stubbornly on. He had no idea how to work this stuff, and for all he knew he might be making it worse.

"*I can show you.*" Aka Manah whispered.

Gabe started and glanced around quickly, but nothing around him had changed. He was still there, and time hadn't stopped. He saw the hob look over at him, and something curious seemed to pass over the thing's face.

"*Shut up,*" Gabe thought back. "*Nobody likes a pushy salesman.*"

"*There is so much I can give you. So much knowledge and power. Why resist?*"

"*I don't want what you have to give.*"

"*Perhaps another sample?*"

"*I said no,*" Gabe thought. His eyes started getting heavy, and a bead of sweat ran down his temple.

"*Perhaps it is not your choice. Allow me to—*"

"Pay attention," Heather said.

Gabe's eyes snapped up, but she hadn't been talking to him. He felt hot all of a sudden.

"We need information," Heather went on.

The hob tore its eyes from Gabe, then bowed his head in an absurdly courtly way. His hand went to his necklace as he bent. "You overmatch my strength by several orders. I am happy to offer anything you desire."

Heather rolled her eyes. "Knock it off. We're not going to rob you. We'll pay for information. We're just new in town, so we need to know—"

The hob abruptly threw himself to one side and scrambled on all fours to hide behind one of the big green dumpsters. Heather watched the thing struggle for an instant, then she sprang forward and pushed the dumpster aside as if it was made of cardboard. The hob was crouched in a patch of tall yellowed weeds, its hands scrabbling at the dirt like it intended to burrow down to safety. It had actually made a surprising dent in just that short time.

"Mercy!" the thing screamed as it rolled to its back.

Suddenly Gabe could see that it was no longer nearly so human-like, having apparently dropped its glamour entirely. Its eyes were now bright and huge, and the teeth had curved inward in a mouth that was far too wide to fit properly on a normal human head. The hair was lank and long, running straight down to disappear into the kimono like a pelt, and small dark red claws tipped the three fingers of his hands. As Heather approached, the hob held up his beaded necklace like a shield.

"Enough!" Heather said, and the force of the word hit Gabe hard enough to make him stagger back. The hob, in the direct line of it, flattened as if slapped by a giant hand, and the necklace slipped from his grip to reveal a small black pouch attached. Heather eyed the creature for a moment, watching the distended stomach rise and fall rapidly, then she shed her aura of force and shrank back down into herself, becoming as petite in spirit as she was in physical form. She knelt and carefully plucked the pouch from the necklace. "A gris-gris?" she asked, holding the thing like a scorpion. "Hoodoo only works if you have complete confidence in it, friend. You should get your money back."

Gabe glanced around to see if anyone was watching the weird display, but the few people walking by did so without a second glance—like they knew this was just where the fairy-tale creatures had their duels. The damned glamours again.

"A bedevil only," the hob said, his voice shaking. "From Mama Tempe. A stun. I assure you, I didn't mean to jinx—"

"Save it," Heather said, pocketing the pouch. "Do you fear me, goblin?"

The hob hesitated, then nodded.

"Good," she said. "I told you why we're here. I even offered to pay. Why run when you knew I could catch you?"

The hob glanced at Gabe and winced like he'd been struck. Heather turned and her eyes widened. "Gabe," she said, her voice suddenly quiet. "What did you do?"

He opened his mouth to answer, but realized that he didn't feel quite right. He was hot and getting jittery. He felt over-caffeinated or sick, and he hoped he wasn't coming down with the flu on top of everything else. The door flashed nova bright in his mind, and a soft subvocal rumble sounded somewhere inside him. His stomach dropped. Not sick then—at least not physically. He looked down at himself and was horrified to see a faint haze of red-gold power surrounding him like an aura. It looked like liquid malice, and it was everywhere.

He tensed at once, but Heather met his eyes and nodded significantly toward the hob. She didn't want to talk in front of the thing, so Gabe mastered his fear and tried to look passively menacing. The tremble of his lips hopefully lent a nice subtle grace note to the whole effect.

Heather turned back to the goblin. "Scary, huh? Now would you like to help us?"

The hob seemed torn between agreeing or dying of sheer terror, but he eventually nodded. Once the momentum got up, his head looked like it might fly right off if he agreed any harder.

"Great," she said, her voice gaining a little sweetness. "Let's start with your name."

The thing smiled, its fish-hook teeth making the expression far more menacing than was apparently intended. "Uklek, at your service."

"Uklek," Heather repeated. "We need someone who can supply us with basic information: Current events, positions of power, the current Umbral Council members, and so on. Can you do that, or introduce us to someone who can?"

The hob brightened. "Yes! I am actually employed by just such a man. Jacob Jimenez."

"Uh..." Gabe said. Heather turned to him and he subtly shook his head. He'd never had any dealings with the criminal kingpin, but he was confident it wouldn't result in anything good.

"How about a third party vendor?" Heather asked. "Not that we don't trust you or your employer."

Uklek hesitated, as if he'd been trying something and it hadn't worked. He finally nodded again. "Of course. There is someone else we may try."

The hob rose and dusted himself off, then walked toward the sidewalk in full view of anyone who cared to look. Gabe watched cars drive by without so much as slowing down for a second glance. Apparently Heather's glamour was working flawlessly to hide the goblin. It was no wonder he'd never noticed these creatures around him before.

"We'll drive," Heather said, making it a command. "You sit up front to navigate."

The hob turned and followed them toward Gabe's car.

"Where to?" Gabe asked as they settled in. He tried to make the question sound neutral, but the goblin reacted like he'd just had a gun pointed to his head.

"Th, th, the university library is the closest entrance," it stammered, pointing vaguely toward the campus a few blocks away.

Gabe sighed and pulled out of the parking lot, pointedly ignoring the way his hands now glowed against the steering wheel.

"Who are we going to see?" Heather asked from the back seat.

"The Locust," Uklek said. "He'll know what you need."

Maybe the thing thought he was being subtle about it, but Gabe definitely heard another layer in the statement, and it made him wonder what kind of trouble they were willingly walking into. It was another indication of how deep into this he'd fallen: He was in a car with a succubus and a hobgoblin, and was now glowing like a firefly, and the idea of seeing a little locust was what had him on edge. He turned onto Vine street and pointed toward campus. At least it couldn't be any weirder than anything else he'd seen in the last twenty-four hours.

CHAPTER EIGHTEEN

"It's hard to shut myself off in regular life. Sometimes there's even an easier way to get something, and I make it elaborate and convoluted by sheer habit. That's left me always expecting to be conned myself, forever looking for an agenda and planning how to counter it...and then counter the counter. I'm like a human Rube Goldberg machine, only less fun, and it doesn't leave much brain power for idle chitchat or honesty. As a result, I don't get invited to many dinner parties."

-Excerpt from Chapter Five, CONscience

  The university campus was largely closed to vehicles, so Gabe found the closest parking spot and they walked the rest of the way. The hob had resumed his human approximation at Heather's request, and though a few of the students eyed them more closely than might have been polite, nobody appeared to suspect them of being anything other than the normal weirdos who gravitated around college campuses. Heather's glamour seemed to be spackling over the worst of their oddities, and he hoped it was something she could keep up for a while.
  He couldn't help but glance down every few seconds at his own weirdness swirling around his skin. The power seemed to be leaking directly from his pores, and no matter how many times he wiped at it or tried to will it away, it just kept coming. It even seemed to trail behind him like a bad scent in a cartoon. He wanted nothing more than to ask Heather what the hell was going on, but he didn't dare with the hob so close. He'd even tried to think the questions at Aka Manah, but the god had been infuriatingly silent. So he did what he did best, and just pretended it wasn't there.
  Love Library was smack in the center of campus, and it spanned two buildings connected by a wide overhanging walkway. Gabe hesitated at seeing that, given his recent luck with glass walkways, but Heather stayed right on the hob's heels and entered the building. Rather than be left behind, Gabe followed. The library was quiet and smelled like old paper, and the memories of his time

studying there came flooding back. And while there weren't many of them, given how quickly he'd dropped out, they were fond. He'd had a place to sleep and plenty of food and people who treated him like a regular guy. It had been a turning point in his life from his interesting childhood—and the dark days after—and it would have been heaven if he'd only had the money to pay for it.

They entered into a foyer dominated by a large reception desk next to a second series of glass doors. "IDs, please," A young woman said from behind the desk.

Gabe turned to face her. "I'm sorry?"

"Student IDs. I need to scan them, please."

Gabe nodded and reached for his wallet despite the fact that he hadn't brought a fake with him. Nothing killed a con like hesitation though, and it was always possible he might come up with a plan while he stalled. He glanced at Heather but she just shrugged, effortlessly conveying that glamours weren't invisibility cloaks. He needed some kind of instruction manual for her abilities, but he shut that thought down before his personal subconscious demon could offer him one. A quick glance at the hob told him he'd be getting no help there either.

"Yikes," Gabe said, digging into his front pockets, "what if I left it at home? We have a research paper due tomorrow."

The young woman knitted her brows and looked over the three of them skeptically. "I'm sorry, but it's the rule."

Gabe smiled and moved closer to the desk. It wasn't hard to read her. The girl had the harried, uncertain look of a freshman only a few weeks into her work-study program, and she was wearing a shirt from a high school production of The Sound of Music. Her plastic glasses were a shade of bright turquoise that she probably thought made her look carefree, but she was standing near a shoulder bag packed full of textbooks, ready to be tackled when she got a spare moment. And all around her, fellow library workers chatted and slacked off while she alone sat at the desk dutifully scanning in books and students. He didn't bother digging any deeper.

"Can I ask you a hypothetical question?" he asked. He mentally went through his list of charming personae and decided on a brainy, earnestly likable one named Geoff.

She continued scanning books into her system and stacking them neatly on a cart. "I suppose."

He leaned on the counter and tried to act about ten years younger—while also hoping that her optical prescription was badly out of date. "Let's say a friend of yours came in and forgot their ID. Hypothetically, would you be able to let them in?"

The girl glanced up at him then. "Be able to? Yes. Would I? No. I could get in trouble."

"Fine, fine," Gabe said, holding up his hands. "But say it was a really good friend. Your best friend. Or, maybe your *boyfriend*."

The girl placed a final book on the cart and then sighed. "Is there a point to this?"

"Of course. Just answer honestly and I swear I'll get to it: would you let your boyfriend in?" He held up a finger, ignoring the waft of gold power it brought with it. "Be honest."

She rolled her eyes, then nodded reluctantly. "I suppose, but only because I assume I would trust him. Okay? But that doesn't matter here, because I don't know you, and you are definitely not my boyfriend."

Gabe smiled brightly and spread his hands. "Yet."

The girl started to laugh at him but Gabe went on. "Hold on! Hear me out. Imagine that time is cyclical in the infinite universes so that everything we're experiencing or ever could has already happened and will again."

"Oh lord," the girl said.

Gabe moved closer to lean over the desk. "In that case, we already know each other as well as any two people can, because versions of ourselves have been through this conversation an uncountable number of times. We might live lifetimes together or have never met. We might love or hate each other beyond all reason. All these strings play out a billion billion times, and we, here and now, are just living one of them. Who's to say which we're on?"

The girl sighed, but a hint of amusement colored her expression. He was at least entertaining her.

"It all hinges on what you say next," he went on. "But in at least one universe, you agreed to go on a date with me. It's already happened somewhere, so it's not unprecedented. And it will definitely happen again, which makes it practically routine." He gave her his best shrug-and-chagrined-smile combo, playing up the awkwardness a little to dilute the charm. "So what do you say? Will you go on *another* date with me?"

The girl looked flummoxed but in a good way, and she slowly shook her head in disbelief. "Is there something wrong with you?"

Gabe shrugged. "Would it help if I promised to take you out for karaoke?"

She continued to shake her head, but a smile crept over her lips. "How would that help?"

"Oh trust me," Gabe said, "if you hear me sing, you'll definitely want a second date. It's kinda my super power."

The girl unconsciously licked her lips and leaned forward just a little. "Okay, you're very weird, and admittedly cute for an older guy, but—"

"Oh my god!" a man's voice from the back room called. "Just let him in, Julia. If he's that desperate to do research he must be in real trouble."

Julia turned back to reply. "Hey! So he has to be desperate to want a date with me? You said I wasn't—"

"New girl," the man interrupted again, "Don't put words in my mouth. I know what I said. But listen to what I'm saying now: it doesn't matter. This isn't CIA headquarters. Is he cute?"

Julia turned back to Gabe to appraise him. "Fairly," she called back, her confidence clearly growing.

"Good enough, honey. Let him go. And get his number. Any boy that tries this hard is worth at least one date. Just don't give him yours, okay? He could be a weirdo—or...more of one. That's a free lesson for the big city."

Julia shrugged and smiled awkwardly up at Gabe. "I guess my boss says you're good."

"Thanks, Julia," Gabe said, pronouncing the name like he was working to commit it to memory. He grabbed a nearby notepad and hastily jotted down one of his phone numbers. "Seriously. Call me, okay? I'm Geoff."

Julia nodded as she gave him another appraising look, then waved him to the glass doors. "I might."

Once they'd entered the library itself, Heather patted Gabe on the shoulder. "Not terrible."

He shrugged off her hand. "We can't all use magic to hack directly into the sex cortex. Some of us have to work for it."

She nodded sagely. "Some harder than others."

Gabe couldn't help but laugh. "You know, good old-fashioned persistence is a viable—"

"Excuse me," Uklek said, with painful respect. He stood at a stairway leading down.

Gabe brushed aside his original point. "Right. Lead the way."

They passed two floors before reaching the lowest level and coming to a large space filled with tall rows of books. Gabe vaguely remembered being down there at some point, but didn't recall anything out of the ordinary. The hob seemed to know what he was doing however, and led them to an old steel door set into the far wall. It looked like the mechanisms were caked with decades of industrial paint, but when the hob touched it, the big bolt slid easily and the door opened soundlessly toward them.

The space beyond became far less modern, harkening back to the military origins of the building, and the staircase leading down was nothing more than steel steps and a handrail lit by bare bulbs. They followed the goblin as he took them down three uninterrupted flights where they finally reached a large, damp-smelling concrete storage room filled with dozens of crates and plastic totes.

"Did I seriously just walk blindly into a basement again?" Gabe asked. "What is wrong with me?"

Heather shushed him while the hob negotiated the rows, searching for something. After a few minutes of weaving through the room, the creature stopped at a large crate stamped with an eye-bending symbol like a crescent twisted halfway through its arc. Heather gasped when she saw it, but didn't explain. The goblin placed his hand there as if to feel the texture of the wood, and the whole thing slid back to reveal a narrow spiral staircase buried in the floor. The hob went down without hesitation and Heather followed eagerly, leaving Gabe behind. He considered raising more of a fuss about how poorly mysterious stairs had turned out for him, but he didn't think it would do him any good. Nobody seemed to actually pay attention to him when he whined. So he followed and kept a sharp lookout for maniacs and/or the demon-possessed.

As they descended, Gabe started hearing something new. At first it was just general noise, like fans running in the distance, but then there was the unmistakable sound of people talking. There was someone down there, and they weren't being shy about it. At the bottom of the stairs, they came to a single metal door, and Gabe stood well back as the hob fumbled at the latch to open it. But nothing came bursting out to kill them, and the air blowing toward them smelled even fresher than the mildewy stuff they had been breathing so far. The hallway beyond was well-lit and clean, and looked more like a high-tech office building than a library sub-basement. There were even words and logos printed on the doors that dotted the length of the halls, as if it made perfect sense to advertise services five stories below the earth.

It sounded like an office building too. Gabe heard phones ringing and people chatting all down the long corridors, and a filing cabinet closed somewhere several doors down. A distant toilet flushed a moment later, and behind it all, something rhythmic was beating in the background. He half expected to find a real estate logo embossed on the first door they came to, but it was something unrecognizable and vaguely arcane, like a sickle surrounded by hand-carved runes.

Heather, for her part, seemed fascinated by the place, and she silently inspected every door as they passed. Gabe could only make out a few names among the rest of the meaningless symbols, but she appeared to know what she was looking at. He tried to catch her eye to get an explanation, but she was in her own world. And after he spotted some bubbling chemistry equipment through one open door, and what looked like an entire dried and preserved goat carcass through another, he resolved to just ask for a summary later. He hoped context would make it less creepy.

Just then a door opened, and a beautiful young woman with a plastic nametag reading "Jenny" popped out in front of them while still talking to someone back in the office. "Tell Esme I'll forward those Beijing purchase agreements—Oh!" She noticed them in time to prevent a collision, but still dropped several papers as she jerked to a stop.

Gabe instinctively bent to help her retrieve them, only to be hauled immediately back up by Heather's hand on his collar. He turned a questioning glare to her, but she was staring straight at the young woman, who was now bending to pick up her own papers.

"Excuse me," the gorgeous woman said, rising. She met his eyes and flashed him a bright, mossy green smile, and there was an unmistakable invitation there that Gabe suddenly wanted very much to accept. But Heather's hand clamped down hard on the back of his neck, holding him fast, and Jenny's smile slipped and turned into a pout. Then she tossed her copper curls and moved past them to continue down the hall without a backward glance.

After another second, Heather let go. Gabe started to argue with her, but then couldn't remember why. He shook his head to clear the cobwebs from his mind and realized the woman might not have been as beautiful as he'd thought. She might not have been a woman at all.

"Why do I suddenly feel like a piece of steak that two dogs just fought over?" he asked.

Heather searched his eyes, then nodded. "Hamburger, maybe. Come on, lover boy."

They passed several more mysterious rooms and branching hallways as the hob led them toward a pair of steel doors at the end of the main corridor. As they approached, Gabe realized that the rhythmic sound he was hearing originated there, and it was weirdly familiar. In fact, it sounded very similar to seventies rock music, blasting loudly enough to carry through most of the structure. But when the hob knocked, the sound quieted almost at once. A moment later, the doors clicked, and the hob pulled them open to reveal a room full of total nonsense.

Gabe's mind actually shut down for a few seconds as it tried to process the mix of images he saw. Creatures shaped like crickets but the size of small dogs scurried through a room that looked larger than the footprint of the entire library. Computer components and monitors hung from every available surface, and cables ran in great bunches all over the ceiling and floor like the roots and branches of a massive tree. Monitors flickered too quickly to comprehend the information on them, and huge server banks lining the walls filled the room with a constant background buzz of cooling fans.

And in the center of it all, suspended high above the floor by a web of gossamer filaments, and skewered by dozens of computer cables jacked directly into its head, was a monster insect the size of a minivan.

CHAPTER NINETEEN

```
"The trick is to stay under the radar. Be good-
looking, but not gorgeous. Be intelligent, but
not a genius. Be willing, but not desperate. If
you get the balance right, they'll never see you
coming. Of course, a boat-load of talent doesn't
hurt."

-Excerpt from Chapter Three, CONscience
```

"Whoa! What—" Gabe began.

Heather elbowed him in the ribs. "Not now," she hissed.

"But look at—" She pinned him with a glare, and Gabe closed his mouth. Then one of the cricket things stopped and chittered at them angrily while waving a foreleg, and Gabe's first instinct was to kick it hard and run away.

The hob bowed low, then gestured to Heather. "They insisted it be now," he said, the texture of his voice indicating very clearly how little he had to do with their apparent breach of etiquette. "They *strongly* insisted. I am not here in an official capacity."

Heather stepped forward. "We need information and assistance. Can we find that here?"

The cricket waggled its head back and forth as if dithering, but eventually responded with a long string of the chittering nonsense.

"Thank you," Heather said. "That is most kind."

Gabe leaned close. "You understood that?"

"He's going to ask the Locust to give us an audience, despite the early hour," she said. "Apparently it's nocturnal."

Gabe just grunted and looked back to the bustle of the room. It was like the command center for the insect rebellion, and he had a feeling he'd be having nightmares about it for a while. But for now, he was keeping it relegated to just another drop in the weird bucket. Once you're already carrying ten gallons of crazy, another cup or two is mostly academic.

A moment later, the cricket came back, and Heather translated that they would be granted a few minutes, despite the early hour.

"Really pushing that 'early hour' thing," Gabe mumbled. "I guess passive aggressiveness is universal across every species."

The cricket led them to a kind of platform at the center of the room, near where the Locust hung suspended a few feet off the ground. It felt like they were going to address an emperor or the Wizard of Oz, and Gabe had to keep himself from kneeling. Up close, he had a much better sense of scale, and he could now tell the thing was at least ten times his size. The shiver he barely suppressed would have been a big one.

Suddenly the room began to buzz and thrum as if the lowest notes on several dozen guitars had just been plucked simultaneously. Gabe moved to cover his ears, and then thought better of it, gritting his teeth against the discomfort instead. He didn't want to seem weak from the outset. He could try to make it through at least half a conversation before that became obvious.

"Our apologies," Heather said, bowing. "We are only recently arrived and do not know the proper customs."

Again the world buzzed and shook, but this time it was less intense. "Of course," Heather replied. "We would not have presumed to come to you without proper recompense. May we discuss terms?"

Gabe gave her a subtle questioning glance, but she ignored him. He wasn't sure what her idea of proper recompense was, but somehow he didn't think a giant bug would accept his credit card. The thing buzzed again, and this time he could tell it was mollified.

"Excellent," Heather said. She turned to the hob. "You may wait outside."

Uklek seemed torn between relief that he was still alive and annoyance at having been dismissed so easily. But he went quietly, leaving Gabe and Heather alone with the bugs.

"First things first," she said after the door had clicked closed again. "Is it within your power to help my master understand you?" The thing thrummed and Heather smiled. "I'm not sure either. That's part of why we're here."

The Locust waved a foreleg, giving the impression that it was thinking. Then it perked up, and Gabe felt a pinprick of pressure in his mind that reminded him of when Aka Manah had pushed his way in, only much less violent. This was more like a piece of string being passed through the eye of a needle—a bit of something much greater being handed to him rather than forced upon him. He mentally reached out to touch the line and instantly felt the presence of the Locust there within him. It felt like the equivalent of a pair of tin cans on a string, and when the thing buzzed again a moment later, the words entered his head fully formed and understandable.

"How's that, buddy? You better?" The Locust said into his mind.

It took Gabe a minute to process it, but when he did, he almost sat down on the spot. Whether it was a weird product of the mental link or the thing's legitimate voice, Gabe couldn't say, but it came out exactly like a stereotypical stoner from a Cheech and Chong movie. It was weird.

"Fine," Gabe finally said aloud.

"Are you good?" Heather asked, studying him.

He plastered on a cocky grin. "Yep. Really fine. Giant grasshoppers and psychic links. No problem."

"Hey, man," the Locust said. "You people all look alike to me too, but I don't go around calling you gorillas, right? Acrididae all the way. Have a little respect for the taxonomic family."

Gabe turned to the thing and gave an awkward bow. "Of course. I say stupid things. My apologies, uh, man."

The Locust waved a foreleg. "Call me Dale, brother. It's so much better than *The Locust*. I hate all that grandiose shit. Plus, there's like, eighteen 'The Locusts', so we have to keep ourselves straight somehow, right?"

Gabe nodded, finding himself perfectly willing to accept a giant bug named Dale now that he'd already made it this far. "Can I ask," he said, watching for Heather's flying elbows, "what are you?"

Dale stirred a little, but didn't seem upset at the question. "Ain't no thing, brother. I'm what you might call an embodiment of the swarm. Like a personification of humanity's eternal fear of nature's wrath, or some shit. Every time a bunch of bugs ate up a poor Roman farmer's crop, boom, I loomed a little larger in the... Whatsit? Collective consciousness. *Zeitgeist*. You dig?"

Gabe dug only shallowly, but he nodded anyway.

"So," Dale said, settling in to his giant shiny hammock, "What can I do you for?"

Heather, who seemed perfectly at ease now, switched seamlessly from careful formality to Midwest rural casual. "It's a bit of a sticky one, Dale. And a little sensitive..." She glanced at the few dozen crickets buzzing around the room.

Dale waved away her concern with a long leg. "Girly, I've been here for over fifty years, and I haven't had a single problem with loyalty. It's like a hive-mind thingy, dig? Without me they're just, kinda, you know. They're an extension of my will or whatever. They can be smart puppies all together, but they don't tell no tales. Swarm thing."

Heather nodded. "Okay by me. Can you start by telling us who's in charge nowadays?"

Dale spread his arms in a sort of shrug. "Newbies, huh? Okay, well, you've got the Hags that want the power, but aren't quite in charge—least not yet. Most of us hope they never will be, but they have their dirty little fingers in almost everything. Couple offices up the hall, even. Scary ladies. Schemers and politicians, mostly."

At the mention of the Hags, Gabe noticed Heather tense ever so slightly, but Dale went on before he could study it further. "Then there's The Chamber. It's all over the place but doesn't do much except talk. Think the U.N. if that helps. Then you've got little Barons that run things locally, sometimes as far down as neighborhood by neighborhood. They're maybe the most reliably present in the day-to-day. Your hob friend works for one of them, by the way, in case you didn't know. Jacob Jimenez, Baron of South Lincoln. Vampire, drug dealer, and sleazebag extraordinaire. He's actually a pishtaco from Bolivia if you want to get exact, but who cares, right? He sucks."

Dale chuckled at his own joke, and the cords plugged into his head rustled at the movement. "Then there's the rogue outfits that run independent communities like the Twenty Brothers or the Maerrywell Clan—though, the latter is more like a terrorist group anymore."

An image of a burned out shell of a building somewhere in the Middle East suddenly popped up on one of the largest monitors, and Gabe took it to be supporting evidence. The next picture was of a half-collapsed sign showing that the place had been some kind of hospital.

Dale barely slowed his lecture. "And I guess you could count the Jade Host, but they pretty much stay in their little corner of China and don't give a crap about anyone else. Lots of old power but no motivation to get involved in the modern machinations. And it goes on and on and on. All kinds of groups that want to call themselves an empire or a new society, but few of 'em ever stick. It's not great—actually, it's a shit sandwich most days—but it does seem to work. And that's what you get for free. My appetizer platter."

Heather let out a breath. "But," she said, pausing in apparent confusion, "who's the leadership? Oberon? Zeus? Who runs the Umbral Council now?"

Dale laughed in earnest this time, and the clicking sound that hit Gabe's ears jarred oddly with the human translation of it in his head. "Those guys haven't been around for at least a century, darlin'. The last few hundred years haven't been kind to the old ones. They putter here and there, sure, but they ain't got much juice left. That happens when a bright star falls. Fizzles right out."

Heather shook her head. "They're the gods. Someone has to be in control."

Dale turned to fully regard her. "You've been out for a while, huh? Look around, sweetie pie. This technology stuff changed everything. Airplanes and telephones shrank the world to a manageable size, then TV and the internet put the whole thing in a box and gave everybody a key. Gods and monsters aren't confined to regions or cultures anymore. Everything's all mixed up together like a stew, one thing influencing another until what comes out of the Ether nowadays is most often some kind of crazy mutt of old folklore and half-formed fantasies some screenwriter thought of on the toilet. None of it's neat and orderly anymore. Purebreds like you are a rarity. The collective will is just too spread out. A kid in Tokyo might have more in common with a retiree in Toledo than he does with his own next-door neighbor. Cultures are all chaos, and it's largely up for grabs for whoever can snatch it. Hell, most Barons are self-appointed. If they have the power to take power, they take it. It's beautiful anarchy, man."

Heather seemed thunderstruck. "But that's just chaos. What about the precepts and the Council?"

Dale hissed, and the sound was identical through both streams. "The precepts are still there in broad strokes, working in the Ether to keep the big bads at bay. Most of us obey them here to one degree or another because we don't want the world to implode. The Chamber is about the only group that holds the precepts as fully sacred, but if you put wind generators in their meetings you'd be able to power the world forever. They're the closest thing to the old Umbral Council that still exists, but they don't have anything like a standing force anymore. They didn't rise from the ashes of the mighty Council so much as stitch together a few body parts. They periodically issue decrees that most of us choose to follow or not based on convenience." He paused and appeared to think. "That's actually been awhile, now."

Heather nodded slowly. "I've been gone a few hundred years. This body had memories from the last thirty, but before that it's pretty fuzzy. And no information about our kind."

"Whew," Dale said. "You missed some stuff. Not even in the big wars, huh? That was a frenzy. Well, let me know if you want me to keep going. Just remember that the meter's running."

Heather looked like she wanted to accept, but then glanced at Gabe and shook her head. "Maybe another time, thanks. Can we ask our questions?"

"What else have you been doing?" Dale asked. Then he relented. "Alright, hit me."

"First, we need to know what happened to my friend here," she said, pointing to Gabe.

Dale turned to him and stared before giving the locust shrug again. "No clue. He's got some power, but it's all wonky, leaking out all over the place like he turned it on without knowing how to turn it back off. You in an accident or something, hombre?"

"Or something," Gabe replied. "Can you tell me anything about a guy called Aka Manah?"

Heather sighed, which, for a professional con, was about as dramatic as a palm to the face. But Dale moved right to work, buzzing in thought while a huge control panel started lighting up with pictures and data.

"Sure enough," Dale said. "He's bad mojo. Practically invented it, actually. Trickster, manipulator, liar, thief, betrayer—a real go-getter. Pretty much all the bad stuff humanity wants to blame on something else all rolled up into a nice neat ball. Probably not a good choice to invite to poker night if that's what you're asking."

"No," Heather said, taking the lead again. "We'd figured out most of that on our own. We're trying to learn why someone might have summoned him. Or, at the very least, what powers he might possess."

Dale cocked his head again. "I can't say why someone might want him here, other than to wreak havoc on the world. He's basically pure corruption. Let him loose and watch the whole place burn, I guess. A suicide cult, maybe? Some fundamentalist wackos trying to force the end times. Who knows? The precepts should prevent someone like him hopping a ride over, but, like I said, it's kind of wild here now. There's all kinds of jokers running around without anyone left to smite them from on high. Crazy times."

"As for powers," Dale went on, "he's one of the old, loosely defined variety. In the original tales he could do whatever was narratively expedient. He was a god in the true sense, in other words. Of course, in other ways he was almost hilariously inept. Got himself hoisted by his own petard once or twice. He could be anything now, you understand, legends shifting as they do." He paused and eyed Heather. "But you know all about that."

Heather ignored him and Dale seamlessly moved on. "Unless this cat is one of the old originals; that would be a different story. But hey, the oldest ones don't manifest anymore. It's too real for them here. They collapse under their own weight on the physical, so they're, like, integral to the Ether now, man."

"What about an Umbra named Gwendal?" Heather asked. "She's the reason—"

She had barely gotten out the name when Dale visibly shuddered. "Wait, wait, wait," he said, "I can't do anything for you about that one."

Gabe jumped in, finally sensing something in the water. "Why not?"

Dale waved him away. "Because I can choose who and what I sell, and she isn't for sale, man. I wish I could help, but no can do."

Heather held up a hand to forestall him, but Gabe ignored her and plowed on. "She almost killed us last night. Then sent two Hunters at us today. We might leave here and find more waiting. We need to know as much as possible about what kind of mess we're in or we don't stand a chance of ever getting out." He waited, but Dale didn't respond. "Come on, man. We bumbled into this by accident, and we're not equipped for it. Can you please help us?"

Dale held up a foreleg. "Kid, I like you. You're like a, what are they called? One of those monkeys. Capuchin. But the only person I like well enough to risk dying for is me. And, as it happens, selling information on her and the people she's running with would be bad for my health. No go, boy-o."

"I get it," Heather said, giving Gabe a significant look. "Let me ask you this then: Imagine that an Umbra tried to manifest inside a prepared body, but the original spirit somehow fought back and trapped it within. What would happen?"

Dale seemed amused at first, but it soon turned to curiosity as his head swung back to Gabe. "Wild," he said. "That explains a little."

"So this happens?" Gabe asked.

Dale nodded his great head. "Sometimes, but only with minor Umbras. Nothing like this. You guys are usually put straight into the nuthouse as it is, but if you have a big boy crammed in there? Well, I'll just say you're lucky your brain meat is still in one piece."

Gabe sighed. "That's very helpful, thanks."

"No, no, don't take it the wrong way," Dale said. "It's just crazy, you know? I mean, man. So you're just a vanilla human with god juice bursting out of your seams?"

Gabe spread his arms. "I guess."

"Trippy. At first glance, you're like, kapow! Powerful. But you probably can't even use it, huh?" Dale shook his great head. "Well, let's see: he might have wedged himself in the veil when he tried to push your soul out, got himself tangled up into a kind of... Like a..."

"A door," Gabe offered.

"Sure," Dale agreed. "If that's the case, then he's stuck there under his own steam. The harder he pulls the harder it pulls back. In lots of ways the veil is thin and weak, easy to slip through. But in other ways it's, like, merciless. He needs the balance shifted to drop back in here or back out there. He can't go nowhere without help from somebody on this side."

"Is it possible to dumb this down any?" Gabe asked. "I feel like I accidentally stumbled into the wrong classroom here."

Dale looked to Heather, who shrugged. "We haven't had time to cover anything but the basics," she said. "He doesn't know much yet."

Dale settled into his hammock and thrummed in thought for a moment. "Not even the basics, really. He's like a little baby."

Heather crossed her arms. "Kinda busy running for our lives."

"Okay, Mr. Human," Dale said. "Here goes: Reality is like a cruise ship in the middle of the ocean, dig? Everything you see, touch, smell, and taste is on that boat. The Ether is like the water. It gives the Umbra a place to live, and it holds that ship afloat. It's home and mother, the stuff of life, but it's raw and sterile. When you're there, nothing matters or makes sense. It's all fuzzy and slow, you know? Compared to that place, the DMV waiting line is a disco sex carnival.

Or so I'm told. I don't drive." He held up his forelegs as if they were the only problem.

"So you can see why an Umbra would want to get here, right?" he went on. "Physically manifesting is like waking from a coma into an LSD trip. You go from nothing to everything all at once. There's only one catch: We don't have physical forms. To get here, we need to borrow or hijack something real and ride it like a pony. Sometimes that means finding an animal or somebody on the verge of death. Sometimes," he gestured to himself, "it's an insect, though that's rare. Other times, it means physical intervention from a magic user or another powerful Umbra on this side to prepare something. Thing is, human spirits aren't exactly nothing, so they need to be removed to make room. That takes skill, and not just anyone can do it. A turtle might be weak and slow, but try to get one out of its shell without damaging it. Same thing. A spirit is never stronger than when it's at home."

"I understand so far," Gabe said, surprised to find it was true.

"Good. So take your little succubus here. She was just a wisp of notion in the Ether recently, outside of time and physical space. Then she landed in this classic carriage and took the reins. Power of one kind or another pierced the veil and bridged the gap. Then they enticed the old spirit out into the Ether, and girly here was free to take up residence. That's how it works most of the time. But it seems like your passenger jumped into you a little early, and you were still at the wheel."

Gabe nodded, numbly. "He tried to push me through, but fell in himself. I think it's holding him there, and he wants out."

"Of course he does. He was probably trying to push you into the Ether via some overly complex construct. Needlessly clever seems to be his modus operandi. Instead, he wedged himself in-between where there's no purchase to go forward or back. He's hanging by his own weight."

"So what do I do about it?" Gabe asked, trying not to sound as desperate as he felt.

Dale looked him over. "Finding somebody who knows more about this stuff than I do would be a good start. Preferably preceded by burning off some of that power you've got wafting from you like stink on a hippie—unless you like the idea of going supernova and killing everyone in a ten-mile radius. In which case, do me a favor and drive eleven miles first."

Gabe looked down at his hands and watched the soft glow swirl for a moment. "But it's not my power to use. He lent it to me to kill the Hunters and it just keeps coming. I don't have any idea how to burn it off."

Dale buzzed high and long, almost like a whistle. "You killed Hunters? That's impressive. Now get the hell out."

"Wait," Heather said, holding up a hand. "Nobody's on our trail right now. We made sure. Please finish."

"Nope, chicka. You've got troubles," Dale said, "and I don't want to catch any of them. I wish I could do more to help, but I'm not Mister Miyagi, and regular business hours start soon."

"Wait!" Gabe said. "We're not walking away with anything useful here. Give us something we can use. Something worth the money."

Dale made a chirping call and several of the cricket things surrounded them. "I'm not going to charge you. I feel like I got enough in return to make up the payment."

Heather took a step forward. "You're going to sell us out." She tried to approach even closer, but several of the crickets blocked her way.

Dale made a disappointed noise. "Nope. Not yet, anyway. But I think you two are going to be big news soon, one way or another, and I like that I'll be the one with an inside track on the story. Whether you're news for causing a big mess or being one, is all up to you."

"Bastard," Heather said under her breath.

"Careful, hot stuff," Dale said. "I can choose to sell you to the next person who walks in. You are in hiding, right?"

Gabe reached out and gently took her arm to pull her back a step.

"There you go," Dale said. "That was dangerously close to harshing my mellow." He sighed, and a printer began working somewhere off to Gabe's right. "I made up a quick list of some people that might help you. They're vendors like me, but not all are as scrupulous. The first one's local here. A *doctor* in the loosest sense of the word. Efrem Reznick. Try him first, would be my advice. If you can find him that is. He moves around and I lose track. No address, sorry. But he'll sell anything for the right weight of silver, and maybe that includes a way to de-god your noodle. Also, he's the least likely of the bunch to kill you on sight."

A cricket brought the list over and Gabe stuffed it in his pocket. The name sounded vaguely familiar, and he made a mental note to ask James for more information. Lincoln wasn't so big that people could stay hidden for long.

Dale looked at Heather. "I recommend you whip him into shape before you see any of these folks, though. That power coming off of him makes him a big fat target. So he'll need to either hide it or back it up. One way or another, you need a good old-fashioned training montage."

"Got it. Thanks," she said.

They turned to leave, escorted by a battalion of crickets, and Dale spoke up behind them. "Take care, Mr. Human. I sincerely hope you don't explode or die a raving lunatic."

Gabe raised a hand. "Nicest thing I've heard all day. A pleasure doing business." Then he followed Heather out through the doors, which closed behind them with a very final click.

CHAPTER TWENTY

```
"Everyone has their limits, but few people truly
know them. When is a burden too heavy? When will
you collapse beneath the weight of what you've
sought and sown? When do you give in and reach
out for any offered hand, regardless of how
soiled? Answer those questions unequivocally and
you'll know yourself well enough to become
someone else."

-Excerpt from Chapter Six, CONscience
```

    The hobgoblin was nowhere to be found when they exited, but Gabe was glad of that—especially now that they knew the thing worked for a drug dealing vampire Baron. They made their way back through the weird office complex and up the stairs into the library proper, and Gabe was so distracted that he completely forgot to look for the girl working the desk. He glanced back once, but left it alone. It seemed unlikely he'd actually be keeping that date.

    "Is it safe to talk now, do you think?" he asked.

    "My glamour is up," Heather said, clearly distracted too.

    "You'll have to actually explain how that works sometime. Are things really that bad?"

    She laughed bitterly. "They're not good. Do I need to recap?"

    "No," he said. "But we have the names of these people, right? There's a doctor right here in Lincoln. We can find him and get some answers. We're way farther than we were at lunch."

    "Right," she said, "that's great. Now we just have to worry about the fact that the entire world is in shambles and I have no fucking clue what I'm doing anymore!"

    Her raised voice caught him off-guard, and he glanced around to make sure nobody was paying attention to them. Luckily the college kids out in search of dinner all seemed perfectly content to mind their own business. Maybe that was the glamour, or maybe it was the natural inclination to not see upset people having awkward conversations.

    "Relax," he said. "If things are running as well as they ever have, it can't be that bad."

She shook her head vehemently. "You don't understand. It's like feudal states or something out there. Nobody's in charge. There are no rules anymore. I mean, it was never great, but this... The only reason Dale likes it is because he's an information broker. People don't buy secrets when things are predictable."

"See, and here I thought you were worried about the time bomb I have in my head," Gabe said.

"And that's the other thing," she continued. "You're too ignorant to know how much trouble we're in, and too powerless to release me from my bond and let me run. So now I'm a babysitter to the world's most dangerous toddler."

Gabe stopped at a light post that hadn't yet lit for the evening. "Whoa! Where the hell did that come from?"

Heather kept walking. "Move it, idiot. What don't you understand about being a gigantic target?"

Gabe felt his anger rising, and though he tried to redirect it, it was a half-hearted effort. He pushed away from the post and caught up to her. "Are you kidding me? You Umbra things pulled me into this! You think I like it? *Your* people did this, and now you're blaming me for saving you from being some kind of sex slave to an insane murder-wizard?"

She stopped and turned on him, but brought her voice down low and cold. "I've saved you too, Gabriel. Don't forget that. I've honored the bond despite the fact that it chafes me like a hemp noose. You would already be dead if it weren't for me, and all you've done is whine about yourself. You didn't save me. I'm still a slave, just to a different master."

"I didn't know!" Gabe said, throwing up his hands. "But, hey, nobody asked you to stick around. I told you to get out of my life once already, remember? So go, lady! Leave! I'll figure this out and save myself, like I always, *always* do." He waited for her to respond, but she only stood there expectantly. The sight of her just staring at him, studying, infuriated him further. "Go!"

Heather stood there waiting a little longer, then her shoulders slumped and she smiled wryly. "Damn. I really thought that would work. Come on, hot-head. Let's get some dinner."

Gabe unclenched his fists and stared at her for a moment, unable to follow her sudden u-turn. "What?"

She shrugged and punched him playfully on the shoulder. "Can't blame a girl for trying, right? I thought maybe if you got upset and ordered me to leave, it would, you know..." She made a clicking noise and then trailed off.

It took his brain another few seconds to catch up. "You got me angry to trick me into releasing you?"

She shrugged again and batted her eyelashes dramatically. "Don't be mad, Gabey. It was an experiment. Now we know that anger alone won't help you burn off that leaking power. If you could harness the magic out of sheer rage, your words would have carried enough will to free me. So we'll have to try something else. See?" she said sweetly. "I'm helping."

Gabe started walking again, slowly. "So everything you said..."

"Come on, you're a pro too. Sort of," she said. "You know how it is: say what you need to say to get the job done. Of course I'd like to be free, but the rest of it—meh."

Gabe felt a new surge of anger try to swell, but this time it all drained away to be replaced with annoyance. "That was a dick move."

"Hey," she said, in mock-admonishment, "a little anatomical equality for the gender please? Men don't have the market cornered on being assholes."

Gabe shook his head, and they walked in silence for a few beats before he finally chuckled. "'Chafes like a hemp noose?'"

Heather laughed. "How about a wool scarf? You have an admittedly light touch as a master." She reached up and ruffled his hair playfully, doing precisely the right thing to dispel the rest of his anger. "Though a girl might occasionally like a little noose action. Free advice."

When they got to the car and were situating, he turned to her. "Were you really going to bail on me if it had worked?"

She looked into his eyes, and he felt the true weight behind them for the first time. His ability to see through glamours seemed spotty at best, but suddenly he could gauge a little of how old she really was.

"Of course not, Gabe. I'm with you forever."

He knew he only heard the false note in it because she let him. It was her way of saying that, yes, she probably would have bailed, but she couldn't, so why pick at it? He suddenly felt like he was in a sham marriage that neither partner could afford to end. To his surprise, it was an oddly refreshing notion. At least he knew where he stood. He couldn't trust her, which seemed like the right call anyway.

Gabe started the car and left campus. They pulled up to Honest Abe's just as the dinner rush was getting into full swing. Luckily it looked like the line wasn't quite to the door yet, so he got out and let Heather follow or not. A second later, she caught up to him.

"I'm going somewhere else to eat," she said, walking close enough that their shoulders touched.

Gabe stopped at the door. "What? Where?"

She spread her hands. "You can ask me to tell you and I'll have to, but I'd prefer not. I spotted some familiar symbols back under the library, and I think I know how to get some more information. Let's say it's reconnaissance and leave it at that, okay? Let me have the list."

"When are we going to that Reznick guy? This isn't really something I want to procrastinate."

Heather sighed. "That's what I'm doing. You want to walk down random sidewalks yelling his name until he pops his head out of a window? Me neither. I'm hoping to find some other Umbras who can help us tonight. There are some *social clubs* back down there, and they'll probably come to life in a few hours. But dragging you along with that leaking power is just asking for trouble in a place chocked full of those who can see it."

"We could ask James," he said. "I swear I've heard this Reznick name before, and he'll know if anyone does. Plus, I'd really like to pop James in the mouth a few times for sending me to the magic murder mansion. Two birds with one stone."

She raised an eyebrow. "While watching you get your ass kicked by a man who's prettier than me would be fun, I don't think it's the best option right now. James probably didn't know what was going on, but we don't know that for sure. We can't take the risk. Besides, Reznick might have his fingers in human business, but it's his magical knowledge we want. We need to come at it from that angle. James can't help us there. We'll keep him as a backup plan though, in case I strike out tonight."

"Fine. Whatever," Gabe said. "But how are you going to find me if we split up?" He realized then that he was arguing because he felt safer with Heather nearby. It was a weird sensation.

She tapped the side of his head. "The bond, remember? I can find you. Ain't no mountain high enough, and all that. And that's also why I need your explicit permission to leave for a bit. I'll only be a few hours."

He almost asked for more specifics, just on principal, but he stopped himself before the words came out. In the end, he really didn't want to know what her idea of a better dinner was. There was a good chance it would turn out to be something he couldn't unhear.

"Fine. Go," he said, handing her Dale's list of contacts before opening the door and slipping inside to get in line. He waited a few beats, then checked over his shoulder to see which direction she had gone. But Heather was still there, watching him through the window. And for that one brief instant, he saw a flicker of genuine emotion on her face as he caught her staring. Her eyes only lifted a bit in surprise and her lips parted ever so slightly, but it was enough for him to notice and wonder about.

Then she collected herself like a consummate pro and dropped him a hugely exaggerated wink and kiss before turning like a dancer and strolling away. He watched her go, moving as if through an English rose garden instead of a big gray parking lot. She made for the first lone man she spotted—a round little guy just getting out of his car who immediately stopped for her. She tossed her hair and touched his arm before laughing like he'd just said something hilarious, then leaned in close to whisper in his ear. A moment later, they were kissing. Gabe sympathized with the guy, understanding what was probably happening in his head right then. Soon they were getting back into the man's car and driving out of sight.

He turned back to study the menu above the register and push the image from his mind. He wasn't sure why the idea of Heather kissing another guy bothered him so much, but it did. Maybe it was the stress of the ridiculous day and his brain flailing for some kind of normalcy, or maybe it was the lingering influence of what she'd done to him earlier that morning. But she was a succubus. That was what she did. And, if she was to be believed, she was doing it to help him. He certainly couldn't blame her for using her advantages. That would be crazy. And it wasn't like she was his girlfriend or anything. That would be even crazier.

"It is not madness to covet what is yours," Aka Manah whispered. *"Take her while you still can."*

"Nobody asked you," Gabe mumbled, then smiled and shrugged when the guy in front of him turned back in confusion.

He took his burger to-go and ate in his parked car. As usual it was huge, a little messy, and completely worth it. It dominated his entire attention, which was a nice distraction from the overwhelming madness of the last twenty-four hours. And it was also why he didn't notice the figure approaching until the window next to his head exploded.

ELSEWHERE

"I want him found!" Gwendal screamed, smashing a chair over a Hunter's head. The one she'd chosen to hit was ostensibly the leader of the thirteen, but had only a deep slash across its neck to set it apart from the others in the grisly group. It took the blow with no reaction and simply stared blankly back at her.

The news of the loss of two of their allies seemed to have affected the remaining eleven Hunters minimally, if at all, and Gwendal wondered again if the things felt any kind of pain. From their flayed and bloody bodies she guessed not, but it certainly didn't make her want to try any less.

She stormed across the hotel room to come face-to-face with Paul. "You do it this time. The Sanguine Fetter is no longer upon him. No doubt the work of the succubus. Can you find his trail without the blood scent?"

Paul nodded."If I know where to start."

"Good. Take this worm with you." Gwendal reached over and lifted the hob by the back of his neck and threw him to the ground at Paul's feet. "Since he is so eager to prove useful."

Uklek covered his head with a hairy arm and tried to shuffle away. "I was told to come to you! My master wishes to make peace so that—"

Gwendal kicked him hard and sent him sprawling. "Your master is a petty drug dealer who fancies himself a Baron of this backwater. He only sent you as a sacrifice, meant to keep me from eating up his flock as he watches in terror from his walls."

The hob blubbered a reply—something about the university and downtown, then the Warrens.

"If you want to serve," she said, her tone cooling further, "then you will lead my Hound to where you last saw the pair, and help him find the trail. If I am satisfied with your contribution, I may yet see fit to lend your master my ear for whatever he wishes to discuss. You will be seen as quite the diplomat." Then she kicked him again, though this time not nearly so hard. "Now go."

Paul dragged the hob bodily from the room, and Gwendal leaned out to call after them. "Do not confront them alone. They have some power that we didn't foresee." She turned to the Hunters and gritted her teeth. "It was my understanding that you were invincible?"

The Hunter she addressed just stared back blankly, either unable or unwilling to respond to what was obviously an insult. And from the feel of the power simmering within the thing, Gwendal knew she'd be hard-pressed to force it. It had been born of primal fears, just like her.

"Tell me," she said, "how do a human and a succubus defeat two Hunters?"

There wasn't much there, but for a moment she thought she spotted a flicker of something behind the thing's yellow eyes. It was like concern, or fear... Or hunger. She noted it for future consideration. There was something deep in that shell after all—some kind of emotion or weakness—and if it was there, she could find it. Just because they were allies today was no reason to dispense with prudence.

She had no doubt that her Hound would track down the missing human, but how quickly he could do it was another matter. She didn't have unlimited time if her plans were to work perfectly. The Chamber might be slow to move against her in any official capacity, but the Hags or Knights of Solomon had token agents nearby and could respond more quickly. And now that she'd breached the magic of the precepts so brazenly, one or more of the groups would surely be seeking her soon. Without Aka Manah's power behind her, she wouldn't stand a chance. And he couldn't possibly have much time left before the fragile human mind broke beneath his exquisite weight. It was all about to fall apart.

She needed more resources, but every time she called Phillip she sank deeper into his debt. There was no telling what he would require in return when this was over, and if she failed to get her love back, she would have no choice but to pay. Aka Manah was to have been here to help. Together they could clear the field with little effort, choosing from among the fallen to slake their thirst. But alone, she was fighting for scraps. And that, above all else, galled her. They might have a little time yet against the Emptiness and the end of all things, but her own pride was not so patient. She wanted the full measure of her power back now. She wanted her true form and her love at her side.

Gwendal turned to the Hunter with the slashed throat. "Make it known that we want the human and succubus," she said. "Offer a reward. Phillip can pay. I don't care who brings them in."

She smiled wistfully at the thought of dozens of desperate Umbras scouring the city for her, doing her bidding. It was a ghost of the true feeling of godhood, she knew, but it was a start. And it was something she would need to grow accustomed to if she was to lead the whole of reality against the Endless Dark.

Gwendal licked her lips. "And bring me two more men."

The Hunter nodded and turned to fulfill its task, its eyes lit with intelligence now that it had a command.

Gwendal reclined back into her nest of soiled sheets and closed her eyes. She reached out into the world again, and again found nothing. The Sanguine Fetter had winked out some time that morning, and the human's blood in her belly had lost its power. So instead, she slipped into memory.

Aka Manah. The only thing she'd ever loved. The god who had found her in that feral, primal place and pulled her up into the light of true consciousness. He had shown her that she could be so much more than the bleeding tit from which a thousand stinking dog-people sucked, and that being a goddess could be greater than what she'd been in that shit-crusted cave. He had lifted her up, set her free, and made her new. And with him, she would finally fulfill the purpose for which she had been born.

Gwendal brushed the Ether with her thoughts, but instead of attempting to break through, she slipped atop it, sliding along the inner edge of the veil like a drop of water. Distance meant nothing in the Ether, and with a thought she traversed the length of it, the supposedly infinite expanse, to where it ended abruptly in a dark, ragged swath. The veil there was tattered and flailing at the edges of the abyss, and the substance of the Ether bled out in huge plumes to be consumed and rendered into nothing by the Eternal Hunger. The Endless Dark. The Emptiness. The thing for which even gods and monsters had no true name.

She watched the substance of life slowly disappear into that maw for what felt like decades, imagining that she could see the void growing by inches for every bit of potential it devoured. There was no knowing what lay within the vast black, or what, if anything, drove it. Most guessed that it was simply the end, chewing its way across reality —the final balance readying a new birth. But for now it was busily absorbing the vastness of all that *could* and *would* be, and soon it would find its way to the center, and begin in earnest on all that *is*.

She and Aka Manah would not accept that. They had seen first the coming dark, and they alone had acted when all others had done naught but deny. There would be no end for them, nor for the world they would make their own. There was too much to do and to be had to allow it all to simply disappear. They would save this universe from consumption, close the breach, and in so doing be worshiped as the only true gods. If in the process they had to sacrifice most of creation, so be it.

A handful of humans had given birth to her those millennia ago, seeding the womb of the Ether with their hatred and malice and fear and lust. But she was only now close to giving them what they had begged and promised. Soon she would have the strength to grow into what she was truly meant to be. She backed away from the edge, leaving that battle for another day. For now, it would be enough to begin taking her true form.

The first bones inside her broke with audible cracks, and her scream of agony and pleasure filled the entire floor.

CHAPTER TWENTY-ONE

"Occasionally I catch myself imagining what I might have been under other circumstances, and I try to pinpoint how I got here. My childhood was pretty crazy, and I have plenty of issues as a result, but it mostly boils down to laziness. I couldn't hack it in any real jobs, so I got a fake one. Despite the occasional legal and moral hiccups, it's just way easier. Sorry I don't have an epic origin story for you. It's just a regular old sad one."

-Excerpt from Chapter Two, CONscience

Gabe woke and noticed three things: First, that he was bound hand and foot—which was a pretty terrible start. Second, that the left side of his head felt like someone had pounded it with a sack of roofing nails. And third, that he was lying in the back of a large SUV traveling at what felt like roughly ten thousand miles per hour. Try as he might, he couldn't come up with a *good* scenario that involved those three things simultaneously. The only two bright spots were that his hands were cuffed in front of him and that the seats were leather—which would make vomiting on them in a minute that much more elegant.

He glanced up to the front and spotted two men facing forward, both dressed in casual but expensive clothes. There was no obvious sign he was dealing with anything legitimate like the police, which left only a few choices for what kind of trouble he could be in. None were good, so he didn't spend a lot of time parsing the options. He considered holding onto the element of surprise for a bit longer by pretending to be unconscious, but then he almost laughed out loud. About the only thing he could do with surprise was yell "boo" and hope they died of heart attacks. So instead, he used his only reliable weapon and cleared his throat.

"Fellas, there's a chance I called the wrong kind of escort service."

The passenger looked back in alarm, then reached back to tug hard on the handcuffs. Gabe grunted in pain, but the man relented as soon as he was satisfied that they were still secure. He smiled down, showing off an impressive set of fangs.

"You were easy to find, human," he said, lisping a little around his teeth and a tongue that seemed too large. "The trail of your energy is like a stench."

Gabe tried to nod, but the pain in his head immediately made him stop. "Good feedback. So you're vampires, huh? Isn't that a little cliché nowadays?" He did everything he could to sound mildly bored. Yesterday he would have been terrified, but a couple near-death experiences in a row seemed to have thickened his skin.

The driver spoke up without looking back. "Not vampires. Pishtacos. All you need to know is that you've been summoned to speak with Baron Jimenez.

"Look," Gabe said, wearily. "I don't care what kind of tacos you guys are. Why don't you just tell me what you want so I can figure out how to give it to you?"

"Not us," the driver said, "the Baron. He has questions for you. Mostly about the way you dealt with his hobgoblin accountant."

Gabe laughed for real this time, and almost didn't care about the pain. "Uklek is an accountant? That's... Of course he is."

"It's not great for you, man," the passenger said as he faced forward. "The Baron takes care of his people, and you royally pissed him off. Unless you have something up your sleeve, you're gonna be—" He cut off and gestured out the windshield. "Now what the hell is this?"

"Shit," the driver said, pulling the vehicle to a stop. "Goddamned Knights again. They better start respecting jurisdiction or the Barons are gonna order another cull of those fuckers. Fuck their shit up for another decade." He pulled out his phone.

Gabe was already fighting to regain his balance after the sudden stop, so when the passenger pishtaco reached back and pulled hard on the cuffs, Gabe could only follow as he was pulled straight to the floor. Then a sharp fingernail was at his neck.

"You say a word and I'll slit your throat," the pishtaco said. "That's a bona fide promise. Stay quiet, and you might live long enough to get back to your lady friend. We'll tell the Baron you cooperated. That's not nothing. Got it?"

Gabe knew he was in no position to argue. While most people weren't capable of the kind of casual murder that the general lexicon of threats almost always suggested, he couldn't lump his captors into the same bucket as "most people". Gwendal had proven that. He very carefully nodded.

"Yeah Jacob, it's Joseph," the driver said into his phone. "We got a Knight here. Any advice?" Someone briefly spoke on the other end. "Oh yeah, we got him. License says, uh, Gabriel Delling. That's why we—" He paused and listened again. "Whoa. Got it. Okay. Hey relax, we'll be safe." Then he hung up and stuffed the phone back into his pocket. "Jacob says the Knights don't get this guy under any circumstances. He wants him pretty bad. Full contact if we have to."

A few seconds later, the driver rolled his window down. "Good day, Knight," he said, his tone polite.

"Good day," a male voice said from just out of Gabe's sight. "You two with Jimenez?"

The pishtacos exchanged a brief look that might have been annoyance, then the driver turned back and nodded. "We are. Just running some errands. Is there a problem?"

There was a long pause, and Gabe considered yelling for help. But before he could muster the courage, the Knight spoke again. "I see. Mind if I take a look in the vehicle?"

Gabe could immediately feel the tension ratchet up several notches, and the driver seemed taken aback. "I don't think our agreement with the Knights allows for you—"

"I know everything about the local agreements," the Knight interrupted, his tone full of easy authority. He sounded like a man completely confident in his dominance, and Gabe guessed that the guy must be holding at least one ace up his sleeve—probably a gun-shaped one. "There are allowances for imminent danger. And whatever you're hauling here is leaking volatile power like a broken oil tanker. I can't just let you drag it all over town, let alone back to your den. Open up."

The driver started to respond, but then there was a distinct click and hum of electronics coming to life. Both pishtacos went very still.

"Step out of the vehicle, leeches," the Knight said, his voice suddenly cold. He definitely sounded like a man with a gun.

Gabe watched from the floor as both pishtacos moved carefully to exit the SUV, keeping their hands in sight and away from their hips and jackets. A moment later, three sets of footsteps were moving toward the front of the vehicle. Gabe seized the opportunity and wriggled himself around to his back, then up into a sitting position. He ignored the muffled voices outside and focused instead on wrestling himself up onto the back seat without being seen. By then, the voices outside were growing louder, and he had a bad feeling he was running out of time. He fumbled for the door handle with his shackled hands and found it locked. He tried to manually unlock it, but it wouldn't budge. It only took a second to realize he was being foiled by a damned child safety feature.

Gabe risked a glance through the windshield and saw the two creatures angrily confronting a man in a red shirt and leather jacket who was holding what had to be some kind of model space gun. Fortunately, none of them were paying any attention to the vehicle at that exact moment, so Gabe carefully reached past the passenger seat and clicked the power lock button on the front door. All the locks clicked audibly, and then all hell broke loose.

The confrontation outside had grown into a shouting match by then, but the minor sound of the power locks came at just the right moment of silence to ignite the situation. The pishtaco on the right looked back suddenly at the sound, and the quick movement made the Knight jerk his weapon to the side in response. The other pishtaco, apparently seeing an opening, lunged toward the Knight with arms outstretched as if he intended to wrestle him to the ground. It was a mistake.

There was a minor pop of light and the soft thunk of a discharge, and Gabe instinctively ducked down behind the seat just as something large and heavy fell against the hood. The sound of a quick scuffle followed, and then the driver's door flew open to reveal one of the monsters climbing inside. A second later, the engine roared back to life and they were screeching away. Gabe panicked and shouldered open his door even as the SUV raced up to speed, and he caught a brief glimpse of concrete and grass moving by much too quickly.

The driver shouted a curse as he wrenched the vehicle hard around a corner and over a curb, and the SUV bounced violently as it fought with momentum and gravity. It slowed for just a moment as it got back under control, and in that instant, the ground looked a fraction less deadly. So Gabe shut off his brain and let himself fall.

He hit hard and rolled along the concrete, which probably saved him from breaking anything, and he came to a stop next to a large dumpster that looked like it had seen better days—even for a dumpster. He used the last of his momentum to shimmy partially beneath the thing, and had only barely gotten under when a motorcycle sped around the corner in pursuit. Then everything went quiet and dangerously still except for his breath and the rustle of gravel beneath his back.

Gabe wanted nothing more in that instant than to lay there, letting his brand new pains come to terms with the leadership of the larger ache in his head—but he knew better. According to all the new friends he was making lately he was leaving some kind of trail for them to follow, and that meant that staying in one place for too long would get him found. He had to move.

He slid out from under the dumpster and found that he was on a back street in one of the more run-down neighborhoods, but he couldn't quite tell where. Luckily his feet had only been bound with rope, and a few minutes of work had the knots undone and the rope tossed into the trash. His handcuffs were still a problem, but his heart rose with sudden hope as he looked back around the corner and noticed the body lying in the gutter.

It was one of the pishtacos, the driver named Joseph, and Gabe rushed over to it with a surge of relief. It was clear from the burned hole through its chest that the thing was dead—or more so, at least—and a part of Gabe wanted to study it to satisfy his curiosity. But the sound of a passing car a few blocks away knocked him back to his senses, and he bent at once to rifle through the creature's pockets.

He wasn't lucky enough to find a handcuff key, but he did find his cell phone and wallet, which he hadn't even realized were missing. He also found the vampire's phone, and he pocketed that too for no good reason. Then he wrestled the thing's jacket off to drape over his hands, and in so doing revealed a gun holster. He left that untouched. Even if it would make him feel safer, the last thing he needed was to run around handcuffed and carrying a gun.

He rose and situated the jacket to cover the cuffs. It would work. He looked weird for sure, but at least he didn't look like an escaped criminal anymore. Just a normal man walking normally with his hands folded beneath a coat over his crotch, like normal. Gabe sighed and took a step past the body, then jerked to a stop as a hand reached up and gripped his ankle.

The pishtaco had him. He reflexively tried to pull away, but the grip was like iron. The thing's eyes were still closed, and it still had a softball-sized hole in its chest, but the grip only continued to tighten.

He could feel his ankle joint protesting with the strain, and he tried again to pull away, but the creature wouldn't let go. Then the real panic set in. He pulled harder, dislodging the jacket in the process, but only hurting himself where the iron hand held him. He grunted in pain as he felt the joint separating and the bones creaking while the tendons screamed their warnings. He tried to toss himself free, using his whole weight to wrench the fingers open, but all he got was a hard fall onto his side, cracking his hip and elbow on the concrete.

"Just ask for help," Aka Manah said.

Gabe was suddenly angry, and he started kicking. He lashed out with his free foot, scoring easy hits in the pishtaco's stomach and groin before moving up to its ribs. The thing didn't try to fight back, but nothing worked to force it to let go either. He ground his heel into the creature's side, pushing with all his strength to break the bones, to shatter, to pierce the organs beneath, but even then the thing held on tight.

"I can save you. A trade..."

This time the outline of the door drew itself on his awareness even before he thought of it. A gift of power was waiting for him there. He kicked again and again.

"I can help you. Help kill it. Power."

Gabe felt himself shouting incoherently, trying not to listen, trying to drown out the whispers. But it didn't help. He didn't need help. He didn't. His thoughts were suddenly coming apart.

"You need to kill. You need help to kill it. I can help. So much power. Use it. Take it!"

He refused to listen and refused to touch the power at the edge of his awareness. He contorted himself to get at the pishtaco with his hands—first prying at the fingers then ripping at the flesh with his nails. But it didn't work. Nothing worked. He knew he was breaking, slipping irretrievably into that red rage... But he couldn't stop it.

"Kill it. Kill it. Kill it. Kill it. Kill it..."

He screamed and lashed out again and again, blindly ripping and crushing and hating. But refusing the power. Refusing! He flailed and smashed and welcomed the fury until it filled him and there was nothing left of him but rage and pain, and his sanity was a distant memory left far behind, and the fire of his new self burned bright and terrible and... And... And then he was falling.

Gabe fell back into a soft patch of grass next to a pale blue house. He scrambled back on his hands, then rolled up to his feet to take several stumbling steps away before he even thought to suck in a frantic breath. His chest burned as he pulled in air, and his legs shook so badly that he could hardly stand. He was free. In fact, he wasn't anywhere near the vampire anymore. He glanced around and found that he was now somehow about a block away from the body, down and across the street beside a house that mostly hid him from view. He had no memory of getting free or of moving away, but there he was.

He looked back to the body and saw that a group of people were crowding around it, with several bending down to check on him. Gabe watched them for a few minutes, catching his breath and trying to snatch the thread of what had just happened, but nothing came to fill the vacuum.

He felt the weight of the jacket over his handcuffs, right where he had put it, and when he tested his ankle for injury, he felt nothing. There was no sign of the struggle, no sign that any of it had been real. But it was vivid in his memory all the same. He waited for Aka Manah to rise and supply an explanation for the trick, but the god was silent. It felt almost as if neither one of them had been themselves in that moment—as if they had both lost control. It was happening, then. They were starting to crack. He wondered what would have happened if he had taken the power.

He did need help. Now.

CHAPTER TWENTY-TWO

```
"The big scores aren't always the hardest;
sometimes you get lucky. And then sometimes you
work yourself sick for nothing. Once I posed as
a Music Therapist seeking funding for a study on
the therapeutic effects of low frequency sound
waves on intracranial hypertension. Yeah, I
know. It was all made up of course, but I still
had to sound like I knew what I was talking
about. It took weeks of prep. Then I found out
that the competing study was something to do
with pediatric neuroblastomas. Kids with cancer.
That night, I threw all my work away. I haven't
managed to become a monster yet, so I've got
that going for me."

-Excerpt from Chapter Seven, CONscience
```

    Gabe got home a little before midnight, but not before retrieving his own vehicle and joyriding around town to confuse the trail for whoever might be following. He didn't understand how the whole thing worked, but he hoped the tank of gas had bought him some time. It had also given him a chance to pull himself back together. There was nothing quite like a good violent hallucination to really take the wind out of your sails.

    It took twenty minutes and all of his hacksaw blades, but eventually he got his cuffs off and was able to pack a bag. He could stay with his dad for the night, then ask James to find this Reznick guy in the morning. It was a plan at least. He didn't know if Heather would come through or not, and he honestly didn't completely trust her. She wasn't human after all. She was a wild card, and James was a known quantity. It was the safe play, and he needed more of those in his life.

    He spotted the nursing home envelope on the counter where Heather had used it to illustrate the Ether. He flipped it over and saw the address, then stuffed the thing in his bag. No sense making it too easy for anyone to find him. Then he zipped the bag closed and tossed it by the front door with his keys.

He had just gotten down to the basement to grab some plastic sheeting to jury-rig a repair for his window, when he heard several motorcycles come to a stop somewhere nearby. After midnight in a neighborhood of retirees and soccer moms, the sound was basically an air raid siren. His first instinct was to break out one of the small windows set high in the wall and cram himself through to safety, but he scratched that pretty quickly as too noisy and too self-eviscerating. And before he could come up with an alternative, his front door slammed open, and heavy, booted feet tromped over his threshold.

Gabe picked up a wrench from the work bench, then crept up the stairs to cautiously peek around the wall. Six large men in biker leathers were standing in his living room, and unsurprisingly, Heather moved among them. She had changed clothes again, this time into a loose gray top and tight jeans with black flats, and she had a little designer purse across her shoulder like a messenger bag. He could only guess where she'd gotten the ensemble without the shopping bags that were still in the back of his car, but it had probably happened around the same time she'd visited a salon, given her crimson nails and artfully piled tresses. She looked like... Well, she looked pretty damned great really, standing framed in front of his bedroom door. But she also looked like she had just led a platoon of maniacs into his foyer, which tempered it a bit.

One of the men stepped forward suddenly and grabbed her arm, pulling her around and close and leaning down to her face. For just a second it looked as if he had unhinged his jaw like a snake's, but then he was normal again an instant later. "So where is he?" he hissed.

Heather squealed in pleasure at the treatment, then sank into the man. "Pretty close," she said, her voice carrying a long, lazy drawl. "Maybe downstairs."

"And you're sure he's not packing heat?" the man asked, staring at Heather like an animal barely in control of his hunger.

She shook her head and smiled. "Positive. He's weak, and stupid. Which is why I don't mind you collecting the bounty. Go see for yourself." Then she pointed right to where Gabe was hiding.

Gabe felt the blood rush out of his legs and he almost dropped to the floor. He ducked back around the corner and pressed himself against the wall, wondering frantically if Heather had really just sold him out.

"She used you."

She'd positioned him perfectly to pull a double-cross, and now he had nowhere to run. He couldn't believe it.

"She fears what I am and what you could be."

Gabe wanted to weigh his options, but it didn't take long to weigh nothing. He had to create a solution out of whole cloth, and quick.

"Oh, there are options. It is time to cut her loose and do this on our own. I will be your guide."

"Shut up," Gabe mumbled. "I'm thinking." He pressed the whispers back and listened to the booted feet approaching. Then he took a deep breath and walked confidently around the corner without even a hint of a plan in his head.

He almost ran directly into the double-wide wall of men in the hallway, but just before the collision, he used his voice to stop them a pace away. "Whoa!" Gabe said, letting his face grow alarmed, but not scared. "Who the hell are you?"

The one on the right reached for him, but Gabe gently slapped the hand away like a child trying to steal a cookie, and for some reason the guy pulled back as if burned. Up close, Gabe could tell that both were wearing imperfect glamours that let a snake-like quality seep around the edges. He couldn't tell what they were, but he knew at once they were Umbras. He marveled for a second at how infested the world apparently was with the things now that he could see them, but he didn't dare gawk for too long.

"Can I help you with something?" he asked, pretending like he didn't notice or care about the way the second man's bifurcated tongue was now flicking out to taste the air. "Or are you more strays she brought home to munch on?"

Gabe wasn't sure if it was the question itself or the hint of bitterness he'd injected into it, but something seemed to confuse the men for a moment, so he used the beat to push between them and get to the center of the living room. The men inexplicably jumped back like he had the plague.

There were eight of the things in his house, and Heather made nine. He inspected them quickly, all terrifying and dangerous-looking as hell, and then he turned at last to Heather as if she meant the least to him. Her expression was part amusement and part defiance, and Gabe got absolutely nothing from it. She could be playing an angle, or she could be selling him out for real. With a pro like her, it was hard to tell where "real" ever began.

"I thought you said you couldn't do anything to harm me?" Gabe said, ignoring their audience for a moment. "Getting the crap kicked out of me by Hell's literal angels seems pretty freaking harmful."

Heather gently pulled herself free from the biker thing and shrugged. "They're here to take you in, Gabe. For the bounty." She let that statement hang for a second, then she sighed. "Better them than someone else. Trust me, I won't let them kill you. We need you alive to collect."

Gabe took a step closer to her. "How generous of you. There's a bounty now?"

Heather nodded. "Just tonight. Lots of people want it too. Half a million dollars makes you quite the popular guy. My new naga friends here happened to find me first, and we made a deal. You understand, of course. Maybe if you hadn't been such a dick to me."

Gabe expected to be tackled at any minute, but the whole crew seemed frozen while they spoke. So he rolled with it and turned to the biker next to Heather, who he took to be the leader. "Can you believe this?"

The man squared up to Gabe and cocked his head to the side. He looked like he was readying for a fight, but something about his body language was off. He was big and covered in tattoos, and was apparently some kind of snake-monster. But if Gabe's guess was correct, he was also scared. Gabe took a slow step forward and was rewarded by the man leaning the tiniest bit back.

"What?" the biker asked, his aggressive tone trying to put the lie to his true disposition.

Gabe moved a little closer and surreptitiously eyed the rest of the room before continuing. Every other man there was reading the exact same way: wary. And all at once he understood why he wasn't already beneath a pile of punching fists. *They* were scared of *him*.

That changed things. He plugged in the new information and let himself straighten. He didn't know if he could control Aka Manah's energy leaking out of him, but he mentally pushed it to expand and work in his favor for once. Then he shaved some of the indignation from his demeanor and subtly replaced it with a hint of boredom, as if this was unacceptably jostling his evening routine. The disdain for

Heather, though, he kept. And he added a touch of malice for good measure. It was a nice emotional gumbo.

"This," he said, pointing to Heather with the wrench and moving another step closer to her. "I save her ass, and she sells me out. What a bitch, huh?" The bikers seemed confused, but Gabe went on before any group decisions could congeal. "I mean, I put down two Hunters for her, and this is her thanks? Turning those things to ash wasn't that hard, but it isn't my favorite way to spend a morning. You'd think the least she could do is forget she knows me."

It had been a guess, since Gabe knew nothing about anything, but apparently it had been a good one. At the mention of the Hunters, he saw several glances flit between the group members, and a few even took a step backward. His reputation was preceding him, it seemed, and for the first time in his life that was turning out to be a good thing. He took another step closer, and Heather eyed him carefully. She had no idea where he was going with this.

"So what, sweetheart?" Gabe asked, following his instincts. "Are these ignorant shits for you to eat or me to kill?"

The question finally lit a fire in the group, and voices rose all around. Fists came up and at least two revolvers came out to swing uncertainly between Gabe and Heather. Glamours wavered and the men began to change, taking on more snake-like traits—some heads flattening, some eyes narrowing, and some fangs growing. The leader of the group, still the most man-like of them, shouted everyone down, screaming that the bounty specified that Gabe be taken alive. But even his fangs now showed past his lips, and the men were right at the edge. They needed one more push.

And Gabe needed a moment of chaos. So he raised his voice above the din as he took the last two steps to Heather. "Is that what you want?" he shouted. "Because you know I'll do it! These fuckers are nothing to my power! You want me to kill them? Fine!" He raised a hand palm-upward as if collecting energy there, then let out a wordless scream of rage as he thrust it forward in what seemed like an appropriately epic spell-casting move. And then things got messy.

Nothing came out of his hand of course, but the nagas all flinched and ducked anyway, making it appear believable in that instant. A gun fired and drywall dust fell from the ceiling, and suddenly none of them wanted to be there. Their simultaneous attempts at flight tangled everything up enough that nobody could go anywhere quickly, and in that space Gabe turned and brought the heavy wrench up and around into the leader's mouth. He connected solidly with a fang, snapping it and sending a spray of something thick and black across the room. The biker fell back screeching in rage with his hand to his face, and black ichor ran between his fingers to burn any skin it touched.

Gabe brought the wrench around to confront Heather, but she was already grabbing him by the collar and pulling him sideways into his room. She lifted him with ease, and he flew five steps before catching himself on his bed. The door slammed behind him, and he spun with the wrench to face her next attack... But she wasn't there. Instead, she was bracing the door with her back.

"Go, stupid!" she shouted, nodding to the window.

Gabe took a second to reconcile what was happening, but the sound of a strong body hitting the far side of the door spurred his understanding. She was trying to save him.

"What about you?" he asked, trying to sound honorable and brave while he fumbled with the window locks.

Heather grunted as another heavy thud hit the door, but her surprising strength held it fast. "I'll catch up. I have to protect—" she grunted again at another blow, "you, remember?"

The window miraculously slid open on the first try, and Gabe glanced out to make sure it was clear. He raised his leg over the ledge and tried to push himself out, then glanced back to Heather just as she stoically took another blow. This time he heard wood splinter somewhere, and he knew that though *she* might be able to hold out indefinitely, the house itself wouldn't. The interior door would take one or two more hits, tops, then the nagas would be on her. He really wasn't sure he could leave her like that.

A moment later, he learned the answer when he found himself pushing his dresser toward the door. Heather eyed him angrily, but didn't argue when he slid the thing behind her and helped her brace for the next hit. It came, and the top of the door cracked, sending little bits of wood raining down on them. They waited for the pause between blows, but then glass shattered in the other room, and the angry shouts and hisses became far more urgent. Gabe heard several electric discharges that sounded similar to what he'd heard a few hours before in the back of the SUV, then there was too much noise to sort anything else out.

Without so much as looking at one another, they both moved at the same time. Gabe jumped head-first through the window like he was a gymnast and not a sort-of in-shape thirty-two-year-old, and he landed gracefully enough to avoid breaking anything. He turned back in time to see Heather effortlessly throwing his entire bed toward the door. Then she turned and dived out onto the grass next to him. She rolled up into a crouch and grabbed his shirt to pull him up into a run alongside her.

"I'll take my applause later," she said. "We need to go."

"What was—Gah!" Gabe stopped abruptly as they rounded a row of hedges and found Paul crouching calmly in the middle of the next yard.

"Stop," the Hound said, his voice gruff and low. "Surrender."

Heather slipped in front of Gabe, one hand coming up in a defensive stance and the other holding her little handbag like a weapon. "Not a chance, Pauly. Not easy, anyway."

Paul grinned and let his tongue fall out of his mouth in a disturbingly canine way. "I appreciate that."

"Wait!" A voice called from behind a nearby tree. A familiar hobgoblin reluctantly shuffled out, panting as if he'd just run several miles. "We are not supposed to confront them!"

"Plans change," Paul growled. "The Hunt does not break, but flows around. The female is nothing, but the Knights cannot be allowed to have the male."

"Yes," Uklek said, gaining confidence, "but Gwendal was very clear. You heard her. My master wishes us to forge a peace, and I intend to see it happen. The Baron Jimenez has also expressed his fervent wish that they remain *alive* to be questioned. Let's hold them here and wait for the Hunters as instructed. I do not have the luxury of —"

The movement was so fast that Gabe couldn't follow it. One moment Paul was crouching calmly, then there was a blur and a squeal, and suddenly he was bent over Uklek's body, holding the hob's trachea between his teeth. The Hound shook his head viciously, sending gore across the grass, then he backhanded the goblin's remains aside to roll several feet into a flower bed. The hob didn't so much as twitch as he came to rest atop a patch of pink mums.

The sheer speed and horror of the violence was underscored by the casual way Paul then trotted back to settle in his previous position.

He rested on his haunches while his tongue worked to lick the blood from his face, then he cocked his head to the side as if to ask if there were any further arguments. Through the whole process, Gabe had barely had enough time to suck in a shocked breath.

Fortunately Heather seemed better off, and she squared her shoulders in defiance. The Hound's bloody grin answered back, and his easy crouch became something presaging a lunge. Heather stiffened, but in that moment, Gabe's front door flew off its hinges and a naga came stumbling out. Paul's eyes flicked to the thing as it sprinted for one of the motorcycles on the street, and Heather used the distraction to produce a small black pouch from her purse and toss it to the Hound's feet.

Uklek's confiscated gris-gris hit the grass with a soft thump, and at first nothing happened. Paul's eyes snapped back to them, and all his muscles went taut for the attack. But when he tried to lunge, the air above the pouch pulsed with a sickening lurch, and the Hound fell back to the grass in a heap. A tiny fire kindled inside the pouch, and it turned to ash in an eyeblink.

"Go!" Heather said, pushing Gabe hard into a stumbling run. "We've got a few seconds!"

Gabe found his balance and ran hard, but they had only made it to the other side of the street when another voice called out from behind them.

"Hey! Get back here! In the name of the—shit!"

A motorcycle fired up and Gabe glanced back to see the man in the red shirt and leather jacket exiting his house and pointing his gun at the escaping naga. The weapon fired once and the muzzle lit like a welding torch, then the cycle peeled away too fast to follow. The man cursed again, then turned his gun onto them.

"I am damned tired of following your ass all over this fucking city, dude," the man yelled across the street. "We're going to have a nice talk about—" Just then Paul got back to his feet, shaking his head woozily, and the man caught the movement. "Are you kidding me?" he said, shifting his aim to cover the Hound.

Gabe pulled Heather behind his neighbor's trees to break the line of sight, then they ran. There was another electric discharge behind them, and a loud growl. Then a yelp, and another motorcycle engine. Then silence. Soon there was nothing but the sounds of their steps and breath as they sprinted along fences and through the yards of his darkened neighborhood.

"What the hell?" Gabe panted when they'd covered some distance. It was all he could muster while focused on keeping up with Heather's easy strides. She was shorter than him, but her pace was punishing.

"Not now," she said. "I have a car a few blocks down."

Gabe ran with her for another minute until they found a white Lexus quietly idling with a middle-aged man behind the wheel. It was the guy Heather had nabbed in the parking lot. She met Gabe's eyes and lifted a finger to her lips, then she approached the driver's side of the car with a smile and a little saunter. Her hair was barely mussed.

"Hey, honey bear," she said, her southern drawl back again. "I know you've been waitin' so long, and I love you to pieces for that, but can I ask you one more teensy weensy little favor?"

She leaned forward and reached through the open window, and Gabe felt something familiar pass through her. He smelled vanilla and contentment.

"Of course, sweetness," the man replied, his voice thick with emotion.

"Thanks, big poppa. You just walk on home then and wait for a few days, you hear? I'll be 'round shortly to..." She ran a single finger under his chin, then drew it up to rest on his lips. "Reward you."

With that, the man got out of his car and obediently started walking down the block, his expensive loafers slapping the pavement in a steady rhythm.

"You drive," she said to Gabe, her voice back to normal. "It's exhausting saving your ass all the time. I need a little nap."

Gabe couldn't stop shaking his head as he got behind the wheel. "Are you actually insane?"

Heather pouted theatrically as she got in, then pulled down the visor mirror to check her lipstick. "You're hurting my feelings, Gabey Wabey. Now drive, unless you want to meet up with one of the dozen things after us."

He hit the gas and the car lurched forward. "Where?"

She settled back into the seat with a sigh and closed her eyes. "Just around for a while."

"No you don't," he said, clicking on the overhead light. "You get to explain what just happened."

She grimaced and reached up to turn it off. "I hate you." She groaned and stretched, then let out a long breath. "Suffice it to say that I found much more in the warrens beneath the library than just that giant cricket. It goes on for miles. I went down there tonight to get answers, and what I found pretty much sucked. But it's too much to tell right now."

"Summarize," Gabe said. He couldn't tell if the bond had reinforced the command or not, but he was too worked up to care.

She yawned hugely before continuing. "Fine. I went out to verify the leads Dale gave us, and I found three things. The first two were the bounty and the bikers. The description going around was your height and weight and winning disposition, and word is all over the city. Everybody wants a piece of you, Gabe, making you pretty much screwed. Gwendal's got every Umbra in a fifty-mile radius on your personal ass. So I told the bikers I'd trade your address for a share of the reward. Nobody's going to be our friends right now with that kind of money and heat on the line, but I figured if we let those guys 'capture' you, they'd be your guardian angels until they could turn you in."

Gabe scoffed and Heather blindly reached over to smack him on the arm. "It would have worked if you hadn't screwed it up," she said. "At the very least they would have been good cannon fodder. Now we're back on the run, only this time from every Umbra in the city."

He rolled the whole thing over in his head, wincing at all the sharp angles, but eventually his nature won out over his fear. "Is it really half a million dollars?"

Heather snuggled her head against the door. "Yep. Must have been recent too, otherwise we'd probably be Dale's unwilling guests right now. Needless to say, almost nobody is your friend anymore, Gabe. Hell, for five-hundred-thousand you're frankly lucky I'm bound to you."

Gabe found himself suddenly trembling, and he went silent.

Heather opened her eyes and glanced over at him. "Geez, I'm just joking. It would take a cool million for me to..." she broke off and really looked at him. "What?"

"I can't do this anymore," he said.

She sat up and her expression went from curious to sympathetic—then finally to resigned. "Fine. Kill yourself." She met his eyes for several heartbeats, then pointedly turned from him and closed hers again. "I'm free either way."

It was like a slap in the face. Crappy as his life might be sometimes, he'd never wanted to end it even at the worst. And giving himself up would probably be suicide. There was nothing to gain from that. Running away was a different matter, but then he'd be leaving his dad and he couldn't do that either. He wasn't a hero, he was sure of that, but he didn't leave people behind when they needed him. Not ever. It was an irritating trait that was earning him most of his trouble lately.

"You're right," he said. "Thanks. So what should I do?"

One of Heather's eyes opened and examined him, like a lizard inspecting a strange bug that had just landed nearby. "Did you just agree with me, thank me, and then ask me for my opinion in the same breath?"

Gabe sighed. "Do I look like I'm overburdened with other options here? You said you found out three things. What was the third?"

Heather's answering smile was barely short of luminescent. "Okay, this I can work with." She reached over and slipped a hand into his pocket, grabbing his phone but lingering there for a fraction of a second longer than was strictly proper. Gabe tensed and she laughed as she withdrew.

A moment later, she handed it back with a mapped location via a ridiculously circuitous route. "Follow," she said. Then promptly fell asleep.

CHAPTER TWENTY-THREE

```
"There are bad guys and then there are Bad Guys.
I'm the former, which makes me a lovable rogue.
The latter are the murderers and rapists. I draw
the distinction here because the law rarely
does. A guy who skims a few thousand dollars
from the church fundraiser can often go to the
same place as the guy who beats his own brother
to death with a can of pork'n'beans. Time served
is the only difference. This book is about guys
like me. I can't explain the real psychos, and I
resent being lumped in with them. I'm just as
scared of those crazy shits as you are."
```

-Excerpt from Chapter One, CONscience

    They pulled up to the apartment complex just after two in the morning. It was one of the nicer places in town and had the thorough landscaping and brick facade to prove it. It was the kind of place that well-off singles rented before settling down, or that rich college kids ruined as they stumbled through school on their parents' dime. Gabe had never lived anywhere like it, but he'd done plenty of appreciating from afar.
    "Hey," he said, nudging Heather awake, "we're here."
    She stirred and looked around drowsily. "Already?"
    Gabe glanced at the clock. It had taken him forty-five minutes to follow her path, and she had slept the whole time. He oddly didn't feel tired himself, which he attributed to the more-or-less constant stream of adrenaline. "I think that's enough beauty sleep for now," he said. "Give the other girls a fighting chance."
    She cracked a smile. "We don't all have engines of pure evil stoking our furnaces, smart ass." Then she saw Gabe's smile falter, and she backpedaled. "I mean, I assume that's what's going on. I don't know for sure, obviously."
    Gabe watched the red-gold energy play over his hands as they gripped the wheel, then he sighed and pushed the thought away to freak out about later. It was getting disturbingly easy to do that, and he knew the pile of worries would eventually come toppling down to bury

him. "It seems a likely scenario," he said. "Terrifying, but likely. Of course, I'm pretty used to taking advantages wherever I can. Anyway, you want to tell me what we're doing here?"

She stretched and groaned, pressing her palms against the roof of the car and arching her back until the metal creaked in protest. Then she yawned and blinked at him. "Getting help."

Gabe rummaged in his pocket until he found his pack of gum. He freed two pieces and offered her one. "Descriptive."

"Oh, you spoil me," she said, taking it.

"I don't think vinegar spoils," he shot back. "Now seriously, I've had one dose of your 'help' already tonight. Why don't you give me a little heads-up on this one?"

She smirked. "I can see why you're such a hit with the ladies. What girl wouldn't like to be told she smells like pickles?"

"Oh, your breath is fine," he replied. "I was actually talking about your personality. But great job proving me wrong. Answer the question, please."

Heather laughed and popped the gum into her mouth. "Fair enough. But did you know smell is the sense tied most closely to desire?"

He nodded. "You've demonstrated it well enough for a lifetime. Did you know being cryptic and evasive is the behavior tied most closely to being left alone in a parking lot?"

She held up her hands in surrender. "I found Reznick. I think it's what nerds like you would call our main quest." She sighed, and the humor slipped out of her voice. "There are so many of us now. It's unreal. There was a time that you could go for months without spotting another Umbra, but tonight I've seen dozens. Maybe it's not quite a representative sample, but Dale was right: things have changed. I just wish I knew why."

She seemed lost in thought for a moment, but snapped back into focus. "Anyway, I met a very nice tengu named Austin who had the most beautiful red hair, and he told me all about Mr. Reznick while we danced. Dale called him a doctor, but he's a bokor—a Voodoo priest—which isn't even a real Umbra. He's more like that sorcerer we met, bending stolen magic to his own use, and he specializes in the dark stuff. He has a reputation for getting anything for enough cash: snuff films, body parts, sex slaves, you name it. He's the go-to guy for uglier tastes around these parts, and that very much includes black magic."

Gabe snapped his fingers. "That's where I've heard the name! I knew some people a few years ago who tried to rope me into this counterfeit Nazi memorabilia thing, and he was mentioned as a buyer. Interested in occult stuff, I think. But much as I would have liked to screw over the kind of trash looking to buy Himmler's jock strap or Hitler's nose trimmer, I steered clear and never met the guy. We really want to deal with him?"

"You like the alternative better?"

Gabe let out a long breath. "Good point. I guess we ask him for the demonectomy and get out. No impulse purchases."

"That's the hope."

He eyed her carefully. "And bonus points if he can figure out how to break your bond, right?"

She seemed caught off-guard by the question, as if that hadn't actually occurred to her. Then she found herself again and shrugged. "I'm not a complicated girl, Gabe. I've tried to make that clear. Sex, food, and freedom: that's all I want. All at the same time if possible. Let's go."

Gabe followed her up to the glass door of complex B and watched her push the button for apartment sixteen. After a few seconds, a man's tired voice came through the intercom. "What the hell?"

Heather leaned in to the microphone. "I'm here to pick up the stuff Austin left last week." Then she leaned close to Gabe and whispered, "Code phrase."

"Tricky one," he replied. Her closeness sent a little electric buzz through his spine, and he regretted it when she pulled away. She smelled like mint and raspberries this time, and the twinkle in her eyes told him that she knew it. He was letting too much slip too often and was being careless lately. He could only really blame the evil deity in his head for maybe fifty percent of that.

"Fine," Reznick said. "I mean it's late, but whatever."

The door buzzed, and they entered. The common hallway was temperature-controlled and well-lit, and apartment sixteen was just a few doors down. Heather took the lead and rapped her knuckles on the door, then she carefully pulled a lock of hair from behind her ear and let it fall over her cheek. They waited almost a full minute, but then finally heard the click and scrape of bolts on the other side. Gabe found himself tensing for a fight, succumbing to the fallout of paranoia that the hard lessons of the last two days had taught him. But then the door swung open to reveal an unassuming man in a black t-shirt, boxers, and rubber sandals. Gabe relaxed. He had a hard time believing that even the most powerful evil creature would start a fight in his underwear and the kind of footwear you could get in a bin at a truck stop.

"You bring cash?" Reznick asked. Then he caught sight of Heather and his eyes widened cartoonishly. It was like he'd never seen a woman in person before.

Heather clearly noticed too, and she slowly brushed the loose curl from her face, making the simple movement look somehow sensual. "Can I come in?"

The man's expression brightened, and he stepped back in overwhelming invitation. "Hell yeah. You can do whatever you want, baby."

Heather went in and favored him with a sweet smile, and Gabe almost had the door shut in his face when he didn't move fast enough. He eyed the place as he entered, and his heart sank. Fast food containers and dirty dishes covered most available surfaces, and old laundry seemed to take up all the rest. A computer desk was the lone oasis of relatively clear space, and Gabe suspected that was only because the man occasionally swiped it clear for his newest round of future trash. There might have been a carpet somewhere in the mess, but it likely hadn't surfaced in years. To say the place looked nothing like a doctor's office was an insult to things that looked nothing like doctor's offices—the aftermath of a hurricane, for instance. Or the lone port-a-potty at a chili cook-off.

"To what do I owe the pleasure?" Reznick asked. He collapsed into a deep leather recliner and gestured for Heather to take a seat on a couch that might have been constructed entirely of old pizza boxes and socks.

She smiled her refusal and pointed to Gabe. "I think that would be self-evident to someone with your skills."

Reznick seemed to notice Gabe for the first time and his upper lip curled in something between a sneer and a smile. "Whoa, dude. You're pretty fucked up."

"Is that the technical term, *Doc*?" Gabe asked. "I imagine you don't meet many people who aren't."

Reznick hoisted a leg over the arm of his chair, apparently unconcerned that his boxers were far from formfitting. "Doc, huh? Naw, just an observation. You've got energy spilling out all over the place. It's weird. Is the human soul trapped in you or vice versa?"

Gabe felt a twinge of relief that he wouldn't have to explain the whole thing. "It's a god, actually," Gabe said. "He's in me, and I want him gone."

Reznick raised his eyebrows. "Sounds like you're screwed. Something with that much power won't be easy to pop out. Who sent you? Mama Tempe? Don't think I don't smell that old-style hoodoo on you."

"Dale sent us," Heather said. "You might be sensing a gris-gris we encountered tonight, but the Locust gave us your name."

Reznick watched them for another few seconds, the slick smile never leaving his face. Then he groaned and leaned over the edge of the chair to rummage through the trash. Heather tensed, but a moment later the man came back up with a small plastic drink bottle filled with a thick, dark yellow liquid.

"Here we go," he said, holding it up to the light. "Catch." The bottle flew to Gabe, but he sidestepped it. "Dude!" Reznick said, sitting forward in his chair. "You hold that or you get the fuck out. Your choice."

"What is it?" Heather asked.

"Piss mostly," he said with a chuckle. "But other stuff too. It's a legit potion. Sach Taral is the technical term, but I call it Truth Juice. Catchier."

Gabe bent to inspect it. "I'm not drinking this."

Reznick snorted. "You better fucking not. That shit's worth more than your life. I just need you to hold it, pretty boy. It won't bite." He looked to Heather. "Unlike me."

She raised an eyebrow and met his lecherous stare with one of her own. "I'm sure a handsome man like you can see fit to helping us. My gratitude would be *substantial*."

Reznick used a thumbnail to pick at something between his teeth, then spit out whatever he'd unearthed. "You can save the sexy mojo, babe." He reached down to his collar and used the same thumb to lift out a chain holding a bone charm. "Did this little ward myself. You're not talking me into giving you nothing for free. You got great tits though, so I might be interested in a trade out."

Gabe glanced at Heather for the play call, but she only had eyes for Reznick. He looked down at the bottle, then bent and gingerly picked it up between two fingers. He didn't die immediately, which was nice, but he thought he felt a slight tingle in his fingertips, and the thing seemed too heavy for its size. Nothing else happened, so he gripped it tighter. It felt like holding a bottle of warm, electric syrup.

"Good," Reznick said. "Just hold that nice and high so I can see."

Gabe complied and Heather tensed.

"Now," Reznick went on, "Are you an asshole?"

Gabe stared at the man for a second. "No. What the hell does this—" Then he stopped as the liquid in the bottle went bright red beneath his fingers. "Whoa!"

Reznick laughed. "Truth Juice! I didn't need to establish a baseline or anything, I just wanted to see your face. Those personal epiphanies are fun to watch. Now, the real questions: Did Dale send you here?"

Gabe stared hard at the bottle, which was already turning back to yellow. "Yes."

Reznick watched carefully, but nothing happened. He nodded. "Good. Are you working for, or in any way affiliated with any branch of Knights, the Chamber, or any other precept or law enforcement agencies, supernatural or otherwise?"

Gabe shook his head. "I don't know what most of that means, so no, I guess."

The bottle again stayed yellow, and Reznick nodded. "That's very good. Last one: how much money do you have?"

"Hey," Heather said, stepping forward. "Do you want to deal or not?"

Reznick lifted a forked stick from the folds of his chair and pointed it at her chest. Shiny metal caps tipped both ends, and Gabe could feel a buzz from it even at seven paces away. "Don't, sweetheart," the bokor said. "This is virgin hazel, silver-tipped and loaded with a pain hex strong enough to drop a rhino. It probably won't kill you dead, but it might make you wish you were. Just answer the question, guy."

Gabe shrugged. "Thirty bucks cash and a few hundred on my credit card."

Reznick watched the bottle, then lowered the wand. "Shit. You're not even worth robbing."

Heather relaxed again. "Then can you help him?"

"Not for thirty bucks." Reznick rose and nodded toward the door. "See you later, sweet thing."

"We don't have a lot of options here," Heather said. "What do you want?"

Gabe started to ask what else they had to give, then he saw the look on her face. "Wait, this is not how you protect—"

"Let the grown-ups talk for a minute," she interrupted, not bothering to look at him.

Reznick smirked and moved up to her. "There are lots of ways to pay. Lots of clients want lots of things, and I sell it all." He eyed Heather appraisingly. "You're a succubus, right? You've got that look. Real naughty, I bet. Video of you could be worth a couple thousand easy to the right market. Maybe I make my own film debut with you, give you a little extra for combat pay. That would cover half."

"Half?" she asked. Gabe could hear the anger creeping into her voice.

"You heard me," Reznick said. "But you might make more cash depending on how good you are with your glamour. A succubus video is good, but it wouldn't be the first. Mostly fun for me. The illegal stuff is where the real money is. Humans are, after all, pretty sick fucks." He laughed like they were sharing a joke. "So that's an option if you want. How young can you make yourself look? Hypothetically. My regular source is getting expensive for the real thing."

Gabe's fists tightened, and he suddenly felt hot.

"So crass, this one. No subtlety at all. He can be safely slaughtered."

Gabe wasn't sure whether that had been Aka Manah's thought or his own, but just then he didn't care. Every other emotion was burned away by a white-hot anger that flared to life in his chest, and his world narrowed as he watched the little man move toward Heather and lift her chin, inspecting the meat, assessing his purchase.

"She is yours, ours, mine. Protect her. Use this. All you need do is take it."

Gabe felt the unmaking power surge into his awareness, and this time he didn't bother to resist or question. The magic ran over him like molten iron, and it blinded his mind with an incoherent rage that was all too familiar. He belatedly tried to give it back, but it was all he could do to keep himself from flying apart before he could loose it at Reznick and wipe that smear of a man from the earth with the strength of a living god—which is what made him miss the takedown.

The sound of a body hitting the floor was the first thing to register, followed by a high-pitched squeal of pain. The magic suddenly receded as quickly as it had come, and Gabe felt Aka Manah curling back up into his hole. Then Heather was standing over the fallen Reznick with one of his hands bent onto itself in a painful hold and the heel of her black flat pinning his crotch to the ground.

"Be nice, and I promise I won't crush them," she said, almost kindly.

The bokor yelled and lifted the wand toward her, but she snatched it from him and crushed it in one swipe. There was a loud snap and spray of sullen green sparks, then the pieces hit the floor in a tiny cloud of smoke.

Gabe was still trying to clear the killing rage from his mind, but even so he knew the situation had tanked hard. "Wait. This is a bad idea. What are you—"

Heather's head snapped around and Gabe took an involuntary step back at the warning in her eyes. He could suddenly see the demon in her, and it stopped the question cold in his throat.

"You don't know who you're dealing with!" Reznick screamed. "I know some scary fucks who are going... Ahhhhrrgggg!" His words devolved into a growling spray of spittle as Heather leaned into him.

She turned back to drop that demonic gaze on Reznick, and his growl fell to a whine. "I've learned so much in these last few days," she said, her mild tone belying the fact that she was poised to castrate a man. "And it's all a little overwhelming, to tell the truth. But I'm frankly amazed at how depraved the world has become."

The force of the moment drove the rest of the fog from Gabe's head, and he was able to string a full thought together. "Okay, do you think this is smart?"

She ignored the question. "I've seen terrible things in my lifetimes, so don't think that I'm ignorant of what it means to be a woman or child in this world. I've made peace with it. I am also aware that I'm very much a product of that depravity, so spare me any allegations of hypocrisy. What I can't abide are those who would profit off of that misery and desperation. I may have been born of it, but you actively choose to perpetuate it—and innovate *new* travesties. Scum like you are paid to facilitate atrocities so those with enough money can be monsters by proxy. You thrive on making the world worse, enriching and encouraging villains."

Gabe searched frantically for something to do or say, but his brain returned only a blinking cursor. Heather had gone far afield, and he was way out of his depth again. "I thought we were supposed to get in and get out?"

"That was before I met him," she said. "I've seen his kind before, far too closely for comfort, in fact. We'll find another way. He's too vile to let live."

Reznick blubbered and Gabe talked over him. "We are not qualified to handle—"

"Shut up," Heather said sweetly. Then she raised her head and scanned the room. "There, I think," she said, pointing to what looked like a closet. "Open that and then try to defend him."

Gabe reluctantly moved to the door, and it felt like nearing a high-voltage power supply by the way it made his skin prickle. There was something magical in there, and it didn't feel nice. He wished he knew enough to know whether he should be scared.

"Wait!" Reznick said.

But Gabe ignored him and carefully pulled the door open—then immediately wished he hadn't. The room was tiny and meticulously clean compared to the rest of the apartment. It was arranged like a curio shop with hundreds of items displayed as if for sale. It was all dried or bottled or tightly wrapped, and all was neatly labeled with printed tags and hung on hooks or fanned out on shelves. But regardless of the presentation, there was no mistaking human body parts. He moved closer with a kind of sick fascination and studied one item hanging near the door. It was a small jaw bone, very white, and very clean, and with teeth that were tiny and close. The tag read, "Ashley -Female- 6 yrs".

Gabe stumbled back and fought down a rush of bile in his throat. His eyes flitted of their own accord between severed fingers, and dried scalps, and femurs hung up like toys on a rack. There were amulets and wands and jars of dark liquid too, and all of it seeped a malevolent power that made him want to vomit. He looked away before he lost it, then fled from the room to find Heather waiting and nodding grimly.

"Dark magic," she said. "This is not a good man." She turned to consider her captive. "Hexes, curses, blood arts, carnal sways... And necromancy. Tell me I'm wrong."

"Fuck you, bitch," Reznick snarled. "The market existed long before me. Before you too. I'm a fucking vendor, is all. A whore succubus has no right to judge."

Heather held out a hand to Gabe. "Give me the bottle."

He numbly handed her the Sach Taral.

"You asked your questions, now we get ours," she said to Reznick. Then she slapped the bottle into the hand she held, crushing his fingers closed around it. The bokor yelled again, but she ignored it. "Now, my friend has a god trapped in his head. How can we help him?"

Reznick's jaw flexed, but a little twist of Heather's foot killed the defiance. He sagged into himself. "You can't," he blubbered. "Or at least, I can't. Not without an equal measure of power to balance the god. A counterweight, right? You'd need another god or the equivalent in sacrifices. Human. Dozens. Also a magical catalyst to break the stalemate, and it has to come from him. Fucking impossible. Magic his human ass doesn't have. Then a sacrificial Umbra, a new human vessel, and a ritual to contain the whole fucking thing so the backlash doesn't tear the veil a new asshole. That last I do have, alright? But the rest... It's out of my league."

They watched the bottle the whole time he spoke, but nothing changed, and Gabe's hopes drowned in that yellow sludge.

Heather sighed. "Fine. Then what do you suggest we do?"

Reznick managed a bitter little chuckle, then seemed to regret it. "Nothing to do. He can try to burn that leaking power before it kills him, but that god stank will just keep coming. He'll have to burn it off for the rest of his life—which probably won't be more than a day or two, fuck you very much." Again the bottle stayed yellow. "Killing him now would be faster. Probably kinder. I can certainly volunteer—"

Heather leaned into the man again, and his teeth slammed together. "Treat the symptoms then," she said. "How does he burn off the power for now?"

Reznick coughed before responding. "Gaaah, bitch! I'm gonna fucking kill... Magic! How the fuck else? Perform a miracle, pull a rabbit from a hat, I don't give a goddamned shit. Just use it!" He coughed again. "You got your answers. Let me go!"

"One more thing," she said. "Who's your supplier? Where do the body parts come from?"

Reznick looked for an instant like he might try to lie, but the Sach Taral was still in his hand, and Heather was leaving no doubt as to how much bullshit she was prepared to take. Gabe had never seen her so serious, and he wasn't sure if he preferred this new version. Yet another layer of the woman unfolded, and yet another rethink of his two-dimensional picture of her.

The man spluttered out the address, and the liquid remained a sickly yellow. It wasn't far.

Heather looked up at Gabe, and her expression was perfectly blank. "Go outside."

Gabe searched her eyes and didn't like what he found. "I'll go when you do," he said.

She took a deep breath, and he could feel her power gathering. He had a hard time keeping hold of the sensation, as if it was psychically slippery, but for one fleeting moment he'd had an impression of a blooming rose, delicate and thorny and beautiful beyond reason. Then it slammed into him.

"GO OUTSIDE, GABE."

The words hit him like a tidal wave of warm honey, pressing him down hard beneath comfort and sweetness until his own thoughts were too smothered to argue with the simple suggestion. But somehow knowing that it was coming made a difference, and he managed to keep a bubble around his thoughts long enough to allow the tempting offer of mindless obedience to pass over without taking hold. He shuddered hard and took a ragged breath. "No thanks."

Her mouth opened in surprise, then she shook her head. "Good job." They stared at one another until her eyes softened and she looked away. "Please?"

The word was so simple and vulnerable that Gabe almost gave in. But something told him he shouldn't let her do this. A minute ago, he had been prepared to squash Reznick like a bug, but that had been a product of creeping insanity and an evil god—not good logic. His opinion of Heather straddled a thin line between necessity and respect, and he suspected that the next few moments could lead to something irredeemable. The man deserved it, certainly, but that didn't make it right.

"No," he said, trying to sound understanding but implacable. "He's disgusting and terrible, but this is not our job."

"That's the problem!" she said, her voice rising. "We can't leave him at our backs, and the world is a worse place with him in it. But there's nobody for assholes like this to answer to anymore! The Umbral Council is gone. *Gone!* You can't understand how bad that is. They were never perfect, but they held the worst of this shit at bay. There are supposed to be stronger and wiser Umbras out there. Gods in control and fixing what's broken. Now, nothing? Fucking Barons that don't seem to care about the filth thriving in their little city? If we don't take care of him, who will?"

Gabe shook his head. He'd never seen her lose control. "You know that I don't understand any of what's going on, but this wouldn't be defense or protection or even justice. It's murder. We don't execute people in cold blood based on a glimpse of evidence. Maybe your old council did that, but we don't. That's not who we are."

Heather laughed bitterly. "You have no idea who I am."

"You're right," he said, spreading his hands. "But I have a rough outline. And it doesn't change anything. I'm not going to let you sink to his level. For your own good, we need to leave *now*."

He saw real anger blossom on her face, and he braced for it. But an instant later, she deflated and moved to join him. Gabe suddenly remembered the bond and cursed himself. He had just forced her to drop something she clearly felt strongly about. He wanted to apologize right there, but feared it would only make things worse. He certainly couldn't change his mind and watch her execute the man, but he had to make it right.

Reznick was cursing and writhing in agony on the floor, holding his groin for dear life. He still held onto the bottle like a lifeline, and the contents sloshed as he rocked back and forth. The scum did deserve to be punished. Maybe it wasn't their place to murder him, but that wasn't the only option for someone with a little creativity.

Gabe consciously refrained from looking back at the body parts as he moved past Reznick to sit at the computer. The password was auto-saved, and it took him no time at all to find what he was looking for. Seven minutes later, he wiped down the keyboard and picked up the man's phone.

"Nine-one-one, what is your emergency?" the voice said on the other end.

"My name is Efrem Reznick," Gabe said, doing what he thought was a fair impersonation. He coughed and cleared his throat just to cast some doubt about the recording if this somehow ended up in court. "I'd like to confess to some murders. I have body parts in my closet. I just... I can't take it anymore." He gave the operator the address, then hung up.

Reznick pulled himself to a sitting position, but Heather moved up beside him, a silent, waiting threat.

"I'd say you have ten minutes," Gabe said, wiping the phone before he threw it against the wall. That felt good. Then he reached down and snatched the Sach Taral from the man's hands. He opened it and poured the disgusting yellow sludge onto the computer keyboard. There were no dramatic sparks or smoke, which was disappointing, but he doubted the keys were functional anymore. That was really the point.

The man snarled, but the effect was minor coming from someone tenderly holding his own crotch. "They won't find anything," he said. "You don't think I've prepared for this? I'm a bokor, you ignorant shits! I don't even need to find you to fuck you up!"

Gabe nodded for Heather to follow him out. "I'm sure you're right. The police probably *won't* find anything. You're too good for that. But they'll be seen coming here."

Reznick stopped frothing, and for the first time looked genuinely perplexed. "What?"

Gabe opened the door for Heather, then wiped his prints from the handle with his shirt. "You really shouldn't leave your invoice lists right on your home computer. What if somebody wanted to e-mail every one of your personal and professional contacts about your intention to turn your records over to the authorities? You'd be super screwed."

Reznick's face went white and his breath caught.

Gabe used his deadliest smile. "And then the human police show up to investigate on the same night? I know how this game works. Word gets around. I imagine some of those scary fucks you were talking about might be concerned. They might not feel great about their names being dragged into the legal system, records getting out, everybody learning the twisted bullshit they bought from you. Those people might want to talk to you very badly. Very soon."

Reznick made a sound somewhere between a whine and growl. "You didn't. You said you couldn't kill me... Not your place..."

"Yeah," Gabe said as he pulled the door closed, "but I'm an asshole, remember?"

He stopped to wipe the outside handle clean, and when he turned, Heather was standing right behind him.

"You did that for me," she said, her face unreadable.

"I mean, I did that for humanity. But yeah, I thought you seemed—"

Everything stopped as Heather pressed him against the door and kissed him. For an instant he considered pushing her away, until he realized that there was no power woven behind it, no enticements or seductions. It was just the moment. Just a girl kissing a boy because she wanted to, and that was its own kind of magic.

A few seconds or hours later, Heather pulled away and took a deep breath. "Thank you," she said. "I don't get many gifts that aren't solicited."

Gabe nodded dumbly, then was startled to remember that they were still standing right outside the door of a Voodoo wizard who really wanted to kill them. He grabbed Heather's hand and pulled her down the hall.

"So you are good for something," she said.

Gabe started to laugh, then glanced over at her. "Wait, the e-mail thing, or the kissing?"

Her eyes sparkled, but she pointedly refused to answer as they ran back to the car.

CHAPTER TWENTY-FOUR

"I understand the gateway crime argument. It seems like once you've crossed that line, everything on the other side should be easier. Stole a candy bar? You're a potential murderer. But that only holds true if you've never glimpsed the real dark side. Those of us who live over here know it's more like a series of islands, each one a new wrong, and all of them tenuously bridged with increasing desperation and fraying justifications. It's all accessible with the proper motivation. Even for you."

-Excerpt from Chapter Seven, CONscience

Heather insisted they check out the address Reznick had given them, and Gabe had agreed for some reason that had absolutely nothing to do with the kiss. It was only a few minutes away after all, and it wasn't like he could head home. There might not be a home to head back to.

Their next logical step was to skip town to chase after the other leads Dale had given them. Just because Reznick had been a bust, didn't mean the others would be. It killed him to leave his dad behind, but he had already started mentally drafting a letter to the people at the care facility. And he could only hope the few hundred dollars he could scrape together would be enough to tide them over. He just needed his dad safe until this was finished. One less thing to agonize over. One less person in harm's way. He could track down Dale's contacts until he had his solution, then he'd come back and fix everything. That was the plan. So he figured he might as well indulge Heather's request before dragging her out on a quest to save his life.

The place turned out to be a big dilapidated two-story number with attached garage and a yard that looked like it was faithfully watered with urine. It sat nestled between another house that looked nearly as bad and the gravel parking lot of an abandoned mechanic's shop. The house was dark, which wasn't much of a shock at three in the morning, but the whole place had the shimmer of what he'd come to recognize as a glamour.

"Should I be worried that I'm starting to sense and see magic stuff more clearly?" he asked. "I can still see in the dark too, and I'm not tired at all. I feel... Stronger, I guess. I can't help but think those might be bad signs."

"You're not going to tell her about our little episodes?"

He squashed the whisper. Heather was the only person in his life that was helping him right now. He wasn't about to test the limits of the bond by letting her know he was already going insane.

She was studying the house as she replied. "Every Umbra is different, and so is every set of powers. Some can see in the dark, some can't. Some don't need any sleep at all, some hibernate for entire seasons. Just depends on the legend."

"Except I'm not an Umbra," Gabe said, making it half question.

Heather shook her head dismissively. "Right, of course. But you are being exposed to his power. A *god's* power. It must be juicing you up. You're like the moon to Aka Manah's sun and you can't help but reflect some of him—for better or worse. Maybe your body is instinctively using some of that leaking energy for your benefit, and all the rest is overspill."

"Maybe," Gabe said. He lifted his hand and studied the red gold aura. It looked brighter than before. He felt hot again. Then he slapped the hand back onto the steering wheel and bounced his head off of the headrest a few times in irritation. He knew she was right, but hearing it out loud didn't feel good. "I just wish I knew what the hell was going on, you know? I wish somebody could tell me what to do."

"I wish that too, Gabe. But Gandalf isn't real as far as I know. You have to figure out the exposition for this story yourself." She turned and gave him a sympathetic look that took any sting out of her words. "I will help you if I can. By any means possible. I mean that."

He nodded, and she gave him a tight smile and patted his leg. It was another little sincere moment between them, and it seemed like a good time to talk. His feelings for her were complicated and had been evolving every hour or so since they'd met. He wanted to see where she stood and make some apologies—maybe hammer out what this partnership might become. "Hey," he said, feeling the moment line up just right, "when this whole thing started... I'm sorry for acting like—"

Right then she threw open the car door and jumped out into the street, crossing the distance to the yard in a few quick steps before Gabe could even process what was happening. By the time his brain caught up, she was already crunching through the dead grass on her way to a gate in the chain-link fence around the back yard.

"...an ass," he finished. He jumped out of the car and muttered to himself, "Thanks, Gabe. I forgive you. Let's be best friends."

He crossed the street to the yard, and the grass beneath his feet was like walking on potato chips. He tried tiptoeing to compensate and ended up looking like a cartoon villain. Heather had already slipped through the gate by the time he made it that far, and it was standing open just enough for him to wiggle through without testing the noise of the hinges. The backyard wasn't in much better condition, but it had less actual grass and more mud, which seemed better somehow. He spotted Heather inspecting the safety bar on a sliding door.

"What are you doing?" he whispered.

She ignored him, and Gabe cursed himself. Despite his better judgment, survival instincts, recent experience, and a general feeling about her that wavered between high-school lust and toilet-full-of-spiders terror, he kept following her without thinking. He normally calculated his plan before taking a bath, but lately he just did whatever popped into his head. It wasn't an upgrade.

He moved closer and whispered in her ear. "You said you wanted to look."

"That's what I'm doing," she hissed. "I don't have any better ideas, do you?" Then she turned and went up the stairs of a big deck to another sliding door. This one was slightly ajar.

Gabe followed her and looked around. Empty beer bottles and food containers littered the deck, and a half-covered hot tub steamed off to one side. The interior lights of the tub were still on and they illuminated everything in a soft blue glow. It looked like the residents had left the remnants of a party to be cleaned up later, but otherwise the place looked fairly innocuous. Throw in a half-busted ping pong table and maybe an inexplicable mannequin, and it was a carbon-copy of half of the houses near campus. It certainly didn't look like the lair of black magic contraband dealers. Gabe turned to whisper this to Heather, but only glimpsed her as she disappeared through the door and into the house. He hesitated, then plunged in after her.

The place didn't look any better on the inside. Torn and overturned furniture littered the living room, and the hardwood floors sported a vast array of deep gouges and dark stains. The house itself smelled like an unwashed toilet, but the vileness extended much deeper. Just from where he stood Gabe could feel the sickening weight of depravity soaked into walls, and he couldn't force himself to take another step against that press. Heather had gone ahead and stopped at two sawhorses and a sheet of plywood that was serving as a kitchen table. Some of the stench was coming from dark crusted plates there, but she didn't seem to notice as she gingerly lifted a pair of silver handcuffs. She dangled them from the chain, letting them twist to display the lines of dried blood along the edges.

That was it for Gabe. He turned and left the house, and the cool air felt like salvation as it hit his face. He went straight to the back railing and wrapped his hands around the wood to keep himself standing. Then he looked up to the night sky for something clean and pure to focus on to let the feeling of sick dread bleed away.

Heather appeared a minute later with spread hands and a quizzical expression. Gabe returned the same gesture, and her face slipped into annoyance. She marched out to him and leaned in to whisper. "They're passed out. Two Umbras. Lots more shady stuff in there. Weird tools, medical tables, shackles. These are our guys."

"What guys?"

Heather gestured back into the house. "For you to burn up that power on. Let's go."

"What?" Gabe hissed.

She sighed and took up his hands, showing him Aka Manah's energy soaking through his skin. "Gabe, the ignorant puppy thing was cute for a while, but you need to catch up. This is not good. Human's don't have magic of their own. Sorcerers, bokors, hexen—they all steal or co-opt the magic of others for their own uses, but they have mechanisms to store and use it. Rituals and charms and stuff. You don't have those, so this power will eat you alive. Forget that it makes you stand out like a beacon to all the people who want to crack your head open. In another day, it will make you dead. Okay? That's not speculation. I can't lie to you. You're special insofar as you're still alive at this point—which is amazing—but you're not special enough to ignore this indefinitely."

Gabe swallowed and opened his mouth to protest, but she gripped his hands hard. "No," she said. "This is it. This is the way. The noble antihero thing you have going on is fine for normal circumstances, but for me to keep you safe I need to help you burn off that power. And the only thing we know it's good for is destruction."

The implication sank in and he shook his head. "Wait..."

"No!" Her anger was hot and quick, and it burned out just as fast. Her eyes softened and she let his hands drop. "No, Gabe. We've found some real bad guys. Grave robbers definitely, but you don't handcuff dead people. Kidnappers, slavers, murderers—maybe lots more. They need to be shut down. Reznick had fetishes and flesh charms back there. Bones and body parts. These are the suppliers. They get it from somewhere, and the magic is strongest when it's fresh. They deserve it, and you need it. Turn your misfiring conscience off, because this is the only way."

"You want..." He paused and lined up his racing thoughts. "You want me to kill them?" Heather tried to speak to justify it further, but this time Gabe pressed over her. "You want me to walk into a house and use magic to murder two people? I thought *I* was supposed to be the insane one?"

She tried to take up his hands again, but he threw her off. "No. Just, no."

"Gabe, this is the only—"

"No!" he said, louder than he should have. "You want to run a con on these guys? Screw them over? Fine. I'm your man. But this Rambo stuff isn't me. Got it? The Hunters were self-defense. This is... I *don't* freaking kill people!"

Her expression darkened and her voice went razor thin. "What don't you understand about this? You're on the verge of splitting in half like an egg, and nothing will be gained from it. Your death will be a waste, and that's assuming you don't turn into some kind of monster that's the worst of both of you."

"What do you care? You're free either way!"

That brought her up short. "I'm just... I guess I don't know."

He threw up his hands. "I get it, okay? But I'm not a killer. I'm not equipped. You may be strong enough to throw a dude through a window, but I have to take a nap after unloading groceries. We should be driving out of town right now. Getting real help. That's the smart play."

"Smart play, right. And have every Umbra in the Midwest following us." She scoffed. "But let's stand here and argue about this some more, huh? Like it or not, Gabriel, your life is about more than running now. Doesn't your name at least mean anything to you? There are blood-soaked demons in there. Act like an archangel and smite, for God's sake."

Gabe crossed his arms. "You're thinking of Michael. He's the fighter. My guy shows up early and plays a horn."

Heather stared at him for a few seconds, then shook her head in disgust and turned back to the house to disappear inside. He supposed he had won the exchange, but he felt worse off for it. He lingered on the deck for a few more minutes, hopeful she would come storming out and they could come up with a real plan that didn't involve frontal assault, but she never returned. So he started making his way back to the car, feeling wise, but also like a coward.

"She's not wrong. Using the power would keep you alive longer."

"Shut up," Gabe muttered. "I trust you less than I do her, and that's saying something."

He made it as far as the bottom of the stairs when he heard a noise from inside. It was muffled by the walls, but it sounded like fighting. He wavered there for a moment, considering going back up to see if there was anything he could do to help, but then his long-absent common sense took over and got his feet moving toward the car again. She didn't need him. Living through the night was the thing to do. He could figure out the rest later. He'd get out of town, find help, and lie low. There were other ways. There had to be.

As he passed the lower sliding doors, the choice was taken from him when a screaming mass of bare skin and fury blasted through the glass, just barely missing him on a tumbling path to the middle of the yard. Gabe threw up his hands against the flying shards and dropped to the ground just as another shape came spilling out of the empty frame.

Heather's shoes crunched over the debris and she held another of the naked, fleshy things suspended by the neck. It writhed and hissed in her grip as they moved away from the house, but she held it fast. She met Gabe's eyes as he stared up at her in shock, and she managed a sly smile that told Gabe everything he needed to know: checkmate. Then the creature she was holding slammed a fist into her head that sent her sprawling back into a bed of shattered glass. She didn't rise, but the creature did.

CHAPTER TWENTY-FIVE

"I play fair with my colleagues, but I can't tell you how many times other con artists have tried to double-cross me. It's almost like a game to see who's best. And I've never been beaten. At least, not since those early days with my dad when I didn't know I was playing."

-Excerpt from Chapter Three, CONscience

    Gabe's senses focused of their own accord, rapidly feeding him information as he backed away. The thing was almost man-sized, but horribly deformed—its back bent in a drastic s-curve, with a neck that was too thin and limbs that were far too long. It was hairless and pale like something subterranean, and its huge hands and feet ended in ragged nails that were more like animal claws. A wide mouth split its face and brimmed with jagged, broken teeth.

    The thing lunged for him, and Gabe dived to the right just as one of those long arms swiped in. Somehow he managed to roll up with his feet under him, and the shock of even accidental physical competence made him almost pitch forward with the momentum. He turned it into a long step, then found his balance and ran to the gate before he dared a look over his shoulder.

    But the thing hadn't pursued him. Instead, it had loped over to help its friend gain its feet, and Gabe could now see that the trip through the plate glass hadn't done that one any favors. Dark blood oozed from dozens of cuts, and the thing looked shaky as it tried to stand. Gabe looked back to Heather. She was still lying motionless near the house, and for the first time she looked truly helpless. He could escape from yet another terrifying situation if he just turned and went through the gate, yet he froze with his hand on the fence. He knew he couldn't leave her, and he didn't even try to fight it this time. This was clearly her fault, but she'd thought she was helping him in her own weird way. He hadn't had that in his life since...ever.

    He let go of the fence. But before he could move toward Heather, the creatures stumbled in the same direction and closed the gap to her with alarming speed. Gabe could only watch in horror as the uninjured monster reached her, then bent to tug forcefully at her jeans.

A button popped on the second pull and the tight denim slid partly down her right hip. At first Gabe couldn't believe what he was seeing, then he couldn't believe he was doubting it. He didn't curse often or particularly well, but the last two days made him want to get better at it. Every rational fiber in him kept screaming that he should just let Heather leak out of his life, but then things like this kept coming up to force him into being some kind of stupid freaking hero. It was getting old.

He ran his eyes over the yard looking for something to use as a weapon, and spotted the glint of a long metal shape nestled in the dead grass. The safety bar from the shattered sliding door had flown into the yard and had miraculously landed only a few paces away. It was better than nothing. Gabe sprinted forward and scooped up his new club mid-stride, hefting it confidently as if he had any plan other than swinging hard. The bleeding monster had started mindlessly pawing at Heather's pants as they stubbornly resisted, and the second creature had to push its friend away to have its own try. The bleeding one fell back in a heap, and the second monster straddled Heather to fumble for her zipper. It never heard Gabe coming.

The metal was hollow but heavy enough to do the job, and Gabe brought the thing around like a baseball bat into the monster's vulture neck. The thud of contact jolted through his hands and arms, and for an instant he feared that the sound of cracking bones had come from him. Then he watched numbly as the monster's head flopped to one side, and the creature slumped down right on top of Heather. He stared at the thing in disbelief, shocked that something had actually worked as intended. It seemed too easy compared to what he'd been through lately, and he wondered if he might be finally getting the hang of things. Then the universe answered him as a bloody arm took him full across the ribs.

Time and space went fluid for a few seconds before Gabe came around to find himself sprawled on the lawn and fighting for breath. He tried to sit up to get his bearings, but the sky above him suddenly darkened as a bleeding sack of skin blotted out the stars. Gabe instinctively rolled to his right just as a clawed hand struck down to where his stomach would have been. He heard the impact hit earth, and the terror of losing his entrails gave him a burst of panic that shot a breath down his throat and propelled him to his feet.

The monster followed. Even slowed by its injuries, it was still depressingly fast. And Gabe barely dodged its swiping attacks as he scrambled toward the back fence. He ducked an awkward slash at his head, then backpedaled to keep the thing in sight as he searched for options. He could feel the fence looming up behind him, ready to pin him, and in desperation, he lashed out with an awkward kick that amazingly connected with the thing's thigh. The creature stumbled and fell, planting a hand to the ground to catch itself, and Gabe used the moment to get another two steps away.

But he knew it wouldn't be enough. In his haste, he'd fled to the far side of the yard, putting the creature between him and the only gate. Heather was still down as well, and he'd already established that he couldn't leave her. The monster was regaining its feet, and even bleeding as it was, it still looked more than capable of tearing him apart. He feinted left and then took a few steps to the right, but the monster matched him and lunged forward with those ragged claws. Gabe danced away, thanking his luck one more time just as he felt the wood of the fence press against his shoulders. There was nowhere left to go. A mindless desperation started thrumming in his chest.

"I am good at opening new ways."

Gabe had spent his entire life erecting walls within himself, blocking out his real emotions and thoughts thoroughly enough to convincingly play fictional characters. But as he stared into the face of monstrous death, none of it prevented the panic. It wasn't fair. None of this was supposed to be real. His legs turned to water, and the roar of his own pulse filled his ears until his brain could do nothing more than flash one-word concepts up like emergency road signs in a blizzard: Run. Fight. Die.

"I can help. You have power to burn."

The creature shifted its weight, and Gabe could already see the attack playing out. He would try to dodge or block, but he had no training, and the thing was strong enough to lay out Heather. He'd been running on pure luck so far, and that was used up. It was all over except for the dying.

"You have but to ask. This is a chance to save her. And yourself."

Gabe closed his eyes and lifted his arms to protect his face, ready for the pain and release of death. He heard the crunch of grass as the thing began its attack, and he held his breath without knowing why.

"Yes," he said.

The world shattered, and he was once again in the frozen moment of his own mind. It took him a beat to process it, but he acclimated better this time. The white door was just as he'd left it—closed and more real than reality. Then the indistinct outline of Aka Manah was there in its place, and Gabe could see the wisps of the goldish glow like a heat haze coming off of him. He seemed more present this time, and his power filled the expanse of Gabe's mind like smoke from a dying fire.

"I have a notion you could use my help again," Aka Manah said, casually inspecting the frozen monster with its clawed hand hanging mid-strike.

Gabe almost agreed wholeheartedly, then remembered who he was dealing with. "Not really," he said. "I've got this guy pretty much where I want him."

Aka Manah sighed. "Of course. You appear to be right on the verge of a great victory."

Gabe matched the god's movements to keep his distance, but tried to make it look casual. "Maybe I am. What do you want this time?"

"So abrupt. We needn't hurry this. I enjoy the dance."

"I do too, under normal circumstances. This doesn't qualify."

"Oh, excellent," Aka Manah said cheerfully. "Then I needn't rouse myself in your defense."

Gabe knew he was being manipulated and that the god had just as much to lose here, but he didn't have the energy to spar anymore. "What if I just ask for advice? What would that cost?"

Aka Manah grew serious again. "You know very well what I want. What we both *need*."

"Look, I want you out as much as you do, but I have more information now," Gabe said. "Apparently it's going to take a crap ton of power to budge you. Freaking human sacrifices. Or I can die and maybe we both go down the drain. We have to come up with another way."

Aka Manah tutted and seemed to drift off. "There are always options. Do you know how powerful the human subconscious is? Much stronger and more capable than you'd think. Gabriel Delling could never have tricked me into this situation nor have survived the pressure of it, but the imprint of proto-humanity written into your bones, that's another matter." He laughed, the sound like an aristocratic hyena. "Humans were once far more formidable. Masters of both Earth and Ether before the first Umbra ever materialized. Sorcerers are perhaps a faint echo of that heritage, singing snippets of the old Music of Making, but nothing near to what you once were. Your blood is so diluted now. Weak." He raised a hazy finger. "Yet the power remains. Your minds and souls have forgotten how to use what you have, but it is still there, untapped and wasted except to birth Umbras from the Ether. A byproduct of your former glory. That's why sacrifices are so useful. You are spiritual cattle. All that psychic meat just hanging from your soul, ready to be gobbled."

Gabe finally understood the tangent and shook his head. "If you think I'm going to kill people to free you, you're barking up the wrong tree. The wrong forest, even, on the wrong freaking planet. Not an option."

Aka Manah waved a hand. "An awfully virtuous stance for someone whose life hangs in the balance. But just an observation. I thought you'd like to know more about your situation." He turned back to the frozen monster and inspected. "Ah yes. I can help you. Here is my offer. I will answer one question for one sense. Sight, sound, smell, touch, in that order."

Gabe's mind raced ahead, trying to plan out his steps in advance. "You seem pretty well informed as it is. Why ask for this?"

"I get impressions and notions, but nothing definitive. I can listen but not really hear here. Look but not really see, you see? And it's all filtered through your thoughts before I get a look. Like a secondhand account of an event. All I'm asking for is direct input. No control, no tricks. Just pretty pictures and sounds."

Gabe almost laughed. "An entire sense for one measly question? That sounds like a slippery slope to you taking over my body. And if you think I'm going anywhere near that again, you're insane."

Aka Manah chuckled. "Oh, I'm certainly getting close, but that puts me in good company, doesn't it?" He flicked a long hand to one side, and suddenly the shimmering outline of an hourglass carved itself into the air. The bottom was already two-thirds full. "I give us another day at most before one or both of us are raving maniacs. Won't that be fun? But very well. Make me an offer. Or you may leave and die. I'm starting to believe that a thousand more years walled behind the precepts in the Ether would be preferable to your company. Your universe may face the Emptiness alone for all I care."

Gabe flailed for a response that would give him the upper hand, but he could only stare at the grains of illusory sand that hung suspended above the huge pile at the bottom. Eventually he just took a shot in the dark. "An even trade," he said. "A question for a question."

Aka Manah seemed to seriously consider before responding. "No. But not bad. The problem comes in quality. There is no single thing you know that will be anywhere near as valuable as anything I know. It would be like trading a diamond for a stone. Technically they may be the same size, but in terms of value—"

"Got it," Gabe said, cutting him off. "So what then?"

"Memories," Aka Manah replied smoothly. The suggestion felt a little too quick, as if it had been prepared well in advance. "For every question you ask, I get to see a year of your life. If I can't have sight, I can at least use your experience to catch up to the outside world. The Ether is *hazy*. We only get impressions. Normally the memories are right there waiting for me to absorb, but this time, alas, all did not go as planned. I got your language and some concepts and a few pictures, but precious else came to me before our little tussle. I would like to fill in the gaps. Simple."

Gabe rolled the offer around in his mind and inspected it for holes. It felt gross, like letting a stranger read his diary while wearing his underwear, but he couldn't see the actual harm. He still haggled by reflex. "One day."

"Oh no," Aka Manah replied. "As much as I love negotiation, I'm afraid these terms are set. One year or nothing."

Gabe glanced again at the monster outside, and then at Heather's still form in the grass. If he was going to die anyway—in the next few seconds or next few days—his memories weren't really that valuable. "I have additional stipulations."

Aka Manah's shape seemed to firm up for a second and he looked eager. "I wouldn't respect you if you didn't. Go on."

"First, only questions posed after the deal has been struck are eligible to be tallied. There's no retro pay here. Second, only questions beginning with the phrase 'my question is' are reimbursable. I'm not going to pay you when I accidentally ask you how your day was. And third, all answers must be truthful to the best of your knowledge. No half-truths or slippery responses. The spirit of the question must be satisfied, and it must be done immediately following the question. Agreed?"

Aka Manah hummed as he mulled the terms. "Agreed. I must say, human, you are admirably adept at this for an idiot."

"Great. Thanks," Gabe said. "You'll also have to teach me how to give you access to my memories."

"A simple thing. Ask your question and I will guide you."

Gabe had portioned off a sliver of his mind to set to the task and had it prepared already. "My question is: With the resources at my immediate disposal, what is the easiest and quickest way to subdue the thing attacking me?"

Aka Manah gestured to the monster like a lecturer. "You are facing a preta. I know you didn't ask that, but I'm feeling magnanimous. It is a spirit of deep hunger and desperation, and this one appears wounded, which will make it even more rabid. It can be killed by conventional means, though I assume that none of those are easy options for you. In that case, I suggest taking an offer of power from me, and rendering the creature down to its component parts. Obviously there will be an additional cost."

Gabe cursed himself for not considering that angle. Of course the god would try to upsell him. Then a thought occurred to him. "This is energy here, isn't it?" he asked, running his fingers through the diffuse mist. "I've been told I need to take care of this somehow. To burn it off. You even said so yourself."

Aka Manah was very carefully silent, and Gabe took that as confirmation that at least one part of his theory was correct. "You're leaking it, aren't you?" he asked. "Maybe trying to get a prybar through the cracks? Or leave a breadcrumb trail for Gwendal? Or maybe you can't help it. Regardless, it's in my best interest to shut it down."

Aka Manah didn't speak, but his aspect seemed to grow less distinct.

Gabe's confidence went up another notch. "My question is: How can I use this power myself, at-will, and without your future help?"

There was no sound, but Gabe felt the pressure of Aka Manah's presence increase, like someone looming over him menacingly. He couldn't describe how he knew, but it was clear that this was something the god would rather not answer. Then the form suddenly expanded and became a massive shape, at least ten feet tall with a long sharp muzzle and huge horns curving out from each temple. The fingers on its hands extended like spider legs, and the bottom half of its body turned to writhing smoke and fire. It opened its mouth and the darkness inside was total.

Gabe swallowed his terror and held his ground. It wasn't real. "I could clarify for you if that was too complicated," he said.

The god took a huge breath as if intending to breathe fire down on him, and then he laughed. It was long and loud, shaking the foundations of Gabe's mind with real pain directly in the center of his brain. It rolled out like a thunderstorm of mirth to every corner of their shared space until it felt like the walls would crumble from the strain. Gabe tried to cover his ears, but it did no good.

Then Aka Manah stopped, and the space fell silent as he shrank back into himself until he was roughly human again. "You have absolutely no idea what you just asked for," he said. "You are far smarter and slightly braver than I gave you credit for, but I will genuinely enjoy seeing how this plays out. I told you that your blood is diluted. Now we shall see precisely how much."

Without another word, Gabe felt something pass from him to Aka Manah: two years of memories. But it happened in an instant, and it wasn't what he expected. It was like the god had reached into him to sift through his thoughts like an archivist, picking and choosing what he wanted and discarding the rest—and Gabe understood the mistake at once. Aka Manah hadn't taken two years *in whole* as Gabe had intended. He had taken two years *in total*. It was a highlight reel of Gabe's entire life, all the best and worst of his memories, and it was already too late to stop.

He started to protest, then realized that he now stood alone in an empty hallway. Stone walls surrounded him, and at the end, there was a small table holding a single closed book. He knew it had to be another construct of his psyche, like the door to the Ether and the frozen moments with Aka Manah. Something too big was happening, and this was the overlay. But before he could study it further, the book opened.

In it was...nothing. Not merely blank paper, but an utter emptiness that stretched swollen and suffocating down into eternity within the pages. It was as if the night sky had devoured every thing in it and wanted more and had been bound in leather. Gabe took an involuntary step back from the book before remembering he wasn't physically there, but then couldn't help it and took another. Staring into that nothingness was more terrifying than anything he'd ever imagined, and just the impression of something beneath his feet kept him from panic. It was too much empty, too much unbroken dark, and yet he couldn't shake the overwhelming feeling that there was something there within. Something watching.

The Long Hollow. The Emptiness. The Endless Dark. The names dropped like rocks into his gut, unfamiliar and jagged and ready to consume him, but his mind rejected them like viruses and cast them back out. It was too much. All of existence was gone into its gullet, and it—*It*—was still hungry. And It saw him. And reached.

Gabe recoiled from the edge of that madness, and his thoughts flailed for purchase. It was some kind of trick. It couldn't be real. It was the afterlife or insanity. When had he gone wrong? When had he died? When had he broken?

Then Aka Manah's voice came through the stone and spoke a word that etched itself in flowing lines across the black: *"Kraklehm."*

Gabe felt the word enter him, sinking into his bones in a way that would forever be his, and lighting an azure spark that dropped below his perception to be forgotten until he needed it again. As it went, it cast a light on the nothing, and the Emptiness receded from it as if afraid. The Endless Dark pulled back and down into the pages, going for now but never forever, and the book began to close. It shut with a soft thump, and Gabe was left standing there as something both new and very old.

CHAPTER TWENTY-SIX

```
"It's easy to split people up into sheep and
wolves, but I'm more like a shepherd. At the end
of the day, the shepherd still eats the sheep,
but he does so quietly and smiling. And the rest
of the flock still runs to him after."

-Excerpt from Chapter Eight, CONscience
```

 Gabe watched from the motel window as his dad got out of the car with an unfamiliar woman. Another new town and another new lady who wasn't his mom. Though she would eventually run away just as surely. He nearly turned back to the comic book he'd found in the lobby, then noticed his dad reach into the trunk and pull out a long, black case.

 "Got something for you!" Alexander Delling said as he pushed into the hotel room. He turned and planted a quick kiss on the new woman's cheek, then nudged her roughly to the side as he reverently laid the black case on the bed. "All yours, kid."

 Gabe flipped open the latches, then stared open-mouthed at the guitar inside. It was the most beautiful thing he'd ever seen. That made him worry it was a trap. "For real?" he asked.

 Alexander grinned broadly. "For real. Time you start earning your keep. We can charge more for a father and son act. And when we don't have gigs, we set you on a corner with a torn little hat out for donations. Cute kid like you? People will eat that shit right up. Might as well cash in on the easy money while you're still young enough for it to work."

 Gabe fought back the flash of disappointment and forced himself to smile and nod. For a second he'd thought his dad had given him a real gift. But this was still good. He'd never owned anything so nice. "Can I try it?" he asked.

 In answer, Alexander lifted the guitar from the case, and set it in Gabe's hands. "Now careful with that," his dad said as he gingerly let Gabe take the weight. "That's an investment, not a toy."

 Gabe couldn't help the surge of elation as he stretched his eight-year-old's hand around the neck of the adult-sized guitar. He knew he probably looked foolish, but he felt wonderful. He carefully strummed the strings just as he had always been shown, and they rang out with a slightly ill-tuned chord.

"I'll tune that up and everything," his dad said. "Pawnshop asshole didn't take care of it. But for now I want you to practice until you—"

Gabe reached up without thinking to turn one of the tuning pegs, and the string snapped with a sharp twang. His heart stopped.

"Goddamnit, Gabe!" his dad shouted as he snatched the instrument away. "I fucking told you *I'd* do that!" He pulled the guitar to him like a child he was defending, then skewered Gabe with a glare. "You never fucking listen. I talk and talk and it's like you're deaf. Now this is worthless until I spend more money on a new string. Pretty stupid. Money we *don't* have."

"Sorry," Gabe mumbled, hoping quick contrition was the best way out this time.

"*Sorry*," his dad repeated. "Yeah, me too. For thinking you were ready for a responsibility this big. You may have your mother's smarts, but you got all her common sense too. All none of it." He blew out a long breath, then turned toward the open door. "We're leaving. Find your own supper. And in the process, maybe you'll find a way to follow a simple fucking instruction."

He went out, and the new woman followed after giving Gabe an apologetic glance. The car started, and the door gently drifted closed.

Time snapped taut, and Gabe found himself back in his adult body, and back in front of a nightmare about to kill him.

He moved. It was like a deep instinct finally got tired of his crap and decided to take over, and a jolt of energy coursed through his body to propel him to one side just as the preta's claws curved in. A flash of pain lit along his right hip from the slash that had been intended for his gut, and the preta stumbled into the fence behind him. Gabe tamped down the remains of the unbidden memories he'd just relived and forced himself back fully into the present. There was something new in him that suddenly made sense, like a package delivered fully assembled, and he couldn't afford to let anything obscure it. Not now. This would save him.

Gabe twisted to face the monster, pushing past the sudden pain from the wound at his side. The same instinct dropped his right hand out and to the side where it curled around nothing. It was all part of it.

He let his body move as it would, and the red-gold aura around him swirled and ran together, brightening as it coalesced. Aka Manah's word flashed again, and the energy coursed across its sinuous length to pool raw and unformed in the palm of his hand. Becoming real. Becoming magic.

He knew now that he'd been using it unconsciously this whole time. A little sip to keep himself awake, a little dash to see in the dark. But now he actually understood the mechanism, and he was the one in control. By the time the preta recovered and turned to bear down on him, Gabe had a golden sphere in his fist that he raised with a defiant shout. And nothing happened.

The preta hit him hard at the waist and Gabe's feet came off the ground as the thing bore him into and through the fence. Wood shattered at the impact, and they landed heavily on the other side, struggling together in the debris. Gabe caught another clawed swipe on his arm, then managed to knee the thing in the gut and send it rolling away. He scrambled up to his feet and sprinted for the old tin building, feeling every step in his ribs and bleeding hip and arm. He hit the wall with a ringing thud, then turned with his back to it, holding out his still-glowing hand like a shield. But the preta was already on its feet and loping toward him. Gabe knew he couldn't take another hit like that to the ribs, and one good rip from those claws would be deadly. He lifted his hand, hoping for a miracle, willing it to do anything. And the preta snarled as it came on.

"Kraklehm." The mysterious word filled his mind again, but this time it resolved into something that made sense: Will. He needed to give the power a shape. Of course. So he turned himself inward and fed the power the first image that came to him. It was probably the years of reading fantasy books and playing video games that did it, but with no time to consider how cliché it was, Gabe threw a fireball.

In his head, the thing blazed into a comet of destruction that engulfed the monster in an explosion of righteous fury. But as with so many other things in his life, his imagination was far more generous than reality. What he got instead was a tiny flare the size of a pencil eraser that languidly drifted from his hand to float forward on the breeze like dandelion fluff. He stared incredulously, half-amazed and half-embarrassed as he scrambled for more magic that wasn't there. He'd used up *all* of the god's leaking power for something that wouldn't scare a bunny rabbit.

But apparently the preta felt differently. The monster tried to pull up short of the little mote, but its speed and injuries hardly left it dexterous. The best it could do was reel back a step as the little flicker splashed against its chest and then fizzled away with about as much drama as a spitball. But to Gabe's shock, the monster didn't act relieved. The preta howled in agony at the touch, and its momentum sent it crashing down onto its stomach to thrash in pain as it tried to extinguish a fire that wasn't there.

Gabe circled wide as he watched. He knew he should use the chance to run, but he couldn't pull his eyes away from the scene. The preta raged and rolled like a rabid animal having a seizure, and it clawed at its own chest like it wanted to dig into its ribs. Then it flopped back onto its stomach like a landed fish and began weakly reaching for its back to tear at its skin in desperation. It thrashed again and again, each one slower and weaker than the last, until finally it gave one last hideous shudder and slumped to the ground to remain still.

Gabe watched in horror and fascination as the tiny mote of fire then burned its way out of the creature's back and continued its slow progress up into the sky. It stayed shockingly bright for a long time as he watched, looking like a distant airplane passing overhead, until finally it either burned out or rose too far to see. He looked down at the preta to find wisps of smoke curling from its mouth and eyes, then the body collapsed in on itself with a bloom of acrid ash billowing from a thousand cracks in the dried skin.

The yard was suddenly silent, and Gabe realized that they must have been making enough noise to wake up the entire neighborhood. He scrambled back through the hole in the fence and glanced around furtively, finally spotting Heather calmly dusting herself off by the gate. Shards of glass fell from her back, and her clothes were still disheveled, but she seemed fine otherwise.

"Not bad," she said, giving him a shrug and a nod. "We'll keep working on it."

"We have to get out of here!" Gabe said, rushing over to her. His legs felt weak all of a sudden, and all he really wanted to do was sit down and replay what had just happened.

Heather held up a hand. "Relax. There's a glamour over this place. We'll work on seeing those next. The people around us probably heard a little drunken reveling, and I doubt it's anything new for them.

The glamour should fade now that these two are down for the count, but we have some time."

Gabe finally took a breath, and then another. "You manipulated me."

Heather smiled, then belatedly heard Gabe's tone and switched to an embarrassed shrug. "For your own good. I thought we were allowed to do that for each other now?"

He shook his head. "No. No way! I had just decided to trust you, and then you—"

She slapped him. It was more sound than force, but it stung his cheek all the same, and it knocked his mind off the furious track it had been building steam on.

"What..." he began.

"This isn't a joke," she said. "The people after you are terrible, and that thing inside of you is worse. There's nowhere for you to run that they can't follow. I'm trying to do what I can to keep you alive while you do practically everything you can to stop me. If I have to trick you into learning how to defend yourself, I will. Because that means you'll have at least a fighting chance when the real bad guys show up. You think a few pretas are scary? How about Paul? How about the Hunters? How about Gwendal and the evil god you have in your brain?"

"I can always help." The whisper came. *"You are something new now. We don't need her anymore."*

"Look at yourself," she said, snatching up his right hand and holding it in front of his face. "Look!"

Gabe saw her meaning at once. The glow of power had completely gone, and he was himself again—at least on the outside.

She dropped his hand. "There are probably better ways, slower and kinder, but we don't have the time. Do you understand?"

Gabe didn't know what to say. Regardless of her methods, she was right. Despite everything, his head was still stuck in the world as he'd known it just a few days ago. He was trying to plug all of this new information into the framework he already had, and he kept finding that there were no slots for the new realities. It wasn't that he didn't want to face the truth; his old mental operating system just wasn't compatible. He needed to upgrade his thinking.

"You still could have..." he began, but his spare indignation fizzled before he could even finish the sentence. "Nevermind. Thank you, I guess. I can't seem to come to grips with any of this, no matter how many times I see the proof. I hate that... I'm sorry you're stuck with me."

Heather nodded and lowered her eyes to the gash on his side. She reached down to inspect it, but Gabe recoiled. "Hold still, big baby," she said. She peeled the bloody shirt and pants away, hissing at what she saw. "Not terrible, but not great. We should get it bandaged. Sanitized for sure. Those claws have been nowhere good." Then she let the cloth fall back and started gently probing his ribs. "Now can I ask you something?"

Gabe grimaced and waved her on. "Sure."

"Why didn't you leave me?"

He had to take a moment to switch mental gears. "I... What? Ah!"

"Sorry," she said, moving her finger to trace the outline of the broken rib she'd found. "I mean, you had a clear exit when they were on me. Why didn't you go? Why did my manipulation work when it shouldn't have?"

Gabe felt his expression darken again, but Heather went on. "And at the mansion when you followed down into the basement. And when you took me from Trevor. And at the mall when the Hunters had me. And at your house when the window was open and waiting. And just now. We both know why *I'm* here, Gabe. Why do *you* keep staying?"

He had been asking himself the same question pretty much constantly for the last two days but hadn't come up with an answer he liked. "I don't know," he said, finally. "I'm getting stupid, I guess."

"You couldn't leave," she said, her fingers still gently searching.

"I guess," he replied. He really wasn't prepared to have this epiphany there and then. "I just couldn't watch you get raped, or eaten, or whatever. Good enough?"

She looked up and studied him hard for a few more seconds, then mercifully broke the stare and stepped back. "I think it's more than that, but you can believe whatever you need to right now. Also, you have three broken ribs." She turned and made for the car. "Incidentally, for your lexicon, the pretas wouldn't have killed or raped me. That's not their thing. They might have fed me a nice dinner."

Gabe followed her out. "Then why rip at your clothes?"

Heather pushed through the gate. "Desperation. There are several kinds of pretas, but all of them have some kind of intense hunger for something, usually horribly degrading. It's their punishment for whatever terrible stuff they did in life—at least, as far as the legends go. These bastards are Umbras, so they just drew a bad hand when the HMS Zeitgeist sailed through their neighborhood in the Ether."

Gabe gingerly pulled the keys from his pocket as he crossed the street. "So this species, or whatever, wants to feed people? How is that degrading?"

Heather opened her door. "They only have to feed people so they can continue to harvest the, uh, final consequence of eating. Didn't you smell it in there?"

It took Gabe a moment. "They eat—"

Heather held up a hand to stop him. "Yes. But I'm ready for breakfast now, so let's not talk about it anymore."

He shuddered and glanced back at the house. "Yikes. What do we do with the bodies?"

"Hey," she said, grabbing him and turning him back to face her. "Don't feel bad for those assholes. You saw a bit of it, but it's better you didn't see the rest. Keep your lily white sensibilities intact. The cops will show up eventually and somebody will take care of all this. There used to be the Templars for that, but who knows now. Either way, it's not on us. We can't afford to stick around here now that your homing beacon is deactivated."

Gabe nodded and pointed the car in the direction of an all-night diner he knew. They drove for a few minutes before he finally spoke again. "'The final consequence of eating.'" He chuckled. "I don't think I've ever heard it put so eloquently."

Heather grinned. "You should hear me explain sex. It's so much dirtier."

Gabe turned to her and smiled, but she held his gaze too long to be joking. "I'll pass," he said, quickly putting his eyes back on the road. "I don't want to have lived through poop-monsters just to die of a heart attack. Of course, I might only have another day to live, so ask me again in twenty-three hours."

"Suit yourself," she said. "Food it is. Then we'll hit the road and find some real help."

ELSEWHERE

Gwendal ran her fingers through the dead man's hair, petting him like a dog. He had lasted much longer than any of the others, and she almost regretted wasting him on a simple sacrifice. It had given her the strength to further mold her flesh, but he might have made a good Hound. They did work better in packs. She met his sightless eyes briefly, smiling down at him, then turned to her current Hound who knelt before her dais.

"His name is Gabriel Delling," he growled. "I found his den—home—but a pack of minor demons arrived before I could report. A Knight of Solomon followed." He turned to show that his left arm was missing a chunk from the shoulder and that it now hung uselessly. "I escaped death. The house was damaged in the battle, but I circled back and found this."

He slid a duffel bag forward and pulled a wadded envelope from inside. Gwendal glanced down at it and raised an eyebrow. The meaning came at once. She smiled and called a Hunter to her side to give him instructions, and the creature slipped its glamour on and went quickly to its task as a human police officer.

"Call when it is complete." She shifted on her throne, toppling her most recent meal to the ground, then turned back to her Hound. "Well done."

"There is more," he said. He barked a command, and a Hunter came in dragging a man by the collar of a heavy coat. The captive tumbled into the room, coming to rest almost at her feet, and the Hound bared his teeth in disgust. "I found him while following the trail. He was preparing to flee. He is weak, but perhaps useful."

Gwendal watched the man try to rise and gather a few scraps of dignity, but when he looked up at her, he prudently stayed on his knees. "Your name?" she asked.

He bowed his head. "Efrem Reznick, mighty one. I've come to offer..." he paused and looked to her Hound, then cringed. "I've come to beg your assistance. In exchange, I offer my service."

Gwendal extended her leg and slipped her bare foot under his chin to lift his face. "Why were you fleeing?"

Reznick shuddered but didn't move away. "That Gabriel asshole you were talking about. He and his succubus bitch, they ruined me. I'm dead unless I find a safe harbor. I want to serve someone strong and wise like—"

"What did they want from you?" she interrupted.

Reznick licked his lips. "They wanted to know how to get a god out of his head or some stupid shit. The trapped Umbra is seeping out, and the human's psychic framework is buckling under the strain. Honestly, I give him a day before he collapses and both of them crap out. Good fucking riddance!" He laughed and then stopped when he saw her face. "I... I told them it would take an insane amount of power to move a god like that. Out of my hands. Not like parting the veil, see? Plus there are a dozen other stipulations, and the ritual—"

Gwendal lowered her foot and sat forward. "How much power to get the god out?"

Reznick seemed at a loss. "More than anyone has. Big god stuff. You can kill the host to maybe send the trapped Umbra back to the Ether, but there's no guarantee he isn't lost in the process. The precept wards aren't meant to be traveled across in either direction. Anything could go wrong. If you absolutely want the god out and solid, and you used the right rituals and took the steps, you'd need dozens of lives. *Hundreds*, maybe. And it would have to be soon before it's too late for either the god or the host. Like I said, a day, maybe." He stopped and licked his lips nervously. "I mean, if that's what you're after, I may know a way, if... If you keep me safe."

Gwendal rose and walked past the man, running a hand over his head as she moved. "You have done well," she said to her Hound, letting him lean forward to nuzzle at her thigh. "Arrange a safe place for this man. We will have need of him. Then take me to Gabriel Delling."

CHAPTER TWENTY-SEVEN

"I didn't mean for this book to delve so far into my personal life, but maybe that was inevitable. I'll end the chapter with this: My father didn't like me, but I think he loved me. When my mother left us, she said it was his fault, but she abandoned me just as easily. My dad stayed and kept me alive until I could do it myself. Then he split. I was fifteen. But I still think he did the best he could. Ten years tied to someone isn't just obligation. There has to be love there, even if it is covered in bitterness and deceit. I know that because I fell into the same trap with him, just on the opposite side. It's not an excuse for what I've done or who I am, it's just… I don't know. Depressingly poetic, I guess.(Note to self: Rewrite this freaking chapter, Gabe. You're losing the funny tone.)"

-Excerpt from Chapter Nine, CONscience

With only one day left to live, Gabe insisted that they take their food to-go. So at five in the morning, they found themselves eating in their stolen car and heading out of town. Heather had already gone through two steak and egg burritos and was working on a third by the time they hit the city limits. He stared out at the recently harvested corn fields and picked up his cup of hot chocolate. The movement barely hurt his wounds, even after only an hour, and he was disturbed to find one more reason to be thankful for Aka Manah's magic. He added super-healing to his list of ill-gotten gains. It was almost enough to make a guy *want* to keep an evil god in his head.

"How's the cut?" Heather asked, somehow knowing he'd been thinking about it.

Gabe slipped his cup back into the holder and lifted his new shirt to show that the bandages beneath were still a pristine white. "Doesn't even hurt anymore. I think I diverted some power down there and stopped the bleeding. Or something. There's a slight chance I'm figuring this crap out. If I could study the rulebook sometime I might even be a useful member of our little dynamic duo."

Heather rolled the wrapper down on her burrito and nodded as if impressed. "Magic is just like life, Gabe. The rules are all fluid if you're creative enough." She smiled, then took a huge bite.

He stared back out at the headlight of an oncoming motorcycle and an otherwise empty highway. They were really leaving. They'd stopped at an ATM and maxed out his credit cards, then dropped most of the cash off in the nursing home mailbox with a note for the staff. It would barely cover two more weeks, but he kept telling himself it was the best he could do. He'd either come back and sort it all out, or he'd be dead in a day. The image of the hourglass flashed back across his thoughts, and this time the sand was hissing down rapidly. Hopefully he had even that long.

"There is a way..." Aka Manah whispered.

Gabe ignored it. Heather hadn't asked about the detour to the nursing home, and he hadn't offered. His life with his dad was the one thing he'd always kept for himself, for better or ill, and explaining it just felt like too much at the moment. Maybe he'd let her read the meandering thoughts in his book sometime. That would catch her up pretty well. But he couldn't quite manage it out loud. He could only assume she had sensed his discomfort about it through the bond and had left him to his task in uncharacteristic silence. It was a kindness he knew he should reciprocate in honesty.

"Do you think I'm going crazy?" he asked suddenly.

She turned to him with a full mouth. "Hmmm?"

Gabe gripped the steering wheel tight and sighed. She deserved to know. "It's just, I've been getting these flashes. Like dips where I get angry for no reason, or start to lose control, or relive old memories that I haven't thought of in years. Then I wrestle it back." He shook his head. "It's hard to explain. Also," he sighed as the motorcycle passed them in the other lane, "he whispers to me. I mean, know I'm still me right now, but I'm afraid I might..."

"Crack?" she finished, plucking the thought from his head. She raised her soda straw to her lips.

"Yeah. Soon. I thought I should tell you before this went any farther. While there's still a chance to turn back. We're going to hunt down the people on Dale's list, but what if we can't find them? Or what if they're worse than Reznick? What if there's no solution and you're just stuck with me while I go insane? I wanted to say that I'm, uh... I'm willing to turn myself in. You know, to Gwendal. Get it over with."

Heather finished her drink and pointed to a gravel road. "Pull over."

"No, I'm not suicidal or anything. I'm just—"

"Gabe," she said. "For one minute."

He slowed and turned onto the side road, the rocks crunching under the tires as he came up alongside a harvested field. She got out, and he followed.

Heather met him at the front of the car and faced him square on. "Let's list your possibilities, shall we?" She held up a finger. "First option: you die. Let's call that a backup plan for now."

"Thanks," he said dryly.

"It probably isn't Gwendal's preference either, truth be told," she said. "The precepts are there to keep the biggest baddest wolves at bay, and there's serious mojo behind them. God with a capital G stuff. Clearly Gwendal has ways around that if given enough power, but according to Reznick it's mighty hard. Her sorcerer is gone, and I don't think she can do it herself. It would certainly explain why Aka Manah has been so willing to help you defend yourself. It buys him more time to find a way out while he has one foot in this plane. The odds of you screwing up and accidentally letting him out in the next day are way better than a guaranteed exile."

"Thanks again," he said.

She shrugged. "Second option: You run until you die. Keep searching. Keep hoping. Maybe that's a day, maybe it's longer. Who knows? That's the path we're on, and it's not bad. Third option: you try to negotiate with Gwendal and allow her to remove Aka Manah. I honestly don't know if it's possible, and I don't think it's a good idea, but we can try. There's a chance you make it out alive, but we're also loosing an evil god on the world. We don't come out like heroes in that scenario."

Gabe nodded slowly. "That sounds slightly less terrible than it did yesterday. I've never claimed to be a hero. But how would we start? And then how could we trust Gwendal to keep her word? She doesn't seem like a handshake kinda gal."

"These are just basic plans, Gabe. I don't know all the details yet. Let's find one you like before we spend time fleshing it out."

"Is there a fourth option?"

She met his eyes, and he knew what was coming before she said it. "You could always fight."

He scoffed. "Seriously? Fight Gwendal and Aka Manah? Just burn up two gods with my little firefly of death? That sounds super likely."

She took a few steps back. "You were able to use some of Aka Manah's power. How did you do it?"

Gabe thought back to the echoing word and the ancient instincts it had awakened. There was more there, buried, but it was beyond him now. "I don't totally know."

"That's fine," she said. "Most of us are that way, I think. It should happen naturally. No spells or wands or whatever—just intent. Every Umbra has a set of powers assigned to them based on the conditions of their creation. The specifics can vary, but essentially it's all the same rules. But you're a regular human—or, you used to be. You don't have any outlines or barriers. If I'm right, you should be able to do anything you want as long as you have the power to fuel it. You should be limitless. Aka Manah's strength and your potential... You could be a god yourself."

Gabe shook his head. "I think that's what he was talking about when he said we would join to become a monster. I don't think the combination works."

"So says the god of lies, right? What if you *can* control it? Maybe he's afraid of that. It's what sorcerers do. They steal magic from other sources and use it. Except you didn't even need their training or that creepy singing thing they do. You just did it. All you need is practice." She straightened. "Let's try something simple. If it doesn't work, we'll get back on the road. Deal?"

He reluctantly nodded, and she closed her eyes. A faint glimmer surrounded her, and suddenly Gabe was forcefully struck by how beautiful she really was. Everything about her was flawless and artful, even down to the tiny spot of hot sauce on her perfect chin. He loved her more than anything, and it was all he could do to keep himself from falling to his knees and begging for her to stay with him forever.

She smiled at his expression and the shimmer faded slightly. "A little strong, sorry."

Gabe's head cleared, and he was able to force a few thoughts through the haze. "What... What happened?"

"The glamour," she said, her voice like blossoms cascading from a cherry tree. "I'm giving you the good stuff. Try to see through it."

Gabe shook his head like an angry horse, then rubbed his eyes. When he looked again, Heather was still a goddess-made-flesh, waiting for his adoration. He concentrated harder, searching his mental control board for the levers that made this work, but nothing changed. It certainly didn't help that he had no desire to see through it.

She took a few steps backward, and the effect lessened some more. She prompted him again, but it was still too hard.

"I'm sorry," he said. "I can't."

"Yes you can. Just not with any reliability. It's all the same thing, Gabe. The ability to pierce light and shadow, to resist mental and chemical manipulation, to spot power and auras—it all comes from the same place. I've seen you do it in bits. Focus on that."

Gabe tried again, but this time he let his mind relax. Maybe it was like an optical illusion. There was another picture of Heather in there somewhere, and he just needed to be flexible enough to see it. For several seconds nothing happened, but then a shimmering heat haze appeared around her, and he latched onto it, prying at it like the lid on a paint can. But as soon as he focused, the glamour snapped back into place and was once again smooth as glass.

He sagged in defeat. "Isn't there a school for this kind of thing?"

She cocked an eyebrow. "Why would there be? Umbras start off already knowing how to use our gifts. Sorcerers are... Well, I'm not sure where they come from. But as far as I know you're the only weirdo with stolen power he doesn't know what to do with. Not exactly worth building a Hogwarts for."

Gabe almost begged off the exercise. Now that he'd burned through most of the excess power, he was actually getting tired again, and he didn't see what there was to gain. Then he realized that he had started to think clearly. "Does your sex magic lose strength over time, or did I just gain immunity?"

Heather made a sound of annoyance. "Both. I can't keep a focused glamour like this up indefinitely, and it wouldn't do any good even if I could. Your brain gets tired of sensations the same way your tongue gets tired of flavors. To keep looking like pure sex to even one man I have to pump out more and more power. Pretty soon I hit my limit, and he gains blood flow back to his brain. That's why I generally don't just stand in the middle of a road letting a guy stare at me while we chitchat. It's all about layering on the distractions. The ambient glamour is different. People see what they want to anyway, and they usually aren't paying devoted attention to strangers. So I can keep that one going much longer provided we're not trying to sneak past a prison security system or something."

"Got it," he said. He decided to try once more. He set his shoulders and relaxed his mind, searching for the haze he'd seen before. This time it came more quickly, but instead of pouncing on it, he let it mature and soften. Soon it was as if the edges of a plastic sticker were peeling up and curling under a heat gun. And just like that it became easy, and he could see what was hidden beneath.

Heather, *Shanti,* was still beautiful and dark beneath her glamour, but she was very different from the Heather he knew. Two black horns curled up and out from her head like a crown nestling in her silken hair, and her skin glowed faintly red even in the blue starlight. Her body faded in and out of focus like a bad camera shot, but he thought he caught glimpses of naked flesh, and a tail, and of cloven feet. But then it changed too quickly for him to be sure, like her form itself wasn't exactly certain what it was anymore. Maybe she had cloven hooves, maybe bare feet. Maybe her horns were thick and spiraled, but maybe they were delicate and barely there. There were competing identities in her, and only one constant remained through all the misty transformations: the black, endless eyes staring directly into him.

He pressed through that image, afraid of seeing any more, and he passed into a hazy, electric mist of power that spun about her like a weather pattern. Clouds of emotion and memories lit along that aura, changing color and texture, and he could almost make sense of them as he stared. He could almost read her. There was pain there, and anger, and lust, and fear, and confusion... And a small packet of something else that sat at her center like a nucleus. It was open, inviting him to read it and know her completely, and he felt the sliver of himself there within it. Something in *him* responded in kind. Souls bound by more than magic.

The moment he thought of bonds, a thin white line presented itself and pulled him all the way back to the surface of his perception where it joined others there to splay out like a bundle of wires soldered to a million points on the intricate grid of her spirit. It looked exactly like a nest of marionette strings, but as it left her, it bunched into a single cable of power that ran unerringly across the distance between them and back to him. This, he realized, was the magic bond. And he could suddenly feel his own side of the connection. It was just a single point, but it was easy to see now that he knew how. He reached for the spot with a thought, then stopped. He didn't dare touch it. Not yet. He couldn't afford to.

Gabe left the bond and focused back on the glamour. It was why he was there. He'd gone deeper than he should have, and that somehow allowed him to come up from behind and peel the thing away like a wet piece of paper. He gathered it up as he went, and the power around Heather fell away in a rush. His vision of the bond and her aura and her soul all faltered and fell with it, and Heather gasped and dropped to her knees, her glamour now entirely gone.

She looked just as she always had. There were no horns and no tail. Only her. "How did you do that?" she asked, her breath ragged.

He smiled to hide his own shock. "Didn't think I'd pick it up so fast, huh? I can see right through you, lady."

She shook her head, then took a minute to catch her breath. Finally, she stood and brushed herself off. "You didn't just pierce it, Gabe. You tore it off of me."

He let his smile slip, then took a few steps toward her. "I'm so sorry... It just happened."

She waved him away and rose to steady herself on the hood of the car. "I believe you. I just didn't know it was possible." Then she chuckled and shook her head. "Though I should have guessed you would skip past the easy thing and do the impossible instead. Idiot man can't even fail correctly."

He watched her to make sure she was okay. "So what did that achieve?"

She took a deep breath and looked up at the stars. "It means you might have a chance if you choose to fight. Your ability to use magic isn't a fluke; it's in there if you try hard enough. Or we can keep running." She stood straight and stretched. "Or we can rent a cabin in the mountains and hump like bunnies until you die *really* happy. It's up to you, master."

Gabe laughed, but her use of the word suddenly made him uncomfortable. "Have terrifying sex while a demon king eats my soul from the inside out? No thanks."

She shrugged regretfully as if the suggestion had been serious. "Your choice. I know what I'd pick for my last day on earth."

"Yeah, well, why do I have the feeling that you'd get tired of my flavor pretty quickly?" Heather's eyes widened in delight, and Gabe felt his face go red. "Not... I meant..." he stammered. "Because you said about the flavor thing for glamours! Ugh!" He let out a breath and sat heavily on the hood. Heather slid closer to him and batted her eyelashes, but when he shook his head, she mercifully ended it with a suggestive wink.

They sat there in silence for a while, listening to the crickets chirp until Gabe finally worked up the courage to change the subject back to something serious. "Hey," he said, struggling to get the words out for fear of how she might react—for fear that this might be the last thing he ever said to her. He felt his side of the bond waiting for him there, ready to be untied at a thought now that he had the means. "I might have figured out how to—"

"You two are pretty loud for fugitives," A low voice interrupted from out in the darkness.

Gabe turned and found only a spot on the road that wavered and shimmered like a glamour. He started trying to pierce it, but it fell of its own accord to reveal the man in the red t-shirt and leather jacket. He was holding a motorcycle helmet under his left arm, and at his right hip was the large, ridiculous handgun.

"You've been following us," Heather said as she put herself between Gabe and the newcomer.

The man nodded. "And you've been running pretty well." He stopped several paces away and held up his hand in a friendly wave. "I'm Leopold Deminov," he said, adding a little Russian flair that didn't seem to otherwise be present in his speech. "I'm a Knight of Solomon, and I've been looking for you, Mr. Delling."

Heather took a step forward. "You're the new Templars?"

Leopold moved his hand a little closer to his weapon. "Yes and no. They still cover Europe and Asia, but only have a small presence in the U.S. The church still runs them. We're an independent agency contracting directly with governments. One of several really, but we're the best."

Heather nodded as if she understood, and Gabe wished he felt the same. "So you're human?" Gabe asked.

Leopold smirked. "Of course. That's the whole point. The Knights of Solomon and her sister organizations are the last line of defense between the wild Ether and the soft underbelly of Earth." He said it as if reciting from a pamphlet. "We control and process the flow of Umbras onto this plane and ensure that the laws of this world are obeyed. We represent humanity to Umbras in all things diplomatic, judicial, and punitive. Registration is compulsory, cooperation is appreciated, and ass-kickings are complimentary." He grinned like a little kid. "I added that last part myself."

Gabe nodded as if suitably impressed. "Charming. You'll have to excuse me because I'm pretty tired right now—and all full-up on ass-kickings, thanks—but can I ask what this has to do with us?"

Leopold raised his eyebrows. "Come on. I've been tracking you for two days, so I'm not in the mood. This lovely lady is a succubus, class two, maybe class one on a good day, but definitely an old original from Eastern Europe or Persia. No horns or hooves yet, and not one of those new crazy-ass variety from the goddamned comics, so she's already on my good side."

Gabe glanced at Heather and watched her give the man a small, careful nod. "And me?" Gabe asked, willing to draw out the conversation longer just for the nice change of pace it made from running for his life and having terrifying personal epiphanies.

Leopold's confident grin slipped as he turned to Gabe. "You're a mystery. That's why we want to talk to you. I see you're taking care of the little power leakage problem you've been dragging all over town, but my superior still wants to ask you a few questions." He casually adjusted his belt near the holstered gun. It wasn't a threat, but it was the precursor. "I need you to follow me."

"And where are we supposed to be going?" Heather asked.

"A temporary office for processing. Quick and easy. A few questions and we'll be out of your hair."

"And if we don't want to?" Gabe asked.

Leopold grimaced and acted as if he was genuinely considering it. "Well, that would make things pretty tough. See, I've already tried to bring you in twice now, and had to make some messes along the way. Those pishtacos in particular were real assholes. Messed up a whole truce we had going with one of the so-called Barons of this little city, and my boss is a ball-buster about that kind of thing. So if I show up a third time with nothing to show for it, I'm kinda screwed."

Before they could respond, he turned and trudged back down the road to a motorcycle that had materialized out of nothing. "Just follow me, okay? It won't take long, and you'll be back on your way soon—only this time, in the good graces of the Knights." He smiled brightly as he donned his helmet. "Just don't run off or fall too far behind. My brother died in the line of duty a few weeks ago, and I'm not in the best of moods lately as a result. It won't help if I have to start my morning off by killing you." He straddled his bike, then held up a small black device with a red button on top.

Gabe groaned, but it took Heather a moment longer to get it. "Detonator?" she asked.

The motorcycle fired up, and Leopold gestured for them to get moving. They scrambled to get into the car, and Gabe winced as he started the engine. When they didn't explode, he hit the gas hard to keep up as Leopold shot away.

"I'm accepting any ideas," he said, keeping his eyes on the single red tail light.

"I don't think we have a choice. I get no read off of him whatsoever, yet he had some kind of powers, including a good set of glamours. Charms, I guess. No telling what flavor. For all I know he really did wire the car up while we were distracted. Besides," she said, leaning down to rummage through the food sacks for anything left, "there's always the chance that we've finally found some people who *don't* want us dead."

The motorcycle hit the highway and shot ahead, and Gabe growled as he struggled to catch up.

"A slight chance," she said.

CHAPTER TWENTY-EIGHT

```
"'Affection makes you vulnerable. Relationships
make you weak. Love makes you both and stupid
besides.' That's a quote from my dad. Alexander
Delling, ladies and gentlemen. I wish I could
say I've seen the error of that dark wisdom, but
the guy wasn't wrong. Though it is a hell of a
thing to hear when you're twelve."

-Excerpt from Chapter Nine, CONscience
```

    They pulled up in front of The Smoothie Criminal a little after 5am. At first Gabe thought their guide had stopped to get breakfast, but then he noticed the juice place was closed for refitting by a new owner. Dark plastic sheeting covered the windows behind cheery "Coming Soon!" banners, but Leopold opened the door anyway and gestured for them to follow.

    The shop was in the middle of a strip mall, situated between an optometrist's office and a Greek restaurant that looked long-abandoned. When they entered, the smell of fresh fruit and yogurt was still light on the air despite the half-painted walls and bare light fixtures that seemed to indicate very little food prep was taking place these days. The lone employee behind the counter, a young man in a tight t-shirt, only glanced up to nod at Leopold before going back to staring at his phone. They went through to the back room where stainless steel appliances gleamed against white tile, and the walls were covered in big, colorful decals of anthropomorphic fruit grinning toothily next to word bubbles proclaiming the finer points of customer service. The whole thing gave the impression of some kind of nursery school for stoner college kids, and Gabe had to tear his eyes from a bleach-blonde banana dude as they stopped at a silver prep table in the middle of the room. Leopold asked them to wait a moment, then disappeared through an interior door.

    Gabe glanced at Heather, and she flicked her gaze up meaningfully to a corner. He let out a deep breath, as if resigning himself for a long wait, then stretched idly and made a casual sweep of the place like any curious visitor would. And once he looked past the kindergarten decor, he spotted what Heather had seen. At least eight cameras covered the room from every possible angle. It was far more technology than a few wayward blueberries would warrant, and the units looked new and comprehensive. So Leo didn't just have a hankering for a parfait after all. Whatever this place was, it wasn't a smoothie shop anymore. Gabe completed his inspection with a big yawn, then gave Heather a tight smile to let her know he'd taken the warning. She nodded in return and started drumming her fingers on the table just as Leopold reappeared trailing a tall woman who looked like she was ready to break someone over her knee.

"Welcome to Earth," the woman said, extending a hand as she approached. "I'm Catherine."

She was bulky like an athlete, and tall, topping Gabe by a few inches and likely more than a few pounds. Her short, steel gray hair aged her a bit, but the resolve on her unlined face put the lie to that. Gabe took her hand on reflex, then regretted it when Heather pointedly refused to do the same. Catherine sized her up with a deep frown, but Heather ignored it with the bemused expression of a champion boxer being challenged by some street kid. Gabe and Leopold, comically, both took a small step back.

"I'm told you recently arrived," Catherine said, wiping the unspoken exchange away. "Can you spare a few minutes to talk while we prepare your paperwork?"

"First, how about you get the bomb out of my car?" Gabe said.

Leopold grinned and pulled out the detonator. In the bright light, it was clearly the severed handle to an old Atari controller. The Knight tossed it on the table and chuckled. "Had to get you here somehow."

"A few questions?" Catherine asked again.

Gabe fought down the urge to reach over and deck Leopold. But getting his ass kicked in a juice kitchen wouldn't improve his morning. He swallowed his anger and shrugged his acceptance. "Why not? It's not like I have anything else to do, like sleeping or reading over my constitutional rights."

Catherine ignored the sarcasm. "Excellent. I also find rising early to be pleasant. Sneak up on the day that way. Hit it while it's napping. Can I get you anything to drink? Strawberry Slammer? PinePeach Punch?"

Gabe shook his head, and Catherine didn't bother looking at Heather before continuing. "Very well." She rubbed her hands together and looked him over. "What in the Ether are you?"

He considered and discarded several responses before deciding to play it casual. He'd been a "person of interest" often enough to know a polite police interrogation when he saw one, so he played dumb. "I'm a guy. A human man. Is that what you're asking?"

Catherine smiled like he'd just told a lame joke. "No you're not. If that's all you were I'd send you home with a Blueberry Bomber and a Branana Brownie and wish you a great day. But there's a couple things about you that make that scenario unlikely. Would you like to know what they are?"

"By all means."

"For one, you're with her." Catherine pointed at Heather with her fingers in the shape of a gun. "That's strike one. A succubus isn't necessarily evil, especially the old ones that just like a lick and a taste, but they're certainly no angels. Hell," she laughed, "even angels are no angels!" She turned to Leopold who smiled knowingly. "But you get the point. She's a parasite. Being in her company makes you either stupid or just as bad."

Catherine started pacing along the length of the prep table, like a general delivering a speech to her troops. "Now, that alone isn't enough to raise suspicion. You two are disgusting, but still technically legal. If," she raised a finger, "it wasn't for the energy wafting off of you like stink from a daycare dumpster." She paused and rolled her hand in the air. "You know, that hotdog and diaper smell?"

Gabe furrowed his brow. "I can guess."

"It's like that, just coming off you in waves. Much better now, but still there. You reek of it, but it doesn't fit any profile we've ever seen. You're something new." She stopped and put her hands down flat against the table. "So I'll ask nicely one more time: what are you?

Gabe spread his hands in surrender. "I honestly have no idea what you're talking about."

Catherine sighed and stepped back. She shot a glance to Leopold and the man suddenly drew and leveled his gun at them. It was like a sawed-off shotgun, but festooned with latches and gears that Gabe couldn't imagine a purpose for. It also had a large bank of what looked like batteries along one side, and little tubes that glowed ominously. It looked like a movie prop, but Leopold's stance made it clear the thing was no toy. The Knight flicked something on the side of the weapon and it made the familiar electric hum.

Gabe considered flipping the table and making a break for the door, but a rustle back that direction alerted him that the apathetic smoothie employee had just filled the exit. Probably with a gun of his own.

"We don't want any trouble," Gabe said, keeping his hands in plain sight.

Catherine ignored him. "Let me tell you a story. The Knights Templar were the ordained protectors of Earth from all supernatural threats for thousands of years. Different names here and there, but the same job. But after the American revolution, they started leaving whole swaths of this continent undefended. Like they had a grudge. Then about a hundred and fifty years ago, around the Civil War, Umbras started coming over in record numbers. We don't know why, but America was a gaping hole in the fence around the material plane, and every deviant boogeyman in the fairy tales started sauntering in as if they owned the place. It was chaos here, and the Templars couldn't have cared less. Probably laughed about it even. They left us for dead."

She closed her hand into a fist. "The Knights of Solomon formed in that vacuum. After World War Two and the demons the Nazis brought through, only a few agencies remained to clean up the mess. The Templars have never recovered from it, but we rose to the top. Now we sprawl across this continent like a security blanket, ensuring the safety of humanity from those foreign to the sphere. Umbras are not unnatural, per se, but they're not natives either. You are guests in our house. We're here to make sure you behave as such." She stopped and stared at him expectantly.

"Great," he said. "Good story. Though, I do think the Templars have a cooler name."

Catherine's expression grew indulgent. "It's what we do that matters. We protect humanity, and we've been doing it for a very long time. We're not vigilantes; we're the law. So tell me, Gabriel, do we need to protect anyone from you?"

Gabe smirked. "Not unless there's a man made out of pie or pillows. And right now I'd take the pillows first, so that guy should watch out." He spread his hands. "See? You can tell how tired I am by the waning quality of my jokes. You should probably let us go before the puns start flying."

Catherine nodded as if taking him seriously. "I've introduced my organization. Will you *please* return the favor?"

Gabe started to babble for more time to think. "Well, I don't have an organization, but—"

Catherine slammed her hand down hard on the table, making it ring through the tiled room. "Stop it. We know you sought information from the Swarm Spirit Locust. We believe you are connected with the deaths of two Hunters yesterday at the mall. Two pishtacos affiliated with the Jimenez cartel were found to be carrying someone or something very close to your energy profile late yesterday, and it suddenly disappeared in the pursuit, setting off a near-collapse of a four-year peace. A group of nagas were forcibly returned to the Ether last night shortly after ransacking your house. Immediately thereafter, a Hound of the Immortal Hunt confronted one of my agents in combat, suffering an injury, but escaping. Sixteen human men have been reported missing in the last week, and there was also a call in this morning about an elderly woman finding her neighbors dead on their back lawn—neighbors who, I might add, were unregistered pretas. I think that was all you two, and I'm prepared to take you into custody for it."

Gabe hid his shock with a mask of polite attention. "Ma'am, I admit to running from the nagas because I'm no fighter, but I can honestly say I'm not responsible for any of the rest of that. Though I'm duly impressed by how thoroughly you have your ear to the ground."

Catherine sighed and crossed her arms. "Information is our edge." She paused and let her cold eyes linger on his face for a while, then she spoke very quietly. "Tell me about Gwendal."

Gabe felt his face flicker at the mention of the name. Catherine noticed, and the corner of her mouth went up. He felt his pulse speed up, and he begged his brain for any kind of plan. Heather had yet to break her silence, and he didn't know enough about the situation to craft a plausible con on his own. He could tell the truth and throw himself on their mercy, but that was assuming they had any. And he'd have to explain Aka Manah in the process. It didn't seem wise to tell these people that he had an evil god sleeping on his cerebral couch. He needed a way out. He needed help.

"Hey man," Gabe thought, *"we're both screwed here if I can't get out of this. Do your time freezy thing and let's make a deal, huh?"*

As if in answer, the room erupted in chaos—followed instantly by darkness.

Gabe couldn't parse what had happened at first. One second, he had been trying to sell more of his soul for a miracle, and the next he was suddenly beneath what felt like most of a wall. Then the pain came on, hot and strong, and his brain finally started catching up. His right shoulder hurt like hell, and his right hip felt like it might have torn back open. But the worst part was that he couldn't move to check any of it since he was now trapped beneath a pile of cinder blocks.

He pulled in a panicked breath and got a mouthful of dust, setting off a coughing fit that felt like a linebacker was using him as a trampoline. He added re-broken ribs to his list of complaints, then stilled himself enough to take in a few shallow breaths that were mostly air. That cleared his mind and let him think. He could feel that the debris atop him was just light enough to avoid killing him outright but was too heavy to move alone. It was a depressing stroke of luck, he supposed, and it meant his only hope was Heather's help. But that was assuming she wasn't in worse shape herself, and he had no way of knowing.

Gabe experimented with a small movement of his legs to get in a better position, but the concrete above him shifted, and the pain of the fresh pressure drove out his breath and filled his mouth with a rainbow of curses that he couldn't voice. Then the sound of gunshots suddenly cracked his shell of shock, and the pain receded as he realized he could hear the struggle all around him. Grunts and curses and shouted orders filled the room, and he scratched any hope for help. This was a battle, and he had to get himself out. That meant power.

He reached inside to the reservoir, hoping to pull enough of Aka Manah's magic to somehow augment his strength, but he found it almost bare. The god's leaking power apparently hadn't yet replenished in him, and what little had, seemed to be pooling in his wounds of its own accord. It was already working to keep him alive and conscious—which, he supposed, *was* a good idea. Of Aka Manah himself however, there was no sign.

"Now you're leaving me alone?" Gabe thought. But there was no reply except the sense of a presence passing just outside of his psyche—something gliding behind the closed door like a shark through dark waters. Waiting. There would be no deal this time, it seemed. He didn't have to wonder why for long.

"Take the Knights first!" Gwendal screamed from nearby. Her voice carried high over the gunshots. "I have the human trapped!"

Gabe felt the paralysis settle over him then, and what little resistance he'd been able to exert on the rubble disappeared. The concrete pressed him even farther down against the floor, and the pain ratcheted up until it was too much. Even with the magic bolstering him, he could feel consciousness slipping away. There was nothing he could do. It was over.

It was a fine way to end the entire mess, really: back on the floor and helpless. They'd come full-circle. Just when he'd thought he had a handle on his situation, he was about to go out like Wile E. Coyote. All he was missing was a big sign to hold up that said "Ow". The thought of cartoons made him remember his childhood and his dad, and a fresh wave of agony filled him. The little money he'd left would run out quickly, and his father would be alone. Abandoned. No money and no hope. It was where his dad had left him seventeen years ago, but there was no solace in the bitter poetry of it. He'd tried to be better than that. He'd tried to have a family.

Gabe wanted to cry—just for something to pass the time until his brain finally gave up. But then an azure flicker brushed over his awareness. It was tiny and frail compared to the pain, but it flitted back again and again like a curious butterfly until he finally acknowledged it. At first he assumed it was his mind pulling the emergency brake on his sanity, that he was finally cracking all the way just like everyone kept saying he would. But the thing turned out to be nothing more than a wisp of energy trying to make itself seen. It barely qualified as a drop next to Aka Manah's ocean of power, but the little thing was insistent and refused to be dismissed. And it did feel remarkably familiar—like traveling a new route to an old destination. It felt like something he'd already seen once and forgotten. Like something buried in him, rising when it was needed. That felt true, and as he reached out to take it, the light unfolded.

"*Ahhh, I suspected as much,*" Aka Manah said from behind the door. "*There is no telling what you've dredged from the depths. Beyond even my memory. It changes...everything. But remember the price. And remember who brought you this far.*"

Gabe marveled as he studied it. The flavor and feel was completely different from the toxic ambrosia he was used to. It didn't burn or thrum with malice, and it didn't pull away from his touch or settle thickly in his mind just when he needed it. It felt clean and correct. And though it was vastly smaller, it shared the same basic geometry. Which he knew was impossible. They'd all said that humans couldn't have it. It had to be stolen like a sorcerer, or bought like a bokor. Yet as he reached through to the in-between place where it lived, it came to his call and filled him with a rush of joy and relief. It was his. *His magic.*

Far away, a Titan awoke and wondered. A temple, long dormant, rumbled to life. And a gray thread snaked through a tapestry dyed black at the dawn of time. The Emptiness knew change, and paused.

But Gabe knew none of that. A burst of strength and clarity filled his body like a shot of adrenaline as his magic flared to life, and it was enough to keep him conscious. He sucked in a few shallow breaths, then used Heather's lesson to search for the paralyzing geas. The new power was like a tool that finally fit his hands, and it only took a moment to find Gwendal's dark energy where it sank into him. It was surprisingly like a glamour or the bond: a heat haze hovering around him and trailing back to its source. Only it was less complex in that it didn't need to create any kind of picture or emotions. All the magic did was tell his brain that there were no muscles in his body to activate. A fairly simple trick, and he knew tricks now too. He was finally grasping the outlines of how this stuff worked, and it felt like understanding calculus for the first time—only deadlier.

Gabe took up the flicker of his magic and threw it unfocused against the geas. And though it didn't shatter as he'd hoped, it did begin to peel away just as Heather's glamour had. He snatched the edges to slip the force of his raw will beneath like a crowbar, then wrenched back with all his strength. Gwendal was far more powerful than Heather, but less flexible too, and obviously unprepared to defend against such an amateur attack. Her magic suddenly fractured at the pressure, and Gabe felt it snap back like a rubberband as his body returned to his control. He heard Gwendal scream, then a loud crash and a lone gunshot. A door slammed. Then nothing.

The pain came back in a sudden jolt as the cinder block pinning his right arm lifted, and a bolt of dusty light rushed into his prison. His last bit of magic burned away in a fitful blue flicker to keep his eyes open, but it left him with nothing else. He was spent. Gabe gritted his teeth to hold back a scream and to brace himself for whatever was now unearthing him, then almost sobbed in relief when Heather's bloodied face appeared in the hole.

"Shit," she said, moving back out of view to shift more blocks. Her strength was incredible, and she had him free in a matter of extremely painful seconds. "Can you move?" she whispered.

Before he could answer, she shook her head and slipped her arms under him, lifting him like a child. The pain was far too much without the magic, and he felt himself dropping straight toward unconsciousness. Heather vaulted a body that might have been wearing a red shirt and leather jacket, then she sidestepped two Hunters sprawled out nearby. One looked like it had been dragged across the pavement face-first, and the other was lying on top of its own severed arm and a long chunk of melting ice. There was no sign of Catherine or Paul.

Heather seemed to read his thoughts. "Catherine ran out with the Hound on her tail," she whispered. "Coward bitch."

He tried to ask about Gwendal, but then she carried him through a huge hole in the wall into the interior of the abandoned Greek restaurant next-door. It was where the rain of cinder blocks had come from, and just inside, Gwendal was sprawled out on the floor. At first she looked dead, and his heart sang with the sight. Then he saw her eyes moving in her head, wild and roving like a rabid dog's.

Even in his barely functional state, Gabe noticed that her body looked much different. She was too long and thin in places, and her features were hollow and malformed as if she'd undergone some terrible plastic surgery. The flesh sagged on her, and her hair was lank and plastered to a misshapen head. She looked incomplete and broken —almost alien. But most importantly, she seemed unable to move.

Gwendal spotted them and hissed. "Cheap shot, whore. If he hadn't distracted me..." She moved her eyes down to Gabe. "You are becoming more interesting by the day, Gabriel Delling. I *felt* that magic. But do not delude yourself into thinking you are a match for me. You will return what is mine, or you will never again see what is yours."

Gabe forced out his reply. "Hey, I'd love to give him to you, but I'm not dying for it. I don't care what you have, lady. Keep it."

Gwendal's whole body was motionless, but there was still a terrible presence about her as the amusement entered her eyes. "Really? You care so little for your own father?"

Understanding hit him in the gut. "What?" Then he started fighting weakly to free himself from Heather's grip. "Where is he?" he demanded.

"Tonight," Gwendal said. "Midnight. Time is short for both of us to get what we want. Come to the ruins of the estate where this all began. Trade life for life. You may even survive it."

Then she laughed, and black tendrils of power snaked from her fingertips to whip across the room in great destructive arcs. One shattered a chair near them, and Heather pulled him close and ran.

Gabe tried to fight and tried to scream, but the last bubble of his strength finally popped as Heather sprinted through the parking lot. He held his consciousness aloft for one moment more, picturing his helpless father in the hands of a monster, then dropped into oblivion.

CHAPTER TWENTY-NINE

"I remember my mom. I know she was pretty, and nice when she wasn't drinking. And she was tired all the time, but that was near the end. She was a school librarian or something painfully noble like that, and I think she fell for the same bullshit my dad spun everyone in his life: big stories and bigger promises. She just had the bad luck of getting tied to him before his paint and glitter wore off. A kid is a hard shackle to shed.

Part of me even understands why she left. It's possible she fought a whole fight I didn't see and felt like she had no choice but to run. Maybe she was afraid of what he'd do if she took me. Maybe she was a good person with a good reason. But I think it's more likely that she saw in me the very thing she was running from, and couldn't bear to take even a piece of it with her. I think I disgusted her for how much like him I really was…and would be. And I think that made her disgusted with herself. I hardly even blame her anymore."

-Excerpt from Chapter Nine, CONscience

"We are coming apart," the whisper said.

His dad scratched at the stubble on his jaw as he looked around the little apartment. Then he shrugged and zipped the duffel bag closed. "That's it. You can have the rest."

"The cracks are widening. Everything leaking together."

Gabe glanced at the old lamp, ratty couch, and assorted trash that made up the bulk of "the rest". All told, the whole inventory of their home for the last year might get him fifty bucks. Maybe seventy-five if he threw in a decent sob story. "So you're just leaving?" he asked. He kept his voice carefully controlled, just as he'd been taught.

"Not much longer now."

Alexander hefted the bag and pasted a fake frown on his face. "Afraid so, kid. I got a tight little widow back in Nebraska waiting to take me in, but she doesn't think I have a kid. The whole scam's primed and ready, and a teenage son would screw that right up. I can't waste six months of phone calls and letters for nothing! You understand?"

"Hours, perhaps."

Gabe balled his hands into fists, fighting back the urge to finally hit the man. "And I'm supposed to do what? Live here by myself? Show up to school tomorrow like nothing's changed when you're four states away? What the hell do I do?"

"Maybe less."

Alexander chewed his lip, then moved over to slap a hand to Gabe's shoulder. "Kid, I stayed with you for fifteen years. Most dads would have run when your mom split, but that's not me. I'm better than that. I fed you, clothed you, and raised you. Even when you were a little shit, I never kicked you out." He squeezed harder. "I'd be a rich man by now if I hadn't been weighed down. You know that? So now it's finally time to get mine. This is my retirement plan. The big one. This gal has a few years left at best, then I'll be set for life."

"These memories..."

"And me?" Gabe asked, barely able to get the words out.

"So much deceit."

His dad squeezed even harder, and the pain was alarming. "That's what I'm trying to tell you, kid. I did for you already. Plenty of times and ways, and that's done now. This place is paid up for another two weeks, then you're cut loose." His frown turned hard. "I don't *know* what you're supposed to do. Nobody fucking does. And that's the big secret, Gabe. You just do something until it works or it doesn't. Then you do something else until you die. No plans you don't make for yourself, nobody there to hold your hand. The end."

"A truth beyond his understanding. I am impressed by... This place is too small..."

Gabe reached up to pry his father's hand from his shoulder, but the grip had become iron.

"Too small... Must get..."

Fire filled his arm and chest as something started bending too far.

"...Out. This will not be where I end. Must get..."

He tried to cry out with the pain, but his voice was suddenly gone.

"MUST..."

He desperately searched the room for help or a weapon, but found only an old hourglass sitting on the counter. Its sand had nearly all run to the bottom.

"Bye, kid," Alexander said.

"...OUT!" Aka Manah screamed.

Gabe woke up screaming too. His shoulder hurt like hell, and he reflexively pulled away, thrashing up through a blanket and rolling directly off of what turned out to be a kitchen table. He landed hard on the floor, adding yet more pain and confusion to his growing supply.

"Damn!" a man said over him.

Two sets of strong hands grabbed him and held him down long enough for Heather to put her face in front of his. "Relax!" she said loudly. "Gabe, it's me! Relax."

He swallowed hard and tried to talk, but nothing came out except a rasping breath. A dark hand gave him a glass of water, and he took it gratefully. He downed half of it in a single gulp, then started coughing violently before he could finish. The rest spilled to the floor as he held his head with his left hand until the room stopped spinning. Finally, he looked up to ask for another, and was surprised to see James standing there with his arms crossed.

"Hey, man," Gabe croaked.

James shook his head and took the cup back to the kitchen. "Don't 'hey, man' me. You've got some damned explaining to do."

Gabe looked over to Heather and saw that she was still bloody and filthy from the attack. The rest of it came back to him in a rush. "She has my dad!" he said. He managed to get his feet under himself to stand, but then a wave of dizziness dragged him face-first into the carpet.

James helped Heather get him back up into a sitting position. "You're not doing shit until you talk," he said. "And probably heal for three weeks. But talk first." He pushed another glass of water into Gabe's hands.

Gabe almost tried to stand again, but then realized the futility of it and sat back against the legs of a kitchen chair. He paced himself this time, and managed to avoid coughing any of the water back up. Then he looked to Heather. She was bloody and covered in grime.

She shrugged, plucking his questions from the bond without needing the words. "They know us now," she said. "Names, addresses, all of it. Neither of our places would be safe. I thought maybe a hotel, but... Look at us. So I called James."

Gabe realized that if Heather looked like she'd just been hit by a truck full of masonry dust, he had to be twice as bad. Her options had been limited.

"I checked the nursing home already," she went on. "They say a police officer took your dad into custody a few hours ago. Probably a Hunter. Maybe only a few minutes after we were there. I'm sorry, Gabe."

"How did you know that's where my—" Gabe began.

"I told her," James interrupted. "And don't give me any shit. It's my job to know. I'm not comfortable working with people unless I own at least one weakness. Yours turned out to make me trust you a little more. That's why you and I have been cool... Till today, obviously."

Gabe felt his brow furrow in anger, and he didn't bother to suppress it. James had pried into his life and found his biggest secret, and... He stopped himself. James wasn't the enemy. There was no reason to take out his anger here. "Got it," he said finally.

James nodded and turned to Heather. "He's awake, girly. Spill it."

Gabe looked up, and Heather shrugged. "I told him we'd explain everything once you woke up. He got tired of waiting, so he decided to go ahead and reset your dislocated shoulder."

He reached up to his shoulder. It hurt like a burning bag of rancid hell, but it was technically where it was supposed to be. "Great alarm clock. Where did you learn to do that?"

"You're welcome for returning the use of your arm, smart-ass" James said. "I learned in the military."

Gabe rolled his shoulder and grimaced. It was functional at least. "I didn't know you served."

James crossed his arms. "Not in America. Believe it or not there might be one or two personal details I've kept squirreled away from you. Now get talking or I'll throw you back to the wolves."

Gabe glanced at Heather to get some kind of read on what she thought their play should be here, but she was blank. James was almost as savvy at reading people as they were, though, so Gabe decided to go with his gut and just tell the truth for once. He didn't think he had the energy to lie anyway.

Forty minutes later, they were sitting in James's living room, drinking fizzy water and carefully avoiding eye contact. The story was done. Gabe had left out several of the biggest things, like the fact that he had an evil god in his head that was talking to him and occasionally making him hallucinate down a quick path to insanity, but the rest of it had been more than enough to paint the picture. James had initially asked plenty of follow-up questions as he tried to find the punchline in the ridiculous story, but when he finally realized that they were serious, he had only been able to scowl and nod along.

"I know it sounds crazy," Gabe said, remembering how he'd felt about the whole thing just a day ago. "It's true, though."

James sat back into the cushions of his chair. "Crazy?" he asked. "It sounds monkey-shit, cuckoo-bird, send-me-to-the-nut-house-and-throw-away-the-key *insane*, Gabe. This is not what I expected to be hearing over my lunch today. Do you..." He scowled again, and then just shook his head and snapped his mouth shut.

"I could show him something," Heather suggested.

Gabe nodded reluctantly. "Whatever you think."

Heather put on her glamour, and this time Gabe saw her curves start to fall away. Her body grew leaner and harder, and her jawline strengthened and hair shortened, giving her a slightly masculine cast. She was still Heather, and still beautiful, but now in a kind of fae, androgynous way. She hadn't changed shape, just *changed*. James's eyes went a little glassy, and a stupid smile formed on his face. Then Heather let the glamour slip away like a dropped robe, and James's pleasure fell with it.

There was a moment of confusion written on his features, then it slipped beneath a wash of anger and James shot to his feet. "What was that?"

Heather held up her hands. "A glamour. Made for your tastes. I can read desire and let you see it. But I dropped it right away. I'm sorry if it bothered you."

James put a hand over his mouth and moved behind the chair, putting it between himself and Heather. "Okay, okay, okay. This is... Fine. Complicated." He nodded to himself like he was trying to force the information through his brain.

Gabe leaned forward on the couch and was pleased to find that his ribs only protested a little at the movement. "James, I'm so sorry, but I don't have time for you to assimilate this in a healthy way. I need you to come to grips so we can work on a plan. It took me two days to get my head around this, but you don't have that luxury, okay?"

James nodded absently. "I need a drink." He spun and walked out the door.

Heather made as if to follow him, but Gabe stopped her. "He'll be back. His keys are right over there." He pointed to a small table near the door. "He just needs to catch up. I can sympathize."

Heather nodded, then folded her hands in her lap and looked down. "I'm sorry about your father," she said, softly.

"Are you?" he asked before he could stop himself. She winced, and he backtracked right away. "Sorry," he said. "I'm just angry." He let his head fall back against the cushion and closed his eyes. "And confused, and tired, and hurt, and really, really freaking confused. This whole thing is a mess. As of a few days ago I thought I had everything figured out, you know? Not great, but working. Now I feel like a kindergartner thrown into a physics class. I don't belong here."

Heather sighed and rubbed her hands together. "I understand," she said. "I honestly do. In the Ether we don't get much information about the real world. People like to think of the spirit world as a huge, heavenly recreation of earth, but it's not like that at all. It's more like the moment right before anesthesia kicks in: you're aware, but everything is hazy and moving too quickly for you to follow. Like that, but forever."

Gabe opened his eyes and watched her. She wasn't playing a game or trying to win his sympathy for anything; she was just talking. He suddenly understood that how he responded in this moment could be important. Like him, Heather was unused to giving things away for free or without good reason. And like him, she didn't know how to have an actual friend. "It sounds terrible," he said. "It must feel amazing to be free for a while."

She took a long breath and nodded, but still didn't meet his eyes. "It hasn't always been a formal summoning for me. Once in awhile there's an occurrence so big that the fabric of reality can't contain it, and the Ether touches this world, making a weak spot. In those places, at those times, we can free ourselves. Like fish swimming through a hole in a dam. Wars do it, so do plagues and other big tragedies. Or sometimes they just exist, like the fairy circle at the mansion. They make it easier to pierce the veil. My last natural breach came during the Thirty Years War."

Gabe felt his eyes widen. "That was what, four-hundred years ago?"

She let a small, wistful smile touch her lips. "Well done. Yes, the world is quite different now. I returned again to a formal summoning about two hundred years ago in central France, to a few members of a revived cult of Bacchus who had no idea what they were doing. But that was fairly brief. A year, maybe less. They wanted me for... Well, what else would I be good for?" She closed her eyes and seemed lost in that memory for a while. There was no hint of a smile anymore.

Gabe wanted to change the subject to something less awkward, but he stayed silent. It felt like the right response.

She opened her eyes and looked up at him with a little of her normal sparkle. "Then I appeared here and now. So I understand what it's like to feel confused and lost in your own world. Try dying in plague-ridden revolutionary France and then waking up in modern America to things like smart phones, the internet, and g-strings. Then you can talk to me about confusion."

Gabe grinned. "Touché." But he couldn't hold the smile for long as he noticed the weariness in her eyes. The concern he felt surprised him. "Are you okay?"

She plastered on a fake grin. "Yeah, of course. Just beaten up. Gwendal is way out of my league."

Gabe sat up at the mention of the name and felt his ribs creak in protest, but not as badly as they should have. He rolled his shoulder and it too felt unaccountably better. Either the magic was still healing him at superhuman speed, or his pain receptors were just giving up. "I still don't know what happened back there," he said. "I could hear, but couldn't see a thing."

"It wasn't good." She winced as she stood. "The wall came down, and it seemed like most of the debris turned in midair to pile right on you. But it wasn't an explosion. More like someone physically pushed through the wall, and those black tendrils were everywhere. I think Gwendal meant to shut you into a nice cocoon and then pick the rest of us off."

"She pushed straight through cinder blocks?"

Heather nodded. "Then three Hunters came through, followed by Paul and Gwendal. Leopold opened up with that crazy gun right away, taking down a Hunter with six quick shots that looked like compressed lightning. It made me glad we didn't try to fight him. Then the other Knight at the door fired shortly after, and everything fell into chaos. I dropped to the side when the debris hit and escaped most of it. I rose to find you, then one of the Hunters hit me."

She turned her face to the side to show him the long purple bruise along her jaw and the split in her lip. "I hit him back, and we both found out at the same time that, with my new fighting skills, I'm a little less than half of a match for a Hunter. He didn't like even that much competition, so he called up his Rime Blade. But before it could freeze, Leopold hit it with a full-body tackle. Saved my life, probably. Turns out the guy might not have been so bad. Neither of them got back up, and when Catherine saw that, she ran through a back door with Paul on her heels."

"I can't believe she ran," Gabe said. "Didn't seem the type."

Heather nodded. "You never know. I don't blame her, really. I might have run too if..." She stopped and grimaced.

Gabe looked down, unable to think of anything to say. Heather could have gotten away cleanly if she hadn't stayed to save him. The bond had forced her to risk her life for him yet again—the bond he now thought he could dissolve if he could only muster the courage.

She shook her head as if to settle her thoughts. "I don't know what Gwendal is, but she's changing. You saw her, right? Already shaping. That can happen after years, but for her to force it... I don't know. Whatever her magic is, whatever her legend, it's black and it's strong. And she's feeding it fast."

Gabe waited several beats for her to go on, but she seemed lost. "How did you beat her?"

"What? Oh. I don't think I did. I felt her working a geas and my legs started to go numb. My only option was to get to her before she could finish. She seemed to think it was funny at first, me stumbling toward her, and she gathered more energy to finish me off. But then some power hit her hard, and she screamed. So I punched her in the mouth."

Gabe spread his hands. "I guess you can add 'glamour smash' to my spell repertoire. I can't make one or see past them with any predictability, but I can run head-first into them until they fall apart."

"That's no small thing. I've never met anyone else who can do it. And for us to have timed it so perfectly... The bond between us must be growing at a rate—" Suddenly her legs gave out, and she fell back onto the couch.

Gabe caught her and guided her fall. "Whoa! Are you alright?"

She seemed dazed, but nodded. "I'm fine. Just...hungry."

Gabe kept holding onto her arm even though she was now safely sitting. He nodded to the kitchen. "I'm sure James wouldn't mind if you grabbed something."

"Not that kind of hungry," she said. "I've used up quite a bit of energy, and I haven't, you know, *had* much of anything since I got here."

He felt like an idiot. She was a succubus. He'd spent so much time judging her for that fact, but hadn't even noticed that she had yet to do much about it. "So you need to..."

Heather smirked. "A little, yeah. And I think James might actually mind if I grabbed some of that."

Gabe blew out a long breath. "Yeah. Didn't you, uh, with the guard at the mall?"

She narrowed her eyes but kept the sly smile. "We were behind that van for five minutes. How long does it take you?"

"Ha ha," he said, dryly. "Okay, what about when you went out last night? That southern guy whose car we still have. You were gone for hours."

"Collecting information in the warrens beneath the city," she said. "I was looking for intel not men. Intel which, I might remind you, saved your life." She angled her body toward him. "Are you trying to find out about my sex life, Gabe?"

He held up his hands. "Just trying to understand."

"I see," she said, "You're just concerned for me. How thoughtful."

He blew out an exasperated breath. "What if I am?"

She studied him and the sarcastic smile slid away, then she bit her lip and looked down at her hands. Gabe looked away too, suddenly uncomfortable, and they sat like that for a long time until the weirdness grew unbearable.

"So," he said finally, "Does it have to be sex? Purely an academic question."

She shrugged. "It doesn't have to be. Any intimate contact will do it, just to different degrees. I grabbed a nibble from that security guard you were so hot on, but it wasn't much. And I pulled in a little more here and there. But they were all just sips. Sex is a steak dinner, and a little peck on the cheek is a single grape. You can imagine the many shades of satisfaction that lay in between. I've had the equivalent of a fruit salad and a cracker in the last two days."

"Would it help if I—"

She held up a finger to stop him. "Absolutely, but you don't have the energy to spare. Young and healthy is best. They bounce back the fastest. But every bit of what you have is bent toward healing. You should probably be in the hospital, actually."

Gabe wanted to argue, but he couldn't deny it. "Maybe James?" he suggested.

"There has to be genuine desire," she said. "I could make it work, but—"

Just then the door opened and James entered, looking dazed but better. He stopped and stared at them for a while, then heaved a sigh. "Fine. I'm caught up. Now tell me what, aside from ruining my day, this shit has to do with me."

Gabe rose with a groan, but found to his surprise that his pains had improved further, and his shoulder almost didn't make him want to die anymore. The magic was working fast.

"Always a price..."

He shuddered and pushed the whisper down. An insane plan had been forming in the back of his mind since he'd woken up, and he needed to start moving his pieces into place. It was reckless, and stupid, and something the old Gabe would never have tried, but it seemed the best course under the circumstances. If he really was going crazy, he might as well make it an advantage.

"I think I need to hire you, James," he said.

James looked nonplussed. "For what?"

"I can't just walk into Gwendal's trap tonight and expect to walk back out with either my father or my life," he replied. "I can't let her be in control anymore. We've been running away this entire time, and now it's time to play some offense and catch her off-guard. But first I need to find out where she lives. I need information."

James's face grew serious. "I swear, man, I don't know anything about that lady. They told me the job was a simple B and E. I thought it was weird they asked for a young man and a pretty girl, but I swear I didn't look any deeper until you didn't report back." He paused and something odd passed over his face. Maybe guilt. "And if we're being honest here—"

Gabe held up a hand to stop him. He didn't need the apology anymore. "I believe you. Relax. From you, I just need people. Terrible actors, if possible. I think I know where to get the information I need." He looked down at himself and grimaced. "I also need to borrow some clothes."

There was quite a bit going on in James's expression as he processed those requests, but of all the unpleasantness the man had endured that morning, it looked like the idea of loaning anything from his wardrobe was the worst.

Gabe knew what he had to do. The heart of the plan was actually stupidly simple, but the trick was in using Heather without her knowing why. She suddenly looked at him sideways, a question entering her eyes as if she'd read even that flicker of deceit from him. He gave her his second-best disarming smile since she'd have seen right through the best one. He still needed her, but hopefully not for much longer.

CHAPTER THIRTY

"I might spend months planning something, only to change it at the last minute. Life is like that too. You can try to account for every detail and every little thing that might go wrong, but something will always surprise you. If you're not good at adapting, you'd better be good at bullshitting. If you're not good at either, you'd better be a fast runner. That's why I know not to rely on other people: I know exactly how much other people can rely on me."

-Excerpt from Chapter Three, CONscience

"You are the distraction," Gabe said, addressing the seven people who'd been able to answer James's summons. He noted that, with few exceptions, they all looked like the type who might be sitting around on a weekday afternoon waiting for a little criminal mischief in exchange for beer money. It wasn't perfect, but he could make it work.

"All you need to do is get in, look casual, and watch for my signal. Don't miss it." He lifted the hood on the sweatshirt James had loaned him and stuffed his hands in the pockets. Then he eyed everyone to make sure they understood. "Obviously I can't send up a flare, so watch for this. When I walk through the study area with the hood up, it's your job to walk out with me."

A girl with a treble clef tattoo on her neck raised her hand. "Won't that look suspicious? All of us leaving at once?"

"That's the point," Gabe said. "We're here to steal a rare book. If they notice it's missing, they'll try to stop me from leaving. But I'll hand it off to this lovely lady on the stairs." He pointed to Heather. "Once we get to the entrance, we'll all cover her exit by being way more obvious. They might search us, but we'll be empty-handed and she'll already be gone. If you don't see the signal, you can make your own way out. Mission abort. Questions?"

A few people exchanged confused glances, but that was good. He needed confused. "Great. James is now the chairman of the Association for Nebraska Undergraduate Studies. You are a tour group from a community college. James will get you into the library, but split up from there and then do everything you can to look casual. But do not miss the signal."

James approached Gabe as the seven other people began to meander away. "What's the goal here? Signals and shit?" he whispered.

"Eh, it's all smokescreen." Gabe said. "Just something to make them nervous enough for this to work. I need them to be obvious, but not too obvious. They're the window-dressing."

James rolled his shoulders uneasily. "You didn't explain how I'm supposed to get them in. Pretending to be someone else isn't really my thing."

"It's your thing today, buddy," Gabe said, clapping him on the shoulder.

James glared back. "Don't push it."

"Don't send me on a job to be murdered by a demon."

James looked like he would argue for the sake of it, but he backed down. "I'm not getting paid for this, am I?"

Gabe laughed. "What do you think? The whole reason I got in this mess in the first place is because I'm flat broke. But for the sake of argument let's call it 'spiritual compensation' okay? Good karma."

James growled, but looked resigned, and Gabe had the sudden feeling that the guy was calculating exactly how much Gabe's life was worth in both karma and cash.

"There you go!" Gabe said. "Channel that annoyance. Do that righteous indignation thing, and the desk attendant will let you pass out of sheer exhaustion."

James started to snarl something, but Gabe stopped him. "You'll be fine. If it gets crazy, just have one of these people pretend to film the whole thing with their phone. You don't even have to say anything. Nobody wants to end up going viral for keeping *you* out of a library."

"Real funny. Because I'm black? What if the desk guy's black too?"

Gabe shrugged. "I actually meant because you're stupid handsome, and that's better than cash on the internet. But sure, the black thing works too. Either way, I'm confident you'll figure something out. Seduce the guy with those puppy dog eyes, or do your secret black guy handshake. Just get in."

James shook his head and walked away. "I don't like you anymore."

Gabe called after him. "You never really liked me that much anyway. And hey, if I had scruples we never would've met." Then he turned to Heather who had been silently waiting by the car. "Ready?"

She nodded and pushed herself into motion like a boat kicked out from dock. Gabe could see she was hurting pretty badly, and though some of the bruising along her jaw had faded to a dull gray, there was no doubt that she looked diminished. He needed her to at least appear imposing for this thing to work, so he searched out the next phase of his plan.

They made it halfway across campus before Gabe spotted a likely candidate, and he gently took Heather's hand to guide her in. The sensation of it was a little nicer than he'd anticipated, but he shoved that thought down with all the others he'd been suppressing lately. His feelings for Heather were way too complicated to examine, and his current situation was way too dire to try—and she was way too much of a demon body-snatcher besides. There just wasn't time to work through any of it.

Gabe distracted himself by slipping into his frat guy persona, Todd. "Hey, bro," he said, calling out to his mark, "Hold up."

The kid he'd picked looked like a brand new freshman still trying to find his feet in the wide world, and more importantly, he looked lonely. He was wearing dark cargo pants, bright green canvas high-tops touched up with a sharpie, and a t-shirt sporting a comic book character so obscure that even Gabe couldn't place it. The lanyard holding his student ID was festooned with tiny colorful pins from some anime, and the wispy attempt at a new beard meant that Gabe could use his best plan. The guy was perfect.

"Hey, wait up." Gabe said, rushing over with Heather in tow. "Question for you, man. Well, favor really."

The kid looked between them, and the moment of uncertainty bought Gabe a few seconds to continue. "I need you to do something for me real quick. No big deal." He smiled in a way he hoped was disarming without breaking character. "I want you to kiss my girlfriend."

The kid's eyes went wide. "What? Why?"

Gabe rolled his eyes dramatically. "Dude, I know. Look, I want to grow a beard for no-shave November, but she say's it'll be like kissing a raccoon. You already have a beard, so I need you to help me prove that it'll be cool. Real quick, man. I mean, look at her. She's crazy hot, right?"

The kid looked incredulous at first, but then covertly eyed Heather. Even without her powers and a little worse-for-wear, Heather was beautiful. It wasn't the kind of offer you stumbled across every day, even at college. Still, Gabe could see the hesitation there and knew he had to keep pressing. Sane people rarely asked strangers to kiss their girlfriends.

"I mean, she doesn't have, like, cold sores or anything. If that's what you're worried about."

Heather smacked him on the arm, just like a real girlfriend, then she exchanged a chagrined look with the kid. "You really don't have to," she said, stepping in conspiratorially. "He's an idiot. But, for what it's worth, I am curious." Then the smile she unleashed on the guy —a little shy, a little sly, a little inviting, and a little scared—was so perfect that a team of psychologists could have written an entire paper on it and still not have fully unpacked it. And that was without magic. Gabe could have applauded.

The effect was immediate. Suddenly the kid was all confidence and unconcern, like he kissed beautiful strangers every day. "If you say so," he said.

Heather let her smile fully blossom and then leaned in for what looked like a quick peck. But as soon as their lips touched, the kid *melted*. He was still there, still participating, but it looked like he'd fallen asleep at the wheel. She stepped into him and slipped her hand around his back, pulling him into the embrace.

Gabe was surprised to find that he could actually feel the feeding. Energy left the kid in a slow roll to sink into Heather, and it was almost like osmosis with the life seeking to fill her of its own accord. Gabe tried to look like a third wheel annoyed by the public display, but none of the passers-by seemed to care about the scene. It might have been the glamour, but again, this was college.

A moment later, Heather pulled away and the effect on her was obvious. She looked brighter and fuller, like she'd been given fresh batteries. She breathed deeply and then shuddered, and Gabe wondered exactly how hard it had been for her to stop before finishing. He knew she hadn't gotten as much as she'd wanted, probably not even close.

Gabe reached between them and playfully pushed the kid away. "Alright, Romeo." He turned to Heather. "Well?"

"Thanks," she said, gently touching the kid's face. "That was nice." She turned to Gabe. "Go ahead, but keep it trimmed."

Gabe clenched his fist in victory, then held up his hand to the guy. The kid lazily slapped it then shook his head like he'd just woken up from a double dose of cold medicine.

"Uh, sure," the kid said belatedly. Then he turned and trudged on with a look of vague surprise.

"How long is he going to be like that?" Gabe asked as they turned back toward the library.

Heather shrugged. "It's different for everyone. A day or two of malaise and a few more of steady recovery. By this time next week he'll just have the lifelong memory of kissing a gorgeous stranger."

"Charming," he replied. Then he held up the student ID he'd unclasped from the kid's lanyard. "Two for one. I'm glad you feel better."

She spread her arms and took a deep breath. "You have no idea. Try going without food and sleep for three days and then eat a plate of ribs followed by a long nap. It's like that, but sexier."

"Uh huh, weird. Anyway, it's nice to have you perky again. Heaven forbid you be quiet and compliant for too long at one stretch."

Heather gave him a sour look. "Don't be churlish, Gabriel. You were dangerously close to being sweet, but there's no reason to overcompensate."

A minute later they arrived at the library in time to see James and his group gathered at the front desk. The whole event with the kid had only taken a few minutes, but it looked as if James had already managed to merit the attention of someone farther up the supervisory ladder. Not wanting to miss his window, Gabe slipped inside.

"...called in advance!" James was saying as they entered. "Now he's telling me you don't do tours. We drove an hour for this. I can't leave without something to show for the time. My dean will kill me!"

Gabe noted that James was shooting for somewhere between indignant and sympathetic, which was a good choice. It left the door open for both routes. Though, he did notice that one of the group was holding up a phone as if recording, just in case. Gabe was only sorry he couldn't watch the whole thing play out. Maybe he'd live long enough to hear the rest of the story someday.

The man James was addressing began replying, and Gabe shared a questioning glance with the silent desk attendant standing nearby. The kid just shook his head. Gabe shrugged and held up the pilfered student ID, careful to keep his thumb partially over the picture. The desk attendant wearily waved them through without even scanning it, and the door buzzed open.

They continued several paces past the doors before Gabe wiped off the ID on his shirt and tossed it to the side. "You up for this?" he asked as they hit the stairs.

She rolled her shoulders in a way that was part seductress, part athlete. "Gwendal knows this face. I either see this through or hide until I die. And I really don't want to live in a cabin on a mountain somewhere. So yeah, I'm ready."

"A cabin on a mountain? Wasn't that one of your suggestions for me? Other than killing myself?"

Heather waved the question away. "For you, sure. But I'm too talented and attractive to hide under a bushel."

"You know," Gabe said, following her down the stairs. "Most people get bitchy before they eat, not after."

"What can I say?" she replied. "You constantly inspire me."

The secret door behind the crate opened at a touch, and Gabe led the way through. No one bothered them in the warrens, and the doors at the end of the hall opened to one of the cricket things coming out to meet them. To his surprise, Gabe found that he could still understand the language.

"No, no, too early," the thing said, waving its forelegs.

Gabe stopped to argue, but Heather moved right past, ducking into the room before the doorman could utter a single chirp in protest. When the cricket turned in alarm, Gabe took the chance to slip in as well. The room was hot and dim, and the soft sound of machine fans hummed in the background. Gabe spotted at least a dozen of the crickets ambling through the room, going about routine tasks, and he noticed for the first time how they might have been something else once—dogs maybe...or children. A few spotted him and seemed to perk up in alarm, but Gabe made his move first.

"Hey, Dale!" he said, yelling toward the huge hammock suspended in the center. "Emergency!"

All the crickets moved at once, surrounding them and brandishing serrated forelegs that seemed much more dangerous than what might have occurred in nature. Gabe pretended not to notice the threat, but Heather took up a casual fighting stance that made it clear she was ready to kick a few of the things across the room if needed.

Gabe wasn't sure what their chances would be in a fight, but luckily he was spared the need to find out by Dale's weird two-tone voice sounding both in the room and in his head. "Cool it," the Locust said, groggy but aware. "Just, everybody dial down the aggression." He moved his great head from side to side, perhaps picking up sensory data that Gabe couldn't perceive, and then he looked down at them. "This is a serious breach of etiquette, man. If I don't get a solid doze I'm a real asshole the next day, you dig?"

Gabe tried to step forward, but a pair of serrated limbs came up right at waist height and helped him change his mind. "Oh, I dig," he said. "I actually haven't slept in a few days myself, so I dig hard. The thing is, I'm trying to suppress my own inner asshole and do you a favor—albeit in the hope that you'll be a pal and do me one right back. Do you dig that, man?"

Dale seemed to sag a little. "Come back when I'm open for—"

Gabe cut him off. "No, see, in about twenty minutes my information will be useless to you, as will your payment be to me. So it needs to happen now."

Dale perked up, either intrigued or annoyed. On the chitinous face it was impossible to tell which.

"I'll even give you a taste," Gabe said. "In good faith." He waved to the computer screens suspended over Dale's perch. "Someone is here to pay you a visit, and I know who."

For the first time, Dale seemed genuinely uncertain, and his air of hippie indifference cracked a little. "What are you talking about?"

Gabe shrugged. "Take a look at the library cameras. Then if you want to deal, we'll deal."

The giant locust wavered for a moment, then brought his monitors to life. He issued a few unintelligible orders, and half of the crickets surrounding them broke off to tend to what looked like a bank of servers. Gabe tried to portray the right balance of unconcern and impatience, but eventually he settled on a standard poker face. This was the critical moment of his plan, and he worried that he had gone too subtle. If the seven recruits didn't look suspicious enough to catch Dale's eye, or if they hadn't gotten in, the whole thing would fall apart.

After a few minutes, Dale looked up. "What am I supposed to be seeing?"

"Are you buying?" Gabe asked.

Dale rolled his head in a kind of resigned shrug. "I suppose, but I can't set a value on it until I know what it is."

Gabe spread his hands. "Of course. You're looking for several people who don't fit in. They're with the Knights of Solomon." He let that sink in for a moment while Dale turned back to the screens. "See, we got pulled in this morning to be questioned on the whereabouts and affiliations of Gwendal. Remember her? Obviously we didn't know jack, but that didn't stop them from asking *insistently*." He tugged on the collar of his shirt to show a little of the deep purple that was still visible on his right shoulder.

He watched as Dale turned back and scanned the screens, and he grew increasingly worried that his hirelings might be blending as students a little too well. Then suddenly one cricket chirped up, saying something that didn't quite translate itself in Gabe's mind, and Dale switched his view to a new camera. In the monitor, Gabe could see one of his people sitting on the edge of a seat with a magazine he clearly wasn't reading and scanning his surroundings every few seconds like a rookie undercover cop. A little jackpot bell went off in his head.

Soon the cameras found more of the same, to greater and lesser degrees of obviousness, and Gabe could sense the tension building in the room. "When they were done with us they started asking questions about you," Gabe said. "Apparently they knew we had talked. Interestingly, they didn't seem to know anything about me from before we spoke, so I can only assume they picked up my trail by watching your front door. I obviously don't know anything of worth, so they must have been out of leads. It sounds like they really want Gwendal, and they're pretty sure you know how to find her." He paused and let that sink in. "I came to trade you that tidbit for more help, and low and behold, who should I spot outside but the same bitch who painted my shoulder this lovely shade of pain: Catherine."

It was all lies and reworked truth, but the name was like a firecracker dropped on an anthill. It was as if they had been hoping it was some kind of mistake until they'd heard that word. Dale suddenly issued what sounded like a long string of orders, and the remaining guards around them began gathering small items and shutting down equipment.

"And that's not all," Gabe said, raising his voice to be heard above the growing noise. "Gwendal and company hit the Knights just as I was being interrogated. The two groups fought each other to a standstill, and we slipped out in the chaos, but she came in just as we were talking about you. I'd put good money on it that she was listening, and that she's going to be paying you a visit soon as well."

Several of the crickets stopped and looked to Dale, unsure of what their next move might be. The big locust waved its limbs, and a winch hummed somewhere above him, lowering the hammock to the ground. When the entire contraption had settled to the floor, Dale rose on legs that looked too thin to hold his bulk. There was a series of rapid pops somewhere above, and the dozens of cords running to the thing's head fell from the terminals and hung from him like dreadlocks. It was a sight to behold. If it was true that Umbras normally changed their shapes slowly over time, Dale must have been working on his for decades.

He turned to regard Gabe. "You definitely got me by the balls, kid. Or," he waved a foreleg, "the equivalent. I can't afford to ignore this or try to verify it or I might get smashed to crunchy bits in this tin can. But we heard about some kind of big showdown this morning that the Knights are keeping hush hush, so I have to assume that much is true. I don't suppose you have any other proof?"

Gabe shrugged. "Are you asking if I stopped to take a picture while I was running for my life?"

Dale sank down on his rear legs like a dog. "I thought not. Alright. We're out of here. What do you want from me?"

Gabe took a few steps forward and stood straighter. This was the gamble of the whole thing. Dale had to believe that Gabe was now more capable than he had been, but also a little bit stupid. He went through his catalogue of personae and found the bits and pieces he needed from his mental wardrobe. It was nice to be doing something he was actually good at.

"I want you to use me as a distraction." Gabe said. "I want to take a shot at Gwendal, and in the process, tie her and the Knights up for long enough to let you go dark. We both get what we want and you come out the overall winner. I just need her location."

Dale went still as his assistants continued making quick work of the contents of the room. Gabe could almost see the thing following all the possible paths of this moment to their eventual outcomes and trying to find one that worked out best for him. It was why Gabe had chosen this method for Dale instead of threats or another kind of coercion: intelligent people—or things—needed the tools and incentives to convince themselves.

Dale finally came out of his reverie. "How do you plan to do it?"

Gabe shook his head. "The how and the why are my problems. Do we have a deal?"

Dale rocked his great head from side to side as a long platform on wheels was rolled out next to him. He turned and awkwardly climbed atop the huge cart, then took several seconds to situate himself. "Like I have a choice," he said, finally. "Damn, I knew I shouldn't have looked into anything called a Night Mother. Curiosity killed the, whatever." The Locust glanced around the room, which had emptied amazingly quickly. Then he sighed in his way. "Well, you're good, man. Also a moron, apparently, but I'm not gonna complain. She's at a hotel downtown called The Briarwood, and she's going by the name of the body she took: Haley Schram. I hear she has a handful of Hunters and at least one Hound. She's got the whole top floor to herself. And that's it. That's all I've got. Truth."

Gabe suddenly felt a little bad about misleading the guy. The Locust seemed to be a relatively honest businessman trying to carve out a place in a world that was far more complicated and hostile than Gabe had ever suspected. If any part of this plan failed, Dale would almost certainly suffer consequences. But there was just no way around it. There wasn't time to put ethics beneath the microscope with his father's life on the line.

"And the people she works for?" Gabe asked, going for broke.

Dale chittered something and a team of crickets hauled on the platform to roll him toward what looked like a freight elevator. "Sorry, chum. No dice. You asked for the Night Mother and I gave her up in the hope that you'll somehow knock her off and win me a pardon. I don't know, maybe she'll choke on your bones or something. But there's no way I'm getting on the bad side of her employers. That she's got even a small part of The Eternal Hunt with her is bad enough, but the big boys at the top make even the Wild Riders look like newborn kittens. The Hunters will just tear your shit up. Her bosses will end you and everyone you've ever known, then build a sewage processing plant over your graves."

"Fair enough," Gabe said. "One more thing, then. Baron Jimenez, is he allied with Gwendal?"

Dale did his clicking laugh. "He's tried, but she couldn't give two shits about having friends in this city."

"Okay, what do you think his disposition would be if he knew that Gwendal's Hound killed his accountant, and that a Knight of Solomon killed one of his men?"

Dale chirped something, and the cart stopped in front of the elevator. "He wouldn't be thrilled."

"Any way you can make sure he finds out about it in the next few hours? The Baron takes care of his people, right? Can't let a fox run loose in the henhouse."

Dale shifted his head from side to side as the cart was loaded into the elevator. "I can spread the word. But if your whole plan is to have the Jimenez cartel at your back, you're deader than—"

"Don't worry," Gabe said, "there are more layers."

Dale chittered. "Better hope a few of those layers are Kevlar, kid." The ensemble finished boarding the elevator, and the overhead door began closing.

"You can't give me any other advice?" Gabe called.

"Sure," Dale said. "If you happen to survive this, stay the hell away from me."

The door closed, and the elevator hummed. Gabe wondered if it was going up to a waiting truck or further down into some kind of bunker. He turned to Heather. "That went alright."

She gave him a half-smile. "Not bad for what you had to work with. Do you think he'll sell us out?"

He started toward the door. "Probably not. If he was going to betray us, he would have grabbed us for the bounty instead of putting on that big show. Plus, that would put him even more firmly on the wrong side of the Knights, and this first plan was based on the impression that Dale likes to ride the thin line in the middle. Besides, it might not matter. Now that my injuries are almost healed, I can feel Aka Manah's magic building back up. And aside from what my body does automatically, I don't really know if I can duplicate my firefly trick to use it up. If not, I'll be leaving enough of a trail for anyone to find us. No betrayal needed."

Heather grimaced. "What do we do about that?

Gabe managed a laugh. "I'm still working on that part."

"So we're right back where we started."

He opened his mouth to agree, but then realized that she wasn't quite right. He felt nothing like the Gabe that had gone into the mansion or that had run through the mall yesterday. Part of that was likely the lack of sleep and bathing, the borrowed clothes, the sliver of succubus soul, and the demon god napping in his brain—but a big chunk of the changes were fundamental. And as much as he hated all of his new knowledge and the things he couldn't un-know or un-see, he realized then that he wouldn't give any of it up if someone offered to take it away. It was all part of him now, and he suspected he'd need every bit to get his father back.

"Let's go," he said, pushing through the secret door into the big storage room. "I have things to buy and a half-assed plan to finish."

Heather followed obediently. "You know, you really don't need to make that distinction when it's the only kind of plan you ever have."

CHAPTER THIRTY-ONE

"People are rarely who you think they are. Even those closest to you. We all posture and pretend our whole lives, trying to get more by being something we're not. It isn't new, and it isn't going away. It's baked into the human condition as surely as lust or greed, and those two things will only die when the last one of us does. You might call that cynical, but I call it reality. And that probably makes me more honest than you. Maybe more honest than anyone. We're all con artists. I just admit it."

-Excerpt from Chapter Eight, CONscience

Gabe pulled up to The Smoothie Criminal at about four in the afternoon, and aside from the plywood where the door to the Greek restaurant had been, everything looked normal. There were a few too many black sedans scattered throughout the parking lot however, and that gave him hope that he'd come to the right place.

"Are you sure about this?" Heather asked, unfastening her seat belt and opening the visor mirror. "These Knights are an unknown. They could be running some kind of protection racket for all we know. Plus—and I can't stress this enough—they definitely hate us now."

Gabe put the car into park. "If I had infinite resources and time to plan, then no, I wouldn't be playing this card. But what choice do I have? The other option is for the two of us to go in after my dad alone, plowing through Hunters and whatever the hell a Hound is. Not to mention Gwendal herself. Are you up for that?"

"Hound of the Hunt," she said. She checked her perfect hair, then produced a tube of lipstick from somewhere. "They're like undead dogs with the loyalty of a golden retriever and the brain of a serial killer. In a human body they become something like a super werewolf, only less hairy. Fast, strong, single-minded: that's what the hell a Hound is."

"Great news," he said. He shut off the car, then worked at opening the package of the little flashdrive they'd picked up on the way. He slipped it in his pocket just as Heather finished applying a coat of lipstick the shade of blood. "We've been running for two days straight. Where did you even get that?"

She pursed her lips at her reflection, then smiled. "Around. Glamours are great, but good old fashion rouge and powder never hurt. I call this shade 'Kiss of Death'. What do you think?" She leaned toward him as if offering a sample.

Gabe held his ground. "I *think* you're the only one who's going to think it's funny. But the 'super werewolf' thing just proves my point. We can't handle all that on our own. Hounds and Hunters and everything else. Enemy of my enemy, right?" He opened the car door, then turned back to her. "Oh, when we get in there, I'm going to give you a significant look. When it happens, do that psycho-girl smile you do, okay?"

She looked like she wanted to protest but then gave it up. "You're the boss. Let's just not get held hostage, or shot, or do anything overly stupid for a change."

The door was locked, but there were lights on in the back room and Gabe could see flickers of movement. He suspected that they already knew he was there, but he knocked politely on the glass anyway. A man in a dark blue jumpsuit stepped around the corner to come striding through the store with a broom in-hand, looking for all the world like a janitor. Of course, janitors rarely filled out their jumpsuits with more muscles than an Olympic bodybuilder, so Gabe suspected that sweeping floors might not be the guy's actual day job.

"We're closed," Not-a-Janitor said through the glass. "Remodeling."

Gabe shook his head. "Not here for juice, bro," he called back. "We're here to see Catherine."

The man paused for a moment, then raised his right hand which now held one of the chunky sci-fi pistols. He was suddenly very focused. He called over his shoulder to the back room, and another guy came through with his own weapon drawn. Once he knew his backup was in place, the first Knight moved forward and unlocked the door, gesturing for them to enter.

"Here's how this works," Not-a-Janitor said. "You tell me who you—"

"I already know," a voice called from the back room. "Stand down."

Catherine came in wearing a new set of clothes and a sling holding her left arm close against her chest. The whole left side of her face was purple with bruising, and she walked with a slight limp. Still, she was alive, which meant that Gabe could use "Plan A". It had a distinct advantage over his "Plan B" in that it existed.

Gabe nodded to her. "Sorry about your men. They seemed like decent guys."

Catherine came halfway into the room and then leaned against the wall with her right shoulder, taking the weight off of her left foot. "Leopold may pull through yet, but he's in a coma. As for Matthew, he *was* a good man. Are you here to turn yourselves in?"

Gabe gave her a disarming smile. "Oh sure, because this morning was definitely our fault. I exploded that wall onto myself to throw you off our trail."

"You certainly do look spry despite it," she replied.

"Well," Gabe said, spreading his hands, "we all have our secrets. Like how *you* managed to make it out alive." He watched her face darken and let his smile broaden accordingly.

Not-a-Janitor betrayed just a moment of uneasiness before suppressing it beneath an air of military discipline. Gabe caught it though, and it helped confirm what he'd hoped would be the case: Catherine had indeed run from the fight, but hadn't given out that detail to her people. Leopold and the other agent weren't around to tell the tale, but Heather had seen, and Catherine knew that.

The woman's face was clean of any guilt or anger by the time she spoke again. "No secret. Fights are messy, and that was a powerful Hound. I drew him out into the open so I could use my weapon, but he was too fast and got my arm in his teeth. He should have finished me, but something drew him back to the store and he left me to bleed out. Do you have a different version to tell?"

Gabe saw the dangerous look in her eyes, and he knew he'd pushed far enough. He'd just needed to let her know that she wasn't in complete control, and that he held a few cards of his own. "That sounds about right," he said. "Probably weren't able to get a good recording from the cameras with all the glamours in the room though, huh? Probably totally fried?"

Catherine's face was stony, but her eyes were growing darker. "Why are you here?"

Gabe glanced at the two other agents. They seemed like they were provisionally subordinate to Catherine, but Not-a-Janitor especially looked like he was ready to take charge at any minute. Gabe made eye contact with the guy briefly as he spoke. "I have a proposition for you."

"We don't negotiate," Catherine snapped back.

Gabe nodded to the back room. "Do you want to find the nice lady who remodeled that wall for you and killed your man? I know where she is."

Catherine went still, but Not-a-Janitor looked like he was about to burst the seam on his zipper. Gabe turned his attention to him. "I'm offering this information dirt cheap too. Just one condition."

"What?" Catherine asked.

"That you make your move against her today. No stalling, no studying, no chance for her to slip the net and go to ground. You hit today, hard and fast, and you take her the hell out of this world."

Catherine watched him coolly for a moment, then pushed off from the wall with a wince. "And why do you care about her?"

Gabe let his own expression darken this time. "Aside from the quarter of a building she dropped on me? Because she has someone important, and I want to be there to get him back."

Catherine considered, then seemed to tire of Not-a-Janitor's insistent stare. "Blake," she said, "call Omaha and see if we can even get a team on such short notice." She turned to the other Knight. "Go help."

The two men left the room, and Catherine took a few steps closer to Gabe. "Ballsy," she said, nodding with appreciation. "You walk in here and make demands like you're holding anything other than your own dick. It's quite a show, let me tell you."

"Not the first time I've heard that," Gabe said before he could stop himself. Heather snickered.

Catherine either missed the joke or ignored it. "We already have our own suspicions about Gwendal's whereabouts, and your little veiled threat about how the fight played out doesn't mean shit to me. So I think we need to have a different conversation. One where I get to —"

Gabe interrupted her by dropping the flash drive on the counter.

"What's that supposed to be?" she asked.

He grimaced like he was playing a great poker hand against someone he knew couldn't afford to lose. "You ran away, Cathy. Left your men to die. Your face just now confirmed for me that you wiped the security tapes like a good girl, but, darn it, you forgot to make sure that none of the neighboring businesses had cameras pointed over here."

Catherine stared at the drive and licked her lips nervously. Bingo.

Gabe crossed his arms. "So it turns out I am holding something else after all. I mean, it's small, but it's really more about how you use it." Heather made a skeptical noise and Gabe carefully avoided giving her a warning look.

Catherine seemed like she was right on the brink, and Gabe gave her a moment to process. He didn't want to push her into a desperate move. Not yet.

After a few seconds, she looked up at him. "I don't believe you. They don't just hand over security footage to anyone."

"To me? No," Gabe said, chuckling. "But imagine you're an unmarried, middle-aged store manager in the middle of a boring day and *she* walks in begging for a favor." He nodded to Heather and met her eyes. Without missing a beat, she gave Catherine the exact sociopathic sex-kitten smile he'd asked for. Gabe pretended to shudder. "It seriously took us six minutes." Catherine's right hand twitched, like she wanted to grab the drive, but Gabe scolded her with an upraised finger. "Obviously that's not the only copy, Cat. A couple people slipped your radar in your dossier of me, and one of them is holding onto a duplicate in case I don't make it through this meeting. Cliché move, I know, but sometimes the old tricks really are the best."

Catherine's expression went through a series of emotional flickers too quick to follow, but eventually she sagged and settled on weary resignation. "What do you want?"

Gabe smiled. "Ah, that's the best part! I want exactly what I said. You take a team in hard and fast tonight, kill Gwendal, and help me get someone out. You get revenge and what I imagine must be some much-needed confirmation of your ability to handle things, and I get what I want."

Catherine mulled the decision over for much longer than Gabe had expected, and for a few moments he worried he had overestimated his hand. Finally she nodded, then reached out viper-quick and snatched up the drive. "To make sure you have what you claim," she said.

Gabe kept his face passive as it happened. "I'm not an idiot, Kitty-Cat. That's empty. What if one of your boys had searched me and taken it? We'd both be up shit creek, wouldn't we? That was more of a visual aid. The only existing copy is on a drive exactly like that. So when you follow through with the plan and the drive is delivered, you'll know it on sight. Give me a little credit."

Her face contorted in anger briefly, then fell into a resigned smile. "So I'm just trusting you?"

"Can you afford not to?" he asked.

The two other Knights came back in then, Blake leading with fire in his eyes. "They can get us something," he said. He gave Gabe and Heather a long look. "If you trust the information."

Catherine turned back to Gabe and clenched her jaw, then she raised her eyebrows expectantly.

Gabe nodded. "Do you know the Briarwood Hotel by the arena? It's brand new. She has several Hunters and your friend the Hound in attendance."

"There's a concert down there tonight," Blake said. "Lots of people. Complications."

Catherine stared hard at Gabe and her fist tightened on the thumb drive. "That means the hotel will be relatively empty. Good timing, actually. Tonight it is."

"What time can I expect you?" Gabe asked.

Catherine snorted, and he could see he'd pushed her as far as she'd go. "You can expect us whenever we damn well please, civilian. We'll pull all the innocents out as we find them. You can come back here and collect whomever you'd like tomorrow morning."

Gabe grimaced and opened his mouth to protest, fully expecting Catherine to talk over him. She obliged. "If you think for even a second that I'll let you tag along, then you're dead wrong. Come back tomorrow and we'll talk. Now get out of here before I decide to send you and your whore to Omaha for observation."

Gabe put on an angry mask and glanced around the room as if searching for some kind of help. When he found none, he exhaled in a huff and nodded Heather to the door. She stayed in character beautifully and kept silent except for a parting sultry glance to Blake. Gabe had been on the receiving end of those a few times, and he felt for the guy. It was like you'd been starving your whole life and someone suddenly offered you a poisoned steak. You knew it was stupid in the long run, but you still couldn't keep your mouth from watering.

They left through the front and got into the car without speaking. He pulled away while she pulled her hair back up into a functional twist knot, using a pen she'd apparently taken from the smoothie shop.

"Obviously you're not going to trust them to get your dad out in one piece, right?" she asked. "Either Gwendal kills him the instant she sees a single Knight, or one of those bozos will accidentally shoot him in the head. Or, most likely, Catherine holds onto him pending delivery of a thumb drive we don't have. So what's next?"

"First, I send a message." He pulled out the phone he'd taken from the dead pishtaco yesterday. He sent five lines to Baron Jimenez, then tossed the phone out the window.

"What was that?" Heather asked.

"Backup plan."

She waited a beat for him to elaborate, but then gave up. "Well, is it a good one?"

He pointed the car toward downtown. "Almost definitely not. But if everything goes to crap tonight, I doubt we'll be in a position to complain. It'll be this or excruciating death." He shrugged. "Can't hurt to try, right?"

She sighed and pulled her seatbelt a little tighter. "You know, I don't think that's true."

CHAPTER THIRTY-TWO

"This can be a hard life. I certainly wouldn't recommend it as a career path if you have other options. It's dangerous, and selfish, and lonely sometimes. But you can make it work if you keep an end goal in sight and really like who you are. You just have to remember that you're spending the currency of the latter to buy the former."

-Excerpt from Chapter Seven, CONscience

Gabe eyed the Briarwood hotel lobby from their bench across the street, then went back to scanning the arriving vehicles. He had given Heather the rest of the details of his plan—save the most important one—and had been shocked when she'd agreed without argument. It was almost like they were starting to trust one another. That made it even harder.

"How long do we have to pull this off?" she asked.

"The concert starts in about an hour and goes until eleven. The Knights will hit in that three-hour window. I'd think they'd be showing up any minute."

She nodded. "So what's next?"

"We need a master key to the rooms upstairs. After that, we wait for the fireworks to start and slip in amongst the chaos."

"This probably isn't going to work, you know," she said. "There are way too many variables."

He watched as several unmarked white vans pulled into the parking garage and started disgorging fit-looking men and women. The Knights had arrived precisely on time. "I know."

"And even if it does work, you'll still have a god-shaped time bomb in your head," she said.

The hourglass flashed across his thoughts once. The top was nearly empty. Aka Manah stayed eerily silent. "Yeah, I know."

"Not to mention that Dale and Reznick both hate your guts, and your house is destroyed, and Gwendal and Paul are way out of our league. And the bounty—"

Gabe took her hand and pulled her into the street toward the hotel. "I got it. You forgot to say I'm flat broke too. Now let's go. If you give me any more confidence I'm going to kill myself."

They slipped into the hotel just ahead of the Knights, and Gabe pulled Heather into the vacant breakfast area. A moment later, the Knights spread out through the lobby behind them, pretending to be loitering guests as they casually set up a rough perimeter. Gabe held Heather's hand as if they were a couple and went straight for the stairwell. He could only hope his trail of power was still dim enough to go unnoticed by the Knights in the busy lobby.

"Give me your phone," he said as the door closed behind them.

Heather obeyed, then she glanced back through the window at the dozens of Knights being casual as hard as they could. "This plan suddenly seems—"

"Too late," he said, hearing the phone pick up on the other end. "Hi, we have a problem in room one-twelve," he said, in his Tony persona's Southern accent. "The toilet is overflowin' like nobody's business. I'm standin' here holding the ball thing so the water doesn't go everywhere, but please hurry. It's definitely broken."

He hung up and gave her phone back. Then they ran to the first floor.

Ten minutes and one smitten maintenance guy later, Gabe had a master key. "I'd say 'good work' but that might be stretching the limits on both words," Gabe said. "Now I need you to go back downstairs. Give me ten minutes, then tell the Knights that Gwendal is on the top floor."

"Is that enough time? What the hell are you going to do if you can't find your dad and get out before then?"

Gabe shrugged. "She needs me alive. If it works, great. If I fail, then the Knights have one more guy to rescue and I'm still there to keep my dad safe. No big deal. Now scoot, little lady. I need to go be a big damn hero."

She sighed in annoyance as he started up the stairs, but a moment later, he heard her descending back to the lobby as requested. Only then did he allow himself to panic. Everything was in motion now, and too late to call back. He wouldn't be able to forgive himself if something happened to his dad, so he had to try—even if it meant running headlong into a wood chipper. Alexander Delling might never have been the man he should have been when he was able to be, but that didn't mean Gabe had to end up the same. He wouldn't run away from this. Not ever. He could do this one good thing in his life, then the world could go screw itself.

That was the part he'd withheld from Heather: there was no way he could find his dad and get back out—not him alone against Hunters and Paul and Gwendal. That had never been the plan. At worst, it would have gotten all of them killed, but even at best it would have left him with the damned god still wedged in his head. He needed to deal with everything at once and come out with the best result possible. But Heather, with her compulsion to protect him, would never have let him go had she known his actual strategy. And he still needed her for a little longer. He wondered if real heroes ever felt as phony as he did right then. And with that thought, he hit the top floor landing and came to a sudden stop. Frost covered the fire door window on all but a small patch, and through that space, a single bright eye was staring back at him.

Gabe's breath caught and his first impulse was to run away, but he squashed that hard and stood his ground. He hadn't come so far just to retreat. Then he found himself instinctively flicking through his personae for a character to hide behind. Viktor was gone ever since Aka Manah had shattered him like glass, but he could use someone else. Anyone would do. But he found a shred of courage somewhere and killed that urge too. He would do it as himself. It was important that he did.

The Hunter opened the door and entered the stairwell with its Rime Blade crackling and steaming in its fist. Its yellow eyes glowed with malice, and its teeth were bared in a rictus grin. It had sensed him coming, as Gabe had hoped it would. It was time for his amazing plan.

Gabe held up his hands to show they were empty. "I surrender."

The creature flicked its eyes up and down the stairs, searching for a trap, then settled back onto Gabe. "So easily?" it asked, its voice like gravel over old leather.

Gabe nodded slowly, being careful not to make any sudden moves. "I know when I'm beaten. And I want my dad back and this monster out of my head. Take me to Gwendal so we can make those things happen."

The Hunter took a step forward and let the door slam closed behind it. "You were worthy prey. Now you would simply roll over and disgrace the hunt? Cheapen the sacrifice of those lost?" There was something wild and unpredictable in its eyes.

"I said take me to Gwendal," Gabe said, fighting hard to keep the fear pressed down.

The Hunter's expression didn't change, but Gabe felt the area go suddenly colder. The light in its eyes was manic. "'Only alive,' was the order. Not whole. You are too worthy for surrender." Its jaw creaked like old wood as it tried to widen its grin. "Run."

Gabe tensed, and it was all he could do to keep from bolting back down the stairs. "No."

"Run!" The thing howled. Then it struck.

Gabe dodged back just in time to miss the first swing, but found himself with his heels brushing the lip of the descending stairs. There was nowhere else to go. The Hunter brought the sword sweeping out low as if to take off his legs, and Gabe's body took over, pitching him to the side and away from the strike. He fell to his stomach, barely avoiding both the blade and a tumble down the stairs, then flipped to his back just in time to see a cloud of brick dust scattering where the frozen sword had sliced a neat groove through the wall above him.

The Hunter flourished the blade in a tight circle to redirect it down at him, and Gabe desperately lashed out with his foot, connecting solidly on the creature's left knee. Then something amazing happened. By sheer luck, the kick caught the creature just as it was transferring its momentum forward, and the knee collapsed beneath the Hunter's weight. The monster tried to catch itself, but its foot hit ten inches of air where the descending stairs started, and it began to topple over. The thing grabbed the railing to stop the fall, tipped just at the point of overbalancing, and Gabe kicked the other leg.

The monster dropped, flying down the stairs in a rolling heap with the sword flailing as it went. And when the jumble came to a stop on the landing below, the thing was sprawled in an entirely wrong shape with the blade rising at an angle through its stomach and out its back. Gabe almost whooped with joy, but caught himself before he could erase his dumb luck with conscious stupidity. He studied the Hunter for another moment, noting that its left leg looked shattered, with bone pressing out against its ragged pants. Even if the thing wasn't dead somehow, it wouldn't be chasing him anytime soon.

Never one to take even a passing glance into a gift horse's mouth, Gabe slipped through the fire door and into the hallway. The first thing he did was survey the area for more Hunters. He had pictured himself surrendering and being taken straight to Gwendal and his father just as the Knights came in to save the day, but apparently he'd underestimated the single-mindedness and batshit insanity of the things. It seemed he'd need to find Gwendal or Paul personally. Their brand of crazy would hopefully be a little more predictable.

He moved away from the stairwell and started opening doors—then stopped at the sight of bodies. Two men were sprawled out across the hotel room floor, motionless and clearly dead. Both were dressed roughly, as if they hadn't been doing well even before meeting Gwendal, and both looked almost like props from a good horror movie. Their skin was desiccated and sunken and a sickly white, and they bore wide ragged wounds across their throats. Gabe had little experience with dead bodies, so he wasn't sure what they were supposed to look like, but these seemed far worse than they should have. They looked used up. Drained. He studied them from the doorway, too terrified to get closer and find his father's features, but even from there he could tell that neither man was familiar to him. He breathed a sigh of relief, then felt bad for it and tore his eyes away.

His only warning was a sudden burst of cold air on his back, but it gave him just enough time to blindly dodge before the frozen sword sliced him in half lengthwise. Instead, the Rime Blade gouged a long furrow down his right arm, and a hideous, searing pain scoured all thought from his brain. Gabe screamed and his instincts took over, propelling him into a charge straight toward the Hunter. He slammed into it hard, and its broken leg crumpled beneath its weight and sent it sprawling backward. As it landed, the blade slid from its grip and skittered past Gabe's feet.

Gabe backpedaled, trying desperately to distance himself, but pain overrode his commands and made the strength run from his legs like water. He pulled at the bare scraps of magic at his command and shunted everything to the wound in his arm to quiet the pain. It wasn't nearly enough, but it gave him a bit of clarity to slap a plan together. He had to salvage this somehow. He couldn't lose now. If he could only find a way to—

Then he was suddenly falling as his heel landed on something hard and his ankle rolled. He tried to catch himself as he dropped, but his injured right arm refused to respond quickly enough, and he took most of the impact to his shoulders and the back of his head. The world exploded in light.

"It is happening," Aka Manah said, rising from his long silence. *"We are fracturing. Impossible to stop now."*

When his sight came back an instant later, he was on the ground and the Hunter was dragging itself toward him. Gabe could see now that the monster's head lolled to one side, and that its left leg flopped worthlessly behind it. But still it came on. It clawed over the carpet toward him, and Gabe knew he didn't stand a chance. Broken or not, anything that could take that much damage and still keep going definitely had the odds in a wrestling match. And it didn't look like it cared anymore about keeping him alive. Something primal in it had taken over, and no mere orders would stop it. Several plans tried to form in his head, but none of them were good. There were no elegant ways around this—just hard and brutal ones. So he gave into the moment and acted.

He reached out desperately to the item he had stepped on, blindly groping with his left hand to where he knew it should be. The Hunter latched onto his leg in the same instant, tearing through his pants and into the skin with ragged nails. The grip crushed his calf until it felt like the fingers would sink to the bone, and Gabe cried out. Then the creature pulled itself up in a single vicious movement. The hideous face rose above him, with eyes wild and rolling, and fleshless muscles working to clench the bare, yellow jaw bone into a snarl. It growled low in its throat and raised a gory fist to smash his skull.

Gabe slapped the ground frantically, desperate to save himself.

The Hunter's fist rose, and the growl became high and feral.

He had one chance, and he couldn't find it.

The monster sucked in a quick breath before the kill.

It had to be there. Where was it?

The thing's shoulder muscles tensed, building force.

He couldn't find it. He couldn't!

The fist moved.

Gabe's hand closed around the hilt of the Rime Blade. And he screamed.

CHAPTER THIRTY-THREE

```
"If you've stuck around this long into the book,
you know my dad wasn't the greatest. And though
I've talked about that relationship for context,
I don't really consider it an excuse for who I
am now. I'm not stupid or a victim. I saw the
paths laid out before me, and I made my choices
as surely as he ever did. I could have been a
Banker, or a Gardener, or a Lion Tamer despite
my childhood. I picked this. That's on me. You
should usually try to make lemonade with what
life hands you, that's true. But other times,
just be thankful you got anything at all and eat
the damned lemons."

-Excerpt from Chapter Nine, CONscience
```

  The instant Gabe touched the hilt of the Rime Blade, his hand froze to it. Then he screamed and swung, bringing the sword into the side of the Hunter's head. The edge sank effortlessly into the skull over its right ear and wedged there to steam sullenly in the dim hallway light. The monster's grip suddenly loosened, and the descending fist only clipped Gabe's jaw before cracking into the floor.

  Still, the Hunter didn't go down. The creature stayed there above him, staring as if he'd just done something stupid. Gabe waited in terror to find out how badly he'd just messed up, then watched in awe as a look of complete peace passed over the Hunter's face. The thing's feral grin slackened and became almost pleasant, and its whole body suddenly seemed to sag with intense relief. Then, with the last of its strength, the monster threw itself toward the blade and sliced off the top of its own skull.

  The creature rolled to one side and hit the wall with a thud, and Gabe quickly pushed himself away. He sucked in several quick breaths and pointed the sword toward the body, but he could already tell that the animating force was gone. The Umbra wouldn't be getting back up. He'd killed another Hunter—or helped it kill itself—and he'd done it with the creature's own weapon.

As the deadly moment frayed and unspooled back into real life, Gabe found himself afraid to learn how bad off he really was. As the first and hopefully least of his problems, he let his focus narrow to the Rime Blade. It weighed almost nothing, but every gram of it pulled and tore his frozen skin, adding a new layer to the pains that were now trying to tally themselves in the aftermath. It was made of an opaque ice in blues and whites and grays, and it looked like it might have been pulled from the heart of a glacier instead of the hand of a monster. A spiderweb of crystalline imperfections ran all along the length, catching his eye until they started to resolve into something very near to runic writing. And even as he watched, small drops of water formed just above his hand as the hoarfrost contended with his living flesh. He experimentally tried to let go, but the stab of agony that followed put an immediate stop to it. It would undoubtedly tear his skin if he tried. So apparently he had a magic sword now—at least until it melted or made his hand fall off.

The pain in his right arm became too hard to ignore then, and he made the mistake of shifting his focus to it next. A wide black gash ran from the top of his shoulder down the length of his forearm, and the muscle had separated enough to show where the bone beneath had been faintly scored by the very tip of the sword. His magic and the frostbitten nerves seemed to be keeping most of the pain at bay, but he could tell that it should hurt much more than it did. He knew he didn't have enough power to heal the wound outright, and he didn't yet know how to consciously start that anyway. So he probably had an amputation to look forward to—if he lived that long.

The hallway started spinning, and Gabe pulled in a long, slow breath as he tried to fight back despair. He'd ostensibly won, but now had two limbs dead or dying. And though he knew he should count himself lucky for surviving at all, he only felt fear. He started shivering uncontrollably and pressed his back hard against the wall for something firm to anchor to. The choices were bad. He could leave now and get to a hospital, but it would mean abandoning his father to whichever side came out on top in the showdown he'd orchestrated. It would mean running away, but he might save his arm.

He waited for Aka Manah to rise and whisper his poison in that moment of desperation, but all he got was a brief impression of the empty hourglass, and then the white door bulging in its frame. The silent images were somehow more frightening than the constant whispers and threats, and they did even less to help him. Everything was turning to complete shit, and that was saying something. It was funny how quickly a turn for the worse could make you miss even the terrible place you just came from.

That almost made him laugh, and the sensation was like a shot of sugar to a starving man. He'd really tried this time and had somehow screwed up anyway. But nothing had actually changed aside from a few ouchies and some fresh self-pity. He was in Gwendal's lair, which was a big step. And he was still alive. This was still the moment, and he still had a chance as long as he didn't give up. He'd spent half of his life conning people into believing he was someone else, yet he'd never once realized how thoroughly he'd been conning himself. The last few days had proven that he no idea who he really was, but fate seemed to be handing him a chance to finally find out.

Gabe used the wall to drag himself to his feet, then leaned there a moment to let the world settle down to a slow rock. He took a step toward a room door, then another and another, until his balance steadied and he felt strong enough to avoid toppling over. He quickly realized that he couldn't use the master key with his lame right hand, so instead he brandished the Rime Blade and stabbed it through the lock. There was almost no resistance as the weapon passed through the metal and wood, but when the door slowly creaked open, he saw that several shards had broken from the edge and were steaming and melting on the carpet. It might even have been worth studying, had it not been for the bodies.

The room was full of them. Nine dead men, all bled out and dumped carelessly onto the carpet or bed like dirty laundry. They looked and smelled like they hadn't been touched in days, and Gabe's throat clenched as he frantically searched the faces for his father. But none of them were familiar. They were dead strangers—lost to someone, but not him. He glanced down the hall at the two dozen rooms on the floor and cursed. His ten minutes had probably elapsed in the fight, which meant the Knights could show up at any point and he'd be right in the middle. It left no time for subtlety, and he felt his inner strategist throw up his hands in disgust as he started hacking open doors and kicking them in.

Eight more rooms went by, with the blade fracturing and melting as he went, and the bodies continued to mount to the point that he had to stop counting. He could only afford to care about one person, and he had yet to find him. There was still a chance. By the time he hit the ninth room, his sword was a broken mess, and he had to work much harder to slash through the lock. He'd allowed himself to grow numb to the sight of death just to make it through the task, but he braced for more as he kicked open the door and leveled the remnants of his sword. What he found was even worse than he'd expected.

The hotel room had been transformed into the set of a horror movie. A stained altar stood in the middle of the room with fat candles burning low and doing little to light the unnatural dark within. Dozens of wicker hoops hung from the ceiling like terrifying ornaments, each one draped with some small bit of red flesh and twisting slightly in its own unfelt breeze. And there was blood everywhere.

Gabe slowly moved into the room and almost tripped over a handful of small wooden figurines that seemed to cover the floor in random piles. They varied in size and complexity—some masterful and some barely roughed out—but all of them were clearly an iteration of Gwendal, and each of them held a whiff of magic. There were hundreds. In some she was portrayed as monstrous: her arms and legs too long, back bent low, and tiny head bowed beneath a thick curtain of matted hair. He recognized in them the precursors of the creature he'd seen that morning. But in other figures she was tall and long and impossibly beautiful, a goddess of sex and secrets. Heather had claimed it took years to mold a body to a new spirit, but Gwendal was already transforming. She was rushing it for some reason, but which of the two extremes she was becoming was unclear.

"Only temporary," a soft voice said behind him.

Gabe whipped around with the sword up to find Gwendal standing in the doorway.

She was taking in the room with the prideful eyes of a master craftsman, barely noticing the weapon pointed her direction. "Of course something more permanent will have to be arranged," she said. "But this has been adequate."

Gabe took several steps backward before finding the strength to hold his ground. She had changed further since that morning, and her skin was now white almost to translucence against hair that was now long, jet black, and stick-straight. She'd developed more of a hunch as well, making her seem far older, and her eyes had grown to twice their normal size. There was no longer any way to mistake her for human.

He took a breath and firmed his resolve. "You know why I'm here," he said, holding the dripping sword steady. "I'm giving myself up. Life for life, like you said. Now where is he?"

Gwendal slowly uncoiled from where she leaned in the doorway and painted her face with a disapproving scowl. She nodded to the sword. "You have an odd way of surrendering. And you're catching me early. I'd hoped to be fully changed for our meeting. You were supposed to be at the estate tonight."

Gabe allowed himself a tight smile. "I didn't think it was a good idea to let you choose the playground. Sorry if I screwed up your game."

Gwendal watched him with her wide, wet eyes. "Not overmuch. We have time to spare, and I will be happy to escort you there, if—"

"No," he said, cutting her off. "Here and now. Show me my father and I'll give you what you want. No tricks, no betrayals. Just the deal." He was pretty sure he needed his dad to be close by for his plan to work. He just needed to see him.

Gwendal's lips curled into a snarl. "Do you think you're clever? Do you think you've won? There is so much more at play here than this small diversion. We are only now unboxing our pieces. The game is yet to begin." She stared into his eyes and held him fast with it. "Though you have seen it, haven't you? The Emptiness? The Endless Dark. I can see its mark in you even now. The war we are attempting is far greater than anything your tiny brain could—"

Gabe felt Aka Manah stir and rise within him at the recitation, and he slashed the sword through the air to cut them both off. "Enough! Give me my dad!"

"Or what?" she snapped back. "You think you can damage me, human? With that?"

Gabe heard the confidence in her voice, but her face betrayed a flicker of uncertainty. She wasn't sure what he could do, and it gave him a shot of courage. "Lady, I've got nothing left to lose. Hell, I barely had the one thing, and you have him. You've backed me into a corner. So either you start talking, or I'll show you what a desperate human is capable of." He took a step toward her, and she flinched back from the blade. He grinned fiercely and took another step.

"I don't pretend to know even a fraction of what's going on. This Emptiness, Ether, Umbra bullshit is mostly nonsense to me, but I know this: I'm not the man I was two days ago. So if you think I'm just going to roll over and let you—"

Just then something caught his foot, and a hoarse scream filled the room. Gabe looked down in shock to find a gnarled hand reaching out from beneath the bed to grasp his ankle. He wrenched himself free, but it was only to find Gwendal suddenly there and wrapping long fingers around his throat. He twisted to bring his sword around, but black tendrils of power rose from the blood-soaked carpet and twined around his arm to hold it like steel coils. They snaked ever tighter as he struggled, holding him still and pulling his arm taut. Then they climbed the blade itself and ripped it from his hand. He tried to scream at the sudden onslaught of pain, but Gwendal squeezed hard and the sound turned into a strangled gurgle. Then she lifted him up onto the balls of his feet and his breath cut off entirely.

She smiled darkly and inspected him, her expression like a cat with an interesting bug beneath its paw. Then she leaned toward him and inhaled, smiling sweetly as she held it in. "He's still in there, isn't he? My love. My god."

"Ahhhh, at last." Aka Manah said, uncoiling in Gabe's mind.

Gwendal tightened her grip further and Gabe felt things grind together in his neck. For a moment he was certain she would kill him right there and extract Aka Manah from his corpse somehow, but then she relaxed her hand and let him take his own weight again. He pulled in a desperate breath and his vision wavered as the blood rushed back into his head, and Gwendal just sighed and turned to look at something on the ground. Gabe reflexively followed her stare and saw that the gnarled hand around his ankle had belonged to a man beneath the bed who looked like he'd lived a thousand years of misery. He was naked and filthy and broken, but his eyes were filled with the dumb, all-consuming fervor of the hopelessly insane.

"Well done," Gwendal said to the old man. "Some of your work was almost acceptable."

"Thank you, mistress. I love you, mistress," The man slurred through fat, split lips.

"Of course you do," Gwendal said. "With my god gone from me, you have loved me best. Now come and take your reward as the final piece of my grand metamorphosis. You have earned it."

The man pulled himself across the floor, his legs dragging uselessly behind him until he flopped over onto his back to stare directly up at Gwendal with unmitigated adoration. Then she lifted her bare foot and brought it down hard on his smiling face.

Gabe tried to recoil, but she held him fast, forcing him to stand there as she stomped the pitiful man to death. She turned her gaze to Gabe as she finished, meeting his eyes and licking her lips suggestively. Then a rush of power poured out of the man and she breathed it in, devouring the spilled life and devotion like a banquet meal.

Gabe saw it all. He felt his own magic recoil from the sensation as Gwendal swallowed the spirit whole, but he couldn't figure out how to turn the perception off. He felt every gasp and tremor in the energy as it died, and it felt more wrong than anything he'd ever known. He was hot all of a sudden and shaking uncontrollably. He could feel the blood running freely from his torn left hand, and the pain in his right arm was growing fierce as the nerves came back online at the worst possible time. He knew he would pass out soon—that, or crack—and there was nothing he could do about it. This was it. This was when he would finally break. And he honestly couldn't decide if he wanted to fight it anymore.

Then he felt Gwendal pull in the last of the spilled life, and all at once her skin began writhing over her frame. She let out an animal cry, and Gabe heard bones grinding somewhere in her body. He watched in horror as her flesh twisted and reshaped itself into something new, and while whole mounds of muscle bunched and tore and swam just beneath her skin. And the whole time, she stared at him, her breath fast and limbs trembling in agony...or ecstasy.

She brought her face close for a kiss or a bite, but then turned to look back over her shoulder. Her huge eyes widened. "You've invited friends," she panted. "I can feel them coming for me. Too late, however. Once again you were..." she groaned in pleasure, "very nearly but not quite clever. A pity though. I would have played so nicely with you." She let out a long, low moan and then her spine crackled like distant fireworks. "Fortunately my plans are fluid. We don't have to go far."

Gabe gritted his teeth and tried to lift what remained of his hand to strike her, but found that his arms no longer obeyed his commands. Her eyes lit with a flicker of delight as she saw his comprehension, then she squeezed. He tried to pry at the paralyzing geas, to tear it off again, but this time the hand around his throat didn't let up. Soon a howling wind was rising in his ears and a dark curtain of smoke was filling his mind. He threw himself against her power as he sank, but his thoughts just splashed over her, too weak and too late as blood stopped flowing to his brain. He grasped desperately for Aka Manah's power to augment his own, but it skittered away from his mental grip as he fell into darkness.

In the end, he managed only a few desperate twitches before the world collapsed around him with a soft hiss and pop.

CHAPTER THIRTY-FOUR

"Remorse is different than guilt, and I'm actually sorry for a lot of things in my life. I never sought out my mom, for one. I guess I've always been too afraid of what I'd find. But mostly I'm sorry for not being able to look my dad in the eyes for more than a moment. I can't help but see both versions of the man in there, and I never know which to hope for. It'll either be the dad I've learned to love over the last decade, or it'll be the one I've hated my entire life. And even though the first is slowly slipping away from me, I can never quite bring myself to wish for him to make a full recovery. It's the real reason I'm always so terrified to visit: a miracle for him would be a nightmare for me."

-Excerpt from Chapter Ten, CONscience

    Gabe woke, and the first thing he did was reflect on how freaking tired he was of getting knocked unconscious. Then he focused long enough to realize he was lying on a bench in a large dark room. His right arm still throbbed, but it moved at his command, and he could see enough of it to know it had scarred over already. That was a hell of a nice surprise when he'd been expecting to lose it. He knew he should have learned already to never underestimate magic.
    He tentatively searched with his fingertips for the damage the Rime Blade had done to his left hand and found the skin intact there too. He breathed out in relief. The only indications that anything had happened at all were a raised rough patch in the center of his palm and an odd chill like holding a cold glass. Nerve damage, he guessed, and he'd definitely take it over the alternative.
    It was only then that he grasped the import of being able to move at all: he wasn't paralyzed, magically or otherwise. But before his brain could lurch into motion and construct a new plan, the sound of a man quietly humming filled the room, and the familiar voice made

Gabe pause and reconsider everything about his situation. He sat up with a heavy sigh. "What do you want?"

Aka Manah stood at the front of a medieval church, lighting the first few candles in a bank of hundreds lined up neatly around the white door sitting atop an altar. He wore a long red robe that covered him from head to toe and cascaded down the stairs like a bride's train, but the loose fabric did nothing to hide the broad shoulders and trim physique beneath. At Gabe's question, he glanced back with a surprised smile that lit an impossibly handsome face.

"Oh my!" the god said. He shook out a match as he turned. "I had hoped for more time to prepare. But then you are full of surprises." His tone was light and affectionate, as if to welcome a party guest that had arrived a few minutes early. He made the match vanish as he descended the steps, then he slipped his hands into his sleeves like a monk.

"I'm a little busy," Gabe said. "So if you could hurry this along I'd appreciate it."

Aka Manah stopped at the bench and bowed his head in acknowledgment. "Yes, you're quite busy recently. Flitting about from place to place, learning new things, killing everything in sight. That's an impressive trophy."

Gabe followed the god's gaze to his arm and saw that the cut was still faintly outlined in the dark blue/black of frostbite, giving it the look of a terrible tattoo. "I had to kill another Hunter. No big deal. Thanks for the help on that, by the way."

Aka Manah raised a perfect eyebrow. "Oh, I would have loved to intervene! Alas, all my energy has been going to keeping us from falling to pieces. You're quite welcome. Still, killing a Hunter is no easy feat. They were old when I was young, though their legend had yet to be properly born." He lifted a hand to stroke a goatee that Gabe hadn't noticed. "They do have some glaring weaknesses for those unafraid to exploit them, however. A certain single-mindedness not the least of which. And a thirst for the Hunt which only barely supersedes the desire for *release*. From the Huntmaster, perhaps. From torment, certainly."

Gabe watched as the god stroked the facial hair once more and then wiped it away as if it had never been. Then a sudden realization hit him, and he stood slowly to meet Aka Manah's eyes. "Why can I see your face now? I thought you were trapped."

The god waved his hand dismissively. "Oh, I am. But I find myself growing more comfortable with my surroundings the longer I'm here. And your memories gave me some much-needed clarity. Thank you for that. It's all allowed me a certain level of freedom to stretch out. I'm really no more present than I was yesterday. I'm just more focused now that I'm fully acquainted with my accommodations. Learning where you keep the towels and how you like your coffee, so to speak."

"Making yourself at home," Gabe said.

"Unavoidable, I'm afraid. And only in time to see the place fall apart around us." He held out a hand, and the hourglass appeared in it. The top was empty except for a single grain of sand suspended in the neck. "I did warn you that this space was too small for us both. I've stretched your psyche as far as I dare in my struggle to maintain cohesion, but neither of us can fight it for much longer. Another hour out there. Maybe less." He smiled then and gestured around. "Do you like the ambiance? A favorite haunt from days gone by. But we can change it if you'd like. Perhaps something more modern?"

Reality flickered like a switched television channel, and Gabe found himself standing at a high-top table in a trendy bar. Strangers milled about, filling the space with a low hum of noise, but none of them had recognizable faces beyond the rough impression of human features. They were like moving mannequins filling a stage set. The hourglass sat as the centerpiece of their table, and the white door behind the bar was the only visible exit.

Aka Manah, now in jeans and a fashionable button-up shirt, smiled at him like a little kid with a new trick. "Better? It's from one of your memories. Though perhaps lacking some verisimilitude for never having experienced it myself."

Gabe suppressed a shudder. "It doesn't really matter, does it? The illusions you throw up? It's all just window dressing in *my* head."

Aka Manah made a huge silver flagon of something dark and thick appear out of nowhere, then took a long pull as he nodded. He smacked his lips and sighed in appreciation. "True enough, though increasingly *our* head. And soon neither of ours—whether by death or something worse. And that's really why we're here." He lifted the flagon and studied the polished surface. Then his face fell as if a joke hadn't quite landed, and he tipped the mug out onto the table. Gabe took a step back to avoid being splashed, but only a wisp of dust fell out.

The god's mouth turned up at Gabe's reaction. "You see, as nice as this all may be, it doesn't come close to the real thing." He tossed the flagon aside. "Reality has a flavor and vigor that can't be duplicated by mere will. This place is much like the Ether: shadow and smoke and nothing else. I can mold it to my will endlessly, but what's the point in playing with a hollow shell? I am dulling my hunger on the smell of real food when what I truly need is sweet wine and dripping meat."

Aka Manah spread his hands wide, as if to show that he was about to bare his soul. Then reality flickered again, and they were standing on a high peak with snow to their knees and cloud-shrouded mountains surrounding them. The door and the hourglass were nearly lost in the blizzard. "Yet, I find that I have a rather unique problem in this," the god went on, ignoring the bitter wind. "And therefore few established options. We should not have lasted this long. I've been waiting for one or both of us to break at any moment, but every time we somehow pull back. We are sustaining what should be unsustainable in your stupidly stubborn skull. In fact, I don't believe there has ever been a pairing quite so resilient as we two. I might even find it a fascinating case study if I weren't so close to the matter."

Gabe was using every ounce of his strength to keep from wrapping his arms around himself in the illusory cold, so he couldn't construct a response.

"We're not completely unique in our misery, of course," Aka Manah continued. "Lunatics, fanatics, the possessed—many have shared our predicament. But I do not believe I need to elaborate overmuch on the consequences that have thus far been universal. Despite our efforts, I fear the final result *will* be catastrophic." Reality flickered once more and this time they were in a dark cave, sitting over a fire. "Any minute now, the thin barrier remaining between our two spirits will split wide, and we will cease to be separate entities. You've felt it, I'm sure. The memories, the emotions. They're precursors. And the best case if we do nothing is that we shatter simultaneously. The worst case is that we don't, and the resulting creature possesses the power of a god with the reckless ignorance of a human. We might destroy the world... Or more."

The fire was thawing him, and Gabe finally managed to speak. "Isn't that why you're here? To destroy the world and the other standard bad guy stuff?"

Aka Manah seemed genuinely disturbed by the idea. "Of course not! What would I gain from blighting this world? The honor of ruling over a barren wasteland? I thought I had made it clear that I am here to save you?"

Gabe shrugged. "You send a lot of mixed messages. But it changes nothing. Your wife has my dad and wants to trade him for you. I agreed. Then she knocked me out for my trouble. I'm already doing everything I can to get free of you."

Aka Manah chuckled like they were old friends having a chat. "Yes, she can be overzealous in her methods. In truth, she is not my favorite wife. But she is powerful—more so than even she knows—though don't tell her that! And she's fiercely devoted to both me and our cause. It's why I groomed her for this. She is to prepare the way for our audacious plan to unpin the wheel of time from its axle and hold the Endless Dark at bay forevermore. It's quite a big deal, actually." He shook his head. "However, you are wrong in one thing: you are not yet doing all you can. For us to safely separate, you must perform one further task."

Gabe smiled then, finally hearing the kind of line he was used to. "Oh yeah? The first time we had this conversation, only one of us could survive and I was about as useful to you as a third nipple. What's so different now?"

Aka Manah met his eyes and frowned. "I would think that quite obvious." Reality flickered again, and they were standing face-to-face in a white padded room. "You are no longer human."

Gabe kept his skeptical mask in place, but behind it his thoughts were running riot. It felt like the hammer had finally come down on him and the broken pieces of his life were falling far away. "What am I?"

"That's the wonderful part!" the god replied. "I don't know! You are something very new made from something very old. And, as it happens, you are just what we need. As a human, the best we could have hoped for was a violent severing with a small chance of us both surviving. You simply lacked the control and strength to manage what must be done. I found that gamble unappealing. But you have magic of your own now. You can tip the scales that bind me here—add your weight to the balance and break the stalemate. And if my wife has secured enough power, she can then use it to pull me free. We all win. This whole nightmare can be over."

Gabe tried to reply, but there was no good response to being told you weren't human anymore. Even if he did come out alive, what would he be surviving as? He tried to push it back to worry about later, but it was too big, and he'd already done that too often. He was over capacity for bad news, and the pile of it was collapsing. What did it all mean? Who was he? How could he fix it? Did he want to? Did it matter? The questions cascaded like error messages on a computer screen, and every one of them demanded an answer before it would go away.

Aka Manah seemed to notice. "I never imagined you would be so shocked. You have been exposed to the power of a god—channeled it, even. That will shape you. Recall that *you* requested the means to use magic, and that you were warned about the price. I forced nothing on you. I couldn't have."

Reality flickered, and they were standing in dead grass over the body of the preta he'd burned. Then they were at the mall watching the Hunters liquefy, then the street by the pishtaco, then Reznick's apartment, then back in the wine cellar where it all began. Gabe desperately tried to deny that he was anything but a regular human, but each location brought back a memory of a small change he'd undergone or a brief nudge he'd ignored. And try as he might to kill the implications, he couldn't deny where it had all left him. He hadn't been considering any long-term consequences from the start. He'd been sprinting from danger to danger, pushing common sense aside and taking any help he could get while he stashed the big questions away to worry about later. He'd been out of his depth since walking into that warehouse two days ago, and everything he'd done and planned since had been woefully naive. And now he wasn't human anymore—which just so happened to be the exact situation the god needed.

The realization hit him like a brick in the face. He'd been conned from the start. Every offer of magic, every trade, and every whisper had all been there to prod him toward this moment. Even the hourglass had been a knife at his back, reminding him of the urgency, piling on the tension. He lined it all up for the first time, and the whole picture became shockingly clear. It had all been Aka Manah driving him to desperation, to need help, to *need* magic. Every step along the way had been another toward this end, and the god had taken advantage of every opportunity to weave the web tighter. All the victories Gabe had thought he'd won were losses. All the truths were lies. He'd been played by a master—maybe *the* master—and he couldn't trust anything he thought he knew. The anger that followed worked well to clear the despair.

He'd forgotten an important lesson: When in a game you don't know how to play, it is always acceptable to take small losses at the beginning to learn the rules. And had he remembered that two days ago, he might not have been pressed into a corner. But with so little left to lose, all he had now was one terrible choice and zero freedom to worry about the larger consequences. If he wanted to break even and walk away, to at least leave with what he'd come in with, he'd have to gamble with one life to win the other. And that meant getting into the same room as his dad.

"Okay," Gabe said, "You've got me. I have no idea what I'm doing here. You are an ancient god of wisdom and sexiness, or whatever, and I'm a guy with an embarrassingly comprehensive knowledge of Star Wars fan fiction. We're not anywhere near the same league. I get that now. So why don't you tell me exactly what you want and what you think I can do to get you there."

Aka Manah smiled, and suddenly the door was there with them again. "I'm pleased that we can work together toward our common benefit. Your job is very simple. I will pit every ounce of my power to balance against the pull of the Ether, and presumably Gwendal will have sorted out a way to pry me free. She is nothing if not resourceful. What we are missing is the middle bit." He gestured to the door. "This side of the portal exists only in your mind. As such, your magic is ideally suited to manipulating it. All you must do when the time comes is open the way. A shred of power only, and I will handle the rest. Once free, I will ensure that your father is returned to you. You have my word."

Gabe stared at the door. "What happens if I don't open it?"

Aka Manah shrugged. "I won't have the strength once we begin. So if you choose to keep this closed... Well, we will see what happens when a broken god and a broken man collide. It should be interesting for those who survive long enough to see it."

Gabe swallowed back his fear. It could just be more lies. "And if I do open it, where will you go?"

The god seemed unconcerned, like a human body to occupy was a trivial detail. "Gwendal will have found a suitable replacement. I will eventually shape it to my liking, so anything undamaged will do. Your only concern is that I will be gone from you and working to save humanity. One day, you will even be thankful for my presence here."

It sounded so simple, and again Gabe found himself wanting to fall into the trap and just accept the instructions to get the whole mess over with. But he had no reason to believe that Aka Manah would keep his word or that he wasn't still playing some bigger game. Gabe knew there would be a catch and something would go wrong. There would be a barb on this hook, but he didn't know enough to predict what it might be. His only hard facts were that Aka Manah was evil, and that Gwendal was probably worse. Without a doubt, he would be unleashing something terrible on the world.

But it was also his best chance to walk away. And he couldn't help but think the world might actually *need* something terrible to finally fix it. It might not be fair or nice, but truths rarely were. It came down to either saving himself and his father today, or stopping an uncertain threat to all of humanity tomorrow. And the latter, frankly, wasn't his job. He wasn't anything special, nor did he have any great reason to love the world. It had never done anything to deserve protecting as far as he was concerned. And he'd never claimed to be a hero.

"Okay," Gabe said. "Let's do it."

CHAPTER THIRTY-FIVE

"My dad wasn't the one drunk that night. The accident wasn't his fault. An ironic twist for a man so adept at hurting other people with terrible decisions. Still, I couldn't squash the hate in those early days, even through the surgeries and the coma. Back then, I only really stayed to prove I was better than him. And yes, I know how crappy that is. But he finally needed me, finally gave me an opening to hurt him back, and I needed to show that family could stick around even when it sucked and there was no reward. Even when the person you were proving it to couldn't remember why it mattered. It was a little vengeance in the only form I could take it. And though it was the wrong reason, I'm still glad for it. I wouldn't have stayed otherwise, and that would've been much worse. Who could have guessed that doing the wrong thing might lead directly to the right? It's almost enough to make a guy take up religion."

-Excerpt from Chapter Ten, CONscience

    Gabe opened his eyes and knew immediately he was back in reality. For one, his right arm hurt like a barbwired bastard. Which turned out to be as much from the damage as from the fact that he seemed to be tied up and hanging by his feet. For another thing, there was a muffled noise in the background like a distant thrum and hiss that rose and fell at intervals. He assumed it was the blood pooling in his head, but he wasn't going to rule out magical hallucinations either. It was tough to tell these days. But mostly, it was because he was slapped awake to the grinning, upside down visage of a naked sex monster. He was sure he wouldn't have constructed that illusion for himself if given the choice.
    "Great," he said, his voice coming out hoarse and heavy, "my luck with women has finally bottomed out."
    Gwendal slapped him hard enough to make his ears ring, and he gritted his teeth to avoid spitting out a curse. Then she stepped back

to appraise him, and suddenly he didn't have to force himself to be quiet. She had finished changing, settling into a form that now seemed complete and completely inhuman.

The lank hair was gone, replaced by dark locks that shone wetly and framed a flawless fae-featured face, and her eyes were now twice normal size and glowing with the amber sheen of a nocturnal predator. All the spare flesh was now pulled taut across a frame that had grown long and lithely graceful, as if the hunched monster from earlier had extended its skeleton to grow into an ill-fitting suit. Her limbs were impossibly thin but corded with muscle, and they now held extra joints along their lengths that lent every movement an ethereal, flowing quality. She had stretched to almost seven feet, and all rules of proportion and realistic anatomy had ceased in her. This was the true Gwendal. She was embodied temptation and consequence, ripe fruit heavy on the branch with hatred, and carnal betrayal made flesh. She was impossible to resist and impossible to desire, and she was staring at Gabe like she wanted to take a big bite out of him.

Fortunately, he still knew better than to let her. He found the glamour she was using and pushed back against it until the effect lessened and he could think properly again. It wasn't that hard now that he knew the trick. She was still undoubtedly beautiful beneath it—in an alien way—but he had always known better than to put too much stock in skin-deep commodities.

Gwendal noticed the moment and magic passing, and her smile turned sour. "Of course not," she said, spitting the words. "You could have been the first man to experience me in my true form, but you continue to be difficult." She considered him for a moment, then stepped closer. The scent that came with her was like perfume and carrion. "Though I suppose it is fitting that my husband be the first to taste of my finished flesh." She stretched out a taloned finger and ran it slowly down his chin and over his throat. "Still, you would have been a sweet fruit, difficult as you were to pluck."

Gabe felt the sharp nail on the skin of his neck and did not doubt the threat it represented. But he had a job to do, and he wanted it done quickly. "Do you listen to yourself talk? You sound like you're waiting for the Power Rangers to show up. I admit that you at least look the part of a proper villain now, but you still sound like all your dialogue was written by a dungeon master on the back of a hamburger wrapper. Seriously, you're an ancient, unspeakable monster, and I'm a regular guy who had no idea what he was doing. This whole thing should have ended with my head on a spike in the first three minutes, but I had to walk my ass directly into your grasp before you started looking competent. Fortunately for both of us, your husband and I made a deal."

It was like pouring water on a hot pan. The anger that had been building in her eyes flared for a moment, then settled to a low boil. "Speak then, or I will tear your arms and legs off. I may need you alive for now, but I certainly don't need you whole. It is no accident that you have been trussed up with your belly at eye level." She smiled hideously with her perfect, gleaming teeth prominently on display. "How is that for proper dialogue?"

Gabe thought of all the nice soft bits that lived in and around his stomach, and some primal safeguards in his mind killed the smart-ass reply before he could voice it. He managed to keep his visible reaction suppressed to a slight shudder. "Yeah, okay. He wants to talk to you."

Her face lit up, and she was beautiful once more—though Gabe knew he'd never look at a smile quite the same way again. He flipped the mental switch Aka Manah had taught him and gave the god a kind of pass-through access to his speech. Now that he was getting a handle on magic, it had taken almost no effort to work out how to do it. Aka Manah had no major control over the body, but even so Gabe could feel the thing's presence inside his mind, reveling in the senses and poking at the boundaries like a backseat passenger reaching up to fiddle with the radio dial.

"Ah, my love. You are more beautiful than ever," the god said with Gabe's mouth.

Gwendal reacted like a school girl meeting her crush in the janitor's closet, and she rushed forward to press herself against him, kissing him long and painfully hard. Then she broke away with a look of horror. "Forgive me!" she said. "I did not know until it was too late!"

"Peace," Aka Manah replied. "There will be time for that later. The human and I have reached an agreement. Have you gathered the components to extricate me?"

"My bokor will complete the ritual," she said. "We have a new body for you. Everything is here, and we will soon have a sufficient sacrifice."

"It must be quite large," Aka Manah warned.

"It will be," she said. "More than enough."

"Excellent. Then bring forth the new vessel and ensure that it is *properly* cleansed. This human can now provide the catalyst to open the way. All the pieces are in place."

"An inspired solution," Gwendal said.

"Yes. We will also need a lesser Umbra to sacrifice. The pull of the Ether will demand completion, and as I pass through to the new vessel, the lesser Umbra must be released to fulfill the purpose."

"He and your new vessel are one and the same. The bokor assures me that you may take the sacrificial Umbra's flesh as he departs it. Very tidy."

"Good. The human and his father are then to be set free, and you and I will finally fulfill our destiny. Do you understand?"

Gwendal bowed her head. "But this human has wronged us. Surely he can't be allowed to go unpunished? What kind of example would that set to a world that must quickly fall under our sway if it is to survive?"

"A means to an end," he said. "Regardless, my bargain is ironclad. Is that clear?"

She bowed lower. "If you say, my love. I will see that your bargain is upheld to the letter. The bokor has prepared the ritual."

She rose and clapped her hands sharply, and lights began turning on high overhead. Gabe saw Paul first, standing by a circuit box like a theater technician who had just nailed his cue, but he quickly found the Hunters spread around the space as well. There were at least seven of them. The place looked like nothing more than a hallway that extended for several hundred feet before disappearing around a bend, but it was weirdly familiar to him. It was large enough for three cars to travel through abreast, and it was all steel beams and unfinished concrete broken only by endless pipes and ducts. At first Gabe assumed it was some kind of factory, but then he listened more carefully to the sound that had been bothering him since waking, and it all came together at once. He'd seen this place before on a tour, just after the grand opening. The muffled sound was music and a crowd. They were below the sold-out arena, with thousands of people above them.

Gwendal's plan became clear, and his stomach turned. He had to remind himself that he'd been expecting something to go wrong, and that this was nothing more than the anticipated bump in the road. He'd known that he'd have to come to terms with the sacrifice everyone had been talking about—it was the only way to be free. There was always a price, and this was it. He could take his freedom and his dad and get out, and all he had to do was let it happen. Wasn't he allowed to be too weak to fight back? Wasn't he allowed to be scared?

Gabe numbly pushed Aka Manah aside and took back control of his own mouth. He licked his dry lips. "You're supposed to yell 'surprise' when you turn the lights on," he said.

Gwendal saw the change and turned to issue commands, and Paul and a Hunter quickly moved a row of boxes aside to reveal a large chalk circle inscribed on the concrete. At the center of it, a terrified-looking stranger was held fast by Gwendal's geas. He was wearing a glamour about himself that flickered between something human and something bird-like, and Gabe guessed he was the sacrificial Umbra and Aka Manah's new body. His hair was a striking bright red, just like the tengu Heather had mentioned getting her information about Reznick from. Austin, he thought the guy's name was. It seemed like a weird coincidence.

"I told you I'd fuck your shit up," a familiar voice said behind him. Reznick walked into view, wearing a dark robe festooned with beads and a cloak covered in black feathers. He also sported the satisfied smile of a man about to see his fondest wish come true. "Your little play almost got me killed, but apparently old Samedi didn't want me yet. I found a patron."

"Look, Reznick," Gabe said, "I don't know for sure what's going on here, but I remember you saying something about this ritual needing a crazy amount of power. A big sacrifice. You're not seriously going to—"

"Fuck you, man," Reznick spat. "I was just doing my thing until you and your bitch came along. This is on you, okay? I might have done some bad shit, but I never would have gotten to this point if not for you. So *know* that. Know that this is on *you*." He sounded like he was trying to convince himself too.

Gabe almost wanted to stop arguing, but couldn't help it. "Come on. There are thousands of innocent—"

The punch was awkward and slow, but Gabe could hardly dodge. He took Reznick's fist full in the stomach and the pain was surprising. He retched and coughed and fought to breathe all at the same time, and the bokor only watched him struggle. Then Reznick spat at him before moving away to crouch by the circle and do something with a flask of dark liquid. He didn't look back.

Gwendal returned with Paul close behind. "Go block the exits," she said. All seven Hunters moved as if choreographed, simultaneously hefting handfuls of chains and locks, then running for the stairs to the upper level.

Gabe coughed once more before finally catching his breath. "Can you cut me down now? I want this asshole out of my head as much as you do, and I surrendered, remember? I'm not going anywhere."

Gwendal nodded to Paul, who stepped over and broke the ropes with one bare hand. Gabe dropped head-first to the ground, and only barely managed to hit with his shoulder to save himself a concussion. Pain screamed across his side, ribs, and arm, and Gwendal stared down at him smiling delightedly.

"Best party ever," Gabe said as he awkwardly got to his feet. His arm flared again, and he clamped his left hand to it, feeling new wetness there. Obviously his fancy healing powers still had limits. For the hundredth time, he wished he had an instruction manual. "Now bring out my dad before I unlock your boyfriend. I want to see him."

She smiled slyly and again nodded to Paul, who turned and ran like a shot. Gabe noted that the Hound seemed to be favoring his left arm, but didn't seem hampered much by it as he returned with Alexander over his right shoulder.

"Dad?" Gabe called, unable to help himself. "I'm right here." He heard a muffled reply that sounded like absolute anguish, and it fed more fuel to his resolve to see this through. The man couldn't possibly understand what was going on. "Dad, just hold on, okay? It's almost over. Everything will be fine."

Paul stood his father up next to the circle, and a haggard Alexander Delling looked around the room like a caged animal. Tears ran freely from his eyes, and his breath came quick and ragged. He looked like a frightened child, and Gabe could see the geas holding him in place against completion of the deal. Paul's hand also stayed on the back of his neck as an extra incentive. There really were no other ways forward, Gabe told himself. This was how it had to be. He *couldn't* save everyone.

Gwendal watched Gabe carefully, then nodded to Reznick. "Let us begin."

The bokor produced a live chicken and a knife from a nearby box, then stood over the circle. In one quick movement he punctured the bird's throat and blood spurted across the intricate markings. It sprayed out to cover the circle far faster and in greater amounts than should have been possible, but stopped perfectly at the boundaries as if held in by an invisible force. The Umbra at the center, Austin, looked like he wanted to cringe away from the flow but was frozen with Gwendal's will. Then the blood stilled and the bokor chanted something guttural, and the whole circle flared to life with a sullen power that seemed to eat at the corners of reality. Austin whined in terror, and Gwendal stepped up next to Reznick to add her own dark energy to the spell.

The ritual was different from what the sorcerer had done back at the mansion, but also somehow the same. Like a new flavor of magic working toward a similar goal, only this time Gabe could actually see it. Half of it was sharpened to pierce the veil—a scalpel of power to cut through the skin and fat and muscle of reality to reach into the womb of creation—and the other half was a hook to pull out something terrible. He watched in horror as a raw, naked hunger reached out from the Ether and up through the beams and concrete, and into the crowd above. Then the circle flared to red incandescence as the hunger pulled, and a vast wash of pure life began draining down to them. That easily, they were killing an entire crowd.

"It is working!" Gwendal said in ecstasy as she gathered the life energy to herself.

Reznick was sweating and breathing hard as he worked the ritual, but Gabe could see the fear and strain on his face. The man was barely standing. "If we're careful," he panted, "we don't have to kill them all. We only need a few dozen—"

"No!" Gwendal screamed. "Take it all! I will not fall short now. Once we've freed my love, we will use the excess to rip wide the veil and summon forth an army with the empty bodies. *This* is why we are here! *This* is how we will save you! Take them *all* for the greater good!"

While she screamed, Gabe felt Aka Manah stirring within his prison, and the closed door reappeared in his mind. This was the moment, he knew. He just had the one task. Yet he couldn't stop thinking about the people dying above. It felt similar to what Heather did, only bigger and worse and they wouldn't leave anyone alive.

"*Now, human.*" the god said. "*Free me. Open the way.*"

This was where the plan was supposed to happen. Gabe knew that. Right here. The idea was to free the god and take his father to safety. But he could also feel the sacrifice. People were dying. Suffering. His thoughts were all fraying, and he was having trouble remembering which thing was the right one.

"More!" Gwendal screamed as the rain of souls enveloped her.

Gabe thought he heard a disturbance in the crowd above. Maybe a scream. Maybe lots of screams. People must be dropping now. He forced his concentration back into a semblance of order, then found his power. It was so small compared to the god's. But he had to stick to the plan. He could save himself and his dad—that was the best he could do. The music far above stopped suddenly and the crowd noise took over. People were panicking up there, he realized. They were losing everything for him to be free.

"*Do it!*" Aka Manah commanded.

Gabe looked at his father, frozen statue-still by the geas but eyes wide with terror and confusion. He *could* do it. He could still have a family. He'd fought for it for so long, and he could get it back with a single thought. It wasn't perfect, but it was his. And it was the easier choice.

"*Now!*" Aka Manah bellowed, the sound sending cracks through Gabe's mind.

Gabe...yes, that was his name. He had to do something. He had to act. But what? The pressure of the god was building, and he had to let it out. That felt like the right answer. The door was bulging, begging to be opened. Wasn't it? He couldn't think. He knew there was a plan, but he couldn't remember why. There were too many things. People were dying. That wasn't fair. He had to do something... But the plan. He had to...

"*NOW!*" Aka Manah screamed, and it echoed through his head like a gunshot.

The hourglass shattered. Gabe's mind went with it.

The door was gone. It had never actually been there. In its place, there was now a writhing mass of power that dwarfed the human consciousness a hundredfold. Aka Manah was spread out like a tumor, tendrils lashed to every corner to prevent being dragged into a wide white rent that led back to the Ether. This had always been the true struggle that his fragile psyche had refused to see. But now that he was broken, there was no sanity left to protect. The door was actually a tear in reality howling for completion and closure as the god within it gripped the edges and refused to let go.

"*Do it, now!*"

The Ether was gorgeous. A sea of pure potential flowed behind the god, undulating and calling in an achingly beautiful song. Harmonies wrapped over and around themselves and filled his mind with the need for his will, begging for an image or a thought or a hope or a fear to imprint upon and become. It wanted nothing more than shape, nothing more than purpose. His mind reached out to the rift, tempted to flow in with it, to join and mold and expand into eternity. And the Ether reached back for him.

"*Free me!*"

A single tendril. That was all. The god had leveraged all of his strength to pull himself out, but one thin line of red-gold power was still tied inextricably to the rift. The balance point. And the pull on both sides was colossal. It was a struggle on the cosmic scale, enough to move planets, and the difference between them came down to that single thread.

"*It must be now!*"

His power was tiny—just a candle compared to the god's nova—but it wouldn't take much. He had only to will the tendril free, and it would be. It was simple.

"*Yes!*"

He reached out with his will and gathered his power. It came, blue and small and sluggish, but it also brought a new thing: guilt. He tried to shunt it aside as he always had, tried to free the god as instructed. But it wouldn't go. Instead, it opened like an origami flower and showed him in its depths another option. His mind was broken, as was the man he had been. But the man he *wished* to be could still exist. For one more moment, at least. There *was* another way, and Gabriel Delling crystallized around it.

"*What are you doing?*"

Gabe could suddenly think again, and he gathered his power to turn his attention to Gwendal. She was focused on the ritual, pulling in more energy and turning it to her purpose. She was already so close. In another moment, she could use the magic to summon Aka Manah into Austin's body. If Gabe opened the way, it could be over in a second. Thousands would die and the monsters would win, but it would be over.

And he couldn't do it.

"No."

He'd never been a great person, but he couldn't steal so much from so many. Not like this. He could be better this one time, and he knew the way.

"No!"

They had all been wrong. The ritual didn't need a big sacrifice. It needed one small one.

"You wouldn't."

His dad stood frozen by the geas—unable to dodge.

"You can't!"

Gabe sighted on his target and brought his will to bear.

"Wait!"

The magic flew from his fist and struck his father full in the chest.

"NO!"

Aka Manah's scream tore down the walls of his mind, and it was all he could do to keep himself standing. Gabe watched as his magic ripped Gwendal's geas from his father, then snapped back onto her like a rubberband. She fell beneath the weight of her own curse just as she had before, and all the life energy surged back up into the arena above. She landed hard and was still, and Paul scrambled over to her. Reznick cried out once in pain as the ritual overwhelmed him, and then he too fell as the magic collapsed and the circle shattered.

Aka Manah went deathly quiet, and in that single instant of peace, Gabe ignored everything else and plucked the white thread from his soul to transfer Heather's bond. "Run, Dad!" he yelled. Then he threw himself forward onto Paul and held tight as his father broke and ran. He could only hope that Heather would find his dad before any of the Hunters did. She might even get him out alive now that she had to. The Hound tore into him, and Gabe abandoned his body to die. For the first time in his life, he was genuinely proud of himself.

"Come on!" he screamed into the ruins of his mind as he gathered the scraps of his magic. "There's nowhere for you to go now! And if I'm about to die, so are you!"

Then his tiny island shattered like glass and he was falling, sinking and dissolving in Aka Manah's ocean of rage.

CHAPTER THIRTY-SIX

"I've always assumed I'll die young. And that's liberating in lots of ways. It means I don't need to actually make something of myself. Pretending is good enough when you're racing against time. And I save a bundle by not worrying about things like retirement or insurance. But mostly I use the idea as emotional anesthesia. Anytime I start to regret where or who I am, I can tell myself I don't need to be a whole person or have a whole life if I'm only sticking around for a bit of it. There's really no sense in getting to know the other guests if you're leaving the party early."

-Excerpt from Chapter Ten, CONscience

"You were listed as his next of kin on the insurance, Mr. Delling," the doctor said. "But we weren't expecting to see you in Lincoln so soon. Your last known address was listed—"

"I moved back here about a year ago," Gabe interrupted flatly. "Why can't I see him?"

She nodded to the doors behind her. "He's actually in surgery now, and the risk of infection at this stage is very high. He's in critical condition, but if you'd like to have a seat, I'll give you a full update on— Hey!"

Gabe pushed past her and slipped through the Surgery area doors just as a nurse used her key to open them for herself. The doctor cried out after him, but he broke into a run down the corridor and left her behind.

He scanned the observation windows into the operating rooms as he passed, and found the first three empty and dark. There were only two more further on. The doctor's raised voice sounded an alarm somewhere behind him, and a nurse looked up sharply from behind a counter. She noted his street clothes, then her face went stern as she said something sharp.

But Gabe had already moved way past caring. He glanced into the fourth room to find only a single person tidying up, then his focus narrowed to the fifth and final window as he made straight for the clean blue light spilling from it. A doctor stopped in his path and looked at him curiously, then disappeared. Hands gripped his upper arm, then became nothing. None of it registered.

The window was partially obscured by a piece of medical equipment, but there was still plenty of space to see the six people hovering around the man sprawled out on the surgical table. He looked so small in there.

And there was so much blood.

Broken beyond repair.

His face was...

Dad.

Someone pulled him away, and he felt himself struggling. They were yelling at him. "Infection," they said. "Arrested," they threatened. "...do everything they could...himself under control...grief...fear...understandable..."

The memory broke and faded.

Gabe woke to find that being dead was surprisingly painful. He was lying on a hard floor and in more pain than when he'd been alive, and his brain felt like it had been dipped in peanut oil and stir-fried with scallions. The blaring alarm was a nice touch too, and the frantic shouting and gunshots really added that terrifying atmosphere that one looked for in a good afterlife. It seemed unlikely that it was heaven, but that wasn't too shocking.

An explosion sounded somewhere nearby, and his left shoulder throbbed in an agonizing counterbeat to the now-familiar ache of his right arm. It all seemed about right for Hell. It was fitting that they'd started him off with one of the worst memories of his life, but he wondered when they planned to fire up the continuous loop of polka music to really hammer it home.

He remembered falling beneath Paul's weight, and the pain of teeth sinking in. Then he had retreated into himself to face down Aka Manah for some reason that had seemed smart at the time, and everything had gone very bright and confusing. He supposed the god and the Hound had probably raced one another to kill him, but he was surprised to find that he didn't actually care how it had ended. His only hope was that Aka Manah was waking up down here too.

"Get up, moron!" a woman said above him. Then hands were pulling at his shirt and heaving him easily to his feet.

Gabe's vision went wobbly for a moment, but even through the shimmer of near-unconsciousness it wasn't hard to recognize Heather's scowl.

"Nice plan!" she yelled, leaning heavily into the sarcasm to make sure it carried over the growing din. Then she was moving him, dragging him to one side around a stack of pallets just as a series of small explosions sounded through the building.

Gabe struggled briefly with the realization that he was alive enough to realize anything at all, but being slammed into a concrete wall by a pissed off succubus cleared out the cobwebs nicely. "I'm alive?" he gasped.

Heather made a noise of disgust. "For now. Can you pull it together, please?"

"Sorry," he grabbed his aching head, "I think I died a couple times. What happened?"

Heather leaned out past the cover, then quickly withdrew. Her eyes were hard and bright as she searched for more threats. "I followed the bond. I got the Knights to chase me here, and we got in just as people started screaming about a terrorist attack. Then the Hunters showed up. The Knights did what they do. Now it's a war zone."

Gabe shook his head. "No, I mean my dad. Did he get... If I'm not dead, then Aka Manah..." He tried to continue, but his thoughts fell apart.

Fortunately Heather seemed to understand, and her expression went tight. "I'm sure we'll find your dad, but you were my first stop. When I came to get you, Gwendal was paralyzed just like last time, and Reznick was out cold. Paul was using your shoulder as a chew toy, so I stomped his throat a little."

A rapid series of shots sounded, followed by a heavy thud, and Heather cursed before slipping out from behind cover without another word. Gabe chanced a quick glance after her, but when he leaned out from behind the pallets, she had vanished. The only thing out there was a Hunter crouched over the dead body of a Knight. And it looked up.

Gabe scrambled back in panic as he reached inside for his power, but a blinding needle of fire dropped him to his knees and filled his vision with an expanse of white light. He caught himself before collapsing entirely, but a wave of agony rolled over him to try to press him down anyway. Even through the pain, he could feel that his magic was nearly spent. It felt either burned up or overused like taxed muscles, and all he had left was a thin thread that he doubted would kill a mosquito. He'd hit his wall—probably burst through it, actually—and he had nothing left. Precisely what he deserved for trying to be a stupid freaking hero.

The Hunter started limping toward him. Half of its face was gone, along with a large chunk of its stomach and the lower part of its left arm, but it seemed merely slowed by the wounds. Its Rime Blade was shattered nearly to the hilt, which was a minor blessing, but it stumbled toward him anyway, brandishing the weapon as if it was just as happy to beat Gabe to death with the pommel. Gabe raised his hands in a feeble defense, then Heather appeared out of nowhere and promptly twisted the monster's head off. The body fell to one side, and she tossed the head to the other.

Gabe gawked as she pulled him to his feet. "Whoa!" he said.

She shushed him. "It was barely functional. Don't think I can do that normally. In a fair fight with a Hunter I'm dead every time. Let's hope I don't have to prove that." She glanced around, then grabbed his hand. "Let's go. We need to find a set of stairs that isn't blocked by fighting."

The air was smokey and dim, and alarms blared as a backbeat to the electric gunshots and periodic explosions. But they made it through the corridor at a quick pace, sneaking past the pockets of fighting that had expanded through the place. There were surprisingly few Hunters to be seen, but those they did encounter seemed to be taking on four or five Knights apiece with little trouble. Gabe hoped Catherine had brought a full platoon.

Heather pulled him into a stairwell, and after a quick check for threats, they ran up and out of the smoke—into a nightmare. Thousands of people were pressed together on the main floor, shoulder-to-shoulder and shoving and screaming to get out. Gabe could see the flashing lights of the first emergency responders through the windows, but it would be a long time before they could get in. Most of the doors looked chained closed, and what few weren't, had the crowd flowing out of them like water through pinprick holes in a dam. As they watched, someone threw a chair through a glass door, and another little trickle of people started pushing to get outside.

"We'll never spot him in this!" Gabe yelled.

Heather had stopped in the doorway and suddenly seemed confused. "We broke the chains on two of the doors to get in," she said. "I figured he would have run that way, but..."

Gabe searched in vain for his father outside in the dark, but saw nothing except running and crying people illuminated by emergency lights. He tugged Heather toward the exit, but she resisted.

"He didn't go that way," she said, flatly. She took a deep breath and her eyes went distant. "I was so focused on finding you, I didn't notice."

"Oh," Gabe replied. When the plan had popped into his head, he hadn't been expecting to be alive for this part. "Look, I'm so sorry. People were dying, and my dad was terrified. The original idea was to let you go as soon as this was done, but then things went wrong. They were murdering everyone, and I couldn't just let it happen. Transferring your bond to my dad was the only way for me to protect him and still save everybody else. I swear, if I could have thought of any other—"

"Explain later," she said, cutting him off and turning away. "Just... Come on."

She led the way by following the bond, and they picked through the crowd to a relatively unused corridor leading to the VIP booths. Nobody was at the ticket-check to stop them, so they slipped into a balcony box above the arena floor. She pulled him to the edge to look down at the stage in the center of the room. The place was deserted by the main crowd, but dozens of people of all ages were still sprawled on the ground near the main stage. Some were writhing slowly, as if desperate to get up but lacking the strength, but a few were disturbingly still. Gabe estimated about eighty people out there, some older, and some far too young. His heart sank. Had he been less selfish from the start and acted sooner, maybe...

"Can we do anything for them?" he asked.

"Yeah," she replied, "get the hell away from them as soon as possible." She pointed to the empty stage below, and there, sitting on the floor and cradling a guitar, was his father.

"Dad!" Gabe yelled.

And from somewhere deep in the arena, Gwendal matched him with a scream of fury.

"Shit," Heather said. "I hate you so much." Then she wrapped an arm around his waist and vaulted from the balcony.

She landed hard among the seats twenty feet below, but softened the impact enough for his fragile human spine that Gabe only lost his breath instead of the ability to feed himself. She stood him up, then led the way down the stairs and to the arena floor. Weakened and hurting pretty much all over, Gabe struggled to keep up, and his chest was heaving by the time they made it onto the stage.

"Dad! he said, picking his way past amps and cords to where the man sat.

Alexander looked up and clutched the guitar to his chest. "Just...holding...it!"

Gabe stopped several paces away and held up his hands. "I know. But we have to go now. Those bad people are coming back. Do you understand?"

His father shook his head, then went back to looking at the guitar.

Gabe fought down irritation and panic. "I know, dad. And I promise we'll play as soon as we get out. But you have to come with me now!" He tried to grab his father's arm, but the man wriggled away with the guitar cradled in his lap and it became an awkward wrestling match.

"Gabe, leave him alone," Heather said softly.

"Give me a minute!" he said. "I can talk to him! Dad, why don't we get a candy bar and go somewhere safer that—"

"Gabe," she said more insistently.

"No!" he shouted back. "I won't leave him!"

Heather took his uninjured shoulder in her frightening grip and turned him. "I know," she said, catching his gaze and forcing him to see her. "I *know*. But it doesn't matter. Look." She pointed to a set of closed doors that were now covered in fine black tendrils creeping over the metal and holding them fast. Every exit was the same. Gwendal was already there. "We're too late."

Gabe's strength finally failed him, and he slumped to the ground next to his dad. "What do we do?"

She blew out a long breath. "You tell me. Your big brain thought us into this mess. Think us out."

"I can't," he said. "The backup plan I told you about was only good for the original version of this rescue. The pishtacos from the Jimenez Cartel are probably back at the Briarwood right now, calling me a liar." He laughed ruefully. "I actually thought I was pretty smart with that one. Damn. And now my brain feels like it took a long spin on puree. There are no more plans. I'm tapped out."

"Fine," she said. "Let's keep it simple. We stand and fight."

Gabe watched the black filaments snake over the doors until they began to creak with the strain. Then he looked at the dozens of people still writhing on the floor, unable to stand or even talk—then at the dozens who weren't moving at all. He'd failed all of them and everything. He sighed. "I did try, you know. To be better. It just turns out I suck at it."

She moved closer to him so that her leg just brushed his shoulder, then she rested her hand on his head and let her fingers trail idly through his hair. "I know. Not your fault. The world is just terrible sometimes, and our best choices one day may be worse than our worst choices another. I wish we could have..." She trailed off and didn't finish.

Gabe wanted to move a little to separate his injured arm from where it rubbed against her leg, but he didn't dare. Instead, he let the feeling of innocent affection wash over him and dampen his hurts. It would almost certainly be the last tender thing he ever felt—from the first real friend he'd ever had. That was a weird thought considering how they'd started just a few days ago. So many things had changed.

Heather had come back for him even though the bond hadn't been compelling her. She hadn't even noticed it was gone until running headlong into danger to drag him out. She'd wanted to save him for its own sake. His throat went tight.

"Run," he said.

She glanced down at him in alarm. "What?"

He took a deep breath and pushed through his reflexive cowardice and self-interest. "I said run. She'll come for me and my dad, and you can slip out. She doesn't care about you. You don't have to be here anymore."

Her fingers never lifted from his hair, but her eyes went back to watching the doors. "Yes I do."

Gabe took her hand and prompted her to help him stand. It hurt more than he expected, but he thought he hid it well. Then he met her eyes and reached out with his remaining sliver of magic to pluck the bond from his father and let it unravel into nothing. He saw the web of it over her aura flicker then dissolve. "No," he said. "You don't."

Heather squeezed his hand, then let it fall. She closed her eyes and took a deep breath that seemed to brighten her color and firm her edges. It was like she had just become a little more real. Then she smiled sadly. "Shut up."

"Please," he said. "I can make a distraction to let you—"

"Gabe," she said, weariness overwhelming everything else in her voice, "You're an idiot. But you're *my* idiot. For some reason. Maybe I pissed off a Fate in another life." She reached up and touched his cheek. "Let's just get through this, okay? We're not dead yet."

He sagged. "I'm so sorry. I shouldn't have used you. I should have found another way and cut you loose when—"

"Hey," she interrupted, "I told you to shut up." Then she leaned in and kissed him.

The warmth of her was like a balm, spreading through him and healing in places he hadn't known were broken. Then their tiny moment of peace shattered as Gwendal's rabid scream sounded outside the doors.

Heather broke away and moved quickly to take up a fighting stance at the front of the stage. She looked tired and beaten, but also like she had no intention of going down easily. It gave Gabe all the courage he needed to move up beside her.

"What are you doing?" she asked, flicking her eyes between the dozen possible entrances.

He raised his hands in imitation of her, ignoring the pain and the fact that he had no idea how to fight. "Not going out like a chump."

She smirked and shook her head. "Goodbye, Gabe."

"Bye," he said.

A set of doors exploded.

CHAPTER THIRTY-SEVEN

"Love is a weird emotion, and one that I'm not great at faking. No good examples to draw on. It can make you stop hating and make you start. It can give you a reason to live and a reason to die. It can build you up into something great, and it can shatter your entire world. Or so I hear. I suppose I probably love my dad, after everything, but I'm not totally convinced I'm capable of it with anyone else. Not that I care. It seems like a bad gamble."

-Excerpt from Chapter Ten, CONscience

    Gabe stared in shock as the two metal doors flew halfway across the arena to skid to halt at the foot of the stage. Gwendal entered, held aloft on ropes of eldritch energy that skittered across the floor and lashed at the walls as she moved. Bloody gashes covered her body, and her chest heaved as if she could barely contain her rage. But she was still darkly majestic, and every inch of her pulsed with stolen power.

    "Give him to me!" she screamed, and the sound of it shook the entire building.

    Aka Manah had been eerily silent for the last several minutes, and Gabe had hoped that meant the god had simply disappeared—gone back to the Ether where he belonged. But as Gwendal approached, he rose again.

    "I grow very weary of you, human," he said. He sounded exhausted, like the strain of holding himself back from the pull of the Ether was finally taking its toll. It might explain why the god hadn't already crushed Gabe's soul. Maybe he couldn't. *"Let...me...out."*

    "Hey, I'd love to," Gabe said aloud in response to both monsters. "But I won't let you two slaughter thousands of innocent people for it. Turns out I'm weird that way."

    Gwendal screeched again, and the black tendrils lashed hard at the ground to dig deep furrows where they passed. "You broke the compact!"

    Gabe actually managed a laugh. "A contract based on lies is void before it's even signed, lady. I didn't agree to mass murder. Maybe that was naive of me to not consider, but that's what you get for working with an amateur. Plus, I *extra* hate you."

Gwendal skewered him with her stare and snarled. "You are the very reason we have come! You and those like you. Your ignorance and apathy are miring this plane in chaos just when order is needed most. We wish only the return of the old ways so that we may muster the strength of this plane and ensure its survival!" She screamed the words. "Your era produces little but empty and fleeting philosophies. You are all poor copies of your ancestors, but we will forge and temper you for the long death on your doorstep. Blind yourselves all you want, but The Emptiness is coming, and we are your only hope against it!"

Something in her posture changed then, and she lifted her head as if hearing a distant call. She smirked. "I could have sent my Hound or Hunters here to bring you back. They are even now finishing the pitiful Knights. But this whole affair has been a significant inconvenience, and for that and so much else, I want this done *now*."

She gestured to a large, odd shape entering the room, and it only took a moment for Gabe to recognize Paul carrying Reznick over his shoulder. They were back to where they'd started—the same pieces back on a new board. It had all been for nothing.

Gabe firmed his features. He refused to let her see him suffer. "So what?" he said, keeping his voice carefully neutral. "You don't have the energy you need. The people are gone, and those remaining here have been sucked dry."

Gwendal's sneer didn't waver for a moment. "Don't you understand? I have already gathered what I need. Look at how magnificent I have become! Yet I will gladly give it up for my love so that together we may become so much more. And your little girlfriend will do just fine for a sacrifice. This will happen now!"

Gabe did the math and realized she wasn't bluffing. By sticking around to retrieve his father, they'd accidentally delivered Gwendal precisely what she needed to finish the ritual. "I think we're about to have a bad time," he whispered to Heather.

"It is what we do best," she replied. "Nothing to lose then."

Before Gabe could respond, Heather was moving fast and leaping from the stage to cross the distance to Gwendal. She made it halfway before the monster realized the threat and started lashing out with her tendrils, but Heather ducked and spun away, never letting them score a hit as she vaulted fallen people and chairs in her headlong rush. Two fat arcs of black energy shot up from the ground and slammed together just as Heather dived out from between them, then she rolled up to her feet directly in front of Gwendal and punched her right in the gut.

The sound was like a fastball hitting a side of beef, but neither woman looked overly affected by it. Gwendal skittered spider-like on her tendrils and circled to return a long-limbed slap to the side of Heather's head. But the succubus was already moving, and her shorter stature allowed her to duck the blow easily and send a quick kick into one of the two joints in the Night Mother's left leg. It did less damage than it would have if the monster had been standing on her own feet, but the crack still rang out through the arena, and Gwendal growled in pain and slithered back several paces.

Then the real fighting started. In the initial exchanges it became obvious that Heather was the more skilled of the two, moving with a grace and confidence that put the final lie to her assertion that she wasn't much of a fighter. But Gwendal quickly caught the rhythm and began using sheer speed to slide past every strike regardless of skill. The Night Mother's power so dwarfed that of the succubus that she didn't need to be good. And soon, Heather was being pressed back as she desperately fended off attacks from every side.

Paul raced up and carelessly dropped Reznick to the ground as he advanced on the battle, but stopped at a quick gesture from Gwendal. Then he turned to face Gabe and bent into a sprint toward the stage. Gabe tried to run through his list of possible weapons, but the Hound was faster than anything he'd ever seen, and it was all he could do to grab a microphone stand and swing for all he was worth. The Hound never slowed as it lifted its left arm to block the blow, but as Gabe had hoped, the limb didn't respond properly. Paul's arm lifted only slightly, and the heavy base of the stand took the creature full in the face. He spun and went sprawling and sliding on his back across the stage with unspent momentum, then finally came to rest near the drum kit—where he immediately sat up.

Gabe knew he couldn't have asked for a more perfect strike, and he couldn't possibly have mustered any more strength for the blow. He'd probably used up his luck for the next decade on that one, yet it hadn't been enough. His blood suddenly sang with the rage and frustration of the last two days, and he finally ran out of reasons to push it away. With an animal cry, he fell on top of Paul, bearing him back down to the ground and using nothing but his fists to pound the Hound's face and neck. Gabe screamed as he let loose all the bile and hatred and confusion and fear he'd been shunting aside, and he poured it into every blow until his hands felt broken and bloody, and Paul was unrecognizable.

"*Yes! More!*" Aka Manah whispered frantically. "*Free me!*"

The red rage didn't relent, but the voice made him pause for an instant—and in that space, a hand shot up and grabbed him by the neck. Paul's eyes opened in the wreckage of his face, and they were bright and wild as he lifted Gabe, then threw him. Gabe went flying across the stage to hit just at the edge and roll off to fall a dozen feet to the floor. Pain flashed as bones broke somewhere, and all the breath left him in a rush.

When there's enough of it, pain eventually becomes noise. And a little more here or there stops being that noticeable. Gabe was just about there, and he knew he had to either get up or resign himself to dying. But before he could even try, Paul was above him, grabbing him by the back of his shirt and lifting him like a kitten. Gabe struggled weakly, but it was no use. Things were grinding inside of him and his brain wouldn't process thoughts cleanly anymore. He was way past used up.

Paul carried him across the arena floor to where Reznick was hurriedly scratching out a new circle, then tossed him to the ground where he could only bleed and watch. He noted distantly that Heather was still holding her own, and he almost rejoiced at that small victory. But then one of Gwendal's tendrils struck her from behind, and the distraction broke the careful rhythm of the fight. Gwendal then stepped forward and slapped Heather down hard to the ground. The sound was like a gunshot, and Heather stayed where she fell. Just that quickly, it was all over.

Gwendal took a step back and laughed. "I'd love to keep playing with you, but I'm afraid I need you relatively intact for another minute."

Gabe tried to rise again, but Paul was there behind him with one arm snaking around to pull him into a submission hold. The Hound brought him up to his knees, then bent him down into a painful bow. And though Gabe fought back weakly with his free left hand, he had no leverage with his right up over his head and his body bent double.

"Now we finish this," Gwendal said. She slipped a bare foot under Heather's stomach and casually flipped her across the floor like an empty tin can.

Heather landed hard in the center of the circle, and she cried out in pain—which was actually a relief. She wasn't dead yet. Gabe tried to turn to speak to her, but Paul tightened his grip and drove him down even further, tearing his wounds anew and forcing the broken bones throughout his body to grate sickeningly. He cried out in pain and the sound of it finally made his father stir back on the stage. Gwendal noticed too, and she sent a black whip across the room to drag Alexander down by his feet. He came screaming and crying as he careened through the prone crowd and toppled chairs, but then he slowed to a gentle landing next to Heather in the circle.

"This is even better," Gwendal said, a cruel smile twisting her lips. "We can sacrifice the succubus back to the Ether and use your father's body as a vessel. You can lose both at once in a beautiful piece of symmetry that my Aka Manah will most certainly appreciate."

Gabe noted that his father had quieted surprisingly quickly, and was now looking up at him with a frown touching his lips.

"Kid," Alexander said.

Gabe almost started to cry. He wondered why now, of all times, his dad had finally recognized him. After nine years of digging for lost memories and fighting the frustration of being seen as a stranger by his own father, why only now had it clicked? The man had to be terrified and confused, yet he had finally found a bit of clarity just when it was all about to stop mattering. Gabe wanted nothing more than to go to him, to tell him it would be okay, and to search his eyes to find out if there was anything of love there. To know if he was capable of it. To know if either of the Delling men were. Then Heather reached out and touched his dad's arm, trying to comfort him even though she herself could barely move. Gabe's heart ached at the simple gesture, and he had at least part of his answer.

"Kid!" Alexander said again, this time pointing.

Gwendal looked to Reznick, who seemed barely conscious himself, and the man shakily cut his own hand and started spreading the blood. A massive power filled the room, radiating off of Gwendal like heat, and her black tendrils dwindled and disappeared as she spent the stolen life energy to fuel the ritual. The circle blazed to life again, and Gabe felt Aka Manah stirring.

"We...are both out of...options," Aka Manah said. He sounded exhausted. "You have...just enough magic...left. Release me and...let's be done."

"Release him," Gwendal echoed, her voice thick with power.

"Bite me," Gabe growled, forgetting for a moment that she absolutely would. Then Paul lifted him and wrenched his head painfully to the side so he could see a Hunter standing just behind him. Gabe stared for a second, not understanding, then he sagged in Paul's grip as the pieces clicked together. "Kid," he said.

The little girl in the Hunter's arms looked no more than twelve. Her eyes were closed, but she was still struggling weakly, and the icy blade at her throat looked eager to do its job.

The threat was perfectly clear all by itself, but Gwendal spoke anyway. "Many of the humans are alive," she said, "thanks to you. Useless for sacrifice as drained as they are, but still worth something. They may even yet recover if you are wise. But I will keep cutting them down until you release my Aka Manah."

Gabe looked to his father and saw that he was turned toward Heather, saying something. She responded, and he nodded calmly. He hadn't seen his dad talk to anyone else since the accident, but Heather was good at getting people to open up. Even broken and defeated she was trying to help. It looked like she would pay for that kindness.

His choice had come down to letting a little girl die along with dozens more like her, or giving up his father and friend. The only two people in his life who had stayed for him when they could have run, or an entire room full of strangers. *His* choice. *His* finger on the trigger. Murderer and Betrayer either way. It was the worst moment of his life.

Gwendal bent low to Gabe's face. "Kill the girl," she whispered.

"No!" Gabe yelled.

Gwendal held up a hand to the Hunter. "Release my love."

Gabe looked at the girl. She was barely conscious enough to know what was happening, but was still struggling. A tough kid. She was wearing a homemade t-shirt for the band, and some of the glittery puff paint had come loose and was hanging from the fabric. She was missing one shoe. She had a name, and a home, and a family of her own. A future. She was innocent.

He turned to Heather and his dad. "I'm sorry," he said.

He freed the god.

CHAPTER THIRTY-EIGHT

```
"I know I'm not going to publish the book like
this. It's turned into a rambling personal
journal, and that's not very marketable. People
want to read about sexy adventures and violent
crimes, not my sad little life. But I might
decide to keep this draft as a memento. Maybe
I'll miraculously have a kid of my own someday
and this stuff can help explain why his old man
was such a weirdo. So I'll write this one last
thing to bring the story to something like a
close:

I actually think my dad did the best he could. I
don't know anything about his childhood or what
made him into what he was, but I think he fought
against his nature every day just to scrape
together enough decency to keep me around. And
that's something. It's what he had to offer, and
after all these years helping to take care of
him, I even understand it a little. So for
everything he lacked back then, I forgive him. I
hope he can do the same for me now."

-Final Note, CONscience
```

If Gabe had held any illusions that he and Aka Manah had formed even a scrap of a bond in last three days, they would have been shattered the instant he used the last of his magic to open the door.

"At last!" Aka Manah screamed with Gabe's mouth as he rushed in to usurp control. "Kill the succubus and cleanse the vessel! Finish it!"

Gabe wrestled control back just in time to see Gwendal turning to focus on his dad, weaving a hook of magic to tear the soul from his body. At the same time, Reznick turned to Heather with a small smile. He chanted a guttural incantation, and suddenly the blood he'd spilled came to life and congealed into a gory rope that lashed around her neck and drew tight. Gabe batted at Paul with his free left hand, but it was like nothing to the Hound and the grip never faltered. A scream of impotent rage tore Gabe's throat as he thrashed uselessly against the impossible strength, heedless of his wounds and broken bones in his desperation to undo what he'd done. But it was too late. He'd just murdered the only two people who had ever given a damn about him, and all that was left was to watch it happen. Heather gasped as she suffocated, and his dad cried out as Gwendal's magic reached for him. It was too much, and Gabe's despair felt like a shard of ice in his soul. And the hatred sharpened it to a razor edge.

The Rime Blade manifested in Gabe's left hand and exploded straight out through Paul's back. The Hound howled in pain and threw himself off of the blade to roll into a heap, and Gabe fell forward, suddenly free. He found Gwendal standing four feet away, her power focused into a tight beam and ready to tear out his father's soul. She drew back her hand to propel it, and without another thought, he pushed himself up on his broken leg and lunged toward her, driving the sword straight into her naked belly.

The scream the Night Mother loosed almost drove Gabe to unconsciousness. But he'd delved deep into greater agonies lately and had come back wielding a blade forged of them. There was no way in hell he was letting go now. He forced himself to stay on his feet, reveling in the exquisite pain of it to feed to the blade, and he followed Gwendal as she tried desperately to back away from her death. Black tendrils lashed at his arms and back and face, but it only honed his edge as he drove it further home. The hoarfrost hissed and spat as it seared her from within, and Gabe pushed closer until his face was only inches from hers. Her claws raked him, and her geas battered at his mind—willing him to fall, willing him to love her, willing him to die. But they were all distant pains as he watched the black energy spill out over his hand with her blood.

Her eyes roved wildly for a way out, and she spotted the Hunter nearby. "Help…me!" she wheezed.

The creature hadn't moved in the chaos and was now staring hard at Gabe. It bore a ragged, half-healed wound across its throat, and its blade was already out and ready. Gabe knew he had no hope of winning if it joined the fight, and he watched in growing fear as it cocked its head to the side, nodded once, and dropped the girl. Then, inexplicably, it lifted its blade in a salute before turning and walking away.

Gwendal sobbed as she watched it go, and the last bit of her power gasped out. A massive wave of energy threw Gabe backward, ripping the blade from his hand as he dropped hard into a row of chairs. The physical pain almost overwhelmed him again as more things broke—then it became almost trivial as Aka Manah finally tore free of his mind.

He first felt as if he would be torn in half as the god burst out into the world, then he was scrambling for purchase as the hungry void of the Ether tried to pull anything back in. Gabe panicked, afraid his soul might be consumed after all his fighting, but Aka Manah reappeared suddenly, back in front of the rift and thrusting in something dark and furious to take his place. The other Umbra fought desperately for a moment, but was quickly overwhelmed and consumed.

Everything went quiet. The void was gone, and with it the door. The hourglass, and unbidden memories, and Aka Manah himself were all gone too. Gwendal was dead, probably. And all Gabe had left was a massive aching hole in his mind where a god had rent asunder the fabric of reality. He could still feel the Ether just on the other side of it, pushing at the thin barrier, testing, calling for him from beyond the veil. The space was already healing at the edges, but he could tell it would never properly close. His consciousness felt ten sizes too big now—if that was possible. Enough to hold a god, perhaps, but too much for...whatever Gabe was now. Without the Umbra to take up the space, he felt like a child wearing his father's clothes.

He wanted to lay there and enjoy the relative peace of that moment, but he knew the terrible day wasn't quite over. He didn't know who had gone through the portal back into the Ether, but he knew it hadn't been Aka Manah. The god was out, and there were dozens of helpless people in the room. He could be anywhere.

Gabe opened his eyes and searched for his blade, but only found a wide puddle and a few ice crystals still stuck to the raised patch on his hand. He halfheartedly tried to summon it again, but it felt buried beneath too much hope and relief. He would get no more help from there. And he'd used the last shred of his power to free Aka Manah. No more magic. No more loopholes. He'd spent everything.

He suddenly realized he didn't know how much time had just passed, and he quickly crawled over to Heather, who was still lying nearby in the circle. Even that much movement made him want to die.

Things grated and screamed inside him, but he couldn't afford to give in to them yet. Almost, but not quite. Her eyes were closed, and she was sprawled as if she'd been trying to crawl away in the end. He reached to her neck to pry the bloody rope off, and was relieved to find it limp and already falling to pieces. But she didn't stir as he turned her over. He put his fingers to her throat and held his breath.

Her pulse was like a song. She was still alive, and that was reason enough for him to stay that way too—for a few more minutes, at least. If she hadn't been the sacrificial Umbra, then his dad had to be okay too. He knew Gwendal hadn't had time to remove his father's soul, and there was no sign of Reznick or his dark magics anymore. And Paul's body was missing. It was over. The only two people he cared about were going to make it out okay, and the thought was a potent painkiller.

Gabe turned and looked to find where his father had landed, wanting to check him next and know for sure, but found him already up and walking back to the stage. Back to the guitars, probably. That was a good sign. Gabe tried to rise and follow, but his broken right leg refused to bear weight anymore. He'd already gotten every ounce of mileage out of it.

"Dad," he called weakly, then coughed to clear his throat. "Dad, we have to go!"

Heather finally stirred at the sound and raised her head. Her eyes were dull and heavy, and a livid blue bruise swelled the left side of her face and nose where Gwendal had struck her. Even her normally flawless hair was a complete mess, and her lipstick was smeared over her mouth in a way that she never would have allowed under better circumstances. She tried to push herself up, then sagged back down.

"What the hell happened?" she asked. "When you killed her... Something... I don't know." She reached up and gently touched her head like she was afraid it might be broken.

Gabe watched her carefully for any sign of difference, any sign that the god might have taken her body, but found nothing obvious. She seemed like herself. That was good. He looked back to his father.

"Dad, we need to go now. Please get down here."

His father climbed the stairs of the stage and walked to the center to look down at the polished guitar. He cocked his head to the side and then bent to pick the instrument up. He held it like a lover.

There was a smear of something dark at his mouth, and he had blood on his clothes from the ritual.

Gabe turned back to Heather. "I think my leg is broken—along with a bunch of other stuff. But we need to get the hell out of here. Any chance you can scrape enough strength together to go grab my dad?"

She groaned and finally managed to push up into a sitting position. Then she gritted her teeth and slowly pulled herself to her feet where she swayed like a drunk. She took a careful step, then another, and moved past Gabe.

"You have what you want. Now let us go," she said.

Gabe used a chair as a crutch and dragged himself up to stand on his left leg. "There'll be police all over this place any second, and I don't know where..." It hit him as his father strummed the guitar.

Alexander ran his fingers lightly over the strings, calling forth an effortless melody. Then a slow, familiar smile creased his lips. "Hello, son. So good to finally meet you *in person*."

Gabe's heart stopped. "No," he said, shaking his head. "It's not possible." He rolled the moment over and around in his mind, trying to find a flaw in the fact staring back at him—trying to find a way to make it not true. "Gwendal didn't take your soul! I stopped her!"

Aka Manah laughed, then tossed the instrument aside as he dropped from the stage on a cushion of red-gold power. He spread his hands as he started toward them. "And yet here I am. The world is complicated, son. Trying to figure out every detail will only get you hurt."

"Don't...call me that," Gabe said. "Just stay back, okay? This can't..." His thoughts started falling apart.

"I won't let you through," Heather said, making a good show of standing in the god's way.

Aka Manah's new face turned down into a frown. "Oh, I have no intention of hurting him. On the contrary. I realized early in our predicament that he presented me with a unique opportunity. He is now far too special to dispose of so carelessly. I'm sure my dear Gwendal will understand if her spirit survived the trip back into the Ether. She may be furious with me for a few decades, but Gabriel was too perfect a prize to pass up. She'll come back to me. Loyalty was ever her greatest virtue...and weakness." His smile reappeared like magic. "No, I have plans for you, my boy. We are going to teach this world how to fear again, and then how to obey. With any luck there might be enough strength left here to hold back the coming end. Like it or not, you are now a *very* important piece of that."

Heather raised her hands and took up a fighting stance. "What the hell. The day can't get much worse. Let's do this."

Aka Manah considered her briefly, then sent a pulse of power into her that carried her to other side of the arena. The crash of her landing sounded terrible.

"Heather!" Gabe cried. He tried to turn to find her, but the movement threatened to topple him.

"She was a distraction, and had served her purpose," Aka Manah said as he held out a hand. "Come with me and I will show you greater glories and darker depths than any human has known for ten thousand generations."

Gabe tried to back away, but the chair was the only thing keeping him standing. "Fuck you."

The god's expression soured. "Come now. You are more creative than that. But if the promise of power does not suit you, how about the miracle of memory? I now know all that your father knew—even that which he had forgotten. Would you like to learn why he was the way he was? I can tell you. How about the reason he left—or the reason he stayed? Yours for the asking. I can even tell if he loved you as a father to a son. It's all here, within me, ready and waiting." He moved his hand a little closer, and his face split into that familiar dragon grin. The dark red smear at his mouth looked like blood. "I can help you find your mother."

Gabe stopped. Everything stopped. Aka Manah and his father: the only two who had ever well and truly bested him, now one and the same. Of course he had known right where to push. He now knew more about Gabe than Gabe did himself. It suddenly felt like all the rest of it had been leading up to this moment—that this was the one that really mattered. And for an instant, he considered the offer.

Then a furnace-blast of heat washed over him, and he threw up his arm in a pitiful defense to ward off whatever fresh terror was trying to kill him this time. But it passed as quickly as it had come, and when he looked for the source, he found a strange little man standing between him and Aka Manah.

"Good evening!" the man said cheerfully. The sound was jarring in the dire quiet. "Am I interrupting something?"

Aka Manah slowly pulled his hand back. "I don't know who you are, but this does not concern—"

The man raised a hand, and the god's mouth suddenly clamped shut. "My name is Phillip. I represent a group of individuals who have a deep interest in the power shifts of our little world. I originally came here to check up on one of our investments, but..." He glanced down at Gwendal's broken body and sighed. "I see this one has rather failed us. A shame. I do hope she didn't waste all of our toys in the process."

The man glanced at Aka Manah, who was starting to visibly seethe as he fought against whatever force held his voice. Phillip pretended nothing was wrong and turned his smile to Gabe. "Fortunately it seems as though I may have stumbled onto something even more profitable. Good day, Gabriel Delling."

Gabe hesitated, but something delicate and pleasant tickled at his mind, and he reflexively spoke the first words to blossom there. "Hi. Is there any chance you can just tell me how much you're going to screw with me right upfront? I'm all done with surprises for the day."

Phillip laughed, the sound rich and musical like something an actor might rehearse to get just right. "Absolutely, if you wish! But first, please excuse me while I address some formalities." He turned to Aka Manah. "You are not supposed to be here."

The god was clearly fighting against Phillip's power, and Gabe could sense massive forces pressing against one another far above his normal perception. The pressure built and the two men stared hard for almost a full minute. Then everything suddenly stopped and Phillip finally clicked his tongue and frowned.

"Very well," Phillip said, referencing something that had gone way over Gabe's head. He made a shooing gesture, and Aka Manah slid back several steps before catching himself on the edge of the stage. "The offer is open. Let me know if you change your mind. But don't flatter yourself that you're a match for us." He turned back to Gabe in what appeared to be a dismissal of the god.

Aka Manah snarled and took a step forward, but several shadows detached themselves from the earth and rose up to bar his way. From behind the stage, two Hunters appeared wielding their Rime Blades. The god caught himself and took in the new odds, and for a moment looked like he might try it anyway. Then he straightened and reached up to run a finger over the scar across his new skull. He pointedly looked past Phillip to Gabe and flashed Alexander's old smile

—all bravado and charm without substance. He stared hard to make sure Gabe saw him—*knew* him—before bowing once as if conceding a match but not the game. He spared a quick promising glance to Phillip, then turned Alexander Delling's body and left.

Gabe watched Aka Manah steal the last vestige of his family, and his heart broke. He'd lost. Nothing would ever be the same.

Phillip patiently waited for the moment to expire and the doors to slam closed before turning back to Gabe. "Lucky I got here when I did! I can feel how used up you are. None of your fancy new magic left, I bet. They certainly didn't give you an easy orientation to this world, did they?" He laughed.

Gabe pushed back against the wave of grief threatening to overwhelm him and found only a vast exhaustion beneath it. "Who are you?" he asked.

Phillip looked amused. "Bold, but not stupid. That's refreshing! As I said: I'm a representative. I make offers. I collect talent. I smooth rough roads. And I just so happen to have an offer for you, Gabriel Delling. Would you like to hear it?"

The man spoke quickly, like a caricature of a professional salesman, and Gabe almost had trouble following. But the touch was there in his mind again, and it nudged him to nod acceptance.

"Excellent," Phillip said, folding his hands together. "We would like to employ your services. You are something unique—shocking even—and we would like you with us. You are clearly in a difficult situation financially, emotionally, and spiritually. You need money, training, and time. We can give you all of that. All we ask is that you assist us in our efforts. We work toward maintaining a careful balance that has been in place since the birth of the universe, and a fascinating subject like you could prove invaluable to that service. Your actions here have set off a few little fun surprises in the world at large, and we would like to help you focus that influence to the greatest good. Entities like that godling are becoming far too common, despite the provisions set in place to prevent it, and I'm afraid that they simply refuse to understand their place in the system. The balance simply *must* be preserved."

Gabe's mouth was getting dry and harder to work. "They claimed to be here to save us."

Phillip waved a hand dismissively. "As if they could. They were referring to an old story that simply isn't true. A belief without evidence. Religion is not strictly the purview of humanity, Gabriel, and even legends have their own superstitions. Think on that and try not to break your brain, eh?" He chuckled. "All they would have done is destroy several centuries of human progress in the interest of fighting an enemy that simply cannot exist. They would have stamped down on your collective neck to muster an army, only to march to a battlefield and find it utterly empty. You, on the other hand, appear to suffer no such delusions. That makes you worth knowing. So what do you say?" He held out his hand just as Aka Manah had. "Can we be friends?"

Gabe felt the delicate touch in his mind again, prompting him to agree and take whatever was handed to him. And he very nearly did. It was the second powerful creature in as many minutes to ask him to join it, and he was fresh out of resolve. But they had pushed him too hard, and his grief was too fresh. Without knowing what he was doing, he seized the thread of Phillip's influence and smashed it against the anvil of his anger. The touch in his mind tried to recoil, but Gabe held tight. He forced the fury to focus his will to an edge, then severed the line and let the stump of it snap back into the little man. The bit of amputated magic tried to wriggle from his grip, but he thrust it deep into the new hole in the center of his mind and it became his.

Phillip's eyes went wide, and his smile finally slipped. "Fascinating," he whispered.

"That's the most bullshit thing I've ever heard," Gabe said. "And I just had the god of bullshit whispering in my head for the last three days. Do you have any idea what we've been through? And now you're saying you *helped* Gwendal do all this? Well, fuck you too! If this is your idea of *maintaining balance,* I don't want a goddamned part of it. Not with you, or anyone else. I'm done being a pawn for monsters. I'm just...done." He took up the bit of stolen magic and shunted it all to his leg to dull the pain, then, in complete defiance of common sense, he turned his back to the man and started limping away to look for Heather.

Phillip's laughter followed him, but there was nothing musical about it this time. "I think you will be my special project," he called.

His voice thrummed with a power that made Aka Manah's feel small, and Gabe was suddenly forced to his knees beneath the impossible weight of it. He felt blood running from his nose and ears. He searched for Heather, but she was gone.

"Two things, though," Phillip went on calmly. "First, you will never stop being a pawn. Not in this world or the next. Your only choice is for whom you play, and even that is...muddy." Phillip was suddenly just behind him then, leaning down to whisper in his ear. "And second, you should be more careful of who you call a monster. You may not be so far from that fate yourself. And monsters are not the worst things in the dark." He patted Gabe lightly on the shoulder. "Rest up, Gabriel Delling. See you soon."

Everything went blank and empty. There was heat. Then nothing.

CHAPTER THIRTY-NINE

"There are lots of reasons why I ended up in this career, but ultimately I just like being my own boss. I hate taking orders, and I really hate having my strings pulled. I need to be the captain of my own ship. If that means I occasionally run it aground, well, at least I know who to blame. The only thing worse than screwing up your life with your own stupid choices, is having it screwed up for you with someone else's."

-Excerpt from Chapter One, CONscience

    Gabe woke up in a hotel room on a real bed and feeling pretty fine. His first instinct was to be thankful that he wasn't regaining consciousness hanging above a wood chipper—given his recent track record—but his relief was short-lived. Something nudged him in the ribs, and he looked over to find Catherine sitting next to the bed. The *something* was a gun barrel.
    "Question time," the Knight said. Her voice was tight and angry.
    Gabe stifled a reflexive comment about waking up next to her. "Okay, shoot—I mean, you know, ask."
    Her frown didn't so much as crack. She reached over and pulled something, and Gabe felt a light tug on his arm. He only then noticed the IV line stuck there, and he followed it up to a bag of morphine hanging above his head. That at least explained why life was suddenly so wonderful.
    "You're broken just about everywhere, and I can make it so much worse if you force me to. So if you want this to keep dripping you won't screw with me, got it?" She almost looked disappointed when Gabe simply nodded. "Fine. Now tell me what the fuck happened in there."
    He cleared his throat, then feigned resituating himself to get a look around the room. They were back at the Briarwood Hotel. He recognized the furnishings. It was actually a pretty nice place without the dead bodies and horrific altars. There was another Knight sitting at

the desk, solemnly cleaning his weapon, and through the open door Gabe could see at least two more of them out in the hall. Four Knights, and him beat to hell and high as a kite. Complete and total cooperation seemed like a decent strategy.

"Of course," he said. "I mean, I don't know everything, but—ahhhh!" He cried out as Catherine shoved the gun into his broken ribs.

"I don't care what you don't know," she said. "Give me facts. Fast."

Gabe started babbling. He recounted the events of the night in unfiltered detail, trying to put together a coherent story through the fog of drugs and his own tenuous grasp of what precisely had happened. He recounted the complete truth—as much for himself as for her—and it came out like the fever dream of a dangerous psychotic on absinthe. By the time he'd finished, he wasn't even sure if he believed most of what he'd just lived through.

But Catherine nodded like she understood. "Explain to me how Aka Manah could take your father's body if Gwendal didn't cleanse his soul first? There are plenty of new things happening here tonight, but that's a pretty damned firm rule for Umbras. Seems like a hole in your story."

Gabe could only shake his head. He honestly didn't know. He knew for certain Gwendal hadn't done it, but everything else had happened so quickly.

"Where did the succubus go?" Catherine asked.

He shrugged. "She's free now, so...gone, I guess. I looked, but she must have slipped out." He knew he'd probably have stronger feelings about that later, but right then the drugs made it about as impactful as overcooked pasta. Heather had run. Good for her.

Catherine sighed and used the butt of her gun to itch her injured arm through the sling. "How about the Hound and that little bokor filth, Reznick? Where are they?"

He didn't even have to lie. "No clue, and I don't care. Dead would be nice on both counts, but I would also accept horribly maimed."

She sat back and blew a bead of sweat from her nose. "Well, that's pretty shitty for you."

For the first time since waking, a twinge of real fear slipped through the haze. "Why's that?" he asked.

"Because," she said, "Omaha wants blood. Eighteen Knights *died* tonight, and twenty-three more are hospitalized. A major mission like this and only four walk out on their own feet? Somebody has to answer for that and it sure as shit will not be me."

The morphine fog retreated further, and Gabe's brain finally started clicking over for real. "Wait, what?"

"You led us into a fucking trap!" Catherine shouted, kicking over her chair as she shot to her feet. She leveled her weapon at him, and her face over the yawning barrel was painted in streaks of hatred. "I'd kill you right now if I could, but you *will* hang for this! Trust me on that. I won't rest until you and your slut and every fucking one of you dirty, goddamned piece of shit Umbras—"

There was a pop and Catherine's head suddenly jerked hard to the side, and she fell to the floor in a heap. A man in a ski mask entered the room, leading with a silenced pistol. The Knight at the desk rose and threw himself toward the intruder, but the masked man dodged three quick punches, then stepped back and shot the Knight point-blank through the heart. The guy was dead before gravity finished with him.

"That was for Joseph and Uklek, fucker," the masked man said.

Two more disguised men came in, and they casually dropped the bodies of the other two Knights on the floor. Gabe sat up and only had time to briefly consider diving for Catherine's weapon before the first man took off his mask and smiled.

"Thanks for the text," James said.

Gabe stared, mouth open and eyes probably as wide as truck tires. "I didn't text you..."

James laughed and turned to the other two men. "See? What'd I say? No clue."

The other two men took off their masks, and Gabe recognized one of them as the pishtaco who had kidnapped him the previous night. The morphine made it take longer than it should have, but Gabe eventually got it. "You work for Jimenez?"

James shared another smile with his men and walked over to the bed. He stopped to spit on Catherine's body and kick away her weapon, then he holstered his gun and bent to help Gabe sit up. "Close. He works for me." He noted Gabe's slack-mouthed expression and apparently took pity. "You're not the only one with alter egos, man."

Gabe shook his head. "No. *You're*... Baron Jimenez? How the... *What?*"

James retrieved a nearby washcloth and handed it to Gabe, then expertly removed the IV needle. Blood welled and Gabe belatedly pressed the cloth to the spot.

"This is some kind of shit, Gabe. Lots of assholes running around here lately, but I never expected it to go down like this."

"*You're* the Baron?" Gabe repeated, still unable to believe the picture the connected dots had revealed. "But... No. The Baron is a vampire."

"Oh, fuck you," James said, tossing the IV line to the side. "A pishtaco is not a vampire. For one—nah, you know what? No time. You do your own damn research. We gotta go before more of these bigoted asshats show up. Can you walk?"

Gabe let James help him remove the sheets to discover most of his body covered in bandages and a pant leg cut away for a compression cast over the bottom half of his right leg. As soon as he saw it, he felt the pain slowly clawing its way back up through the drugs. "I'm guessing no," Gabe said.

James gestured, and the familiar pishtaco came over and helped pull Gabe up. They got on either side of him and became his crutches. James nodded to the last man who then went out ahead of them with his gun drawn.

"*You're* the Baron?" Gabe asked again.

"You're gonna need to shut up with that, Gabe," James said as they entered the hallway. "You're just about the luckiest bastard on the planet right now, so don't fuck it up by running your mouth."

The walk was painful, but it ended relatively quickly at the end of a back stairway and a waiting car. A police officer was standing nearby, looking the other direction and carefully ignoring the running engine and slamming doors.

James got in back with Gabe and then they were speeding away. "Who needs a glamour when you've got cash, huh?" James said. One of the pishtacos up front chuckled, and James turned to Gabe. "You look like a wet shit."

"Thanks," was all Gabe could manage.

"I've got a guy to patch you up. We're going there now. Are you, uh..." he tapped the side of his head.

Gabe nodded. "Gone. Everything's gone or dead. Just me now."

James ran a hand over his jaw and sighed. "What a fucking mess, though. This is what I get for trying to be a nice guy. Make peace and keep people happy. Shit. What does that get? A goddamned slaughterhouse and a war with the Knights of fucking Solomon in my city."

"Sounds like you're having a rough night," Gabe said.

James laughed and started rolling up his sleeves. "Yeah, okay. Point taken. But say, man, I am sorry about this. We listened to a bit of your story before storming in, and I'm, uh, just sorry."

Gabe looked up and saw the truth of it on the man's face. It only helped a little, but it was something. "Why didn't you tell me?" he asked. "I mean, this whole thing could have been avoided if—"

"Hey, I said I'm sorry and I meant it," James interrupted. "I really didn't know what I was sending you into. Honestly thought it was legit. We didn't find out about the Night Bitch until the next morning. Sent an emissary and everything to talk it out. We didn't know who she really was and who she was chasing until my guys picked you up, and I only found out who you were when they lifted your wallet. I tried to get some shit together to bring you in and help you out, but you're an elusive bastard. Next thing I know, two of my people are dead, and there you are at my doorstep to tell me your side of the story. And...fuck, I just didn't know who or what to trust anymore. A succubus in Heather's body and you suddenly tossing magic around and healing your shit like Wolverine? I've got people to keep safe and people to answer to, you know? I've always been careful to keep these two worlds separate in my life, and all of a sudden they were bleeding together and going septic fast. I feel like a real asshole now that I know the whole thing, obviously."

Gabe just shook his head. There wasn't anything to say.

"By then," James continued, "Mama Tempe and Baron Kamuzu were involved. They're my counterparts in the city, and they wanted to wait and see. Find out who was bankrolling the Night Bitch. Find out if they were an enemy or possible ally. There's dark shit coming out of the woodwork these days, Gabe, and we've got a city to protect. I swear I wanted to bring resources to bear for you, but they outvoted me. Said we needed to know who was who. I couldn't just help you outright, you understand?"

"Why didn't Heather notice you?" Gabe asked. "You were with us for hours."

James leaned back in his seat. "She's not quite as smart as she thinks she is. Also, she was in pretty bad shape by the time you got to me. And I'm *old*, Gabe. Tricky. Wouldn't be here if I wasn't. I play these side hustles like James and a few other characters to keep my hand in at the street level, but I've got more resources than a little succubus can handle."

"So what do you want?" Gabe asked, too exhausted to care about tact. "Why are you here?"

James made a noise of disgust, like he was asking himself the same question. "Well, you texted me, didn't you? Told me the Knights killed Joseph, and the Hound killed Uklek. Probably wanted me to storm in and be a good cover for your exit? Keep Gwendal and the Knights all busy so you could slip out between our legs in the process?"

Gabe made a noncommittal noise, and James waved it away as he went on. "Nah, it was a good try. You didn't know who you were using any more than I knew the shit I was sending you into. It was fair play, and might have worked on another guy another day." He sighed heavily and rubbed the back of his head. "But this *is* some shit, make no mistake. I don't know who the hell was bankrolling Gwendal, but she had assets, man. You can't drop a casual half-million bounty and not have pockets that run a hundred times deeper. And throwing Hunters away like dime store toys? That's fucking scary. Then we got the Maerrywell Clan blowing shit up all over Eastern Europe and China, and the Hags suddenly buying up anything that isn't tied down like they're playing a goddamned game of full-contact Monopoly. Plus the Chamber is convening for some kind of secret meeting in Athens, and now we add in whoever the fuck these new people are, and—"

"He said his name was Phillip," Gabe said.

"Huh," James replied. "Pretty lame name for such a scary bastard."

Gabe gingerly touched his ribs and winced. The morphine was already wearing off. "James Jackson. Jacob Jimenez. Damn. I don't understand any of this, J. What kind of trouble am I in?"

James folded his hands and shook his head. "I don't know. Something big is going down at the upper levels. We've been trying to keep it out of this city, but it slipped in anyway. Now we need to lower our profile before the big boys decide we're worth noticing. Lincoln won't be a battleground anymore if I have any say in it, and after being proved fucking right tonight, Tempe and Kamuzu damn well can't argue with me."

"Fine by me," Gabe said. "I don't want anything to do with this stuff."

James eyed him coldly. "Yeah, brother, but it apparently wants something to do with you."

Gabe stared back, letting the silence linger while streetlights passed quickly through the windows. "What are you saying?"

James snapped his fingers and the front passenger handed back a fat envelope. "Here," James said. He almost looked sad. "Ten thousand. That's a down payment on your house. We're buying it off you. You'll get another ninety in a dummy account in a few weeks, but that cash will start you off."

Gabe took the money numbly. "What the hell are you talking about, James?"

Baron Jimenez looked back at him, and there was nothing human in his eyes anymore. "I'm saying that we will patch you up and buy your broken-ass house for ten times what it's worth. But then you need to get the hell out of my city." There was no room for discussion in the statement.

Gabe gripped the cash, wondering at last where Heather had gone, and where Aka Manah had taken his dad. But the morphine was too distant and the pains too many to focus on just one hurt. He nodded and turned to watch the outside world go by, wondering where he should go next...and what his life was now.

"Sorry about your dad," James said.

"Yeah," Gabe replied around the lump in his throat. "Me too."

CHAPTER FORTY

Gabe stared at the new chapter for the hundredth time, searching for an answer that he knew couldn't possibly be there.

```
"I'm a… I don't know. Not a conman, I don't
think. Not a man, probably. Two months ago as I
write this, I changed. And now I'm something
totally different. Something unique, or so the
monsters tell me. Maybe someday I'll find out
what that's supposed to mean, but for now I'm
a…"
```

The cursor blinked at the end of the sentence, mocking him with its unfailing persistence. There were words to finish the statement, he was sure, but he didn't have them or know where to find them. Nor did he know if he wanted to.

He closed his laptop and put it back on the side-table. He'd tried endlessly to finish his book over the last two months, but what had started as a little project to make a quick buck had morphed into something darker and much more complicated—like his life. It was now part journal, part confession, and part research log, and he couldn't imagine anyone actually wanting to read the thing. The act of finishing it was more symbolic at this point.

Gabe rose and moved to the dim fireplace, then used the poker to stab at a log until it revealed the hot embers within. He placed some thin branches in the middle and waited for them to catch, and soon it was burning strong again. The snow fell heavily outside the cabin, almost coming up to the window sills now, and he knew he should soak up as much heat as he could before going back outside to clear the roof and paths. It was his only real job there—aside from staying alive—but with an inch of snow falling every hour some days, it could easily fill his life with honest, simple work.

Fortunately his injuries had healed quickly and well, and the exercise had been doing him good. He barely felt a twinge of pain anymore, and that at least made him thankful for the magic still working for him. Mending dozens of bruises and cuts, several broken ribs, and a shattered leg all in a few weeks was beyond amazing, and he wasn't about to complain. The wound on his arm from the Rime Blade had taken longer to finish healing, but he frankly considered himself lucky to have kept the arm at all. He considered the faded black line of damaged skin there something of a badge.

His fingers felt at the place on his left hand where the raised patch still occasionally twitched with cold, and he shuddered at the memory of the Hunters. He hadn't dared try to call the blade up again, but he suspected it was still there, just waiting for enough anguish. He sincerely hoped to never find out.

Gabe placed the kettle on the hook, then moved the swing-arm over the fire. He'd never been much for tea back home, but the stuff seemed to taste so much better in the mountains. An errant log settled badly in the fireplace, and he picked up the poker again to wrangle it back. But just then, a tentative knock sounded at his front door and he swung around to face it. His mind quickly ran through the list of people who knew he was up there—then through the list of those who might be out in such rough weather. No one good came to mind.

He slipped over to the door and risked a quick glimpse through the window, and what he saw made him grip his weapon even tighter. He knew he wasn't ready for this.

"I saw you, Gabe!" she said, her voice muffled through the glass. "Come on, it's cold as a bastard out here!"

He steeled himself, then wrenched open the door and filled the entrance like a sentry. "What are you doing here?"

Heather shook off her hood and smiled brightly. "I came to see if you'd changed your mind. Remember? Cabin in the mountains? Crazy sex all day? I mean, you could have given me directions, but no big deal. I'm here." She made as if to push past him, but he stood firm and her smile faded. "Come on," she said. "I just want to talk. I came all the way here in designer boots with this crap up to my thighs, so you know I'm serious."

He almost refused, but knew he couldn't. All the memories he'd been trying to run away from suddenly boiled back up, coming too fast and too hot to shove down: her face the last time he'd seen her, Aka Manah's smile on his dad's lips, and the broken pieces of the night that he'd finally puzzled together. Small things, normally—barely worth noticing—but they changed everything. Ready or not, it was time to deal with it. He moved aside, and she stomped off her boots as she stepped in.

"Fine," he said, managing to lay a calm, even tone across his warring emotions. "Tell me why you did it."

She stopped midway through shrugging off her coat and tried to fake confusion, but Gabe met her eyes and squashed it for her. If she had hoped he'd been fooled all this time, she now knew she was wrong.

She sagged, and her voice went soft. "How did you know?"

The image he'd constructed for himself flashed back in his mind: Aka Manah standing there. The dark smear on his father's face. The same color smeared across Heather's. "Your lipstick," he said. "You called the shade 'Kiss of Death', right? And you did once warn me that you could take a human soul like plucking a grape."

She moved past him to sit down hard on the arm of the couch. "It was the only way."

Gabe threw the poker to the floor, and it clattered loudly near the table. "You killed him! You betrayed me!"

She closed her eyes for a second, then anger twisted her features and she rose to meet him. "It was the only way! You killed Gwendal to try to win it all, but you didn't think what would happen when the god had nowhere to go! No body to take and only one path to retreat to, Gabe! You! What else could I have done?"

He turned and slammed the front door, and a mass of snow fell from the awning. Then he stopped and leaned forward to rest his head against the cold glass. *For him.* She had stolen his father's soul and given the body to an evil god...for him. Of course she had. And worse—*much* worse—he'd known it all along. He'd just been too cowardly to face it. Without Heather to hate for it, the loss welled back up fresh as the first day to cut straight through his lie of a life and swallow his heart whole.

A full minute passed and neither of them spoke over the hiss of the fire and the whisper of falling snow. Then Gabe finally sighed, fogging up the window and obscuring the world. "Say it."

There was a long pause before she replied. "What?"

"Say what you did," he whispered. "I want to hear it."

There was a rustle of movement behind him, and Heather's voice was closer when she spoke. "You don't want that."

He let his fists loosen and fall to his sides. He could barely talk past the catch in his throat. "I need it."

Her hand touched his shoulder, and her breath was warm on his neck. "You killed Gwendal before she could...prepare a new vessel. There was an instant when Aka Manah had nowhere to go but back. Into you. You were already broken, and had been through too much, I thought. And... I had one heartbeat to decide. I could barely move, and he was right next to me." She stopped and slipped a hand under his arm and over his chest, gently pulling him back into her. "So, yes. I did it. I took Alexander's soul so Aka Manah would leave you and take him instead. It was the only way to save you."

Gabe swallowed hard. "Why didn't you let me die? I was ready."

She rested her head on his back. "Because he asked me to help you. There in the circle, in those last seconds, he turned and asked me to help you. His boy."

Gabe felt the tears burning in his eyes, and he let Heather take hold of his shirt and gently pull him around to face her. Her own eyes were wet and dark.

"You tried to die for us," she said. "Nobody has ever..." She shook her head firmly. "I couldn't let you."

He tried to back away, but she held him there. "You weren't obligated!" he said, trying even at the last to deny that someone might care for him. "You could have run! You were free!"

She stared at him like he was something fascinating and terrifying and new. "Yep."

She held him as he cried.

****

After an hour of talking and crying and hammering out the dents in their relationship, Gabe finally made tea with the thoroughly boiling water.

"So what's your plan up here," Heather asked, mercifully shifting to normal conversation.

He looked to her and was relieved to feel no more pain or anger. She'd done what she'd done, and so had he. Nothing would change that stuff. In the end, they'd both done things they regretted, but for reasons they had thought were good. And that neutralized most of the poison in the wounds. The only bit of control they had was in how they went forward, and it seemed like they were headed in the same direction for now. Heather might be the only real friend he had in the world, in fact—not that he could ever tell her that.

"Train to fight," he said as he poured the tea. "Heal too. Read every fairy tale and religious text I can get my hands on, and hide from Aka Manah and that Phillip guy until they lose whatever interest they have in me. Hopefully grow old and die of boredom. Whatever keeps me alive."

She laughed, the sound like a balm in the heavy atmosphere. "Another sterling plan from the master tactician. You're going to train to fight up here by yourself? With what, old Bruce Lee VHS tapes?"

Gabe grumbled, but didn't argue. He hadn't really been thinking many steps ahead as he'd fled Nebraska and then the country. He'd just needed to get away, and Canada had seemed like a good start. "Do you have something better?" he asked as he slid a steaming cup in front of her.

She smiled and sipped the tea, making a noise of pleasure that was just a touch too graphic for good taste. The twinkle in her eyes let Gabe know she'd done it on purpose. She seemed as ready as him to get things back on track. It was a very nice feeling.

"As a matter of fact..." She pulled out a slip of paper and tossed it to the table.

Gabe opened it and read the single line written there. "Mikhail Kirchhoff?"

She smiled like a little girl with a secret. "Ask me who he is."

He sighed. "Okay. Who is he?"

Heather put down her cup and leaned forward, pretending to be afraid of someone overhearing. "The sorcerer from the mansion."

It took Gabe a moment to understand, and when he did, he nearly dropped his cup. "The tall guy? Uh, now Trevor, I guess? The one who wanted you for carnal magic, and murdered our team, and helped Gwendal start this whole freaking mess? *That* sorcerer?"

She nodded. "You got it. But his name isn't really Trevor. You may recall that he can wear people like suits sort of like an Umbra, only he can jump at-will. Big mojo. Sorcerer stuff. He's still out there, and I know where to start looking."

Gabe sat back. "Why in the hell would we want that? I want to stay as far away from those things as humanly possible."

She smirked. "Hey, you're not doing much 'humanly' anymore, buster. So don't throw that stuff around so casually. And that is precisely why we *do* need to find him. I assume you haven't spontaneously learned how to use your magic while shoveling snow up here, and I'm afraid that iron poker won't do you any good against anything but a pissed off pixie. If you really want to learn to defend yourself from gods and monsters, magic is the only way. And the best place to start for that in your case is a sorcerer."

Gabe tapped the side of his mug for a few seconds as he considered. "So what? He can turn me into a real boy again?"

"I doubt it," she said. "But I don't know why you'd want to be. I'm hoping he can tell us what you are and teach you how to be whatever it is. Because, as unique a little snowflake as you may be, he and his kind are the next closest thing that I'm aware of. We'll beat it out of him if necessary. Worked with Reznick, right? Their adorable little music magic is slow to cast, and most sorcerers are worse at fighting than you are."

Gabe worked on a flat refusal for a bit, but soon the memory of Phillip's whispers and Aka Manah's last promising look filled his memory and slowly proved Heather right. "*That* guy, though? Isn't there another way?"

She laughed lightly. "Sure. There's a whole world of magic and mystery just waiting for you to discover and screw up somehow. Now that we have a little breathing room, we can explore the options. All you need to do is decide if you're happy with a life of solitude and cowardice, or if you want to find out what the hell is going on."

She raised a hand and started ticking off fingers. "Why is Aka Manah here? What the hell is an 'Endless Dark'? Who's Phillip, and why does he seem to have such a crush on you? Why do you have magic? And what in Ether's name *are you* anyway? I've been out there catching up all this time, and there are a thousand new things I need to teach you. But each one of those has another thousand questions attached that I can't answer yet. The world is crazy, and amazing, and incredibly dangerous, Gabe. And if you want my opinion, that danger will find you no matter where you are. Staying in one place and mired in ignorance doesn't seem like a fitting end to your story."

Gabe took a sip of his tea. She was always so hard to argue with. "How did *you* find me? I dissolved the bond."

Heather leaned forward and tapped him on the chest. "You've still got a little piece of me, remember? And vice versa. If you bothered concentrating, you might feel it too. That's bigger than the bond, and maybe why we get along so famously. A little sliver of succubus is enough to make even you decent company."

"Right," he said. "So I get to look forward to you tracking me down for the rest of my life?"

"You wish," she replied. Then she stood and stretched, rising to her toes and pulling everything taut.

Gabe looked down to study the dregs of his tea. He knew she was baiting him. Heather was still beautiful and still dangerous—and clever, and annoying, and surprising, and basically perfect in most ways—but now there was something much more to her that he couldn't quite get his head around. She had come back for him again, defying every rule about life he thought he knew. She was free of any obligation to him, yet here she was. Here to help him for no other reason than that she wanted to. That was different, and he didn't know how to feel about it. But he knew enough to not risk ruining it by doing something stupid. Their friendship was like a tiny flawless bubble floating on the wind, and he didn't dare breathe for fear of finding out how fragile it really was.

She seemed to see the decision in him, and couldn't help but poke at it by making a final noise of pleasure and drawing it out ridiculously before relaxing. "Well," she said, her voice bright, "you stay out here and do some hard thinking. Let me know what you decide. Tomorrow I'll fill you in on all the juicy details I learned about the magical underbelly of this modern world. But right now I'm going to take a long, hot shower and melt into bed. I assume, gentleman that you are, you don't mind giving up the only bedroom?"

He waved her on wordlessly.

"Such a sweetheart." She moved toward the bathroom, unfastening her dark hair as she went until it fell across her shoulders in a liquid tumble. Then she glanced back. "Oh, and I somehow forgot to bring pajamas. Fair warning if you decide to snuggle with me tonight. You have fun with your *hard thoughts*." She smiled wickedly, then closed the bathroom door just enough to let a shard of light spill out.

Gabe gathered the dishes and dropped them in the sink to be washed in the morning. He needed to get more wood for the fire, and a pillow and blanket for the couch. It was shaping up to be a long, cold night.

THE END

Book Two
FATE LASHED
Now available in print, e-book, and audiobook!

If you enjoyed this book, please consider leaving a review at Amazon or Goodreads. Or anywhere, really. I'm sure you'll think of somewhere good.
Seriously, every review helps me out by letting more people know about this series. There's this whole popularity algorithm on Amazon that I don't understand at all, (I assume it's a gremlin pulling levers in a room full of spinning gears and dot matrix printers) but every positive review I get bumps the book up a little more in that diabolical machine. Plus, I genuinely appreciate your feedback. You are exactly the cool, smart people I wrote this for, so I want to hear which parts landed as intended.

And please look me up at
www.Josherikson.com

where I have a mailing list you can sign up for. I send big updates, deleted scenes, and super secret short stories through that thing.

You can also find me at
https://www.facebook.com/EtherealEarthSeries/

That's where I drop smaller, more regular updates, along with pictures of my day or sandwiches or whatever.

And finally, some real talk. If you pirated this book, would you at least do me one favor? Tell a few friends who you think might enjoy this story. If even one of them decides to buy a copy, you will have helped me out. I want to get the new books out as quickly as possible, and that means being able to buy groceries and stuff. Thanks for understanding.

Acknowledgements

This book wouldn't have been possible without help from a bunch of really great people.

First, I need to thank my wife, **Jenny**. She is relentless in her support of me, and that's really the only reason I was able to give this a shot at all. Having someone believe so completely in you is exactly as motivating and terrifying as it sounds, and that combination turns out to be pretty decent fuel for this job.

I owe the rest of these folks big thank-yous as well, but in the interest of not filling up twenty pages with gushing compliments, I've tried to boil it all down to the vital essence.

Dave, for reading several early (much worse) drafts and still telling me I could do this.

Geoff, for helping me seem like I knew what I was doing with the audiobook recording.

My Editor, Kaitlyn Johnson, for digging so thoroughly into this thing to help me get it up and running.

Anna, Anne, Dan, Carissa, Lacey, Liz, Mike, Missy, Jared, John, Raine, and **my mom**, for reading earlier drafts and saving me from some pretty embarrassing mistakes.

And finally, to **all my family and friends**, for supporting me when this seemed like a nonsense idea, and asking questions even when the answers were super boring, and for buying this book even though it's not something you would normally be remotely interested in. Thank you all. I can't tell you how grateful I am.

About the Author

Josh Erikson spent twelve years in the hospitality industry before life gave him a swift enough kick to propel him toward writing. Now he splits his days between thinking up stories for the awesome people reading this, and spending time with his wife and two young children. He lives in rural Nebraska, does not own any livestock or cowboy boots, and likes corn a perfectly regular amount, thank you very much.

Printed in Great Britain
by Amazon